WARLORD OF AYODHYA

RESURRECTION

BOOK II

What sets Shatrujeet Nath apart from his cohort of neo-mythologists is how well he writes. His words are easy, his images are strong, and given the fact that his books are action packed, his language is practically lyrical. The situations are believable, the characters he creates feel authentic, each with a complex psychological profile, each true to themselves. And this time, the addition of magic to Nath's own armoury of skills electrifies a fast-paced narrative that is a thriller to the end.

—Arshia Sattar, author & translator of
the *Valmiki Ramayana*

BOOK II

SHATRUJEET NATH

JAICO PUBLISHING HOUSE

Ahmedabad Bangalore Chennai
Delhi Hyderabad Kolkata Mumbai

Published by Jaico Publishing House
A-2 Jash Chambers, 7-A Sir Phirozshah Mehta Road
Fort, Mumbai - 400 001
jaicopub@jaicobooks.com
www.jaicobooks.com

WARLORD OF AYODHYA: BOOK II
RESURRECTION
ISBN 978-81-19153-57-2

First Jaico Impression: 2024

Page design and layout by Inosoft Systems, Delhi

Printed by
Nutech Print Services - India, New Delhi

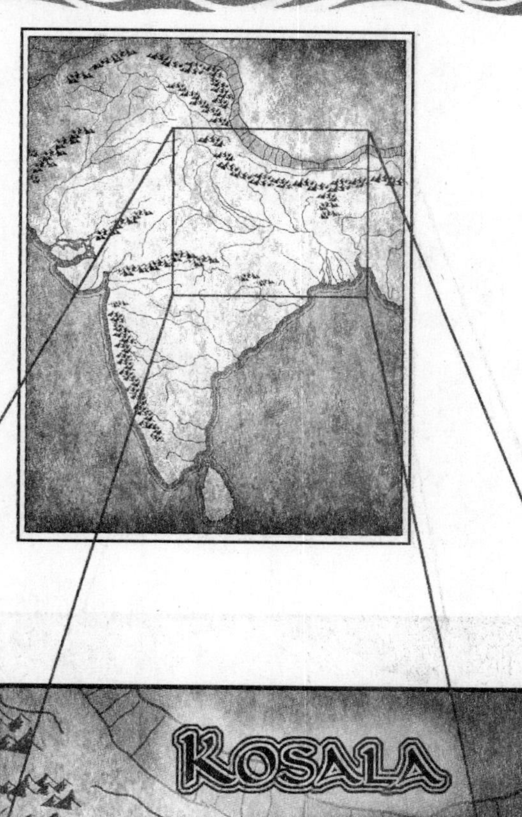

KOSALA
madhupura
Sarayu
Yamuna
VIDEHA
ayodhya
KOSALA
CHEDI
chitrakuta
KASI
ANGA
tamralipti

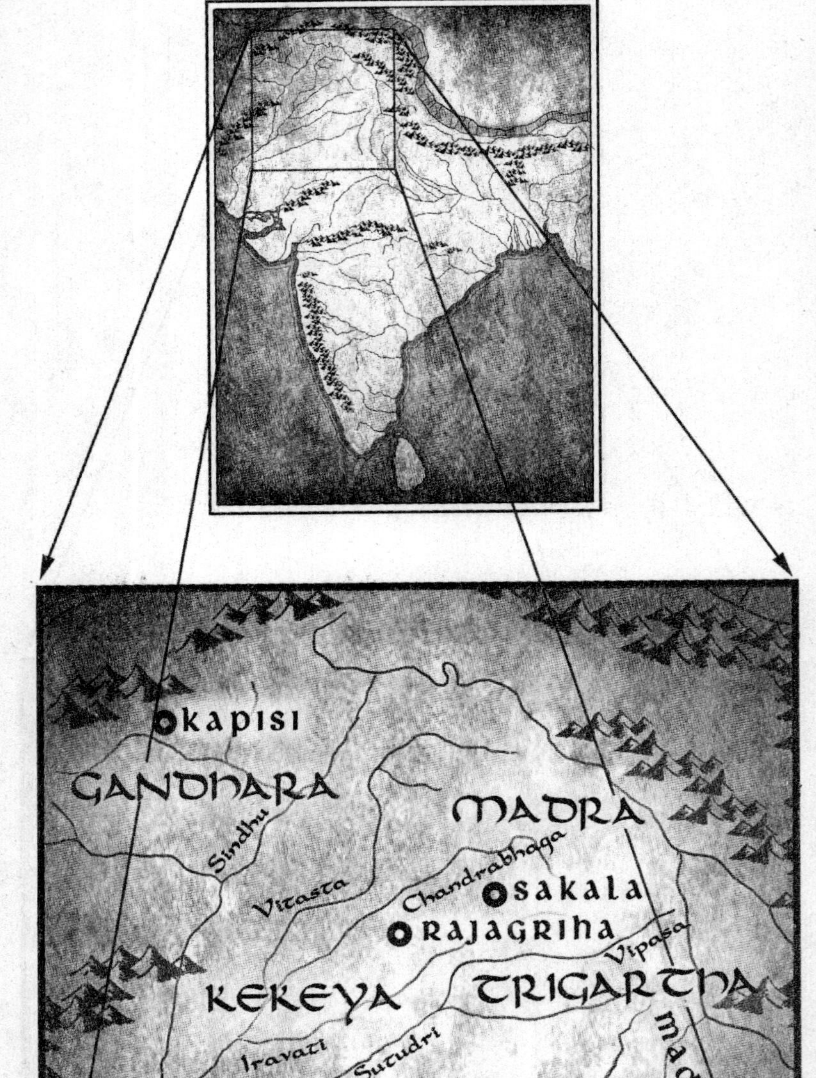
KAPISI
GANDHARA
MADRA
Sindhu
Chandrabhaga
SAKALA
Vitasta
RAJAGRIHA
Vipasa
KEKEYA
TRIGARTHA
Iravati
Sutudri
MADHUPURA
THE RIVER KINGDOMS

To

Ravi Balakrishnan.

For reading anything I write

and telling me it's great.

You are good for the ego.

Glossary

aarati : a prayer ritual with lighted lamps
adhipati : lord, ruler
ajameghya : the acacia tree
amalakam : Indian gooseberry
atayi : kite
been : a traditional Indian wind instrument
chhatra : a caravanserai
dandapala : a palace investigator
dhattura : nightshade
dhol : a drum
dhoti : traditional men's garment
draksha : berry, grape
goparasa : myrrh
grdha : vulture
homa : Vedic fire ritual
homagriha : fire sanctum
jatuka : bat
kakah : crow
karapala : a light sword
khadga : a heavy sword
khanga : a long sword
kshatri : chamberlain
kshurika : a small dagger
kumara : young man, prince; also a form of address
kunta : javelin

mahamuni	:	lit. great sage; also a form of address
mahanayaka	:	a commander
mahayoddha	:	lit. great warrior; champion
mama	:	uncle; also a form of address
manchika	:	a low seat or stool
munivar	:	a form of addressing a sage
nagarapala	:	a member of the city militia
nana	:	grandfather; also a form of address
nayaka	:	a captain
paduka	:	an ancient Indian form of footwear
parshvadha	:	a battle-axe
pranaam	:	salutation
pravara	:	cloak
raja	:	king
rajan	:	king; also a form of address
rani	:	queen; also a form of address
raya	:	another form of 'raja' or king
rishi	:	sage
rupa	:	an ancient Indian coin
sala	:	the *Shorea robusta* tree
sambrani	:	a balsamic resin used as incense
sarikah	:	mynah
sarpa	:	snake
sayyasana	:	a couch
shiraska	:	palanquin
shul	:	a heavy spear
shyena	:	hawk
tulsi	:	the holy basil plant
tvak	:	cinnamon
upanayaka	:	a captain's deputy
uttariya	:	a scarf-like garment draped on the upper body
vaidya	:	physician
vajramushti	:	an ancient Indian knuckleduster
varaha	:	boar
vatika	:	garden

vrischika : scorpion
yashtimadhu : liquorice
yoddha : warrior
yuvaraja : prince; also a form of address

one

EVERYWHERE, ALL AROUND HIM, THE UNRESTRAINED ROAR of rain. Bearing down on the roofs of the palace overhead, pounding the courtyards below, battering the parched extents of the palace grounds, pummelling the very earth into submission. A rampant, overwhelming assault falling ceaselessly from the sky.

But above the rush of the water — dampening it, deadening it — there was another noise.

The sound of Taksha's laughter. Carefree, joyous.

He knew the laughter wasn't real, that unlike the rain, it was only in his head.

Siripala? Angara? Play? Story? Outside?

Everything was a question for the boy, it occurred to him, the prospects of fun, endless.

You are bound to lose something precious.

Anguish lanced afresh through Bharat's chest, and his legs threatened to give way as he gripped the parapet that he was leaning against to stay upright. Screwing his eyes shut, he swayed and forced himself to breathe deep and steady.

The memory of setting eyes on the boy for the first time came groping at him. It was almost a month after his return to Ayodhya that he had been able to visit Rajviraj to meet Mandavi and the baby. He had still been grappling with the aftershocks of his father's passing and the going away of Rama, Lakshmana and Sita, and grief and frustration lay heavy on his shoulders as he was welcomed into the house of Raja Kushadhwaja. Mandavi had emerged from her chambers like a burst of sunshine, cradling the baby, and as he took the little bundle into his arms and looked into the eyes staring curiously at him, Bharat had felt the weight of the world lift and evaporate. What shall we call him, he remembered having asked Mandavi. She had said she favoured the name Taksha.

Taksha, he had whispered, bending over the baby. A moment passed before the baby's lips had twisted in a small smile of delight.

Taksha. The name now left his own lips in a sigh of despair, quickly drowned in the fury of the rain.

All these people disappearing like this... it really scares me. Mandavi's words from a night not long in the past came to Bharat. They had been lying in bed awaiting sleep when she had spoken suddenly of her fears, her eyes wide in the dark. *What if it were to happen to you or Taksha?*

Turning to his side, he had put a comforting arm around her. *Nothing will happen to me, dear, and nothing will ever happen to your son,* he had said. *I promise you that.*

Feeling a hand on his shoulder, Bharat turned to find Kushadhwaja, with Shatrughna standing further behind the old raja. Kushadhwaja's face was drawn, his eyes anxious as he considered Bharat.

"Why aren't you with the boy?" Kosala's *kshatri* tilted his head in the direction of a door down the gallery before which Kausalya, Sumitra and Urmila stood in a huddle, conversing in hushed tones.

"I'm… I can't bear to see him lying there," Bharat shook his head. "What… what if the *vaidyas* fail to —" his voice broke in a sob, the prospect of what he was thinking too terrible to put into words.

"The kid will be fine," Kushadhwaja interjected, his words forceful over the noise of the rain.

"What will I say to Mandavi?" Bharat asked, giving no sign of having heard his father-in-law. He gazed down the length of the gallery with a pained expression. "I… I promised her nothing would happen to Taksha."

"The kid will be fine," Kushadhwaja repeated, strengthening his grip on Bharat's shoulder. "He is in the care of the *vaidyas*. He is in good hands."

"She'll never forgive me," the king hung his head, his shoulders drooping in dejection.

Shatrughna stepped forward to stand before Bharat. "Taksha will be fine, brother," he insisted. "The *vaidyas* are certain the kid wasn't hit by the bolt from the *vajramushti*."

Bharat nodded, but looked miserably at the door to the chamber where the *vaidyas* worked with their potions and poultices. He had carried Taksha into the palace a quarter of an hour ago, and the *vaidyas* had taken charge of the boy. He had watched the *vaidyas* trying to revive the boy, unsuccessfully, and with each passing moment, staring at his son's pallid face, seeing him draw weak, fitful breaths, Bharat had grown certain the *vaidyas* would all inevitably fail.

There is a heavy price attached to the creation of magic…

"He isn't regaining consciousness," Bharat muttered, half to himself.

"The *vaidyas* are doing everything in their capacity," Kushadhwaja said, taking an even tighter hold on the king's shoulder. "You *must* trust them. You can't give up like this." The *kshatri* peered closely at his son-in-law. "What makes you think this won't turn out well? What causes you to doubt the *vaidyas* and lose all hope?"

Bharat blinked, listening to the rain, hearing rishi Surochi's warnings about subjecting himself to the *agnimanasa homa.*

The loss is inevitable. It is a sacrifice that the magic demands and exacts.

The magic had claimed its price. He had known it would, yet he hadn't heeded Surochi's words. He had insisted on undergoing the *agnimanasa*. He had done it for the people, to alleviate their suffering, to bring back the rain.

And the rain was here, a loud and merciless deluge.

The king shook his head. He couldn't tell anyone about the *agnimanasa*. Not now, and probably never. They would never forgive him, especially Mandavi.

"Things will turn out alright," Kushadhwaja was saying, the sharpness dropping from his tone, his grip loosening, his expression gentler. "Taksha will be back on his feet in no time…"

The sound of approaching footsteps pulled Bharat's attention away from Kushadhwaja, and he turned to see a figure come into view at the head of the gallery. The king stiffened immediately, and as everyone else took notice of the woman, a tide of uneasiness surged through the gallery. Shatrughna shot a wary glance at his brother, whose eyes were narrowing in aversion and mistrust.

"She shouldn't be here," Bharat took a step forward, breathing in anger. "This part of the palace is out of bounds."

Before he could make a further move to intercept the visitor, Kushadhwaja stopped him, fingers flat on the king's chest. "She is the boy's grandmother," the old man said under his breath with a small shake of his head. "Let her be."

Drawing a deep breath, the king watched Kaikeyi pass them and head towards the door where the other queens of the palace stood looking uncertain, not knowing how to react to her sudden appearance. Not once did Kaikeyi meet Bharat's gaze, her eyes focused straight ahead, but her tread was firm, her shoulders squared and defiant, daring anyone to come in her way. Reaching the door, she slowed her pace, giving Urmila and Sumitra a moment to make way for her. Then, without a word, sweeping aside the curtains that covered the doorway, she entered the chamber where the *vaidyas* were striving to revive her grandson.

Bharat glared after his mother for a moment longer before wrenching his gaze and his thoughts back to Taksha.

Angara? Play? Story?

"Any news of the attackers?" Kushadhwaja asked Shatrughna, making conversation to fill the awkward silence that had settled around them in Kaikeyi's wake.

"They found one of them in the trees, burned to death," the prince replied. "No sign of the second one though, but the guards are searching the grounds."

"He couldn't have gone far," Kushadhwaja nodded. Turning to his son-in-law, he said, "Don't worry, we will nab him. We will get right to the bottom of this."

Bharat nodded at his father-in-law and *kshatri*, but it didn't really matter if they got the man or didn't, not right now. Taksha was all that mattered at this moment. He just wanted his son back. He desperately wanted his son back, even though he guessed that wasn't how this was destined to end.

You are bound to lose something precious.

Struggling to ignore the jagged shards of despair ripping through him, Bharat floundered in the roar of the rain he had brought to Ayodhya.

There wasn't a street in Ayodhya that wasn't full of people, that wasn't bubbling over with joy.

The rain had come suddenly, unexpectedly, without warning, the clouds forming with uncanny speed, the first roll of thunder surprising everyone so they had stopped in their tracks to listen, not ready to believe what they were hearing. After all, no one had portended rain in Ayodhya; not the fortune-tellers seated on the steps by the Sarayu, not the rishis in the Sanctum across the river, not the old boatmen who could gauge the next day's weather by reading the river currents. Even when the wind whipped through the city's streets, dragging debris along, people had been cautious, not willing to celebrate too soon for fear of being disappointed later. Ayodhya hadn't seen rainfall for so long that the prospect of rain seemed hard to envision.

Children had been the first to burst out of their homes as the first few uncertain drops turned to a drizzle before the sky relented, opening its heart to a grateful land. The womenfolk followed the children outdoors, lifting their faces to the clouds and letting the rain wash away their cares before running indoors to fetch pots and pails to fill with rainwater. Their joy spread to the men of the household, and soon everyone except the hopelessly invalid was out in the rain, dancing and frolicking in joy and splashing through puddles that grew and filled out rapidly to submerge whole streets with water. Lamps were placed inside doorways to light up streets and courtyards, men essayed out of their homes with *dhols*, and feisty folk songs sprang to life in street corners, while children shrieked as they chased one another and went wild. The rain was heavy and the raindrops often painful, but it didn't seem to bother the citizens of Ayodhya. The rain had taken their minds off their anxieties and fears — the rakshasa attack, the eerie disappearances, the daily struggles of life, all momentarily forgotten.

There wasn't a street in Ayodhya that wasn't bubbling over with joy.

As with everyone else, the rain had taken Dileepa and Nandana too by surprise. They had gone to sit by the ruined mansion by the river to watch the sun set, a favourite routine of theirs. Even after it had grown darker, they had sat hand in hand, her head on his shoulder, listening to the distant cries of the boatmen and watching the bobbing reflections of the bargemen's torches in the dark water, when a wind rippled through the reeds and they were drawn to the low rumble of thunder. By the time they had made their way back to the road that led into the city, lightning streaked endlessly across the sky, and Ayodhya was still half a mile away when the rain started coming down in sheets.

There was no shelter to be found, and Nandana had abandoned even the pretence of looking for one, throwing her arms open and allowing the rain to drench her. When Dileepa had tried to hurry her along, Nandana had resisted, pulling the *dandapala* playfully to herself, making light of his diffidence, forcing him to shed his reserve. Putting her arms around his neck, she had drawn him close, and standing in the middle of the road under a vast, wet sky, they had melted into one another's embrace, swooning and losing themselves in a never-ending kiss from which neither had a recollection of surfacing.

Drunk on passion, eyes locked in love, the two made their way back into Ayodhya, but the city was in no mood to let the lovers be. Men, women and children danced everywhere, and Dileepa and Nandana were dragged into one group, from whom they freed themselves only to be drawn into a second one. They eventually gave up trying to escape and joined in the fun and festivities, surrendering to the love and gaiety that had ensnared them in an evening of rain.

There wasn't a street in Ayodhya that wasn't bubbling over with joy that evening.

She stood near the mansion's rooftop and frowned upon the dark, dripping city in frustration.

She didn't understand this rain.

It had come from nowhere, in impossibly large quantities. There was no reason for it to rain so heavily, given the scant levels of magic present over Ayodhya, and this worried Simhika. What had brought the rain if not magic? And if it was magic — it had to be, she knew instinctively — how had the magic in the atmosphere become so strong all of a sudden? What forces were at play here? Who was interfering with her work, making it doubly difficult for her to weaken the foundations of the human kingdom?

Destroy the homa *fire that sustains Ayodhya's magic, Simhika, and you will have the gratitude of every rakshasa, starting with me, Ravana.*

Her lord's words rang in Simhika's ears, uttered the day she had left Lanka with the objective of weaving an elaborate subterfuge in Ayodhya. She had worked hard to put her plans into action. She knew she had made good progress, and she was confident her efforts would soon bear fruit. But now this rain was here, bringing with it a warning that her work was being undermined by something… or *someone*.

Simhika realized she had to quickly counter what was happening. She had to prevent the magic from coming back, from gaining strength and spreading over Ayodhya. She had to locate whatever — *whoever* — was causing this resurgence and put a permanent check on it. Simhika knew what she needed to do. She just didn't know where and how to start. Perhaps she would set her *pets*, her shadows, to the task, she thought idly…

A movement far below by the bend in the street drew the sorceress's attention, distracting her. The rain was starting to let up a little, enough for Simhika to make out two silhouettes darting down the street towards the mansion.

A man and a woman. Huddling together under the pretext of rain, laughing breathlessly, hopelessly in love.

The pair drew near, and light from an open window fell on their faces. Nandana's doe-like eyes were on Dileepa, full of affection. The *dandapala* said something funny, and Nandana laughed in delight as they slipped back into shadow.

Simhika heaved a satisfied sigh. The girl was putting on a very convincing act of being in love, she thought to herself. In fact, had she not known better, she might have believed Nandana was indeed smitten by Dileepa. The poor investigator was taken in by the deception, of course, and the girl had him nicely wrapped around her little finger. Simhika decided it was time to exploit the *dandapala* once again to further her agenda. She needed to gain access to the king next; she had to infiltrate the palace the way she had wormed into the Sanctum. With luck, the *dandapala* might even help her get to the source of the magic that had mysteriously returned to Ayodhya…

The sorceress of Lanka lifted her eyes to scan the city's rooftops, which were becoming more discernible as the rain slowly lightened. She suddenly felt more reassured and less intimidated. She had dealt with impossible odds before and won. She would tackle the magic of the humans.

She would triumph again, she decided, as she watched the thinning rain with grim, challenging eyes.

They ducked under the awning of the mansion's doorway, trying not to laugh too loudly, holding on to each other, not wanting to let go, eyes locked in delirium, their breaths fevered, stretching the moment, willing the night to last for an eternity. Nandana and Dileepa stood in the shadow of the doorway, burning with desire.

Pulling her to himself, the *dandapala* whispered in Nandana's ear, "How will I bear being away from you tonight, my dear?"

The girl snuggled against Dileepa's chest with a sigh. "I wish you didn't have to go," she said, her breath setting his skin on fire. "But we must part for now because the night is growing old, and Ma Parnalata might be getting anxious about me."

"You are right," said the *dandapala*, releasing the girl from his embrace with great reluctance. With a wry grin, he added, "Youth should always defer to the old, whether it be the lengthening night or a worried aunt."

"Stop being mean," Nandana struck him playfully with a lightly curled fist. "Ma means well."

"Of course she does," Dileepa said hurriedly, worried he had given offence. "I said that in jest."

"I know."

"I respect her a lot," he insisted in a mollifying tone, searching the girl's face for a reaction. "I really do."

"I know," the girl smiled, and the investigator breathed in relief.

"Will you come tomorrow?" Nandana asked after a moment's pause, looking at the *dandapala* with expectant eyes.

"I have to follow up on a lead tomorrow," Dileepa began, sounding doubtful, "and I don't know how much time that will take."

"Oh," the girl's voice rang with disappointment.

"But I'll try my—" Seeing the crushed look on Nandana's face, the *dandapala* stopped. With a sigh and a shake of his head, he said, "Okay, yes, I will come tomorrow." He took the girl by her chin and lifted her face to his. "Happy?" he asked, his eyes twinkling.

Nandana nodded, smiling in delight. They pulled each other into another embrace, but disengaged quickly. It was getting late. The rain had slowed to a drizzle, and there was no other sound to be heard. The city had fallen silent, the street around them empty except for rippling puddles of rainwater.

"Tomorrow then," Dileepa said, stepping back, drawing away, still holding the girl's hands.

"Tomorrow," Nandana nodded. Their fingers touched one last time, like the echo of a longing.

He turned and began walking away. Half a dozen steps, and he turned to find the girl still under the awning of the doorway, watching him leave. He imagined he saw her smile. He waved to her. She waved back.

He continued walking. Another ten steps, and he looked back again. This time, the doorway was vacant.

With a sigh that was both happy and melancholic, the *dandapala* set his face towards the street and his mind to the task of getting back home.

There were still twenty paces to the turning onto the main street when a figure stepped out of the shadows of a building — straight into Dileepa's path. The investigator slowed his pace in surprise, wondering who it might be at this late hour. Then, he froze, his eyes widening against the drizzle…

The tall figure held a *khanga*, its long, oiled blade shining dully in the dark.

The figure took one, then two purposeful steps forward, narrowing the distance between them. Any lingering doubts Dileepa might have had about the man's intent were dispelled as he raised the *khanga* and braced his legs to strike.

His mouth, throat and lips too dry to utter a word or to shout for help, Dileepa spun on his heel to run in the opposite direction, but he stopped even before he had turned fully.

Blocking his path in the other direction was another figure, also armed with a *khanga*.

Before he could make complete sense of this, the *dandapala* sensed movement to his right and left. Darting rapid glances out of the corners of his eyes, he saw two more armed men step into the street, cornering him from both sides.

He was surrounded on all four sides. All escape routes had been cut off.

A whimper wafted to Dileepa's lips as the four assailants approached him, swords raised to cut him down in the middle of the dark and deserted street.

Ask yourself, why do we rishis never suggest an agnimanasa, *rajan?*

The rain's intensity had tapered, making other noises audible. The calls of the guards combing the palace grounds, torches in hand, searching for the second assailant. The footsteps of palace hands hurrying in and out as they acted on the orders of the *vaidyas*. And from somewhere in the city, the faint echo of a song and the rhythmic beat of a *dhol*.

Rishi Surochi's words from their conversation at the Sanctum when the king had first broached the subject of the *agnimanasa* kept swirling out of the mists of Bharat's despair.

Nothing can be created out of nothing, and magic needs the strength of the homa *fire to come into being. But during the* agnimanasa, *there is no* homa *fire. So, the magic draws strength from another source: a thing or a person that the one doing the* homa *holds close to his heart.*

What could I lose —

Let it be, rajan. The price is not worth the effort.

People were singing and dancing in the streets, Bharat thought to himself, rejoicing at the coming of the rain. It had been a long while since they'd had a reason to rejoice, and he had given them that joy. But had he done so at the cost of his son's life? Had Surochi been right about the price not being worth —

The yuvaraja has woken.

Bharat frowned inwardly in confusion. He didn't recall Surochi saying anything about —

He blinked once, his eyes widening as hope soared, his heart missing a beat in the sudden flush of excitement that swelled in his chest and burst through his veins. Had he heard right? Was he imagining it, or had someone —

It was Vihari, the chief *vaidya* of the palace, the king realized.

Giddy with expectation, Bharat spun around to face the *vaidya* when he felt Kushadhwaja grab his arm.

"The boy is up," the *kshatri* was saying, sounding breathless as he tugged at Bharat. "Come…"

Bharat, Shatrughna and Kushadhwaja joined Kausalya, Sumitra and Urmila by the door, all six of them looking eagerly at Vihari.

"Is my… Is he alright?" Bharat asked haltingly, afraid of the answer.

"He is mildly disoriented, but he seems fine otherwise," the wrinkled physician said, drawing the curtain aside, inviting them to look. "There he is, rajan. You can meet him."

For a fleeting moment, Bharat felt the strength leave his legs. He had virtually abandoned hope, convinced that the *agnimanasa* had claimed his son — that he had gambled away the boy's life for the good of the land. But by some grace of destiny, Taksha had been saved and returned to him. Bharat, for a fleeting moment, wondered if he even deserved to have his darling son back.

Seeing their king enter, the *vaidyas* withdrew from around the raised platform that served as a bed-cum-examination table, making room for the family. Kaikeyi bent over the boy, a hand on his forehead, gazing into his face, tears shining in her eyes. Sensing Bharat and the others, she looked up and straightened, but showed no inclination to leave her grandson's side.

Assailed by the cloying scents of *yashtimadhu* and *tvak* that lingered in the chamber's closed atmosphere, Bharat crossed to Taksha, his heart beating wildly in relief, his own eyes suddenly moist with gratitude. The boy lay on his back, a compress to his head, his face still sallow but gradually regaining its colour. However, the moment Taksha caught sight of his father, his face lit up and he raised one hand towards Bharat, beckoning him. Sinking down by his son's side, Bharat took the boy's hand gently in his own, wrapping his fingers around it protectively. He held his breath as he stared into his son's eyes, unable to speak, unable to believe his good fortune, and the moment shimmered between them until Taksha broke the silence.

"Ba..." he said, addressing his father in a voice that was barely more than a whisper.

"How are you feeling, brave man?" the king smiled in reply, feeling his voice choke a little.

A ghost of a smile appeared on Taksha's lips. Bharat gave the little hand a reassuring squeeze. Looking around, he said, "See... everyone is here to see you."

Taksha searched the faces until his gaze alighted on Kushadhwaja. "Nana," he said.

"Yes, your nana," the old man stepped forward and beamed down at the boy. "Get well quickly. We have to go out and play."

"Play," Taksha said, the idea already imparting strength to his voice. Then, as a thought crossed his mind, his brow furrowed. "Angara?" he asked, looking at his father.

Angara. Bharat felt a pang of guilt at the mention of the dog. Angara had most certainly saved Taksha's life by going after the second assailant repeatedly, yet he had hardly spared a thought for the dog ever since he had brought Taksha in from the rain. What had happened to Angara? Where was the dog, and was it —

"Angara is fine," Shatrughna spoke from behind in a bright, cheery voice. "It is with the stable boys and is being well cared for, but it is also impatient and waiting for you to get back outside."

"There… one more reason to get well soon," Bharat smiled at Taksha, glad to hear that Angara was alright. He would look up the dog in the morning, he promised himself.

As he kissed the boy's hand and got to his feet, Bharat heard Sumitra put a question to the head of the *vaidyas*. "Do you know what happened to him? Why did he faint the way he did?"

Everyone turned to Vihari in anticipation. The subordinate physicians exchanged looks as their chief cleared his throat. "We don't know for sure, though I suspect it could be a seizure of some sort," he said.

"A seizure?" Kushadhwaja repeated. "Like a fit, you mean?"

The chief *vaidya* shrugged. "Umm… yes, maybe."

"Could it happen again?" Bharat asked in the troubled silence that followed.

The silence in the room deepened to the extent that the physician's voice seemed to bounce off the walls. "It is hard to say," he said. After a pause, he added, "It might recur, or it might not."

"That is not very helpful," Kaikeyi remarked, her tone making it plain that she was dissatisfied with the reply.

"I'm afraid it is not, but it is better than a lie to make everyone feel good," said Vihari, spreading his hands. "We shall observe the yuvaraja to see if we can learn something more about what afflicted him."

The king nodded. "Please do what you can to try and prevent a recurrence," he said.

"It might be good to let the child rest," pronounced Kushadhwaja, and the *vaidyas* agreed.

One by one, everyone came to Taksha's side to shower him with their love and blessings before leaving the room, until Bharat and Shatrughna were the only ones remaining. Shatrughna bent over his nephew and tousled his hair.

"Once you are back on your feet, I have a surprise for you," he said with a twinkle in his eyes. "A gift."

"Gift?" Taksha's face glowed in anticipation. "What?"

"If I tell you, it won't be a surprise, will it?" Shatrughna grinned as he straightened. "Get well."

Bharat knelt beside Taksha one last time. "Yes, get well soon," he said softly, "and… and thank you for not going away." Seeing the look of incomprehension on the boy's face, Bharat smiled. "It's alright. You will understand one day." He kissed Taksha on the forehead and rose to leave.

The brothers made their way through the palace. The rain had practically stopped, though water still dripped from the eaves and awnings. Outside, the search for the second assailant was still underway as torches pinpricked the dark of the palace grounds.

"Let's go and see what's happening," said Bharat, looking towards the grounds.

"Leave it to me, brother," said Shatrughna. "You should set some rest. It's been a hard evening for you."

"I'm alright —" Bharat began, but the younger brother interrupted him.

"No. You *must* rest. And anyway, if we haven't found anyone yet, it's unlikely we are going to find anyone now… at least not tonight."

Bharat considered this and nodded. "Alright. But let me know if they find anyone."

Once the brothers parted, Bharat traversed darkened corridors towards his bedchamber. He was lost in thought, and he failed to notice a figure detach itself from behind a curtain as he passed by. The figure stepped out behind the king and stood in the open, surveying him for a moment.

"Bharat," the figure called.

Startled, the king stopped and turned. But even before he had fully faced the figure, dislike had crept into his eyes and his jaw had stiffened. He recognized the voice that he had come to hate.

"What do you want?" he asked coldly.

"Do you know, had I been the assailant everyone is looking for, I could have killed you a moment ago, when you passed that curtain?" Kaikeyi asked, stepping into a halo of light cast by a distant lamp. "You didn't even *see* me, Bharat. You've got to be more alert. And what are you doing walking alone in the darkness like this?"

"What are you talking about?" the king asked irritably.

"Don't you realize what happened this evening?" Kaikeyi asked, taking a step closer to Bharat. "Those two assailants… What did they want? *Who* did they want?" She paused. "Not Taksha. Definitely not the kid. Why would they want anything with him? No, they wanted *you*, Bharat. *You* were their target. Someone wants to assassinate you. Your life is in danger, and you can't afford to be lax about it. As your mother, I am here to warn you to be careful."

Without another word, without even waiting for Bharat to react or reply, Kaikeyi turned on her heel and walked away. The king watched his mother go, her words ringing loud in the stillness of the night.

You were their target. Someone wants to assassinate you. Your life is in danger.

He stood rooted to the spot, too stunned to string two coherent thoughts together, as they came at him from all four sides.

Who were these men? What did they want? Why were they attacking him? What should he do? What *could* he do?

He could run, Dileepa thought to himself. He could at least try.

But all exits had closed a while ago, the *dandapala* realized. The attackers were closing in and he had less and less room to slip between them. Even if he tried, the long *khangas* would shred him in seconds.

He could put up a fight.

Had the situation not been so grim, Dileepa might well have laughed at the ridiculousness of the thought. He was a *dandapala*, an investigator of the palace, not a *yoddha* in Kosala's army, not even a *nagarapala*. He was trained to solve crimes using his intelligence. He wasn't trained to fight — definitely not trained to fight barehanded against four armed men intent on killing him.

He could scream for help.

The men were almost upon him, the blades of their swords already singing in their downward arcs, and Dileepa knew screaming for help would serve very little purpose. By the time anyone got around to opening their windows and looking out, his sad little life would be over, his blood sullying the puddles in the street. Still, he could try screaming. It was the one thing he *could* do.

So drawing his breath, the *dandapala* opened his mouth in terror, knowing it could well be the last sound to escape his lips —

— when a golden-orange light burst into being over the street, right above his and his attackers' heads.

The suddenness of its appearance took all five men by surprise. Instinctively, all five glanced upwards, their minds turned from the more immediate thoughts of slaughter and survival. And looking up, they stared, mesmerized by the spectacle unfolding before their eyes.

The light was a globule, shaped like a particularly large pumpkin. Suspended mid-air a couple of yards over the men's heads, it pulsed unevenly, its radiance harsh on the eye. Little tongues of fire leaped and flared off its surface as it spun on its axis, slow and lazy.

Then, even as the men gaped in wonder and astonishment, vague forms pulled from the globule in all directions, tearing outwards from its centre, breaking free of its core, ripping away from its surface. In less than a fraction of a moment, the globule had disintegrated into six individual parts —

— the parts transforming into six fiery *shyenas*, their majestic, hooked beaks, curved talons and the undersides of their wings glowing golden-orange, as if lit from within.

Even before they had formed fully, the *shyenas* flapped their wings, twisted their bodies around, and swooped down upon the four attackers, beaks opened in aggression, talons angled to strike. Surprised by the speed at which everything had happened, the attackers were slow to react, and the *shyenas* struck the men's faces, lacerating their features. Blood arced in the half-light shed by the birds, and the men shrieked in pain, one dropping his sword to shield eyes that were already going blind. Dileepa saw thin trails of fire appear where the talons had raked flesh and skin, and the smell of charred flesh assailed his nostrils, making him gag.

Two of the men regrouped and took their *khangas* with both hands in an attempt to stand against the birds. One took a wild swing at the *shyena* closest to him and missed, but the other's sword sliced through another of the birds. Sliced *right through* it, like cutting through a pall of smoke. The *shyena* flapped in the air, unharmed, its ghost body intact. Then, all six birds renewed their attack, even more hostile this time, even more vengeful.

Watching the birds descend, Dileepa staggered away from his attackers, not knowing what was going on, but aware that for some reason, he was safe from the birds, that they had come to his rescue. But before he could put more thought to it, the *dandapala* heard the men scream again and turned to see the ghost birds ravage their faces, throats and chests, laying their bodies open, wings beating the air, bloodied talons slashing in wild abandon. Dileepa saw one man fall, then another, then the third. The fourth attacker, the one who had lost his eyes at the start, was down on his knees, holding his bleeding face and crying to himself, already defeated, but the *shyenas* were not done with him yet. Two of the birds attacked him, striking repeatedly at his bowed head and back, flaying him until he fell on his side. One *shyena* went for the man's throat, his final shriek ending in a ragged gasp that rose from the torn ruins of muscle and cartilage.

The sight of the four men lying dead in the street brought the bile up and Dileepa bent over and retched. He had never witnessed anyone being killed before, and this was a killing of a different level, dreadfully efficient, so without mercy. He was conscious that it might have been his body sprawled in the street instead of the men's and he was thankful it wasn't, but the gruesomeness of the killing was still revolting.

Licking his lips, disgusted by the aftertaste of bile on his tongue, the *dandapala* raised his head to look at the birds. The *shyenas* looped and weaved over the street for one moment, surveying their grisly handiwork before flying down the street in unison, as if in response to a command. Following their languid flight, Dileepa's eyes widened as he noticed the figure at the turn of the street for the first time, standing right under the shadow of Ma Parnalata's mansion.

As the birds drew near the figure, the investigator observed the figure spread its arms, and one after another, all six *shyenas* slipped into its embrace... where they vanished, absorbed into the body of the outlandish figure. Once the last of the birds was gone, the figure exuded a glow for the space of two heartbeats, a golden-orange nimbus that threw the figure into silhouette.

A woman, Dileepa made out, even as the glow diminished and died.

He swallowed hard, his lips and mouth suddenly dry as he stared at the dark figure standing at the other end of the street, immobile, looking back at him. He couldn't believe what he had just seen. He couldn't believe the birds, he couldn't believe the killings, but most of all, he couldn't believe what he had seen of the figure that he was certain had everything to do with the savage birds and his rescue.

The *dandapala* had caught a glimpse of the woman's face just as the birds had slipped between her arms. The glow cast by the birds had lit her features momentarily, features that he had come to regard as the most exquisite, the most bewitching in the whole wide world. Features that he had fallen in love with and spent sleepless nights conjuring in his imagination.

Even though her face had been illuminated for a mere fraction of a second, Dileepa had had no trouble recognizing Nandana.

two

SUMMONS TO ATTEND COURT HAD BEEN SENT OUT EARLY, and the annex to Ayodhya's Throne Room had been abuzz with activity since mid-morning. Courtiers and clerks lounged in small groups, dissecting the previous evening's events, speculating on the identity of the would-be assassins, marvelling at their king's presence of mind at foiling the killers, while thanking the heavens for Taksha's narrow escape. Baladitya, the *mahanayaka* of the *nagarapalas*, was quite in demand as everyone was keen to know if the *nagarapalas* were anywhere close to catching the assassin who had got away. But to everyone's disappointment, the *mahanayaka* revealed little. Mitraka, the head of the *dandapalas*, was also in attendance with her investigators, as was *mahanayaka* Gajakarna of Kosala's army. *Adhipatis* Sudhanva and Sheelabhadra maintained their distance, both pretending as if the other didn't exist, the former speaking almost exclusively to Gajakarna while the latter engaged mostly with the revenue minister, Sheshagupta. Palace hands came and went bearing buttermilk and honeyed lime juice, dispensing refreshments as everyone waited for the king to arrive.

Bharat was held up by a never-ending stream of visitors and well-wishers who, on hearing about the attack, came to the palace to enquire after the king and the yuvaraja. The guild master of Chedi, who was visiting Kosala on business, was one of the first to arrive, offering his king's good wishes and support to Bharat. Representatives of Kosala's own guild led by the new guild master, Sheelabhadra, had dropped in next, followed by Surochi with a dozen other rishis of the Sanctum. Surochi had been circumspect all through the meeting even as the rishis agreed on a special *homa* for Taksha's well-being, and as they were leaving, he had exchanged a meaningful look with Bharat. Even common citizens queued up to meet their king, and though Shatrughna suggested otherwise, Bharat insisted on giving everyone an audience, not willing to turn away those who meant him well. Elsewhere in the city, people flocked to temples to offer special prayers for their king and his son, and men and women underwent fasts to atone for any mistakes of theirs that might have brought misfortune to the palace. That morning in Ayodhya, in whichever direction one looked, there was an outpouring of sympathy and relief directed at Bharat and Taksha.

It was well past noon when Bharat finally reached the court with Kushadhwaja and Shatrughna. With an apology for the delay, he took his seat on a *sayyasana* and everyone else settled around him. The chamber was packed all the way to the back, and people even stood outside, craning their necks to watch and listen.

"My thanks to each of you for your patience and support," Bharat began, clearing his throat. "To all of you concerned about Taksha, the boy is recovering well."

A collective sigh of relief spread through the room. The king waited a moment for the murmurs to subside before continuing. "The not-so-good news is that we know practically nothing about the attackers." He turned to Baladitya. "Please share what you can with us."

The *mahanayaka* rose to his feet, a tall, gaunt man with a long nose and a short beard that was more white than black. "Unfortunately, there is little of value to share, rajan," he said in a voice that rumbled like faraway thunder. Addressing the court, he said, "There is nothing on the body of the attacker who died that can give us a clue to his identity. And unfortunately, his head and face have been burned beyond recognition."

"What about the second man?" someone asked from the back.

"We have been combing the city all morning, but we are yet to find any trace of him," Baladitya admitted. "Checks have been intensified along the riverfront and at the city's gates to stop him from getting out." With a pause, he added, "On the positive side, none of guards at any of the gates have reported an instance of someone leaving the city last night."

"So, the man is still in Ayodhya," said Sheshagupta as murmurs of satisfaction went around the room.

"Yes…" the *mahanayaka* looked at the revenue minister soberly, "…unless he escaped by boat under cover of darkness… or swam his way to freedom across the Sarayu."

The thought killed whatever hopes the *mahanayaka* had raised earlier, and everyone went back to looking crestfallen.

"However, Mitraka and I think the chances of his still being in the city are greater," Baladitya said with a nod in the direction of the *dandapalas*. "We understand that he was attacked by the dog and was badly injured. We doubt he could have swum across the river in such a state. And while he could still have taken a boat out of here, it is our belief that he is hiding in Ayodhya."

"Let us hope you are both right," said Bharat.

"Starting this afternoon, we will be paying visits to all the *vaidyas* in the city," said Baladitya. "One of them might have treated someone for wounds from dog bite." The *mahanayaka* looked at Mitraka with respect. "The idea came from the *dandapalas*, rajan."

With a nod of appreciation, Bharat addressed Mitraka. "I would like you to spare a few of your *dandapalas* to assist the *nagarapalas* in this investigation."

Mitraka, a hefty woman in her fifties sporting a large silver nose ring, bowed to the king. "It is an honour to serve the palace, rajan," she said, "but my *dandapalas* are already quite stretched with the investigation into the disappearances. We are few in number, and our hands are full."

Before Bharat could reply, a courtier spoke. "It's not as though the *dandapalas* are making any great headway with the mystery behind the disappearances," he said, a shot of sarcasm in his tone. "In fact, I just heard about four fresh cases of people disappearing from the city since last evening."

As fresh murmurs broke out, Baladitya addressed the courtier. "There have been *three* cases, not four. One was a boy who had gone to visit his grandmother but had forgotten to inform his parents that he wasn't coming back for the night. The parents thought he had disappeared and panicked."

"Fine, three then," the courtier replied. "It doesn't change the fact that the *dandapalas* are no closer to stopping the disappearances. So, some men can easily be diverted to investigate the attack on our rajan."

Bharat cleared his throat loudly, signalling his intent to speak. "I understand the *dandapalas* are few in number and are burdened with other work, but we could really benefit from their skills," he said tactfully. Looking at Mitraka, he added, "If you can share even some of your resources with the *nagarapalas*, we would all be very grateful."

Mitraka bowed again. "The *dandapalas* will do all they can to serve the palace and the people, rajan," she said, ceding to the king's wishes.

In the silence that followed, one of the older courtiers spoke. "What's important is that our king was attacked." He looked from Baladitya to Mitraka. "Do you have any thoughts on who might want to cause the rajan harm?"

Baladitya and Mitraka exchanged glances, each waiting for the other to reply.

"The matter is being investigated," Mitraka said at last. "We will share what we learn at the earliest."

The head of the *dandapalas* had scarcely finished when Sudhanva spoke. "The threat has to be external," he grunted. Seeing he had everyone's attention, he said. "Madhupura, to be specific."

"Can you elaborate on that, *adhipati*?" the old courtier asked.

"It's pretty obvious to me," Sudhanva shrugged. "Lavanyasurya has something against Kosala. He has adopted an antagonistic approach towards us for quite some time now, raising tariffs at will, seizing our garrison in Madhupura, all with the intent of provoking us. When he sees that we refuse to act, when we refuse to protect what is ours by right, he is emboldened. Seeing our silence as a weakness, he sends assassins against the rajan. It's that simple." Stopping to draw a breath, he shot a glance at Kushadhwaja. "Instead of sitting here and wasting time in talk, we should be going to war against Madhupura. If we are to be taken seriously, *we... must... act.*"

"You may be right about Lavanyasurya," Kushadhwaja conceded, "but action should be based on evidence, not on passion or personal bias."

"The Kosala garrison was taken from us, our men stationed there thrown in prison before being forced to leave Madhupura," Sudhanva said heatedly. "Those men are your evidence." Pointing to Shatrughna, he added, "Your son-in-law was there. Ask him."

"And the evidence that the assassins were from Madhupura?" the *kshatri* kept his cool, refusing to let Sudhanva ruffle him.

The *adhipati* of Sankasya shucked his shoulders. "You will see it is Lavanyasurya's doing," he insisted grouchily.

"The plot to kill the rajan could have been hatched here in Kosala," said a voice, and all heads pivoted to Sheelabhadra. "There are people in Ayodhya who have reason to be dissatisfied with some of the rajan's recent decisions," the guild master pressed on. "The rajan acted to safeguard the interests of his subjects, but it hurt these people badly, so it is possible such elements could have conspired to kill the rajan."

This time, the silence stretched all the way to the back of the room and even spilled out to where people stood looking in through the doors and windows. More than a few pairs of eyes went to Sudhanva as he sat glowering, his head lowered, but no one noticed Gajakarna shift on his feet uncomfortably.

"You speak in riddles," the old courtier remarked.

"Do I?" Sheelabhadra's tone was challenging. "I think what I have said is plain to everyone."

"Speculation of this sort does no good and must stop," Bharat stepped in, his voice ringing with authority and tinged with annoyance. "I have no patience left for idle talk and guesswork. The *nagarapalas* and *dandapalas* will conduct their investigation to find hard, irrefutable facts, and we will act on those and those alone."

The sharpness of the king's words quietened everyone, and Kushadhwaja took the opportunity to address Bharat. "Until the *nagarapalas* and *dandapalas* get to the bottom of this and we are able to counter the threat to your life, you are in danger. Security needs to be tightened around you wherever you go. And you need a bodyguard."

"I don't think one is necessary," Bharat protested. "I am quite capable of—"

"The *kshatri* is right, rajan," Sudhanva interjected. "Not for a moment do any of us doubt your ability to defend yourself. You are a *mahayoddha*. Still, there is no harm in having an able pair of hands for support." He leaned forward in entreaty. "You already have so many cares. A bodyguard will ease the worry of constantly being on one's guard."

The kshatri *is right… the* adhipati *is right…* A chorus of voices rose from all around in support of the idea. Bharat finally had to raise his hands in surrender. "As you all wish," he said.

Sudhanva immediately turned to Gajakarna. "Perhaps the *mahanayaka* could detail one or two of the best men he can spare…"

"Yes," Gajakarna said, nodding, "Indeed I will."

"One man should suffice," Bharat noted.

"As it pleases the rajan," Gajakarna nodded again.

"There is one last thing…" Bharat looked around the chamber. "Some of you might have heard about the strange killings in the city…"

Some heads nodded while other faces looked confused as voices and eyebrows rose around the room.

"Why don't we let the *mahanayaka* tell us about it?" the king said, inviting Baladitya to speak.

"Early this morning, four men were found murdered… *massacred*… in a street in the city's old quarter," the militiaman revealed. "All four had been killed violently, their throats ripped open. They bore distinct scratch marks on their faces, shoulders and hands, as though they had been mauled by a vicious animal… which could explain their torn throats. I know this does not make sense, but the wounds that had been inflicted on them also had traces of burn marks."

"Maybe they were attacked by wild dogs," somebody hazarded a guess.

"No," Baladitya shook his head. "What attacked them was definitely bigger. The wounds were only on their heads, faces, shoulders and hands. Not a scratch on their torsos, stomachs or legs." He paused, considering a new possibility. "It almost feels as if they were attacked from *above*… by a bird of some sort."

"A bird?" the courtier Vijaya asked in disbelief. "What bird?"

Baladitya shrugged. "What is interesting is that four *khangas* were found near the four bodies."

"They must have killed one another then," someone else surmised.

"Except that none of the *khangas* had any blood on them," said the *mahanayaka*. "None of the swords had been used to strike or kill."

"And no one saw or heard a thing?" Sheshagupta asked.

"Well, an old woman living on the street claims she heard a noise. When she opened a window to investigate, she apparently saw a man running away from the street."

"A man, not a bird," one courtier snickered.

"Didn't this woman see the bodies?" Shatrughna enquired.

"It was too dark, yuvaraja. She couldn't see this man who ran away clearly either, but we're trying to find out who it might have been."

"And we don't know who the four dead men are, I suppose," said Sudhanva.

"Not yet, *adhipati*," said Baladitya. "As I said, their faces have been badly mangled, making it hard to tell their features. We are hoping some relations will come to claim them and help make an identification."

"People disappearing and returning mysteriously, our rajan being attacked, people being killed bizarrely in the middle of the street…" a wizened courtier, bent with age, voiced his thoughts in a slow quaver. "What curse is this that afflicts us? What is happening to our beloved Ayodhya?"

A tense silence pressed down on the assembly until another courtier spoke. "Is there any reason to believe that the deaths in the street are in any way connected to the attack on the rajan?"

Grim looks were exchanged all around the room as the possibility of a connection sunk in. The *mahanayaka* of the *nagarapalas* glanced at Bharat, unsure about how best to answer this.

"The *nagarapalas* and the *dandapalas* will get to the truth as their investigations progress," the king said, coming to Baladitya's rescue. With that, he rose, drawing an end to the proceedings.

As he walked out of the chamber, Bharat was conscious of the anxiety that permeated the room, and he couldn't help playing back the old courtier's words in his head.

What curse is this that afflicts us? What is happening to our beloved Ayodhya?

Sweat beaded Dileepa's brow as he elbowed past his fellow *dandapalas* and exited the chamber, heading straight for the door that led to the palace grounds. He felt hot and more than a little light-headed, and he needed fresh air. More importantly, he needed to get away from everyone so that he could think clearly.

When she opened a window to investigate, she apparently saw a man running away from the street.

Panic took a vice-like hold on the investigator as *mahanayaka* Baladitya's words came back to him. Who was this woman, and had it been him she had seen, or was it someone else altogether? Could she identify him as the man who had run? He did remember running, and if she identified him, it wouldn't look good at all…

She couldn't see this man who ran away clearly, but we're trying to find out who it might have been.

Dileepa shivered despite the warmth of the sun falling over him like a curtain as he stepped onto a walkway. He wondered what he should do. Should he confess? That would look better than being caught like a criminal, and everyone would probably treat him with greater leniency. Confessing was an act of honesty, after all. But then, it wasn't as if he had confessed as soon as the men had been killed. He hadn't even confessed when the bodies had been discovered in the morning. He had stood in the king's court with Mitraka and the other *dandapalas* and listened silently to Baladitya talk about the killings — many hours after the bodies had been discovered. There wasn't much honesty he could discern in that kind of behaviour.

And even if he did confess, what exactly would he say? That the men had attacked him, but he hadn't killed them? That they had been slaughtered by phantom *shyenas* controlled by… a young woman whom he was in love with, who was the daughter of a dead records clerk, and who now lived with her aunt on the street where…

No, no, no, the *dandapala* shook his head. No one would believe his story. And why would he put Nandana in trouble when she had saved his life?

But who exactly was Nandana, a voice in his head piped in. What did he know about her? And how could he explain what he had witnessed the previous night? The image of the six *shyenas* melting into her arms — *fusing with her* — would haunt him forever. She certainly wasn't the coy, innocent girl with whom he had fallen in love. There was more to her, aspects stronger and darker than he could have imagined, more powerful, more *forbidding*. He thought back to the darkened street; the fine rain settling like mist around him, the mutilated bodies slowly growing cold, Nandana standing there, dark, motionless and purposeful. He had stared at her, too shocked to move, and then he had heard what had sounded like a window being opened. It must have been the old woman, he now realized. He had turned to look — and when he turned back, the girl had vanished like an apparition. That is when, seized with sudden panic, he had fled from the street, catching the old woman's attention…

In no way was Nandana as vulnerable as she habitually came across, as someone in need of caring. What he had seen yesterday told a completely different story. She wasn't just capable of taking care of herself… *she had taken care of him*. So, what else about her had he misread? How could he trust his judgement of her now, and how could he trust her hereafter when she plainly wasn't who she pretended to be?

"Stop!" The investigator felt a hand grab him by the wrist as a voice spoke in his ear. "What's the big hurry, Dileepa?"

The *dandapala* jumped and turned, his face draining of colour on seeing Mitraka. He had been found out; something had given him away about yesterday —

"Where are you going?" Mitraka asked. Then, taking a closer look at him, she asked in a kinder tone, "Are you alright? You look…"

"Yes, yes," Dileepa replied hurriedly. "It was just a little stuffy inside, and I needed some air."

"It was packed in there," Mitraka agreed, letting go of her subordinate's hand. "I suppose everyone wanted to see and hear the rajan after yesterday's attack."

They stood quietly for a moment before Mitraka eyed Dileepa. "You heard the rajan say he wants us *dandapalas* to help the *nagarapalas* investigate the attack."

The young investigator nodded.

"And you heard me tell the rajan that we are really short in numbers — which we are."

Dileepa nodded again.

"So my question to you is," Mitraka cocked one eyebrow at her junior, "what progress have you made in the special case that you are working on for the rajan?"

"I am making progress," Dileepa replied vaguely.

"Good," said Mitraka, though from her tone, it didn't sound as if she fully believed him. "Whatever this case is, I want you to solve it quickly. You are not contributing to the investigation into the disappearances. There's also this attack to investigate now. I don't have enough *dandapalas* to cover everything anyway, and your absence is crippling us. So, wrap this case up quickly and come back. Am I clear?"

"Absolutely," said Dileepa. "Actually…" his eyes strayed over his superior's shoulder, "I have to see someone in connection with that case right now. So, if you'll pardon me, I must go…" Without waiting for Mitraka to grant him permission, the *dandapala* slipped from her side and jogged after a figure walking down a corridor.

"*Mahanayaka*… a moment please," Dileepa called as he drew closer to Baladitya.

It took the *nagarapala* a moment to place the investigator's face. "Dileepa," he exclaimed, his eyes lighting up with warmth.

"I am honoured you recognized me, *mahanayaka*," Dileepa smiled in return.

"It's not every day that a young *dandapala* is seen in the king's presence," Baladitya remarked. "Tell me, what can I do for you?"

"I have a question pertaining to the allocation of guard duty at the city's gates," the investigator began. Seeing Baladitya nod encouragingly, he went on, "Who at the *nagarapala* headquarters is in charge of posting guards at the different gates?"

The *mahanayaka's* brow furrowed. "How is this important?"

"Oh, it's just that as we are assisting the *nagarapalas* in investigating the attack on the rajan, we thought it might be good to talk to all the guards once again… just to make sure nothing's been missed." Dileepa turned and looked over his shoulder at Mitraka, who still stood surveying him from afar. "Our chief is just being thorough," he said to Baladitya with an apologetic smile. "I thought it would be easier to get the names of all the guards from the person scheduling their duties at the gates." With the slightest of pauses, he quickly added, "So sorry to bother you like this."

"No, no." Glancing in Mitraka's direction, Baladitya nodded politely and Mitraka nodded back. "We need your help with this investigation," he said, turning back to Dileepa. "It's not a bother at all." After a moment's thought, he said, "Assigning *nagarapalas* to guard duty and patrols is *upanayaka* Mahulya's responsibility. Speak to him."

"We are most grateful for your help, *mahanayaka*," the *dandapala* said with a bow.

Watching Baladitya proceed, Dileepa turned to find that Mitraka had also gone her way. He let out a sigh of relief. His little ploy of using Mitraka's name to gain Baladitya's cooperation had worked. He finally had a name to pursue—*upanayaka* Mahulya. The man who had repeatedly appointed the same set of five *nagarapalas* on guard duty at the city's east gate, through which, if his and the king's suspicions were right, food grains and other essentials had been smuggled into Ayodhya and Pushyanta's storehouses.

As the *dandapala* headed for the path leading into the city, his mind returned to the night before and to the old woman by the window. What if she could recognize him? What would his parents have to say? How would they deal with the shame of their son's arrest?

Wait, wait, wait… he screamed at himself. He had nothing to be afraid of. He hadn't killed the men… *Then who had, and why did you run?...* They were the ones trying to kill him… *Why?...* He had no idea why, he had nothing to do with them… *If that's so, why were they trying to kill you?...*

Why had they tried to kill him, Dileepa wondered, recalling the question posed by one courtier: *Is there any reason to believe that the deaths in the street are in any way connected to the attack on the rajan?*

Two sudden, surreptitious attacks on the same night, one on the king, one on him. Who would want to kill him and the king? Why them, what did they share in common? Nothing except the investigation of the food hoarding scam. The king had commissioned the investigation. He had uncovered Pushyanta's role in the racket and arrested the guild master, and Pushyanta had died in custody. Were the attacks a retaliation by *adhipati* Sudhanva or by Pushyanta's own family? The *dandapala* remembered the king telling him that Pushyanta's uncle was Mihiradutta, the *adhipati* of Sravasti…

Or, had someone got wind of the fact that he was continuing the investigation of the hoarding scam at the king's behest? Were the attacks motivated by the fear of being caught and exposed?

But then again, as *adhipati* Sudhanva had claimed, maybe the attack on the king was an external conspiracy after all, and there was no link between the two attacks. So, who were the men who had cornered him last night, and what would they have gained by killing him?

"*Dandapala* Dileepa?"

A woman's voice had hailed him, and the investigator turned to see a palace maid standing by a neem tree. She approached him and offered a *pranaam*, and Dileepa did likewise.

"I bring you a message from Rani Kaikeyi," said the maid. "The rani wishes to see you."

"Me?" Dileepa's eyebrows rose in surprise. "Why?"

"I'm afraid I don't know. But I have been asked to escort you to the rani's chamber."

"Right now?"

"Yes. The rani is expecting you."

"Alright," said the investigator, knowing from the way the maid had framed her words that the option to refuse didn't exist.

Following the maid through a side door, Dileepa crossed countless courtyards and passageways that were silent except for the clack of his wooden *padukas* on stone. The *dandapala* wondered what the king's mother wanted from him, and his mind went over whatever little he knew about the queen. He knew she had been the old king's third wife, the youngest and most beautiful of all three queens. Growing up in Kusinagara, the one story he had heard repeated about Kaikeyi — the one that everyone in Kosala, perhaps everyone in all of Jambudvipa, had heard repeated many times over — was how, as a young bride, she had once rescued Raja Dashratha from the rakshasas. The story was that when she and Raja Dashratha were returning to Ayodhya after a hunt, they were ambushed by a rakshasa horde that had been lying in wait for them in the forests to the city's south. Dashratha and his detail were outnumbered, and the rakshasas started closing in on the king and Kaikeyi when Dashratha's sentient war chariot manifested in answer to his summons. The king and queen boarded the chariot, but before they could blaze their way out of trouble, Dashratha was struck by an arrow and lost consciousness to rakshasa magic. Buoyed by hope, the rakshasas redoubled their attack and the king's capture was imminent, but Kaikeyi refused to give in. Taking control of the chariot, she blitzed out of the skirmish, leaving the rakshasas behind as she transported her unconscious husband back to the safety of Ayodhya.

"The rani saved our raja from the clutches of the rakshasas," Dileepa could hear the admiration in his mother's voice every time she narrated the tale at bedtime. "What is truly amazing is that she gained control over the king's war chariot that day, a feat no one other than Raja Dashratha had ever achieved. Imagine... *the mind-chariot*. Apart from the raja, Rani Kaikeyi is the only person who can get that chariot to bend to her will."

Nowadays, of course, the only story told and heard about Rani Kaikeyi was how she had plotted to have Rama sent into exile so her son could become —

"The *dandapala* is here, rani."

Dileepa noticed that they had reached an herbarium where the king's mother was crouched over a row of *tulsi* bushes, tending to the plants. The rani looked up at him, and Dileepa bowed, awed by the woman's poise and regal bearing even while she knelt in the mud like a common gardener's wife.

Kaikeyi got to her feet and surveyed him in silence, dusting her hands and waiting for the maid to withdraw. It wasn't until the maid's footsteps had fully receded that she spoke. "So, you are Dileepa."

"At your service," the *dandapala* bowed again.

"Good. I need you to investigate last evening's assassination attempt on the king."

Dileepa blinked. "I don't understand —"

"You are a palace investigator, aren't you?" Seeing the man nod, Kaikeyi continued, "Find out who was behind yesterday's attack, who is it that wishes to harm the king."

"The *dandapalas* and *nagarapalas* have begun investigations as per the king's orders," Dileepa began explaining. "The entire *dandapala* force will be —"

"I want *you* to get to the bottom of this," the queen interrupted. "You are doing this for *me*, not for the king or the crown." Reaching into a satchel slung across one shoulder, she extracted a pouch that clinked with *rupas*. "Here," she said, extending her hand.

"No," said Dileepa. "I am paid by the crown and that is adequate. But I will do my best to find out what you want."

Kaikeyi looked at him for a moment before putting the pouch back into the satchel with a nod. "For the duration of this investigation, you will be my eyes and ears. I will expect updates from you every two or three days, and I should be informed whenever you or someone else makes a significant breakthrough."

The *dandapala* nodded. "May I ask why you picked me for the job, rani?" he asked.

"You have the king's confidence. He trusts you, so I believe you have his best interests at heart. Also, from what I have heard, you seem pretty competent. The way you exposed Pushyanta…" She stopped and glanced towards the herbarium's exit. "You should go. You have work to do."

Afternoon had turned to evening by the time Dileepa got back to his quarters. He was tired, confused and frustrated. The king wanted him to investigate the hoarding scam and try and find Pushyanta's killer. Mitraka wanted him to join the rest of the *dandapalas* in solving the mystery of the disappearances and contribute to the investigation into the attack on Bharat. Rani Kaikeyi also wanted him to unmask those behind the attack on the king. Then, on top of all this, he had an investigation of his own to conduct, figuring out who wanted *him* dead and why. And there was the issue of Nandana and the phantom *shyenas* as well…

His thoughts going around in circles, the investigator climbed two flights of steps to the rooftop dwelling he had rented from an aged widower. Slipping off his *padukas* by the door, he washed his hands and feet before entering the sparsely furnished house. Straightaway, his eyes went to the reed mat spread on the floor, pushed against the far wall. In the dimming light of the day, he made out the soft glow of the listening bells as they lay on the mat, pulsing like opalescent moonlight.

A message from Nandana.

Feeling the tips of his fingers tingle, Dileepa went over to the mat and picked the bells up. He walked to the window and opened it, letting the breeze blow in.

Slowly, holding his breath, the *dandapala* brought the bells up to his ears and listened.

Please come this evening, there was a lilt even in the girl's whisper. *I will explain everything.*

"I have already told you, I had *nothing* to do with the attack on the king."

Hidden under the exasperation in Sudhanva's tone, there was a hint of anger as he glared at the men standing before him. "Didn't I tell you that I would work out a plan to remove Bharat and come back to you? Why would I act unilaterally then?"

"I don't know," Mihiradutta of Sravasti shrugged his heavy shoulders and looked at Jayabhama standing to his right. "We thought you might have decided to make a move without consulting us."

"Well, I didn't," Sudhanva said in a huff.

The three men were in one of Sudhanva's sugar factories. All around them, sugarcane juice was being extracted using crushers operated by bionic bulls, and laborers refined the extracted juice into broad vats using layers of fine muslin cloth for the purpose of straining. Away to the right, men stirred the juice concentrate over fires, thickening it to molasses, while in the far distance, bullock carts laden with more sugarcane trundled in from the fields. Feverish activity abounded around Sudhanva, Mihiradutta and Jayabhama, and everyone was too busy to pay attention to the three aristocrats.

"Not that we would have had a problem had the bid on Bharat's life been successful," said the *adhipati* of Sravasti under his breath. "But when we heard that the bid had failed, we assumed you had messed it up. That's why we came in a hurry to see you."

"For the last time, it wasn't me," Sudhanva insisted.

"Alright," Mihiradutta raised his hands, signalling the end of the matter.

"Who do you think was behind it then?" asked Jayabhama, Pushyanta's elder brother.

"Who knows?" Sudhanva grunted unhappily. His attempt at implicating Lavanyasurya in court that morning had failed, and he was loath to go down that path again. The attempt had not just failed, it had backfired miserably on him, thanks to his old nemesis, Sheelabhadra. The wily *adhipati* of Kusinagara had turned everyone's gaze upon Sudhanva by hinting that the bid on Bharat's life might have originated *within* Kosala's borders, hatched by those who had been affected by some of the king's recent decisions. Everyone knew about Pushyanta's arrest in the hoarding scam, and it had been easy for Sheelabhadra to point in Sudhanva's direction without taking names. How he hated the man, Sudhanva cursed Sheelabhadra bitterly for painting him as a suspect in people's eyes. In an effort to salvage the situation, he had tried underlining his allegiance to the king by backing the call for a bodyguard for Bharat, but Sudhanva knew some of the damage done that morning might be irreparable.

"What next?" Jayabhama persisted. "What about the plan to get rid of Bharat?"

"Humph," Sudhanva scowled. He began walking back towards the row of waiting horses. "That plan will have to be put on hold for a while."

"On hold? Why?" Jayabhama sounded indignant as he and Mihiradutta fell in step to the right and left of Sudhanva.

The *adhipati* of Sankasya didn't reply straightaway. His mind was on what Gajakarna had said when they met right after court had dispersed. "Sheelabhadra has laid bare the possibility of an internal conspiracy against Bharat," the *mahanayaka* had said, sounding apprehensive. "Now that the possibility has taken root in people's minds, putting your plan into action will be much, much harder." What Gajakarna had meant was that he would be reluctant to back any rebellion against the king. Sudhanva didn't really blame the commander though. Whoever had made the attempt on the king's life had really messed up the plan to oust Bharat from the throne.

"Why can't we stay our course as planned?" Jayabhama pressed on. "We have all agreed Bharat has to go —"

"Yes, but the attack has changed the ground reality," Sudhanva snapped, sensing dark shadows form at the edges of his vision. He had a sudden, intense craving to dig into Jayabhama's chest and rip his heart out, the memory of Pushyanta's blood, slick and warm over his hands, making his head reel in anticipation. Struggling against the urge, the *adhipati* pushed the hideous black thing rising inside him back and blinked in the late evening sunlight.

"The attack has changed things because it has won the king the people's sympathy," Sudhanva explained. "You should see the number of people lining up at the palace to show their solidarity with the king. You should see the people thronging the temples to offer prayers for Bharat and the kid. That kid has done his father a huge favour… an attack on the king that nearly cost the little yuvaraja his life. What a heart-wrenching story! The people of Kosala are with their king and his son, and at the moment, their affection is paramount. They won't tolerate a bid to topple Bharat, and anyone making an attempt will earn their wrath. It isn't the right time to overthrow the king."

"Your assessment is correct," said Mihiradutta after a moment's thought.

"But the same people have suffered on account of the rakshasa attack, the disappearances, the drought…" Jayabhama argued. "That should make them unhappy with the king."

"People are easily pleased and placated; they are always ready to forgive and forget," Sudhanva replied. "Perhaps it's the rain that has taken the edge off their anger, fear and frustration." With a smirk, he added, "It takes so little to make the poor fools happy and content."

They mounted their horses and slowly made their way back to the road that led to Sudhanva's mansion in Ayodhya.

"How long will we need to wait before we can act?" asked Jayabhama.

The idiot was ugly *and* stupid, Sudhanva decided. He'd just been told the time wasn't right to stage a coup against Bharat. Why couldn't he get it through his thick skull that problems didn't always come with answers attached, and that more often than not, one had to wait for a way to show itself?

"Patience, Jayabhama, patience," Mihiradutta advised, the uncle understanding the complexity of the situation better than the nephew. "We must wait for an opportune moment to strike."

"A predator in a hurry is a predator that goes hungry," Sudhanva nodded in relief. "The moment that we are waiting for will come. It has to. Nothing lasts forever. The euphoria of yesterday's rain will evaporate, and affection for the king will disappear with time. We have to wait for the discontent to return, for the dissatisfaction to set in. That is when we will act." He looked at Jayabhama. "I am not giving up on my plan to remove Bharat from the throne. You have my word."

They rode in silence for a while until Jayabhama turned to Sudhanva once again. "Has anyone learned what happened to the four men who were killed last night?" he asked.

"Not to my knowledge," Sudhanva replied absent-mindedly. "*Mahanayaka* Baladitya had some vague theory that they were attacked by an animal or a bird or something."

"And the four haven't been identified so far?"

"I wouldn't know."

"But there was nothing identifiable that was found on them, right? On their bodies, I mean?"

Sudhanva looked at Jayabhama, taking note of the younger man's tense expression and pointed questions. "Like what?" the *adhipati* asked. Then, looking squarely at Jayabhama, he said, "Is there any particular reason you are so curious about the men who were killed?"

Seeing Jayabhama and Mihiradutta exchange a glance, Sudhanva stared. "You have something to do with them," he said.

Mihiradutta shook his head ruefully. "You might as well tell him," he grunted at his nephew.

Jayabhama coloured as he turned to Sudhanva. "They were… my men," he said. "I mean men hired by me."

"To do what?" Sudhanva asked.

"To kill the *dandapala*."

"What *dandapala*?" Sudhanva looked bemused.

"The one who arrested Pushyanta."

"What?" Sudhanva smacked his forehead with his palm in astonishment. "You hired killers to murder a *dandapala*?" He looked at Mihiradutta in disbelief. "And you approved of this plan?"

"I had no idea of this until he told me this morning," the *adhipati* of Sravasti ventured, frowning in disapproval.

"We couldn't let the *dandapala* get away," Jayabhama countered. "He's the reason my brother died in custody —"

"Are you out of your mind?" Sudhanva glared angrily at the younger man. "Do you know that lines are already being drawn connecting the four dead men with the attack on the king? People are wondering if the two attacks are related… and here you tell me the dead men were working on *your* orders. If anyone finds that out, you know what'll happen, don't you? They will come for you and your uncle and me. They will link us to the attack on Bharat, you fool."

Mihiradutta and Jayabhama looked worried. "But if the men can't be identified…" Jayabhama began.

"Shut up," Sudhanva snarled. "The two of you ride all the way from Sravasti to ask me if I had anything to do with the attack on the king. You suspected me of acting without consulting you, when it is *you* who have been acting without taking me into confidence." The *adhipati* paused to draw a breath and force back the shadows that were closing in around him. "Didn't I tell you our top priority was replacing Bharat? But you had to go after the *dandapala*. I hope you realize you have jeopardized the plan to remove Bharat and put all of our lives at risk."

"How was I to know the king would come under attack?" Jayabhama made another attempt to defend himself. "I acted —"

"Please," Sudhanva snapped. "If you can't admit you've made a mistake, at least keep quiet."

"The boy made a mistake, and he is sorry for it," said Mihiradutta, trying to soothe the *adhipati*. "Aren't you sorry?" he cocked a brow at his nephew.

"I am sorry," Jayabhama mumbled, looking cowed. "I really am."

Sudhanva remained silent for a while, regaining control over his temper. At last, he spoke. "We have to make sure there is nothing on the dead men that can be linked to you." He looked at Jayabhama. "What did you pay the men with?"

"Common silver *rupas*," Jayabhama replied.

"That's good. The *rupas* could have come from anywhere. Were the men from hereabouts?"

"No, they were from the mountains to the north."

"That's good too. No one is likely to come all the way to Ayodhya looking for them." Sudhanva thought for a bit and nodded. "I think we should be okay. But here onwards, do not do anything without speaking to me." Giving Jayabhama a long, hard stare, he added, "And keep well away from the *dandapalas*."

"I know magic."

Dileepa turned to look at Nandana. Unlike most other evenings, today, the lovers weren't seated by the old, abandoned mansion on the edge of Ayodhya. Today, they leaned against a boat that had been hauled onto the riverbank, well inside city limits. Today, they hadn't sought seclusion. Instead, they leaned against the boat, watching children shriek and cavort in the river's shallows fifty yards away, while old women sold flowers and swapped gossip on the steps of the small temple behind them. They leaned against the boat, their faces and postures rigid, shoulders not touching. Even during their walk to this spot, Dileepa and Nandana hadn't held hands or locked fingers, keeping their distance, thoughts of the previous evening's occurrences wedged deep between them. They had hardly spoken three sentences since they had met fifteen minutes ago.

"I have always known magic."

Dileepa simply looked at Nandana. He said nothing, waiting for her to speak. Her message had said she would explain everything. He would let her.

"I knew magic even as a child. I mean I knew I had… something special. A power. I could do things." Nandana paused to gaze at the opposite bank, which was little more than an outline in the deepening twilight. "But when father came to know about it, he scolded me, told me to hide it."

"What kind of power?" Dileepa asked, curiosity getting the better of him.

"The kind you saw yesterday."

"So you… create *shyenas*?"

"I create beings with fire. All sorts of beings. *Shyenas*, *sarpas*, *varahas*… but mostly birds."

"How do you do it?" the *dandapala* asked in wonder.

"I don't know. I just can, sometimes, when I'm angry or desperate. But not always. And I don't have complete control over what form my creations take. Instead of the *shyenas*, it could have been something else yesterday. Still, it would have protected you from the attackers." The girl's limpid eyes turned to Dileepa. "My anger would have made sure of that," she said in a whisper.

Dileepa blinked and looked away. She had saved his life, and he knew he wasn't being grateful enough to her for doing what she had done.

"How did you know there was a threat to my life?" he asked.

"I was at the door of the house, watching you leave, when I saw the men step out of the shadows and surround you. It all happened so quickly." She paused, her voice trembling. "For a moment, I believed it was too late, that I..." she heaved a sigh infused with fear as well as relief. "I can't tell you how happy, how *thankful* I was on seeing you hadn't come to any harm," she confessed.

The investigator was silent for a bit, processing everything he had just heard. The children were wading out of the water to make their haphazard way home, dallying here, delaying there, stretching playtime for as long as it was possible before parental censure put an end to the day's fun.

"Why did you disappear the way you did, leaving me alone in the street?" Dileepa asked.

The girl looked ashamed. "I... was afraid," she stammered. "I told you my father asked me to keep my powers concealed from everyone. He said that people wouldn't understand... that I would be seen as a freak, a misfit. He said this to me so many times that I have come to believe it as true. That is why I ran. I knew you had seen me and... and I was afraid you would see me as a freak and start disliking me." She stopped and turned fully around to face him. "I am not... I am just a normal girl... Please don't hate me for what happened yesterday," she implored, tears forming in her eyes. "I will try not to let this happen ever again, but don't hate me, and don't stop meeting me…"

Dileepa's heart melted. Nandana hadn't just saved his life, she had done it at the risk of her powers being exposed, at the risk of being found possessing a special ability that her father had warned her to hide from the world. She had used her powers to save his life, knowing it might alienate him from her. She had been so selfless, and here he had been wondering whether he could trust her…

"I do not hate you," he said, reaching for the girl. He drew her close, wrapping his arms around her, comforting her as she broke down, sobbing and snuffling against his chest. "There is nothing in this to hate you about. What you did is fine…" he peeled away to peer at her face. "You saved my life, remember?" he smiled. "Tell me, how can I hate you for that?"

Nandana was too overwhelmed to say anything in reply, and the *dandapala* was content to hold her and let her cling to him while she let the tears wash her guilt and fear away. They stood like that until the girl's sobs subsided and she wiped her tears and stepped out of his embrace. She gave him a mildly embarrassed smile, and Dileepa grinned back. "Better?" he asked.

The girl nodded. "I was so afraid I had lost you that I couldn't sleep all night," she said. "Thank you for understanding."

Dileepa nodded. A mild breeze had struck up from across the Sarayu, and for a while the lovers stood close and let it blow over them. The day's last ferries were crossing the river, and behind them, a steady stream of the devout made their way into the temple as the priests readied for the evening *aarati*. At last, the girl looked up at the investigator.

"I have a request," she said. "Don't say anything about my powers to Ma Parnalata."

"She doesn't know?" the *dandapala* asked in surprise. Seeing Nandana shake her head, he said, "But you can tell her… she is your aunt."

"No," the girl said. "I mean, yes, she is my aunt, but no, I don't want her to know."

"Why not?"

"She won't understand, and she will worry for me. I don't want that."

"Alright," said Dileepa. After a moment's thought, he asked, "So, who all know about this?"

"Father did… and now you."

"That's all?" The *dandapala* whistled under his breath. "Makes me feel special."

Nandana smiled at him, then her expression turned serious. "I meant to ask earlier… who were those men?"

Dileepa shucked his shoulders. "I haven't the faintest clue, but it's possible they had something to do with my investigation into the hoarding scam that led to the arrest of Pushyanta. I don't have any other enemies to the best of my knowledge."

The girl's eyes were round with apprehension. "I warned you to be careful."

"I remember," the *dandapala* replied. "It is also possible that the attack was linked to the attack on the king." He looked at Nandana. "You know about last evening's attack on the king, don't you?"

"I overheard one of the women working for Ma saying something about an attack at the palace."

"Yes," said Dileepa. In a few crisp sentences, he explained what had happened. "The attack on the king and the attack on me happened roughly around the same time, so there is bound to be suspicion that they are linked."

"Imagine, something could have happened to the yuvaraja," Nandana gasped. "But who would want you and the king dead?"

"Those affected by the probe into the hoarding scam," the investigator answered. "It might well turn out that the two attacks are unrelated, of course, in which case we are left with not one but two mysteries to crack." Dileepa stopped as he remembered something. "Guess who I met this afternoon?"

"Who?"

"Rani Kaikeyi. The king's mother. She called me to her chamber."

"Why?"

The darkness hid the glow on Dileepa's face, but the pride in his voice was impossible to miss. "She wants me to investigate the attack on the king. She picked me specifically because I have the king's trust, and because she had heard of my competence. Those were the reasons she gave me."

"You are working for Rani Kaikeyi?" Nandana asked, her eyes widening in anticipation.

"I am working for the king," Dileepa corrected.

"But you have access to Rani Kaikeyi. You have her ear."

"I do," the *dandapala* grinned. "Doesn't that make you proud of me?"

"It does," said Nandana, her mind on what Simhika had said about Dileepa and the inroads he was making into the palace.

Let us see how deep he gets into the palace and to what extent we can use him. Those had been Simhika's exact words. And now Dileepa had direct access to Rani Kaikeyi, the king's mother.

"It does," Nandana repeated. She smiled up at the investigator. "It makes me proud and happy."

Angara sat at Bharat's feet, staring up at its master with soulful eyes, its tongue out, tail swishing the ground, waiting to be showered with more love. The dog had been delighted to see Bharat, throwing itself on the king and zipping around in excitement, and Bharat had had to wait until the edge had worn off before he finally got around to petting the dog. He was glad to see Angara was none the worse after the previous evening's encounter with the assassins, and once the dog had calmed down, he had taken its face in both hands and looked into its eyes, whispering his thanks for coming to Taksha's rescue at the nick of time. Had Angara not lunged at the second attacker and thrown his aim, the bolt from the *vajramushti* would surely have struck the kid...

Bharat bent to scratch the dog's head, and the animal's ears folded back in pleasure. Lifting its snout, it nuzzled Bharat's hand, giving it a grateful lick.

"Do you like dogs?" the king asked, cocking an eyebrow at the man standing three yards away, almost directly under the globule of light suspended in mid-air.

"I don't like them, but neither do I dislike them, rajan," the man replied in a formal tone.

The king nodded and petted Angara, pleased with the man's honesty. Everyone knew about his affection for Angara, and the man could have tried gaining his king's favour by professing his own love for dogs. Yet, he hadn't.

"You said your name is Atibhanu?" Bharat asked.

"Yes, rajan." In his mid-thirties, the man was short and powerfully built, with tattoos on his muscular arms and neck. He wore his hair short, cropped nearly to the scalp. He looked at the world with deep, thoughtful eyes that didn't seem to miss much, and which were now focused on Bharat.

"How good are you with the *karapala*?" Bharat asked, eyeing the light sword on the man's hip.

"I was the runner-up at the last sword-fighting championship held three years ago, rajan. When Raja Dashratha was still king of Kosala."

The king frowned, casting his mind back to the championship. Then, his face cleared. "So, that was you?" he said with a small smile. "It was a good fight, I remember. I can assure you there is no shame in losing to a *mahayoddha* of Shatrughna's calibre. I can't remember anyone having bested my little brother in swordsmanship."

"To bear a wound inflicted by the yuvaraja is an honour," said Atibhanu with a bow.

Bharat eyed the scar running the length of the warrior's cheek, Shatrughna's sword having left a permanent mark on skin and tissue.

"I am also competent at wielding the *shul*, rajan," Atibhanu asserted. With a pause, he added, "*Mahanayaka* Gajakarna has charged me with the job of protecting you. I shall not fail his trust in me while I do everything to gain yours, rajan."

"I was not in favour of getting a bodyguard," Bharat said, watching Angara amble off to inspect something in the grass. Off to the right, where the palace grounds met a stand of trees, sentries patrolled, and the ground itself was better lit, with torches placed along its perimeter at frequent intervals. "It's only because everyone insisted…"

"A *mahayoddha* like you is more than capable of defending himself, rajan," Atibhanu inclined his head. "But it is my job to be vigilant, if only for everyone else's peace of mind."

Bharat smiled, warming to the warrior. "I am glad we agree that I can take care of myself," he said. "So, you don't need to be with me all the time. It will suffice if you accompany me only when I'm going out —"

"I can't do that, rajan," the warrior protested, looking worried. "I have been told to be with you all the time. If anything were to happen to you and I wasn't around to help, it would be viewed as a dereliction of duty. I will be penalized —"

"I understand," Bharat nodded in resignation. "Do as you've been instructed to —" He stopped. "What is it?"

Atibhanu wasn't paying attention to his king. His eyes had drifted to something behind Bharat, something that was low near the ground, and his hand had gone to the hilt of his *karapala*, his fingers wrapping around the grip…

Drawing his own *karapala* from its sheath, Bharat spun around. He immediately saw what had caught Atibhanu's attention.

Angara.

The dog stood ten paces away, its face towards the stable yard, towards the line of trees where the assailants had hidden the previous evening. Its ears were up, its muscles wound tight, body braced and alert, a low growl building in its throat.

"Something is amiss, rajan," Atibhanu said, drawing level with the king, sword in hand.

As if on cue, Angara gave a short bark and shot off in the direction of stable, legs kicking mud and gravel into the air.

"Angara," Bharat called as he tore after the dog, a mantra on his lips, his left hand conjuring a shield that sparked with magic. Atibhanu followed, hard on the king's heels.

Having had a head start, Angara increased its lead by twenty paces, its bark turning frenzied as it neared the stable. The patrols had picked up the dog's barks and Bharat's calls, and men were now moving in from all directions, closing in from all sides, forming a loose circle around the stable…

"I think I see a figure in front, rajan," Atibhanu panted.

Bharat strained his eyes, and an outline sprang out of the surrounding dark a dozen yards ahead. At the same time, the dog's yapping changed in pitch from aggression to manic excitement.

Then, with a sudden whimper, Angara fell silent.

Suddenly afraid for the dog, Bharat stepped his pace up a notch, but he hadn't taken more than five strides when a light dazzled into being right where the figure stood in front of the stable. Flinching at its sudden brightness, the king took three more steps before skidding to an abrupt halt, his mouth opening in surprise. Atibhanu also drew up short beside him.

"Rajan?" the figure spoke in a familiar gravelly voice that Bharat realized he'd sorely missed. "What is happening? Why is everyone here?"

Bharat stared back, too stunned to say anything.

Siripala.

Right there in front of the royal stable, where he was always to be found before he had suddenly gone away.

Bathed from head to toe in silvery light, the ostler stood and surveyed the closing ring of guards with great puzzlement as Angara crawled on its belly to his feet, its tail wagging uncontrollably in delight.

three

THE BOATS CROSSED THE SINDHU IN THE FIRST LIGHT OF dawn. There were over a hundred of them; some small, accommodating no more than six men, some large enough to fit four or five horses. Most were trade barges, though, with room to seat twenty. Nearly all the boats had been drafted into service under some form of duress, the oarsmen all bribed and threatened to row Gandhara and Kamboja's troops first across the Sindhu and, later, the Vitasta.

The waters of the river churned under a multitude of oars, and the vessels slid, swift and sleek, from one bank to the other, grinding into the gravel so men and horses could disembark, before turning around to fetch the next load of warriors. Riders and their mounts stomped up and down the banks, raising such a din — chatting, laughing, neighing, whinnying — that they frightened away the animals that had come to drink at the river and sent the birds roosting in the trees into frenzied flight.

The crossing lasted over an hour, and Nagnajit chafed through much of it, goading his captains to speed things up. Beside him, Mahasa, the chief of the Kambojas, sat in near monastic silence, watching the crossing with eyes that were narrow slits in a face the texture of dried leather. The

Kambojas were distinguishable from the Gandharan troops by their chunkier build and the traditional chequered turbans they wore. Also, unlike the Gandharans, the Kamboja horsemen all bore bows in addition to their sabres. Though united in cause, both sets of warriors had kept to themselves in the march from Kapisi, but now, here on the narrow banks of the Sindhu, they were all pressed together and forced to fraternize.

"Faster, faster," Gandhara's raya roared, riding up and down the bank. "We're too slow. Is this how we plan to take the River Kingdoms? Why are the boatmen rowing like old women? We'll all be dead in the Vitasta, our bodies full of arrows, if we can't get any quicker. Come on, hurry up now."

Finally, the last boatloads made a safe landing, and the crafts were all hauled ashore to be carried by porters to the Vitasta, a two-day march to the east. Nagnajit anticipated a need for the vessels to ferry his army across the Vitasta, fully expecting the River Kingdoms to take away their own boats from the river to slow the advance of his invading force.

The sun was right in their eyes when Nagnajit and Mahasa climbed out of the valley where the Sindhu flowed and crested the hills that shielded the river from the eastern plains. The sight of these endless plains greeted the two warlords, the land flat and stretching into the heat haze, out of which the sun appeared to have emerged. Dwarfed trees dotted the landscape, the monotony broken here and there by crude dwellings of solitary shepherds.

"Is this it?" asked Mahasa, squinting against the sun, the disappointment plain in his tone.

"Yes," smiled Nagnajit, the opposite of the Kamboja in almost every way, except when it came to ruthlessness and ambition. In that, they were blood brothers, two peas in a pod.

"*This* is what the River Kingdoms look like?" Mahasa asked again.

"Don't be fooled by what you see," the raya chuckled. "You'll discover the land looks nothing like this, my friend."

"You're sure it gets better?" Mahasa couldn't shed the scepticism. "You've never actually *been* there."

"No, but I have heard it being spoken of," the Gandharan's eyes were dreamy. "A land of great riches. Soil so fertile almost anything will grow. Prosperous kingdoms with cities that span the horizon. Ayodhya, Kasi, Madhupura, Tamralipti. Men and women of great beauty… And then, of course, there's the magic that makes everything work in the cities. I've listened to the traders talk, and I have heard the wonder in their voices."

Both men sat staring east for a moment, a breeze ruffling their hair, cooling the sweat that was beginning to bead their brows.

"Does that mean you won't stop with the River Kingdoms?" Mahasa considered Nagnajit.

The raya shrugged and flicked his horse's reins to get the beast moving again. "The answer lies on the other side of the Vitasta." With a pause and a smile, he added, "Let us first focus on the River Kingdoms, my friend. We can decide the fate of the rest of Jambudvipa once we've taken Sakala and Trigartha, and crushed Kekeya under our heels."

Passing under the arched and newly festooned entrance to the Sanctum of the Fire, jostled along by festive crowds streaming in to witness the consecration of the new *homagriha*, Simhika felt a swell of guarded optimism in her, flush and welcome like the warmth of the sun on her skin. A quiet sense of accomplishment pervaded her at having got here at last. Here, inside the famed Sanctum of the Fire, so close to her targets — Ayodhya's rishis and, more critically, Ayodhya's sacred fire.

The morning was radiant after another rain-washed night, the air cool and laden with moisture. Recurrent rainfall had taken the sting and savagery out of Kosala's unending summer, and city and countryside were turning verdant, the Sarayu slowly filling again, fed by a hundred streams and tributaries. The kingdom's subjects too had become buoyant, renewed with hope as farmers took to their fields and prospects of a good harvest returned while the threat of drought receded. Though the attack on the king was still fresh and the disappearances continued unabated, the fact that Bharat and Taksha had escaped unhurt, and that more of those who had disappeared were returning, were interpreted as fate's benevolence towards Kosala. It wasn't as though the fear and mistrust that had haunted everyone had suddenly dissipated; it was just that the people of Kosala now had things to be relieved about, to rejoice about. So, that morning, packed boats crossed the Sarayu and citizens swamped the Sanctum in the expectation that the consecration would put a permanent end to the miseries afflicting them and their kingdom.

Standing beside Nandana in the looming shadow of the *homagriha*, watching people assemble by the hundreds,

Simhika smirked inwardly. Once she'd had her way with the rishis, everyone here was going to be *so* let down, she thought to herself. Once she'd had her way, there would be no hope left for Ayodhya and its people.

Yes, the coming of the rain and the return of the magic was worrying, she had to admit. There were clear signs that the magic had strengthened over Ayodhya, and while she couldn't explain why, she put it down to the imminent consecration of the *homagriha*. It didn't make sense, but magic, dark as well as pure, didn't always follow the laws of logic. But whatever the cause, the sorceress decided she would deal with it and destroy it. She was here, within the Sanctum, and her magic was also here, with more to follow, she thought, looking at the rishis' wives.

Although the crowds were raucous, the atmosphere in the immediate vicinity of the *homagriha* was austere. The rishis' chants rang deep and sonorous in the air, and aromatic *sambrani* smoke from dozens of dispensers rose and eddied like physical manifestations of the chants. The rishis themselves were inside the sanctorum, while their wives sat in an enclosure outside. Opposite the entrance to the *homagriha*, space had been cleared for the dignitaries of the royal court. Simhika squinted at the king, dark, young and bearded, his face already etched with the burdens of responsibility. To his right was his wife with their son in the crook of her arm. On the other side stood the king's brother, Dashratha's youngest son, Shatrughna, tall, strong and handsome. Nandana had pointed all of them out on various occasions, and she identified Dashratha's older queens, Kausalya and Sumitra, who were both present for the consecration. But the third queen, the one accountable for Rama's exile and Dashratha's death, was absent as usual. That was one acquaintance Simhika wished to make, for she believed Kaikeyi presented an opportunity she could exploit. A stubborn, strong-willed queen at odds with the rest of the royal household, and obsessed about her son's success…

Behind the royal family stood a dozen *dandapalas*, Dileepa among them, along with a company of *nagarapalas* headed by their *mahanayaka*. Many courtiers were in attendance, of whom she knew Sudhanva and his son, Yadudeva, by face, and of course Gajakarna, courtesy Dileepa's introduction. Simhika was acquainted with Sudhanva in other ways as well, having aroused the shadows within him and understood what they were capable of doing. The *adhipati* looked unhappy and distracted, and even at this distance, the sorceress sensed resentment coming off him in waves. She delighted in it, willing it to fester, wanting the rancour to run over her like the season's first rain.

This was what she lived for, creating strife and discord. It was what she revelled in, why she had been sent here to Ayodhya —

A gasp went up from those nearby, interrupting her thoughts. Looking around, Simhika noticed everyone had their eyes trained towards the Sanctum's entrance. She followed their gaze to see a contingent of soldiers come marching down the path that led to the *homagriha*.

"Look," she hissed at Nandana in excitement.

But the girl didn't react. She kept looking the other way, towards the king's enclosure, her face turned from the approaching soldiers. Puzzled, Simhika looked as well to determine what had caught Nandana's interest, but all she could see was the king's household, his courtiers, the *nagarapalas*, the *dandapalas* —

She got it. One particular *dandapala*. Dileepa.

"Nandana," Simhika shook the girl hard by the shoulder.

"What?" Nandana turned, startled.

"Look," the sorceress said, trying not to sound cross as she jerked her head.

"Oh," the girl's eyes widened appreciatively on seeing the soldiers of the Sanctum garrison.

Attired in their new uniforms, the soldiers were a treat for the eyes. Simhika had taken care to incorporate modern designs into Kosala's outmoded uniform in ways that would appeal to the traditionalist in Gajakarna, while being radical enough to impress those seeking freshness. The black dhoti with its plain gold border had been modified, and gold and saffron threads were now woven into the black cloth so that the dhotis shimmered with hidden fire. Jet-black sashes and bright saffron turbans finished off the ensemble, while saffron streamers tied to the men's spears added a dash of flair to the weapons. It helped that the men were among the best warriors in Kosala, young, fit and handsome, the sight of them drawing murmurs of admiration from all quarters. Reactions came from the royal entourage and from the enclosure where the rishis' wives sat… and it was the rishis' wives that Simhika observed most keenly.

Lanka's sorceress wasn't disappointed.

The rishis' wives were pointing and whispering among themselves, captivated by the soldiers' outfits. Soon, they would enquire about the uniforms and learn of her existence. They would seek her out, hanker after her creations… By successfully baiting the rishis' wives, Simhika had moved one step closer to the destruction of magic in Ayodhya and the devastation of the ruling Ikshvaku.

In was mid-morning by the time the boat ferrying the *dandapalas* docked at the Ayodhya bank of the Sarayu, but theirs wasn't the only incoming boat; the bank was swarming with citizens returning from the consecration, so Mitraka decided she'd wait for the crowds to clear before disembarking. The *dandapalas* sat in their boat, chatting, and unsurprisingly, the conversation veered to the uniforms worn by the Sanctum garrison.

"We should get ourselves new uniforms," remarked one *dandapala*.

"But we don't wear uniforms," one of the senior-most investigators pointed out.

"We do have official turbans and sashes though," another countered.

"I wouldn't mind wearing the sort of uniforms those soldiers wore," said a fourth, a portly man in his middle ages.

"Those uniforms were designed to look good on young men," Mitraka said with a grin. Pointing to the man's paunch, she added, "You would need something with a lot more cloth, I'm afraid."

Everyone laughed as the chubby *dandapala* gave his belly a good-natured pat.

"I wonder who designed those uniforms," said the old *dandapala*.

"I heard it's a woman who's recently come to Ayodhya

from Angadesh," another man replied. "It seems she has set up her weaving unit somewhere in the heart of the old quarter."

"That's around where the four dead men were found in the street," someone else remarked idly, and Dileepa, sitting at the stern of the boat, froze in his seat, not daring to breathe.

"How did someone who is new to the city manage getting introduced to Gajakarna?" Again, it was the old *dandapala* who spoke.

"Forget that. How did she even get the *mahanayaka* to agree to changing the uniform?" Mitraka chuckled. "That man can be so stuck in his thinking..."

Listening to the conversation move away from the uniforms and Ma Parnalata to Gajakarna's idiosyncrasies, Dileepa sighed in relief. He said nothing, though, and sat formulating his plans until the crowds on the riverbank thinned a little, and one after another, the *dandapalas* got off the boat. Being the last one to set foot on soil, Dileepa jogged after Mitraka and caught up with her as she neared the shops that lined the riverfront.

"May I talk to you for a moment?" he asked. "In private?"

Mitraka considered Dileepa with raised eyebrows before nodding. "What is it?"

Seeing her subordinate hesitate, she motioned to the other *dandapalas* to go on ahead. Once all of them were out of earshot, she looked at Dileepa.

"I was thinking about our conversation the other day," the young investigator said. "You were saying how the force is understaffed and you would like me to join the investigation —"

"I remember," Mitraka interrupted. "What about it?"

"I want to help the force by doing whatever I can to —"

"Have you solved the case you were working on for the rajan?"

"No, I am still working on it —"

"How do you intend dividing your time? The rajan has entrusted you with something important, and I don't want to be called in and told that I am burdening you with other work —"

"No, no," Dileepa assured her hurriedly. "I can investigate two things at the same time."

"Are you sure?" Mitraka glared in warning. "I don't want any excuses later —"

"There will be none, I promise."

"Okay," Mitraka started walking. "Join the team investigating the attack on the king."

"Actually, I was wondering…" Seeing his chief turn an impatient eye on him, Dileepa stopped. "Please listen to me… I have thought this through."

He *had* thought this through. He knew Mitraka wanted him back on the beat. Meanwhile, Rani Kaikeyi wanted him to investigate the attack on the king. However, he wanted something else altogether. So, he had devised a way to make all of it work.

"Tell me," said Mitraka with a resigned sigh.

"You already have a team investigating the attack on the king. The other *dandapalas* are busy looking into the disappearances. What you don't have is someone following up on the four men they found dead in the old quarter. It just struck me on the boat that that needs to be investigated too. *I* could do that."

"Those four men are not a priority."

"I think they are," Dileepa insisted. "Remember how someone in court asked if the four deaths could have been linked to the attack on the rajan?"

Mitraka thought back to the session in court and nodded.

"What if they *are* connected?" Dileepa pressed. "We *must* look into the four deaths. For all we know, solving that case might help us catch those behind the attack on the rajan. I am not saying that will happen, but we mustn't overrule the possibility."

Mitraka gave the investigator's words considerable thought. Finally, she nodded. "You have a point," she admitted. "Okay, you can open investigations into the deaths in the old quarter. You will work with the team investigating the attack on the rajan and share anything of importance that you find."

"I will," said Dileepa with a grateful bow.

Watching the chief of the *dandapalas* walk away, he smiled to himself. Working with the team investigating the attack on the king would give him access to information that he could pass on to Rani Kaikeyi. Meanwhile, digging into the details of the second attack might provide him with a clue about those who wanted *him* out of their way. And if fortune favoured him and the two attacks were related, he would earn Mitraka's admiration and gratitude... maybe even a promotion or a handsome reward from the king. Perhaps an estate in the countryside where he would settle down with Nandana...

It occurred to Dileepa that he was officially investigating his own case, though he was the only one to know about it.

Flanked by his father and his uncle, holding onto their fingers with both hands, Taksha skipped and trotted along the path leading to the royal stables. The men were saying something to each other about Siripala, but the boy was too preoccupied to even try to follow the conversation. His eyes were fixed on the stable, and he could barely contain his excitement as they got closer, his legs and his heart wanting to break into a run. He had tried to make a dash for the stable the moment they had entered the palace ground, but his father had restrained him, telling him to show some patience. Behind the three of them came Angara, sniffing the borders of the path curiously, and right at the back walked Atibhanu, maintaining a respectful distance between himself and the members of the royal family.

"The *dandapalas* have spent hours talking to him," said Bharat. "He has absolutely no memory of the time he was away from here."

"Just like everyone else who has come back," Shatrughna observed.

Bharat nodded gravely. "He couldn't believe he had disappeared. He was convinced it was the same evening."

"Where *is* everyone going?" Shatrughna wondered, thoroughly mystified. "And what happens to them when they are away?"

"I wish we had an answer," said Bharat. "Maybe we would then find an end to this weirdness."

"Yes, this needs to end," said Shatrughna. "Not a day passes without fresh disappearances. And whatever is causing it is spreading. It seems a couple of cases have come to light in Malla, and at least one disappearance has been reported in Kusinagara as well."

"At least those who are going are slowly returning," Bharat said with a sigh.

Rainwater had pooled in the middle of the path, a patch too wide for Taksha to navigate without getting his feet wet. Bharat and Shatrughna caught the boy by his hands and swung him up and over the puddle. The kid chortled in delight as they set him down on the other side.

"Yes, and those who're returning appear none the worse for whatever they've been through," Shatrughna nodded. "That is a consolation."

Hearing their voices, Siripala limped out of his dwelling and shaded his eyes as he watched the small group draw near.

"Siripala," Taksha called. Pulling himself free of Bharat and Shatrughna's grasp, he ran to greet the old man. Angara promptly joined the race.

"How are you, yuvaraja?" Siripala smiled down at the boy.

"How are you," Taksha repeated. Then, looking around, he asked, "Gift?"

Siripala looked from the boy to Shatrughna and back. "It is your uncle's gift to you. Ask him."

Taksha promptly turned to his uncle with a look of expectation.

Shatrughna grinned at the boy. "Wait here," he said, before disappearing inside the stable.

Taksha shifted from one leg to the other, and the excitement spread to Angara like a contagion. The dog began hopping and bouncing, its tail wagging ceaselessly as it looked at everyone in anticipation.

Shatrughna emerged from the stable, a dark-brown mare in tow, and Taksha squealed in delight at the sight of the beast, knowing intuitively that it was the gift meant for him.

He ran forward and Shatrughna scooped the boy up and planted him atop the horse. Taksha's eyes glistened as he ran a palm lovingly over the horse's back and neck, feeling the velvety softness of its coat, and the animal responded to his touch with a nicker and a gentle toss of the head.

"Gift," Taksha whispered. He couldn't seem to stop smiling.

"You like her?" asked Shatrughna. Seeing the kid's emphatic nod, he said, "Take good care of her, and she will be your most reliable friend for life."

"Friend," the boy nodded again. Even on horseback, he was an inch shorter than Shatrughna.

"Thank your uncle for his gift," Bharat reminded the boy quietly.

"Thank," said Taksha.

"I am glad you like her. But while the horse is my gift, the real gift is the one you will get from your father — the art of riding her well," said Shatrughna. "No one rides better than your father in all of Jambudvipa, so you will be learning from the best." Shatrughna paused, then drew the boy into a huge hug. "I won't be around for a while," he said. Seeing the puzzled look on the boy's face, he continued, "I have to go somewhere far for work. But when I'm back, I hope to see you riding her like the wind." He patted the mare so that the boy understood him.

"Riding," Taksha nodded eagerly.

Handing the reins to Siripala, Shatrughna returned to Bharat's side. The two brothers walked a little way from the kid and the ostler. "The beast is docile," Shatrughna said, as if to allay any fears Bharat may harbour about Taksha's safety. "I checked with the seller before buying her."

"I know you would have," Bharat smiled back. He turned to look at the horse. "She is beautiful. And I can see Taksha has taken to her."

They walked some more before Bharat spoke. "With the consecration of the *homagriha* behind us, we should turn our focus to building the market garrison."

"Yes," Shatrughna replied. "The sooner we start, the sooner we inflict damage on Madhupura's economy." When he turned to his brother, there was a shadow of concern in his eyes. "But are you sure you want to come with me?"

As soon as the decision to build the market garrison on the Yamuna had been taken, Shatrughna had been given the charge of bringing the plan to fruition. Scouts had already been sent to look for suitable locations along the river, and a workforce of four hundred woodcutters, carpenters, bricklayers, masons, builders, boat makers and foremen had been put together, along with three dozen cooks, cleaners and porters, and four hundred men of Kosala's army to escort the convoy and provide security once the building of the market began in earnest. A dozen rishis were also made a part of the endeavour to build magic and hasten the construction of the market garrison. It had been decided that the convoy would set off right after the *homagriha's* consecration, and that Shatrughna would stay until the market was up and running, secure from threats. The whole exercise was estimated to take over two years.

"Yes, I would like to come and see the beginning of Kosala's first trading outpost," said Bharat. "It's been a while since I went anywhere outside Ayodhya. I could do with a break, especially since we now have an able *kshatri* in Raja Kushadhwaja to administer the land in my absence."

Shatrughna nodded. "I shall give orders to prepare for departure," he said, but a troubled frown continued to crease his brow. The frown didn't go unnoticed.

"Is something bothering you?" Bharat asked.

"I somehow…" Shatrughna stopped, struggling to find the right words. "I think it's dangerous."

"What's dangerous?" Bharat raised his eyebrows.

"Someone attacked you, brother. Your life is in danger, even in the relative safety of Ayodhya." Shatrughna shook his head unhappily. "Out there, on the open road west, you will be even more exposed, even more vulnerable. I don't think it's a wise idea —"

The king threw his head back and laughed. "How can I be vulnerable when the best swordsman in Jambudvipa is by my side?"

Shatrughna gave his head an adamant shake. "We are heading for Madhupura. What if *adhipati* Sudhanva were right about the attack having been plotted by Lavanyasurya? You'd be walking straight into danger —"

"It's just a theory," Bharat maintained. Then, clapping a hand on Shatrughna's arm, he grinned. "I have nothing to worry about when you are with me. And though not of your calibre, I'm still handy with a *karapala*."

"I won't be with you on your journey back to Ayodhya," Shatrughna reminded him dourly.

Bharat smiled and nodded. "I am deeply touched by your concern, brother," he said. "But I will be fine, I promise. Especially now that I know someone wants to cause me harm, I will be more watchful, trust me. And lest we forget, I have him with me." The king glanced over his shoulder at Atibhanu. "You remember him, don't you?"

Shatrughna looked at the bodyguard and shook his head. "Should I?"

"Remember the sword-fighting championship three years ago?"

"The one I won," Shatrughna nodded.

"The one you had to fight really hard to win," Bharat grinned.

Shatrughna peered at Atibhanu, eyes widening slowly in recognition and respect. "Was *he* my opponent that day? I remember him being very good."

"Not as good as you, but close," said Bharat. "So I may not have Jambudvipa's best swordsman by my side protecting me, but I have the second-best." He paused to smile reassuringly. "Don't worry about me. I have all of Kosala behind me. Put your energy into building our own market. Let us put a swift end to Madhupura's monopoly and bring Lavanyasurya's pride crashing down to earth."

The youngest of Dashratha's sons nodded. "When would you like to leave?"

"Like you said, the sooner we start, the better."

Thunder rolled in the clouds hanging low to the west as Yuddhajeet walked his horse along the Vitasta, overseeing the evacuation of the river market. The town was home to a hundred people, who were being shifted out of harm's way in the eventuality that Gandharan troops would pick the spot for a crossing, though all the intelligence they'd gathered so far suggested that Nagnajit intended to ford the Vitasta near Mithuna. Still, a change in strategy couldn't be discounted, so the river towns had to be evacuated, homes and shops had to be emptied of stocks and supplies that could feed or equip the invading force, and the boats needed to be secured to the near bank so that they were useless to the troops attempting the crossing. The one thing that didn't need doing was poisoning the wells; the Vitasta was right here, with enough water to slake the thirst of all of earth's armies.

"Quick, quick… get the carts moving," Yuddhajeet urged, chafing at the tardiness and lack of urgency.

In every town he'd been to since morning, townspeople had taken their time clearing out their houses and loading their belongings into carts. Their inertia was understandable; they were exchanging a life of harmony and routine for one of uncertainty. They weren't used to war, but they knew one could last a long time, and many feared they might never see their homes again. Yuddhajeet understood this, but the River Kingdoms didn't have the luxury of time; the last update he had received from his scouts said the Gandharan forces had crossed the Sindhu, which put them a couple of days' march away. The river towns needed to be evacuated rapidly, and there were so many of them on both banks of the Vitasta.

"Easy, easy," said Yuddhajeet, noticing an old woman struggle with a crate. Stopping his horse, he dismounted and took the crate from the woman. Placing it in a cart, he helped her in as well. "Have a safe ride," he said.

"Fight like the storm; kill like the lightning," the woman replied by way of a blessing.

Yuddhajeet had never heard that one before. It sounded grand. He bowed his thanks.

They moved to the next town, then the next, making sure no townsfolk were left behind, trapped in the war zone. Yuddhajeet rode alone, for Ambareesha and the other Bahlikas had stayed back in Mithuna to master some basic mantras for harnessing magic, though there was another, more strategic reason behind Ambareesha's absence. Yuddhajeet supposed Gandhara would have its spies watching the riverfront, and he was keen on keeping the Bahlikas hidden from Gandharan eyes. For the same reason, Kekeya had blocked westbound traffic for a week now, not wanting reports of the large presence of Bahlika troops along the Vitasta to reach Nagnajit. The Bahlikas were the element of surprise that Ashwapati and Yuddhajeet were banking on to even the odds between Gandhara and the River Kingdoms.

Dusk was nigh by the time Yuddhajeet returned to Mithuna. The town had been evacuated, and apart from a few civilians who had stayed to look after the needs of the rishi who'd come from Rajagriha, everyone in the town was there to fight the Gandhara-Kamboja confederacy. The sound of mantras issued from the direction of the town hall, which the rishi had selected to house the *homa* fire. Boats lined the eastern bank, rocking in the river's currents. The sky was heavy with clouds, and a weak drizzle fell over the town as Yuddhajeet rode towards the dwelling he shared with Ambareesha.

Getting off the horse, he was stretching his back to work out the kinks and the stiffness when, out of the corner of his eye, he spied a figure appear from behind a house two doors away. The prince turned to get a better look and was surprised to see a woman; as far as he knew, the women of Mithuna had already been sent off to safety. So, he stared as she set a tub down by her feet and began plucking leaves off a shrub growing outside the house. The woman had her back to him, so the prince couldn't see her face.

"How come you are still here?" he called out sharply.

Startled, the woman turned, a hand to her chest. Seeing it was Yuddhajeet, she relaxed. "I didn't know you were around," she said.

"*You?*" the prince regarded Abhisarika in bewilderment. "What are *you* doing here? When did you come?"

"An hour ago. As to what I'm doing here," she extended her hand, showing him the leaves she had plucked, "These are antiseptics. They help wounds heal faster."

Of course, Yuddhajeet thought to himself. She was a medicine woman; that's how Ambareesha had described her. She was here to tend to the wounded, but a war zone was a dangerous place for a woman of peace. "We have *vaidyas* here to treat the wounded," he remarked, wondering if Ambareesha knew his cousin was in Mithuna, wondering if Ambareesha had known all along that she would show up. "There's a war brewing around us —"

"That's why I came. Once war begins, you will discover that no number of *vaidyas* are enough. Also, my father took your money in return of a promise to send all the help he can in the coming war. I am here to honour that promise."

Yuddhajeet nodded. "I understand," he said. He actually didn't. The River Kingdoms had paid for swords and spears, not for medicines. But if this woman wanted to include medicines in the deal, he wouldn't argue. "Just be careful once the fighting begins," he reminded her, wondering where she had left her daughter.

Before Abhisarika could say anything, a voice addressed the prince from behind. "Don't worry about her. My daughter knows how to take care of herself."

Yuddhajeet turned to see the dark, craggy face of chief Sailusha staring at him, the lips smiling under the big white moustache.

"Chief," the prince did a *pranaam*. "It is a pleasure to see you. I presume you came together?"

"We did," Sailusha replied.

"Does Ambareesha know you're both here?"

The chief shrugged. "I am told he is away learning magic."

"He is in Gandhapuri," Yuddhajeet pointed eastwards. "I could take you to him."

"Let me fetch my horse," the old warrior nodded.

Yuddhajeet turned to ask Abhisarika if she'd like to come along with them, but he was surprised to see she had already gone indoors. No courtesies, no niceties, no with-your-permissions. He frowned as took his horse by the bridle and led it back to the path.

Sailusha appeared with his horse. "Are we prepared to take on Nagnajit's forces?" he enquired as he got in the saddle.

"I'm fairly certain we are," the prince answered, mounting his horse.

His mind dwelled on the woman a moment longer. She seemed to have this suddenness, this abruptness, built into her character. One instant, she was not there, the next she was, then again, she wasn't. Appearing and disappearing at will.

He found her aggravating and annoying. Her poise. Her matter-of-factness. Her unflappability. Her reserve, her resolve. Her unwillingness to fit a type.

His own inability to fathom her, to size her up.

Everything about Abhisarika confounded and exasperated him, Yuddhajeet realized.

It was raining again. Not a cathartic, earth-shattering downpour as on the night of the attack, but a steady, sedate rain, unspectacular and therefore reassuring. The sort of rain that allowed farmers to sleep soundly, secure in the knowledge that nothing was going immediately wrong in their world.

Taksha too was sound asleep in his cot, lulled by the sound of the rain and depleted by a full day's excitement, first at the Sanctum, and later in the palace ground with the mare and Angara. Activity had dulled inside and outside the palace, and only the occasional flicker of the sentries' torches told of vigil and wakefulness. The city beyond the palace gates had also retired for the night, its people giving into sleep with relief and gratitude. The rains had ushered an end to not just the summer heat but also the fear that had laid siege to Ayodhya, entrapping its people's souls.

"I'm so thankful that he is fine and nothing happened to him," Mandavi said softly, shooting a quick glance over her shoulder to check on Taksha as he slept. "I was so scared. Throughout the journey from Rajviraj, I could only think all kinds of horrible thoughts. What if something had —" She shuddered at the memory. "I tried so hard not to, but the thoughts just kept coming and wouldn't go away. I was afraid I would end up making all those thoughts a reality and we would lose —" her voice trembled and cracked with emotion.

"Shh..." said Bharat, putting an arm around her, drawing her close. "Shh..." he repeated. "It is over. The kid is fine. Forget about it."

Mandavi swallowed the lump in her throat. Composing herself, she nodded. "Yes." She looked up at her husband, her eyes following the line of his brow and nose. "I feared so much for Taksha that I hardly spared a thought for you," she said, a note of guilt in her voice. "When it was *your* life they were really after..."

"It's okay," said Bharat. "At that time, even I was concerned only about the kid's well-being. It wasn't until later that it struck me that..." he left what he had been meaning to say unfinished.

"I am sorry," Mandavi whispered. "I should have —"

"There's nothing to be sorry about," Bharat butted in, turning to look at his wife. "It was natural to fear for the kid. He is small, and anything could have happened to him. And he is precious to you."

"So are you."

"I know," Bharat smiled in the dark. "Which is why you don't have to apologize for not having thought about me."

With a sigh, Mandavi placed her head on Bharat's shoulder, and Bharat held her even tighter. They were seated on a wooden swing that occupied a portion of their bedchamber overlooking a garden. The chamber was in darkness, the only light coming from the muted pulse of magic that coursed through the chains of the swing, propelling it gently back and forth.

"Who would want to harm you?" Mandavi wondered aloud. Then, raising her head, she looked at Bharat. "Father says the *dandapalas* haven't made any breakthrough in their investigation."

The king shook his head.

"Don't they even have a clue?" Mandavi pressed. "I've heard it spoken that Raja Lavanyasurya might have been behind this..." She paused as something struck her. "You know, Rani Kaikeyi said something the day I took Shrutakirti to her for her blessings. She said Madhupura, Chedi, and Kasi would betray Kosala when it suited their interests —"

"Don't listen to her," said Bharat. "She can say anything she fancies. It doesn't mean anything."

"But Raja Lavanyasurya *has* been behaving peculiarly towards us," Mandavi stressed. "Father told me about everything he's been up to."

Bharat nodded. "Yes, but there is no evidence that he was behind the attack. All we can say for certain is that the attackers were acquainted with my routine. They knew I took Taksha to play with Angara every evening. They knew the vicinity of the stable was lightly guarded. They had inside information."

"You mean it was planned locally?" Mandavi's eyes widened in apprehension.

"Meaning it was definitely executed with local help."

Mandavi was silent for a long time, pondering the implications of what she had learned. Finally, she looked at Bharat. "You should be very careful," she said. "Now even more so as Shatrughna isn't going to be here, at least for the foreseeable future."

"I already *am* careful," the king replied. He nodded towards one of the torches moving in the palace ground. "And so is everyone else."

Mandavi gave this a moment's thought before looking up at her husband. "Do you need to go?" she asked. "I mean, with Shatrughna? To establish this new market? I mean… Shatrughna can do this by himself…"

"He can," Bharat agreed. "He most definitely can."

"Then why are you —"

"To make a statement," Bharat replied even before Mandavi had framed the question fully.

"What do you mean by that?"

"We were on the verge of going to war with Madhupura over their mistreatment of our soldiers," said the king. "But we didn't. Now, we are building this market, and I want every kingdom and every principality in Jambudvipa to know that this is a strategic decision backed by the throne of Ayodhya. My going with Shatrughna sends the message that this market is not to be taken lightly. This market is Kosala's property, the king's property, and it is not to be messed with. Shatrughna will build the market, safeguard it, administer it, but it is the king's market. Meddle with the market, and you meddle with Kosala."

Mandavi stared at Bharat's profile. When she spoke, there was a smile in her voice. "You sound like a king," she said.

Bharat said nothing. They were silent for a moment, listening to the rain. When Mandavi spoke next, her voice was tinged with sadness. "Shrutakirti is in Rajviraj. Rama, Sita and Lakshmana have been gone a long time. Once Shatrughna has also left, the palace will fall very silent," she remarked. "Only the two of us will be left here with the queen mothers and Urmila."

"Taksha will be around to make up for everyone's absence," Bharat pointed out.

"Yes, but I miss the days when we sisters first came here," Mandavi reminisced. "There was so much activity all around, so much laughter and gaiety. Now, there isn't even an echo of that old joy left. It's almost like it was never there."

Bharat nodded but chose to keep quiet this time.

"I dropped in to see Urmila this afternoon," Mandavi said, brightening a little. "I hadn't sat and really talked to her in a long while."

"She hardly ever leaves her chamber, other than to visit the palace library," said Bharat. "Not that I blame her for choosing to live like a recluse."

"I know. But you know something…?" Mandavi looked at her husband in excitement. "Urmila told me what she's been doing in the library all this while."

"What?" Bharat asked expectantly.

"She has been learning how to weave magic."

Bharat's eyebrows rose in wonder. "*Weave magic*… you mean like the rishis?"

"Yes."

Bharat whistled under his breath.

"She's been mastering the mantras and the techniques for well over a year," Mandavi revealed.

"I would never have guessed," Bharat shook his head, impressed.

"Even father was amazed," Mandavi smiled, her voice swelling with admiration. "But I'm not surprised. Urmila was always the cleverest among us sisters."

The cot creaked as Taksha turned in his sleep, letting out a small whimper. Bharat and Mandavi leaped to their feet.

"Probably a bad dream," Mandavi whispered to Bharat. "Why don't you go to sleep? I'll make sure he's alright."

Instead of going to bed, Bharat went to the canopied balcony that adjoined the bedchamber. Standing by the parapet and locking his hands behind him, he watched the rain descend on the sleeping city with a growing sense of satisfaction.

The *agnimanasa* had worked. The rain had arrived, ending the drought and bringing with it the promise of an end to his people's suffering. The magic was also back in Ayodhya's atmosphere, he could tell. The disappearances continued unabated — some said they were getting more and more frequent, and they were definitely more widespread now — but people were also coming back. So many of them. Like Siripala.

Also, for the first time in over a year — for the first time since the fall of the old *homagriha* — mahamuni Vashishtha was showing signs of improvement. Nothing major yet, nothing drastic. Just an alertness in his eyes, a flush of colour in his sunken cheeks, a steadiness in his breathing that hadn't been there two weeks ago. The *vaidyas* were excited and hopeful, certain that their ministrations were at last bearing fruit. Bharat knew better, of course, but he hadn't said a word about the *agnimanasa*.

Mahamuni Vashishtha was recovering. Siripala had returned. The magic was back. And Taksha was safe. The *vaidyas* had decided that it had been a seizure and nothing worse. He hadn't lost the boy to the *agnimanasa* as he had feared. Contrary to Surochi's warnings, the *agnimanasa* hadn't taken anything from him. It had only given. Given back Taksha and Siripala, unharmed. Given back the magic.

His fears had been unfounded, and Bharat was beginning to see the *agnimanasa* as benign, and not adversarial as Surochi had made it out to be.

Watching the rain, soothed by its sound, the king of Kosala felt an assurance that his kingdom's bad days were behind it now.

four

SIMHIKA HADN'T EXPECTED THE RISHIS' WIVES TO COME visiting so soon. It was the third morning after the consecration of the *homagriha*, and the sorceress was lounging in the inner courtyard, her eyes closed against the glare of the sun, her freshly washed hair spread over a wicker basket to dry, when one of her attendants had run up to announce the arrival of the rishis' wives. There had been four of them, and they said they had dropped in on a whim, but Simhika knew better. The women had made an effort to look for her mansion in the clutter of the old quarter, and anyone putting themselves through so much trouble had to be deeply motivated, the sorceress thought.

Simhika was immediately proved right. The visitors were welcomed and seated, and attendants were still serving them pots of spiced buttermilk by way of refreshments when one of the wives admitted to having been mesmerized by the soldiers' uniforms. Taking her confession as their cue, the other three women had joined in, telling Simhika how much those uniforms had impressed them all. Once they had nothing left to say in praise, the women had looked at each other before one of them hazarded the question: could

Simhika weave them saris that were grand in design, yet stylistically simple?

"Nothing too extravagant," one had stressed. "We are the wives of Ayodhya's rishis, after all."

"So, no silks," another had said. "But anything in cotton would be fine."

"Simple, but not plain," a third had clarified. "Something that catches the eye."

"I know what you mean, and I can try," Simhika had replied.

She had lied, of course. About trying. She knew exactly what the women meant, and she could weave saris of the sort they were talking about. In fact, she had a dozen saris lying upstairs that she could have shown the rishis' wives right away and sold for a tidy profit. But instead, all she had said was that she would *try*.

"Please give me a few days to come up with something worthy of your attention," she had said.

"Can we come back in a week from now?" one of the wives asked.

"Oh no, I am sure I will have something ready before that." Yes, time was critical. There wasn't a moment to be squandered. Her lord in Lanka was waiting for her to destroy Ayodhya's magic. The sooner she began, the sooner…

"So when —"

"I won't bother you to come here again," the sorceress had smiled in reply. "It will be an honour to visit you at the Sanctum. Let *me* bring the saris to you when they are ready."

To Simhika's delight, the wives agreed. The more often she visited the Sanctum, the greater the influence she would be able to exert on the rishis and on the fire burning in the *homagriha*. That was why she had decided against showing the saris that were already in stock. She needed a pretext to visit the Sanctum again.

The rishis' wives left, pleased with the outcome of the morning's expedition, and Simhika was wondering what to do next when one of her helpers came to tell her that the *dandapala* Dileepa was at the door.

"Dileepa," the sorceress greeted the investigator warmly. She had casually moved to addressing him by name a while back, and he hadn't objected. "What brings you here so early in the day?"

"I was in this part of town on work, so I thought I would drop in," the *dandapala* replied.

"Excellent," said Simhika. She turned to an attendant. "Bring our guest some buttermilk."

"You had visitors," Dileepa remarked, sitting on a low *manchika*. "I saw some ladies leave as I turned into the street. From their looks and general demeanour, I gathered they were the wives of some of the rishis."

"Nothing escapes the palace investigator's sharp eye," Simhika chuckled. "Indeed, they were the wives of some of Ayodhya's rishis." After a short pause, she said, "Their visit was the result of *your* hard work."

"*My* hard work?" Dileepa asked, looking mystified.

"You got *mahanayaka* Gajakarna to meet me and hear me out. Thanks to that introduction, the soldiers of the garrison got those fabulous new outfits. The uniforms have impressed the rishis' wives so much that they want me to design saris for them now. I owe you my thanks for this amazing breakthrough."

"I did nothing, Ma," the *dandapala* protested. "Nandana asked me to put in a word, and that is all I ever did. I can hardly take any credit for that."

"That is your humility speaking," Simhika said, shaking her head gently to show she disagreed.

"Speaking of Nandana, isn't she around?" Dileepa asked.

"No. She wanted to visit the temples by the river." The sorceress paused. "She left an hour ago. She wasn't expecting you to come around at this time of the day. I mean, you usually don't —"

"No, of course not," Dileepa said hurriedly. "I dropped in without notice. It's perfectly alright."

"Like I said, she left a while ago, so she should be returning anytime now. Wait a while. Maybe you could have lunch with us..." Ignoring the protests from Dileepa, Simhika called to one of her helpers. "The *dandapala* will be having lunch with us, so listen carefully..." The sorceress reeled of a series of instructions as Dileepa accepted the fact that the fate of his next meal had been decided and the choice was no longer in his hands.

"What else are you up to these days?" Simhika asked once the attendant had left. Eyeing the empty pot in Dileepa's hands, she popped another question. "Shall I ask for more buttermilk?"

"No," the *dandapala* shook his head. Then, replying to the first question, he said, "I am working on the attack on Raja Bharat."

"Imagine, how dreadful," Simhika looked aghast at the mention of the attack. "The raja himself attacked in his own palace." She leaned forward. "Any idea who was behind the attack?"

Dileepa shook his head.

Simhika sighed. "What is this city coming to?" she said. Looking closely at the *dandapala*, she added, "Four men were killed down this street a week ago, the same night the raja was attacked. I am sure you know about it."

Dileepa nodded. "I... yes, it was discussed in court. A very strange occurrence."

"No one seems to be investigating those deaths," said Simhika.

Dileepa squirmed uncomfortably. "I think... perhaps the *nagarapalas* are. We *dandapalas* are looking into the attack on the king."

"Let's hope you make rapid progress and nab those responsible."

"I hope so too," Dileepa looked downcast. "I'm due to give Rani Kaikeyi an update, and I have nothing of significance to share."

"Who?"

Dileepa looked up at the sorceress, surprised by the sharpness in her tone. "Rani Kaikeyi."

"Why do you have to update the rani...?"

"Because she's personally asked me to investigate the attack on the raja. She called me to the palace and..." the *dandapala* paused to consider the sorceress. "Wait, Nandana didn't tell you about all this?"

"No," Simhika shook her head. "When did this happen?"

"About a week ago. The rani called me —"

"And when did you tell Nandana about it?"

"The same day. She must have forgotten to tell you."

"She must have."

"Yes, so the thing is that I have to report on the investigation's progress..."

Simhika smiled and nodded, but she wasn't paying heed to any of the words pouring out of the stupid *dandapala's* mouth. From the very beginning, it had been made abundantly clear that the *dandapala* was a key to the palace and the king, especially after he had won the king's trust by exposing the hoarding scam. She had pinned hopes on Dileepa worming deeper into the palace, and here he was, interacting with Kaikeyi, the king's mother — a candidate immensely suitable for exploitation. But instead of telling her about it so she could use it for Lanka's gain, Nandana had kept this fact hidden from her, not mentioning a word about it for nearly a week...

"...I was telling Nandana how Rani Kaikeyi thinks well of me..." Dileepa droned on.

Simhika's mind went back to the night of the rainstorm. She had been on the mansion's rooftop. She had watched Nandana and Dileepa return to the mansion. She had watched the *dandapala* leave, and watched as he had been surrounded and attacked by four men bearing *khangas*. She had been thinking of intervening — Dileepa was important to her plans — when she had seen Nandana conjure the six *shyenas* and spring them on the attackers. That night, she had ascribed the girl's actions to her love for Lanka: Nandana had gone to the *dandapala's* rescue as he was a critical pawn in the grand plan to bring an end to the rule of the Ikshvakus.

But now, the sorceress looked back on that night and Nandana's actions from a new perspective. Perhaps the girl had not acted out of her love for Lanka after all. Perhaps it was a different love that had dictated her actions… Suddenly, Simhika was reminded of the morning at the Sanctum, when the soldiers of the garrison had marched through the gates. She had tried to get Nandana's attention, but the girl had been looking at Dileepa, lost in thought…

Nandana didn't tell you about all this?

No, she hadn't.

She must have forgotten to tell you.

No, she hadn't forgotten.

She had intentionally concealed vital information that could benefit Lanka and her lord Ravana. Only because she had fallen in love with a human.

As the cold wave of realization swept over Simhika, she shivered in the sunlight coming down from the mansion's sky-lit ceiling. Nandana's loyalties had shifted, and she was prepared to betray Lanka's cause in her love for the *dandapala*.

The chill she had felt passed, and in its place, a seething anger took root at the core of Simhika's being…

Rain — a steady, wet, incessant drizzle — continued to fall from the colourless sky, turning the ground under the horses' hooves squelchy and difficult to walk on. Men rushed about the tents that had been pitched into the damp earth, threading between clusters of doleful horses, hurrying between the armouries and the corrals where more horses waited to be saddled and led out. Swords, spears, bows and quivers filled with arrows waved in the air wherever one looked, and the place rang with the sounds of horses whinnying and snorting, and men shouting encouragement to one another. The children and womenfolk of Gandhapuri stood at the edges of the village, silently watching the menfolk of Kekeya go to war.

Yuddhajeet sat on his mount, eyes narrowed against the drizzle, taking stock of the activity all around. News had arrived that the Gandharan army was marching straight for Mithuna. Having learned from his spies that the town was only moderately defended by a few thousand Kekeyan troops, Nagnajit probably hoped to ford the Vitasta at its shallowest and storm the river market, Yuddhajeet surmised, delighted that the ploy he and Ambareesha had devised to draw Nagnajit to Mithuna had worked. They expected an assault within a day of the Gandharan army reaching the opposite bank… which gave Mithuna's defenders just enough time to put their strategy into action.

There was a stir to the left, and Yuddhajeet followed everyone's gaze to see Sailusha come out of a house. The chieftain struck across the open ground where the tents were pitched, buckling his sword to his waist as he headed for the stable to pick his horse. The man had a commanding presence, the prince had to acknowledge, and eyes followed him all the way to the stable. All the Bahlika warriors were already mounted, men and horses standing motionless in the drizzle.

A horseman ambled out from behind some tents. Yuddhajeet turned to find it was Ambareesha, and they exchanged nods.

"So, we go to war," the Bahlika giant observed as he joined the prince of Kekeya.

"Finally," Yuddhajeet agreed.

They had gone over the strategy a number of times, and everyone knew their role in the fight. If they could execute it as well as they had planned it, Yuddhajeet knew they had a very good chance of beating the Gandhara-Kamboja combine.

He looked at Ambareesha. "You haven't forgotten your mantras, have you?"

Ambareesha dropped his head and gazed inwards as he uttered a mantra. He stuck his hand out self-consciously, tentative about his abilities, but when he closed his fingers, a javelin appeared in his hand, his fingers wrapping easily around its wooden shaft. The warrior's eyes shone with pride and relief as he grinned at Yuddhajeet.

"Very impressive," the prince smiled, clapping the giant's shoulder.

"We'd have done better had we had more time," Ambareesha replied.

"We must make the most of the time we are given," spoke a voice from behind the men.

A woman's voice. Familiar.

Yuddhajeet's eyebrows rose as he turned to find Abhisarika on a saddle. She had tied her hair into a tight bun at the top of her head, and an armour made of thick hide covered her torso. The prince blinked at the sight of the wooden shield in her hand and the sword that hung from her hip.

"We must, sister," Ambareesha concurred in a grave manner. "We must."

Yuddhajeet shot a glance at the giant, then looked back at Abhisarika. "You're riding into battle with us?" he asked. He didn't even attempt to conceal the surprise in his voice.

"Yes."

The prince nodded slowly. "I didn't know," he said. What he meant was that he hadn't expected this.

"I told you the other day," the woman said.

"When?" Yuddhajeet twisted around in his saddle.

"The other evening in Mithuna. I told you I was here to honour the promise father had made."

"Oh yes… right." He had thought she was here to treat the ill and the wounded, he remembered. "But I thought you were a medicine woman."

"I am one."

Yuddhajeet looked at Abhisarika searchingly. "Isn't it strange for someone whose job is saving lives to be riding into battle?"

"There is a time to save lives, and there is a time to take them," the woman replied. "Besides, I believe someone who saves lives is better qualified to fight battles," she added. "If one knows nothing about saving lives, one shouldn't be taking them either."

The prince nodded again, not knowing how to respond. Once again she had befuddled him, left him bereft of words. It was beginning to frustrate him.

"The chief is here," Ambareesha announced, and Yuddhajeet exhaled in relief.

Sailusha rode up to the trio. "The Bahlikas are ready," he said.

"So are we," Yuddhajeet replied.

The chief nodded. Without another word, he spurred his horse, and the beast leaped into a gallop. The Bahlikas all thundered after him, a surge of horsemen with their javelins pointing straight up. Looking around, Yuddhajeet saw Ambareesha and Abhisarika also riding away in pursuit of their tribespeople.

The prince looked at Kekeya's soldiers, who were still milling around uncertainly. "Men," he roared, trying to rally them. "Let us ride to defend Mithuna." He paused, remembering the old woman's words from a few evenings ago. Drawing his sword, he held it aloft.

"Fight like the storm," he exhorted, "and kill like the lightning."

Thunder growled in the distance. The elements sensed a bloodshed coming. The elements were hungering for war. Kekeya's soldiers raised their weapons and screamed back at the sky.

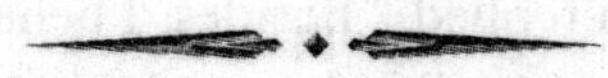

He awoke, ravenous and thirsty.

It was a hunger and thirst the likes of which he had never experienced before. It wasn't a hunger born in the pit of the stomach, where hunger usually lingered; it wasn't a thirst felt in the gullet and on parched lips. This was a hunger spawned deep in the bones, a dark and insatiable craving that permeated muscle and tissue like an ache and seeped out of every pore and spread over his skin like a contagion, smothering him, consuming him. This was a thirst that emptied his mind, emptied his soul, creating space only for itself and the greed to be slaked… not with water, with something darker and richer and more filling. Like blood.

Hunger and thirst. Intertwining, melding together, building on one another's agony and ecstasy, becoming one so he couldn't tell them apart, *couldn't tell anything apart.*

Hunger and thirst and himself. All fused into one. All one.

He wasn't even aware he was awake. All he sensed was a sudden realization that he was hungry and thirsty, that he *was* hunger and thirst, that he needed appeasement, fulfilment, gratification.

He rose and went in search of nourishment. He sought what he wanted not with his eyes though, which were sewn shut, eyelids glued together in sleep. Not with ears and nose either, like some feral, nocturnal creature. Not with any of the senses known to man.

He sought what he wanted from memory. Memory of what he had been told, though he couldn't remember any of the words now. Maybe no words had been said. Maybe there had been nothing but sounds and suggestions.

He sought what he wanted from knowledge. Knowledge of what had to be done when the time came, when he became hunger and thirst.

He sought what he wanted from instinct. Instinct so ancient, so clever, so evil, it knew all things past and future. Instinct that knew where to look, how to look.

So, swaddled in hunger, burning with thirst, and numb to all other faculties and sensations and emotions, he approached the small, dark object that his hunger and thirst sensed — *desired, yearned for* — in the dark. Every step closer to his prey stoked his hunger and thirst, till he was entirely swallowed by his need to feed, saliva spilling from his lips and drooling down his chin in anticipation. The scent of warm blood rose to his nose and washed through him in a euphoric tide, and the thought of the taste of flesh made him weak-kneed, so he sagged and stumbled —

— and woke to consciousness, opening his eyes in the semi-dark of dawn.

He blinked once, then again, trying to get his bearings and make sense of what was happening. Wondering why he was standing in the dark instead of being in his bed where he ought to have been asleep, wondering how he had got to the middle of his room without waking up —

That was when he heard the sound. It came from in front of him, from somewhere down by the floor of the room. A tremulous part growl, part whine, part yelp. Sharp and infused with fright, with terror even.

"Angara?"

This time, he heard a note of plea in the dog's part whine, part whimper. A desperate sound in the dark, desperate to please, desperate for mercy.

He flicked his fingers, and a small, incandescent globe lit up over his head, chasing the shadows out of the room —

— casting its light over Siripala —

— illuminating Angara as it crouched low in one corner, cringing in fear.

The dog had its ears folded back, its tail tucked between its legs, teeth bared, eyes watchful and scared as it watched the old ostler.

"Angara?" Siripala said again, snapping his fingers at the dog.

The animal wagged its tail once and bowed its head in a placatory gesture, but it stayed pressed to the wall, unwilling to trust the kindness in the man's voice.

"What happened?" Siripala asked. Taking a step forward, he went down on his good knee and patted the ground. "Come here…"

The dog straightened slowly and shambled over, still trembling, head still down, uncertain and still looking cowed. Reaching Siripala, it stretched its neck out and sniffed his hand once before giving it a tentative lick. Finally, mustering some courage, the dog drew a few steps closer, and as the old man patted its head and scratched its neck, the animal dropped its guard, wagging its tail and licking his face in relief.

"What happened?" Siripala asked again, gently brushing the dog's coat with his fingers. "What scared you so much?"

It took a minute longer for Angara to fully calm down. With one final pat on its head, the ostler got to his feet and limped into the stable yard. The dog followed him. Standing side by side, they watched the eastern sky turn orange while birds lifted off the trees in the day's first flight.

Siripala remembered nothing of the hunger and thirst that had taken such a terrible hold of him barely minutes earlier, waking him up and sending him on a hunt for prey. No hunger, no thirst. He did puzzle over how he had come awake standing in his room in the dark, in front of Angara. He also pondered the state he had found the dog in, and searched for a reason for its fear. But there wasn't a trace of the hunger or the thirst anywhere in his mind. No recollection of the manic desire to sink teeth into flesh and savour warm blood. No remains, no residue.

Everything wiped clean, everything forgotten, like it had only been a dream. Or blotted out like a hastily repressed nightmare.

The arrows left the bows almost in unison, speeding towards the sky, leaving the synchronized twang of three hundred bowstrings behind on the riverbank. Up they soared, graceful as the flight of a river bird, spanning the Vitasta before dipping and homing in on Mithuna on the opposite bank. Down they tore like a swarm of incensed wasps, like lethal rainfall, hammering into the houses that lined the waterfront, shattering tiles and skewering wood, seeking out life that could be terminated by the cracking of the cranium, the slicing of the carotid or the severing of the spine.

None of those three hundred arrows took any lives, though. The residents of Mithuna had already been moved out of the war zone, and the town's defenders were hidden deep within the houses, waiting for Gandhara's troops to start crossing the river before attacking them, when they were in the water and at their most vulnerable. This was also Nagnajit's reading of the situation upon seeing the deserted town and riverbank. So, as the first batch of boats with Gandharan soldiers headed for the opposite bank, the raya signalled Kamboja's horse-archers to shoot another round of arrows on Mithuna. The idea was to keep the Kekeyans sheltering inside so that they couldn't come out and interfere with the landing.

As arrows rose on one bank and fell on the other in volley after endless volley, the river churned with oars as boatload after boatload of Gandharans made the crossing. At a spot where the river was at its shallowest, horses were whipped and dragged and driven into the water to hasten the landing. The sound of water splashing was everywhere, and the mid-morning sun refracted off the spray rising over the Vitasta. Watching the scene unfold, Nagnajit noted the rapid progress of his troops with satisfaction. Already, the first set of boats were nudging against the far bank, and soldiers were leaping onto land. The lead horses were halfway across, while more were being lined up for the fording. In Mithuna, not a soul moved under the hail of arrows, the riverbank vacant except for the fifteen fishing boats that had been drawn up on the sand, where they lay like wooden carcasses, their bellies opened to the sun.

"Should I get my archers to stop?" asked Mahasa, sitting astride his horse to Nagnajit's right.

The raya assessed the number of Gandharan soldiers massed on the other bank. Still more were needed to make a concerted and effective rush, he surmised. He shook his head at the Kamboja warlord.

"We must be careful," Mahasa warned.

Nagnajit nodded. He understood that they had to quit shooting arrows at the right moment. Too soon, and Mithuna's defenders would grab the opportunity to step out and attack his men before they had even landed properly in sizeable numbers. Too late, and it was the Gandharans who'd be felled by the arrows as they ran in to take the town. Timing was critical, and the raya squinted into the sun to see how the landing was progressing and how his men were faring. His informers had said that they could expect up to two thousand men guarding the town, which wasn't much. His troops could easily take the place as long as they all crossed safely.

Arrows arced over the river, which was now seething with boats, horses and men. In Nagnajit's estimate, close to five hundred men had crossed over and were waiting by the water's edge — swords and spears ready, shields up — for the signal to charge. The sand between the river and town was open, except for the boats sunning in the heat. A rush would take his men to the town in less than ten seconds, the raya gauged, but the question was, were they set to make a rush? Narrowing his eyes, he tried assessing the men, looking for a sign that said they were ready to —

There! He saw three of the men at the front of the attack nod to one another.

"Now," Nagnajit shouted to Mahasa. "Now."

The chief of Kamboja raised both hands above his head and brought them down in a scything motion. At almost the same instant, the men on the opposite bank broke into a run, scrambling up the sandy gradient to Mithuna, while behind them, another three boats bearing Gandharans bumped against land. The last volley of arrows sailed over the Vitasta and over the heads of the charging men to slam into the hapless town.

Letting out a sigh of relief, Nagnajit smiled in anticipation of the bloodletting that was to come. It was time to make Kekeya pay for seizing the tributes that his men had collected from Sakala.

Gandhara's soldiers dashed towards the line of buildings, but expectedly, they were greeted by a shower of arrows that slowed their progress. The men pressed on nonetheless, ducking behind their shields, but four or five of them were lost in that opening onslaught. Then, all of a sudden, one of the boats drawn on the sand caught fire. A moment later, a second boat ignited, followed by a third. Nagnajit shielded his eyes against the glare and watched fire-tipped arrows emerge from the houses and strike the boats, setting them ablaze.

"The Kekeyans are smart," Mahasa growled.

They were, Nagnajit had to concede. He now saw why the boats lay scattered in such a slapdash manner instead of being laid side by side in neat rows, the way fisher folk typically beached them. Filled with hay and cloth and doused in oil, the boats were being employed as flaming obstacles to retard the Gandharan assault, forcing the attackers to mass together so they offered better targets to the town's archers. The raya swore roundly for underestimating the Kekeyans and not seeing through their plan.

"Why are your men slowing down?"

Nagnajit stared. The Kamboja chief was right. Even as his men struggled to get past the burning boats, they appeared incapable of quick movement, stumbling and stalling halfway up the bank, only to be cut down by Kekeyan arrows.

"Something is hindering their advance," cried Mahasa.

Fishing nets.

The raya of Gandhara had no way of being sure, but he knew he had guessed right. Hard to see in the morning sun, unless one was expecting them and knew where to look. A bit like a spider's web. And his men had blundered straight into them.

Flaming boats as obstacles; fishing nets strung along the bank to encumber his troops. But for the fact that it was *his* men who were at risk of losing their lives, Nagnajit would have admired the ingenuity of Mithuna's defenders.

Ensnared by the boats and the nets, the Gandharan units became easy targets for the Kekeyan archers, who slaughtered the enemy without mercy. To complicate matters, fresh boatloads of Gandharans ran up the riverbank to join the fight, not realizing that those who had gone ahead were struggling to get past the strategically positioned fishing nets. So, more and more soldiers massed on the bank, unable to move forward quickly enough to get to the houses and neutralize the Kekeyan archers.

As Nagnajit watched from across the Vitasta in mounting unease, dozens of Kekeyan horsemen rode into view from behind the buildings. Reinforcements for the archers, the riders were armed with bows and arrows meant to annihilate the Gandharan soldiers fumbling on the bank.

"Fall back," Nagnajit shouted, fearing a rout. "Give an order to the men to fall back."

He whirled on Mahasa. "Get your archers to give my men cover," he screeched. "The Kekeyan archers and riders must be stopped."

The warlord once again raised his arms over his head. Nagnajit turned his attention back to the distant bank, where things had gone terribly wrong in a matter of moments. The Kekeyan riders were letting their arrows fly at his men, many of whom were already heading back towards the river, knowing the rush had failed. Others were desperately trying to untangle themselves from the nets, hacking and slashing wildly with their *karapalas*. Dead bodies were piling up already, and even from this distance, Nagnajit could count over twenty men down.

As orders were relayed to the men to withdraw, the raya glanced at the river, which was full of horses struggling against the currents and boats crammed with soldiers. Everywhere he looked, chaos and confusion reigned.

The fact that the landing had been a disaster and his army was in complete disarray slowly sank into Nagnajit. His soldiers were partly on one bank, partly on the other, and partly in the middle of the Vitasta, where they were of absolutely no use to anyone.

With this realization came the rumble of hooves; a thrum in the air above and a tremor in the ground below.

Nagnajit listened, trying to pinpoint the sound. It was coming from his right. *And* from his left.

Then it flashed through the raya's mind that the hooves were on *this* side of the river.

He darted a glance at Mahasa in alarm. They looked at one another, then turned to see hundreds of horsemen thunder out of the surrounding floodplain from both flanks, squeezing Kamboja's archers and the remnants of the Gandharan army in a pincer attack.

Knowing they had been outfoxed once again, the raya peered at the riders, observing their long, traditional *kuntas*.

These weren't Kekeyan warriors, Nagnajit realized.

The riders closing in around his troops and the Kamboja horsemen were Bahlika mercenaries, the points of their javelins flashing in the sunlight.

Yuddhajeet had never been in a full-fledged battle before.

Yes, there had been a hundred little skirmishes in the past, some involving even up to a hundred men on each side. But none of those compared to this, the here and now of the war against the Gandhara-Kamboja combine.

The sheer sound of battle was intimidating. The high, ululating war cry of the Bahlika warriors, no words, all scream. The reverberation of hoof beats. The deathly whistle of arrows, perilously close. The roar of the wind and the pounding of blood in the ears. And the final coming together of bodies and metal and anger as the sides collided into a single heaving mass of malevolence.

Finding himself hurtling straight at a pair of Kamboja riders, Yuddhajeet blocked out all sound and narrowed his vision on his adversaries. One of them had an arrow nocked, which he let fly at the prince's head. The missile came fast, spinning on its axis, barbed head rotating in mid-air as horse and arrow sped towards each other. Uttering a spell, Yuddhajeet threw his left hand into the air, hoping the magic in Mithuna's atmosphere was strong enough to do the rest. With less than two yards between him and the missile, a curtain of shimmer formed in front of the horse. The arrow struck the shimmer, parted and pushed through its field, then exploded into a million tiny fragments, dust that blew past the prince's face as he charged at the two Kambojas.

If the riders were taken aback by what he'd done to the arrow, they gave no sign of it. Instead, the spurred their mounts forward, swords drawn, bodies well balanced to deal the death blow. Yuddhajeet quickly estimated distances and concluded that the one to his right was marginally ahead of the other. Gripping his lance, he swung his hand out hard, flinging the weapon forward so it took the man in front on the chest. The blow was so hard and so well directed that it unseated him and sent him back crashing. The horses were almost upon the prince, and seeing the second Kamboja rider lunge at him with his *karapala*, Yuddhajeet cast the shimmer again. But the magic was weaker, and the sword tore through the shield's resistance. Fortunately, the shimmer held long enough for the prince to get past, so when the sword slipped in, Yuddhajeet was no longer there to receive its stab. The prince turned in his seat and brought the lance around, the extended arc giving the weapon great momentum. The lance smacked hard into the rider's head, the skull imploding on impact. The man went over the saddle like a sack of salt, his light gone before he even hit the ground.

The next instant, the prince was in the breathless squeeze of battle. The magic, however, got harder to conjure as its reserves dipped in the atmosphere, and Yuddhajeet was compelled to draw on it sparingly to conserve his energy. So, he fell back to brawling the old-fashioned way, dodging *kuntas* and ducking under blades as he slashed, speared, stabbed and clubbed a gruesome trail through the enemy. The light turned red with the splatter of blood, and the odours of carnage became stifling. Horses neighed in terror, metal clashed with metal, and screams of agony and anger rang up and down the riverbank as complete strangers fought one another for ownership of a patch of soil that would be around for generations after the warring sides had passed into the anonymity of history. Somewhere in the middle of all the bloodletting, the prince lost his mount to a Gandharan javelin, but he avenged the horse with a brutal stab at the Gandharan soldier's heart.

Hacking and hewing his way out of a melee, Yuddhajeet paused for a matter of seconds to take stock of the situation. All around him, men writhed in combat, Bahlikas and Kamboja warriors evenly matched in skill, strength and determination. Closer to the river, Gandhara's troops were in a state of disorder, while on the other bank, the fight was reaching a premature end with the Gandharans either falling to Kekeyan arrows or throwing themselves into the

Vitasta to escape death. Leaderless and directionless, the Gandharans still in the river watched the battles on both banks as if they were spectators and not participants in this war. Yuddhajeet didn't know what Nagnajit looked like, so he had no idea where the Gandharan king was… if he was present here at all.

Turning to his left, the prince caught a glimpse of Ambareesha, a clear head taller than the men he was fighting. The giant was surrounded by Kamboja warriors who were assailing him from all sides, and though the Bahlika wielded his sword to good effect, his attackers were numerous, their weapons probing. With the ring slowly tightening around him, the pressure began to show on Ambareesha, and the prince sensed it was a matter of moments before the Kambojas found a gap to exploit…

Out of the corner of his eye Yuddhajeet saw a figure run to the rescue of the beleaguered fighter. It was Abhisarika, clutching her sword and shield tight, leaping over the dead and the wounded, intent on taking down those who posed a threat to her cousin. She flung herself into the scrap, slashing with her *karapala*, and Yuddhajeet saw one, then two men fall. Three Kamboja warriors turned to deal with her, but Abhisarika parried them expertly, cutting one's throat and inflicting painful stabs on the others. But the press around Ambareesha was far too great to force a way to his side, and when she spun to fend off a blow, the prince caught the desperation in her eyes.

Magic was the one sure way of rescuing the Bahlika, but with magic running low over Mithuna, he risked —

With a shake of his head, Yuddhajeet thrust all argument out of his mind.

The Bahlika giant needed help, and it was in his power to offer it to him.

Raising a hand and chanting a mantra, Yuddhajeet dashed towards the pack of warriors around Ambareesha, pushing with his hand, channelling all the magic he could draw out of the ether at the Kambojas. The air warped and tunnelled and hummed with magic. The enemy reeled under its blast and was thrown back, and Yuddhajeet and Abhisarika leaped at the Kambojas, cutting a path into their midst, drawing their attention away from Ambareesha. The assault on the giant eased immediately.

The Kambojas turned on the prince and the woman with surprising speed. Refusing to buckle, they redoubled their attack and came hard at the three champions of the River Kingdoms. More and more fighters swooped down from all directions, swords and spears searched for openings, while Yuddhajeet cast shields of shimmer that thinned and vanished as the magic over Mithuna depleted rapidly and the strength drained from the prince's body. Though vastly outnumbered, the woman and the two men fought a valiant battle to keep the Kambojas at bay, displaying a peculiar combination of grace, strength and focus that made it hard for the enemy to beat them.

But the effort that had gone into extracting magic out of Mithuna's ether was beginning to take a toll on Yuddhajeet. His reflexes dulled, his limbs grew leaden, he was overcome with fatigue, and his vision blurred so he could no longer clearly see an attack coming —

— which was how a *karapala* slipped under his defence and sliced his stomach.

As blood oozed from the wound, searing heat coursed through the prince's mind and an orange-filled darkness came over him. Pain flared again, this time along his shoulder and down an arm as another sword found its way to him.

A ram horn blew somewhere, long and mournful.

Incapable of lifting his lance, blinded by fatigue and the fire in his wounds, Yuddhajeet tottered, waiting for a *karapala* to sever his head or a *kunta* to run through him and come out the other side.

Instead, what he heard was a flight of feet accompanied by voices calling in panic, all sounds diminishing as they moved away, withdrawing from him. The din of battle receded, and hands grabbed him to keep him from falling. The horn blew again and again.

"We won."

The prince pried an eye open and looked at the man who was holding him.

Ambareesha. Barely recognizable under all that gore and grime.

"Are you alright?" Abhisarika's face loomed behind her cousin, looking concerned.

"Look, they are retreating," Ambareesha beamed in delight. "Victory is ours."

"He is bleeding," the woman said. "Put him down, gently."

Yuddhajeet wanted to look at the bleeding. He wanted to look at the enemy running from battle. But he was too tired. Victory was theirs. That was good enough for him.

Rani Kaikeyi wasn't in the least bit pleased with the progress of the investigation into the attack on her son. Which was perfectly understandable, Dileepa thought to himself as he stood before the queen, listening quietly as she made her displeasure plain.

"It's been what… eight days now? Ten days?" the rani scrutinized the *dandapala* narrowly.

That was about right.

"And in all this while, there's been *no* evidence found pointing to who could have been behind the attack?"

There was none.

"Absolutely *no* breakthrough?"

None whatsoever.

The rani gave her head a disappointed shake. "I had expected more of you, *dandapala*. I'd been given the impression that you were able and resourceful."

"We're all doing our best," Dileepa stepped in hurriedly. "It is only a question of time. I… We are bound to uncover a lead sooner or later."

"One hopes it is sooner than later," the queen said, sounding caustic and dubious. "I'm tired of hearing about your inability to crack the case." With a toss of her head and a wave of her hand, she dismissed him.

The investigation had indeed run aground, Dileepa admitted, as he left the queen's chamber and picked his way out of the palace. They had had very little to start with. One dead body, the face charred beyond recognition, impossible to identify. And the second assassin had vanished into thin air. No one had seen him, no one remembered ferrying him out of Ayodhya, and no *vaidya* had treated him for his wounds.

Beyond that, what did they have to work with? Mitraka had suggested that they make enquiries at the city's *chhatras* and inns to see if anyone remembered anything or had seen either of the assassins, but no one had. Door-to-door searches had been constituted, but even those had yielded nothing. Every single line of enquiry that the *dandapalas* had pursued had run into a dead end, and not one lead, not one name had come into the open…

Dileepa's own investigation into the attack on himself wasn't faring any better. The four bodies had remained unclaimed, and despite efforts to preserve them, they had started decomposing. So, a decision had been taken to dispose of them. Even before he had taken over the enquiry, the *nagarapalas* had solicited the help of Ayodhya's public to identify the men, but to no avail. Suspecting the four killers to be from other parts of Kosala or beyond, Dileepa had summoned the keepers of Ayodhya's *chhatras* to see if they could tell him anything about the men, but that hadn't been of any great use. "So many people come and go every day," the keeper of one *chhatra* had stated. "Traders, craftsmen, artists, people in search of employment, pilgrims… It is nigh impossible to tell faces apart or remember where who came from…"

If the men were from outside Ayodhya — and Dileepa was certain they were — one thing was plain. They had had local help. The men had known something of his routine. They had known about his evening walks with Nandana. They had known he would come to drop the girl at her doorstep. They had been waiting for him at a spot where he would be alone, when no one was around to witness the attack or to come to his aid. Of course, they hadn't foreseen Nandana

— *he* hadn't foreseen Nandana. But all of it pointed to help from a local hand. Someone who knew about the attack, someone who knew that he had escaped unhurt… someone who was probably watching him even now.

The thought made the *dandapala* shiver every time.

The attack on him and the attack on the king were similar in that way, Dileepa deliberated for the hundredth time as he turned left at the palace gates and took the road leading to the old quarter. In both cases, the attackers had intimate knowledge of their targets' habits and movements. The raja had been attacked when he was alone and his son had been playing with the raja's pet dog. The attackers had known the raja would visit the secluded spot, and they had waited for him in the exact same fashion that Dileepa's attackers had waited for him. Both attacks had also happened within an hour or two of each other…

It all leads back to the arrest of Pushyanta, the investigator told himself once again. Pushyanta's arrest and the unearthing of the hoarding scam — that was the common link between him and the king of Kosala.

Dileepa had begun probing Mahulya, the *upanayaka* who assigned guards to patrols and sentry duty across the city. Mahulya had turned out to be a veteran *nagarapala*, nearly fifty years old and well respected by his fellow militiamen. The man had the reputation of being hardworking, and was a devoted family man and loving father to two daughters, the older of who was wedded to the chief of Kosala's armoury. The *upanayaka* was known to live within his means, and as far as Dileepa could tell, the man hadn't come into any money suddenly. Mahulya lived a rigid middle-class life, and nothing about him seemed to stand out. Yet, the appointment of the same set of five guards at Ayodhya's east gate raised a red flag…

Dileepa was due to brief the king on his investigation into the hoarding scam, but the stars were being kind to him, and the king was away and wasn't expected back in Ayodhya immediately. Dileepa had almost nothing to share. He had nothing on Mahulya to bring him in for questioning — if anything, it would antagonize the man as well as the entire force of *nagarapalas*. Worse still, it could put anyone else involved in the scam on alert. The *dandapala* hoped some lead would miraculously emerge and lead to a resolution of the case in time for his meeting with the king…

The investigator had been so caught up in his own thoughts that he hadn't realized the passage of time and the distance he had covered. It was with a jolt of surprise that he realized he was already in the old quarter and just two turns away from the street where Ma Parnalata's mansion was located. Dusk was falling but light was adequate, and Dileepa noticed that the streets were filled with people who stared at him strangely as he passed by. Wondering what was going on — and mildly discomfited by the attention he seemed to be attracting — the *dandapala* turned into the street where the mansion sat…

…and straightway realized that something was amiss.

A small crowd was gathered near the mansion's gate, and Dileepa recognized a couple of the women in Ma Parnalata's employ. A couple of *nagarapalas* were there as well, everyone talking in low voices. Catching sight of him, one of the women said a word to a *nagarapala*, who turned and eyed Dileepa.

"What's happened?" the *dandapala* asked, scanning the faces in front of him.

"Do you know Ma Parnalata?" the *nagarapala* said by way of reply.

"Yes, I do."

"He does," the woman who had pointed him out added.

"Come with me," the *nagarapala* motioned with his hand, pushing his way through the group.

Dileepa followed, looking thoroughly mystified, a sense of misgiving forming in the pit of his stomach.

Crossing the inner doorway, they entered the mansion, where more of Ma Parnalata's weavers stood in morose groups. A couple of them looked at the *dandapala* before exchanging glances as the *nagarapala* led the way up a flight of stairs.

"What has happened?" Dileepa asked again. "Please tell me."

Instead of answering, the *nagarapala* walked down the gallery overlooking the inner courtyard until he came to a closed door. Stopping in front of it, he rapped on the wood with his knuckles.

"You may enter," Ma Parnalata's voice spoke from within.

With a nod at Dileepa, the *nagarapala* pushed the door open. The two men stepped into a room that the investigator immediately understood to be the old aunt's bedchamber. Ma Parnalata lay on a couch, propped up by silken pillows, while half a dozen silk cushions were spread all around her and another three lay scattered on the floor. Heavy curtains were pulled across the window, blocking the last of the light and trapping the scent of *goparasa* that pervaded the room. Two globes on opposite ends of the bed cast their soft light on Ma Parnalata's heavy, puffed-up face as she turned red-rimmed eyes in Dileepa's direction.

"Ma, what's happened to you?" the *dandapala* asked. He took four steps and sank down by the woman's bedside. "Are you unwell?"

"Haven't you heard?" the old aunt asked, her voice choking tearfully.

"Heard what?" Dileepa asked as cold dread reared and rattled through him. Taking the woman's hand, he gave it an urgent, desperate squeeze. "Heard what, Ma?" he whispered again.

"Oh… Nandana…" Ma Parnalata gasped. "She's gone."

"What —" the investigator stopped, unable to complete the question, feeling the room reel and pitch under his knees.

Ma Parnalata nodded. "She… She vanished this morning. Like the others in this city. Gone without a trace."

Yuddhajeet opened his eyes in darkness that was illuminated by a small source of light coming from somewhere behind him.

He blinked. He was lying on his side. In a bed. But where?

He could see the outline of a window, framing the night outside. He made out the silhouette of a water carafe set against the widow and the night. The carafe and the window were familiar. They told him he was in his room in Mithuna. But how had he got here from the thick of battle, and when had it turned dark?

There was a vague recollection of hands helping him into a boat that rocked in the water. There had been sunlight in his eyes, a canopy of trees, then a drink forced down his throat, sweet and burning with pepper and herbs and cannabis… Was all that a dream? Or was *this* the dream?

He began pushing himself into a sitting position, then remembered he had been cut in the stomach in battle and had to be careful. At the thought of the cut, he felt pain where the wound had been inflicted. Shifting in little nudges, he peered down to find his midriff swathed in layers of clean linen.

So, he wasn't dreaming. This was for real, though he had no idea how —

"Look who's up!"

Yuddhajeet craned his neck to see an outlandish, two-headed figure towering over him. A small, baby-monkey head next to a bearded human head. "How are you feeling?" Ambareesha asked.

The prince grunted. His lips and throat were dry. When he turned to prop himself up, his head spun. His right arm and shoulder hurt where the Kambojas' swords had cut him the second time.

"Careful," the Bahlika giant cautioned.

"Water," Yuddhajeet mouthed, pointing to the carafe.

Ambareesha handed him the jug. "Let me get someone to inform Abhisarika that you are up," he said, and left the room.

By the time the giant returned, Yuddhajeet had emptied half the carafe. He felt less light-headed, his throat was less parched, but the gap in his memory was puzzling. "You said to me that we'd won… how?" he asked. "What happened after…?"

"You remember nothing," Ambareesha grinned. "That's quite a potent sedative she gave you."

"Is it the same day?" Yuddhajeet asked, staring out into the night.

The giant nodded as he sat on the bed. The baby monkey immediately slipped into his lap. "The battle was this morning. You've been asleep all afternoon and all evening."

"How did we win?"

"We won because we fought better," Ambareesha shrugged. "They fled."

"Gone for good? Not regrouping to make a second attack?"

"Gone for good, at least for the time being. We sent scouts after them. They've broken up into small bands. They're disorganized, they're defeated. They're heading home."

There was a moment's silence.

"Did we lose many men?"

"Close to fifty," the giant looked solemn. Then, his face brightened. "But not even half as many as *they* lost. The last I heard, their dead numbered in excess of a hundred, and we weren't done counting yet." He scratched his beard thoughtfully. "We have to figure out what to do with all of their dead."

"Can't leave them in the open, can't throw them into the river," said Yuddhajeet. "We'll have to burn them."

"What a waste of good firewood," the Bahlika scowled, even as he nodded in agreement.

The prince rubbed his forehead, still feeling woozy from the effects of sedation. He glanced at the monkey. "How did it get here?" he asked, pointing to the animal. "Hadn't you left it behind in Rajagriha?"

"We'd sent a rider to Rajagriha, informing Raja Ashwapati about the victory. The rider brought her along." Ambareesha scratched the monkey's head affectionately, and the animal closed its eyes in pleasure.

Yuddhajeet shook his head in wonder. It seemed like the two were inseparable. Peeling back a portion of the bandage on his shoulder, he tried inspecting the injury, but it was too dark to see. "Abhisarika treated these?" he asked.

"Yes. She cleaned the wounds, stopped the bleeding and stitched the cuts back together."

"It looks like she saved me a second time," the prince observed wryly.

"I told you she's skilled at saving people," said Ambareesha.

"She is also one hell of a warrior," Yuddhajeet's eyebrows rose in appreciation. "I didn't think she'd be this good when she rode up armed with a sword in Gandhapuri."

The giant chuckled. "She learned all of her fighting from the greatest warrior I've had the honour of knowing." Before the prince could ask who, the Bahlika's face turned grave. "From holding a sword to taking a life, her husband taught her everything." A heavy pause. "He was my oldest childhood friend."

The 'was' wasn't lost on Yuddhajeet. "What happened?"

"He died a year into their wedding. Abhisarika was expecting Smara when he was taken by the Chandrabhaga." Seeing the shock on the prince's face, the giant gave a sad nod. "It was a flash flood. And despite being so skilled at saving lives, Abhisarika was helpless to save her husband, the man she had loved so deeply, for so long."

The room was quiet.

"The greatest tragedy is that little Smara never got to see her father's face," Ambareesha sighed.

Footsteps scuffed the dirt outside. The giant darted a glance at the door and straightened. "And of course, I must thank you for coming to my rescue and saving my life," he said, changing the subject quickly, his voice brimming with cheer. "I'm told you used magic to repel the Kamboja warriors who had surrounded me, so… thank you."

"In my place, you'd have done the same," Yuddhajeet replied. "That is what friends are for."

The door opened and Abhisarika stepped inside. "And there you are, sister," boomed the giant, rising to his feet. The baby monkey climbed onto his shoulder. "We were talking about you…"

"What were you saying about me?"

"Nothing…" Ambareesha hadn't expected the question. "Just…"

"I was telling your brother that you are a remarkable warrior," said Yuddhajeet.

"That's it?" the woman asked, coming over to the bed. "Nothing else?"

The men exchanged wary glances, afraid she'd overheard them speaking about her misfortunes. "What else? I mean…"

"Just a remarkable warrior?" Abhisarika asked as she began removing the bandage that covered the prince's shoulder. "Not a remarkable medicine woman?"

"My mind lacks the skills to judge that particular talent of yours," Yuddhajeet smiled, sighing inwardly with relief. He tilted his head at the wound. "But this body will always bear testimony to how good a medicine woman you are." It was heartening to see a smile play on her lips. She was capable of emotion, the prince thought idly. "I'm grateful for what you have done for me."

"It's too dark in here. I can hardly see properly," the woman said to the giant over her shoulder. Ambareesha nodded and left to fetch more lamps.

For a moment, there was silence in the room. "Thank you for doing what you did," Abhisarika said softly. "We might have won even otherwise, but I doubt if my brother would have survived had you not come to his rescue."

The prince didn't know what to say, so he merely inclined his head.

"That spell you cast towards the end… that is what weakened you, right?"

"It wasn't just that one spell. I'd been channelling magic earlier during the battle as well, when there just wasn't sufficient magic in the atmosphere. That's a problem with magic. When there isn't enough around, your energy drains in trying to squeeze what little is available." He sighed. "A valuable lesson learned, though. It's unrealistic to use one rishi and expect the atmosphere to fill with magic."

"You knew how badly drained that spell could leave you, how it could even cost you your life." The woman stopped her work with the bandage to look deep into Yuddhajeet's eyes. "Yet you cast it to save Ambareesha. My brother and I will never forget that."

five

WATCHING THE BOATS COME UPRIVER FROM THE DIRECTION of Madhupura, Bharat smiled quietly in satisfaction.

He had been expecting this visit from Lavanyasurya. He had even arranged for it to happen.

From the very beginning, he had known that Lavanyasurya would be intrigued — even irritated — by Kosala's decision to set up its own market along the banks of the Yamuna. He had made sure that Ayodhya's intent was publicly known so that the news could travel to Lavanyasurya's ears, and it had. Even as the caravan from Ayodhya had neared Madhupura, he and Shatrughna had noticed Madhupura's lookouts tailing them from afar, tracking their movements. They had been followed all the way to the site that had been chosen for the river garrison, and they were under observation even after tents had been pitched for the night.

The next morning, the *nayaka* in charge of the garrison had come to Bharat's tent with the news that a courtier from Madhupura sought an audience. The courtier was welcomed and treated to a sumptuous lunch in accordance with Bharat's directives, after which he was told to wait. But as the day drew to a close, he was politely sent away with word that the raja was too preoccupied to see him. The following day, another of Lavanyasurya's courtiers had come calling, and although he too was accorded utmost courtesy, he wasn't able to secure a meeting with Bharat either, leaving empty-handed after a long and fruitless wait.

Now, Lavanyasurya was here himself, approaching the river market's site in a convoy of five boats, Madhupura's tiger-motif flag fluttering on the prow of each craft. The mid-morning sun dazzled off the river's surface, the air humid down by the water but cooler up on the rise where Bharat stood with Shatrughna, surveying Lavanyasurya's arrival. The spot that had been picked to build the market was on the eastern bank of the Yamuna, roughly five miles upstream from Madhupura, at a point that afforded easy access from both banks. Work had commenced, with one set of workers clearing the bank as another excavated the ground to drop the market's foundations. A third group had already started building a road going east, while the boat makers had begun curing timber for the construction of boats and the pier. The rhythmic sound of axes cutting through wood rose from all around, mingling with the sharp chirrup of crickets and the sweeter notes of birdsong that filled the forest air.

"You should be careful, brother," said Shatrughna as he eyed the incoming boats mistrustfully.

Bharat nodded in reply. He understood Shatrughna's concern, for Madhupura's involvement in the attack on him was yet to be ruled out. But even if it had been Lavanyasurya's doing, Bharat doubted the raja was foolish enough to try any tricks far away from the safety of Madhupura's walls.

The boats nudged the bank one after another, and as soldiers, courtiers and sycophants set foot on land, five men began beating small drums while another lifted Madhupura's banner into the air. An attendant laid a plank of wood between the bank and the caparisoned boat in the middle, and a portly figure negotiated the gap on shaky legs.

"Is that him?" asked Bharat, narrowing his eyes against the glare. "It's been a while, but I don't remember him looking so… *strange*."

"That's him, but…" Shatrughna paused, "…you're right. He looks more bent from the time I met him last."

"That was what… less than a month ago?"

The younger brother nodded.

"Perhaps he is ill," Bharat remarked, feeling a little sorry as he watched Lavanyasurya hobble to the head of the little procession, which left the boats and approached the encampment by the river.

"It is a sickness of the heart," Shatrughna scowled, remembering his encounter with the raja. "And it has done nothing to reduce his arrogance. Look at those drummers. Who's he trying to impress?"

"Let us go down to meet him," said Bharat. "We shouldn't be accused of an utter lack of grace."

As the party from Madhupura drew near, Bharat was struck by the transformation in Lavanyasurya. There hadn't been very many occasions to meet while they had been growing up, but Bharat remembered Lavanyasurya from the few times Dashratha had hosted his friends in Ayodhya. Being older than the four Ikshvaku brothers by over a decade, Lavanyasurya had rarely interacted with them, keeping to himself and displaying a sneering sense of superiority whenever the opportunity presented itself. Bharat recalled Lavanyasurya as always having been dumpy, unathletic and predisposed to sluggishness, but the version of the man that was now before him looked sickly and broken from the inside, his complexion yellowing under an uneven stubble. The raja's eyes were red, as though from lack of sleep, but they were the one part of him that looked alive, dancing with barely concealed malevolence.

Seeing Bharat, Shatrughna and Atibhanu approach, Lavanyasurya raised a hand, and the drums fell silent. The *chunk-thunk* of heavy axes on wood was loud in the ensuing silence as the two sides appraised each other, the atmosphere stiff and formal and distinctly lacking in warmth.

"What is the meaning of this?" Lavanyasurya finally demanded in a brusque tone, sidestepping all niceties. Placing one hand on his hip, he glared in Bharat and Shatrughna's direction.

Shatrughna had been right, Bharat realized. It was a sickness of the heart, and it had had little impact on the man's arrogance. He felt sorry about having felt sorry for Lavanyasurya. He cast a lazy eye around, as if searching for something. "The meaning of what?" he asked, looking at the raja of Madhupura with a bored expression.

"You refused to entertain my courtiers."

"I haven't come all this way to entertain your courtiers."

"They were here in their official capacity," Lavanyasurya bristled. "Protocols should have been adhered to."

Bharat shrugged. "I already have plenty to do here. I can't be bothered by such little-little things as procedure and protocol." He paused. "Now, if that is all, I would like to get back..." he half-turned, implying he had more pressing things to attend to.

"What's the meaning of this market?" Lavanyasurya demanded.

"This market?" Bharat paused, looking mildly amused. "It is a market. You know what markets are meant for. What more can I say?"

"You think you will build a market here?"

Bharat pretended to give the question a moment's thought. "Yes."

"You think you can build a market to rival Madhupura?"

"We are building a market to sell the goods Kosala produces and buy the goods Kosala needs."

"By bypassing Madhupura," Lavanyasurya's eyes slanted in outrage.

"You are attaching far too much importance to Madhupura, rajan," replied Bharat. "This is not about Madhupura. It is about Kosala and what Kosala wants. We can't afford to pay high taxes, so we are forced to look at alternatives. Building this market is definitely a feasible alternative."

"And you think everyone will trade with you here?"

"Why not? We have goods that others need, and we are prepared to pay for the things we need." Bharat slipped a note of condescension into his voice. "It's simple economics, rajan. Where is the confusion?"

"You think I will let others trade with you?"

Bharat was pleased to see that his needling was getting under Lavanyasurya's skin. There was anger and menace in the raja's tone. "I don't see how you can stop them," he chuckled.

"Everyone needs Madhupura to trade with everyone else. If we wish, we can keep anyone out. That won't be so good for them. We can force compliance, you see."

Bharat grinned and shook his head. "That wouldn't be a very clever thing to do, rajan," he said. "You wouldn't want to bully and browbeat the very people your city depends on for its income. I think…" he paused dramatically, "I really think you need better people advising you on how to run your economy. Now if I may…" once again he executed the half-turn to suggest he was in a rush to get back to other things.

"You are challenging Madhupura, Bharat," Lavanyasurya snarled in open displeasure. "You're making a big mistake."

Bharat stopped and studied the squat figure of the raja for a moment. When he spoke, his voice was flat and emotionless. "I am making a *big market* for Kosala, rajan. Don't come in my way. *That* would be a big mistake."

Without ceremony or ado, without giving Lavanyasurya the opportunity to get another word in, Bharat spun on his heels and walked away, ending the interview. Conscious of the hateful stare that followed him, the young king smiled at the luxury of having men like Shatrughna and Atibhanu watch his back. Not once did he turn to look at the raja or his crestfallen retinue as they trooped mournfully back to their boats.

The smile on Bharat's face widened as he considered the outcome of Lavanyasurya's visit and their face-off. A face-off that Bharat had anticipated and carefully planned for—right down to the dismissive snub of Madhupura at the end—ever since they had decided to build the market garrison.

All this while, Lavanyasurya had been provoking Kosala by dictating terms and setting the agenda. Now, finally, Kosala had the initiative, and Lavanyasurya was being forced to think and react to the situation.

Gaining the upper hand felt nice and deeply satisfying.

"Which one did you like?" a voice asked.

Yuddhajeet turned to see Raja Ashwapati come limping down the path from the palace, leaning heavily on his staff.

"I like all of them," the prince smiled in reply as he waited for his father to join him by the high paling that encircled the field where the horses were brought out each morning and evening for their exercise. There were seven fine specimens out there at that moment, all tossing their heads and prancing about, kicking dust into the sunlight slanting in through the trees. "They're all equally beautiful."

"Okay, so which one do you like the most?"

Yuddhajeet appraised the horses again, slowly, one by one. "That one," he said at last, pointing to a mare with a shiny coat that was such a deep shade of tan that it almost appeared black in places. The beast's legs were all black, the same colour as its mane, which flowed majestically in the wind.

"You've always had a good eye for horses," Ashwapati nodded in approval.

"I think we will get along well, though I'll know for sure only once I've taken her for a gallop."

Father and son leaned against the wooden fence and watched the horses with affection. Kekeya had always been famed for producing horses of great beauty and strength, but it was only during this lifetime that the little kingdom had started breeding horses especially suited for war. Steeds bred in Kekeya were in demand not just in Jambudvipa; buyers came from across the mountains to the west as well as from Cina on the other side of the Himalayas. It was ironic that the Gandharan and Kambojan troops had ridden into the River Kingdoms on horses born and raised in Kekeya.

"You'll have to take it slowly," Ashwapati cautioned. "Wait till the wounds heal fully."

The prince nodded. "A month at the very least," he said, making a face to show his displeasure.

"The *vaidyas* tell me the girl did a very good job of sewing you up. They were very impressed."

"She's good."

"I gave Sailusha special thanks for that, besides thanking him for coming to our assistance."

"They fought well," said Yuddhajeet. "All the Bahlika warriors —"

"Be careful," a woman's voice called out from somewhere behind them. "Don't fall."

Surprised, Yuddhajeet turned to see a small girl hurrying down the path towards them. The girl had her eyes on the path, her whole mind focused on keeping her balance as she trotted over the uneven ground. A pair of tiny white flowers sprouted from the girl's fist, which she held firmly clenched.

Realizing it was Smara, the prince glanced further up the path to see Abhisarika standing there, watching her daughter. Behind her was Ambareesha. Yuddhajeet switched his gaze back to the child, wondering why she was in Rajagriha, and why she was heading this way with such great intent. He was still working this out when, from the corner of his eye, he saw his father take a step forward.

"Slowly, Smara," Ashwapati said as he dropped to his haunches, stretching both hands to grab the kid in case she fell. "Slowly…"

"I've got you something," the girl twittered, her pace slackening as she drew up to Ashwapati. Coming to a halt, she carefully extracted one flower out of her fist and offered it to the old man. "It's for you."

Yuddhajeet blinked. How did the girl and his father know each other, and how had they become friends? He looked at Abhisarika, who had followed her daughter down the path.

"What about a flower for him?" Ashwapati asked softly, pointing to Yuddhajeet.

For the first time, the child took notice of the prince. Just one look at him and she clammed up, recognizing him from the morning he had taken a knife to her mother's throat. Without uttering a word, she tucked the hand that held the other flower behind her.

"I am sorry," said Abhisarika. "I didn't expect her to come here —"

"Where else would she go?" remarked Ashwapati, eyes shining in delight. "She knows where to find me in the evenings."

"I see you have become good friends, rajan," the woman said with a smile.

Smara seemed oblivious to the conversation as she stared at Yuddhajeet. The prince took a step forward and squatted beside his father. "Can I give you something?" he asked.

The girl just stared back at the prince, barely blinking.

Stretching out his hand, Yuddhajeet reached behind the child's ears, touching her hair lightly. He then drew the hand back and showed it to Smara: a lone white flower lay across his fingers.

The girl's eyes widened. She felt the spot where the flower had appeared magically. She looked at the flower, then at Yuddhajeet.

"For you," he said.

She took it and inspected it, turning it this way and that, as if expecting it to vanish any moment.

Yuddhajeet reached with his other hand and plucked a second flower from the girl's hair. Smara gasped in amazement this time.

"This one is for your mother," he said, handing it to the child.

Smara took it, turned to her mother with a grin and gave her the flower. Abhisarika took it with a nod of thanks to Yuddhajeet. The prince nodded back, smiled at the girl and stood up. Smara studied both the flowers she held, one in each hand, comparing them. Making up her mind, she thrust the one she had originally brought with her towards Yuddhajeet.

"You can have this," she declared solemnly.

Yuddhajeet bent and took the flower. "I will keep it with me for eternity," he said.

Smara blinked, not understanding. Then, with a nod, she dusted her hand on her little tunic and ambled away to watch the horses.

"How did *you* get to know her?" Yuddhajeet looked at his father with a raised eyebrow.

"I came upon her playing in the courtyard one morning. I smiled, and she smiled back. That is all there was to it," Ashwapati shrugged. "We became friends."

"Playing in the… How did she get here?" the prince turned to Abhisarika.

"I left her here in the care of one of the palace matrons before leaving for Mithuna," Abhisarika replied. She looked at the raja of Kekeya apologetically. "I hadn't expected her to bother you."

The old man shook his head vehemently. "No bother at all. She's a sweet kid." He paused. "In fact, I shall miss her once you leave."

"You can see her again when you come to attend my cousin's wedding, rajan," said Abhisarika, with a wave of her hand in Ambareesha's direction.

"What?" Yuddhajeet stared at the woman, then at Ambareesha, who stood looming over them. "*Your* wedding? You are getting married?"

"Can't I?" the giant grinned.

"Well… you never said anything…" Yuddhajeet fumbled awkwardly. "I didn't even know…"

"You didn't know because you'd never given a thought to his being married," Abhisarika said. "Marriage is not one of the things that's top of mind for you."

Yuddhajeet glanced at the woman. She had sounded vaguely accusatory, but there was nothing in her expression to suggest she was being critical of him. Not knowing what to say, he simply shrugged.

"Some friend you are proving to be," Ambareesha snorted.

"Well, I thought you were wedded to that monkey," Yuddhajeet retorted good-naturedly. Both men laughed. "So, when is the wedding?"

"Still a few months away, which is why I hadn't mentioned it. But now that you know, I expect you and the rajan to be there," Ambareesha said with a bow.

"Who is the lucky bride-to-be?" asked Ashwapati.

"The daughter of one of the Bahlika chieftains, rajan," the giant replied.

"One of the sweetest girls to roam this earth," Abhisarika added. She looked at her cousin. "He is the lucky one, winning the hand of such a noble woman."

"That I am," Ambareesha consented. "More so considering how I have been seeking that hand for years now."

"Lucky you," Yuddhajeet clapped the giant on the shoulder.

"Allow me to take your leave," said Abhisarika. Bowing to Ashwapati, she addressed Smara. "Come, child, let us go."

Holding hands, mother and daughter went back the way they had come as all three men watched them. Reaching the top of the path, Smara turned to look at Ashwapati, before shifting her gaze to Yuddhajeet. Her eyes were kindlier and less hostile, the prince noted, her countenance more accepting of him. It felt as though he had finally been absolved of a wrongdoing.

She left the child here, he thought to himself in amazement, as mother and daughter slipped out of sight. He turned back to watch the horses. She left her daughter with a palace matron to fight in a war that wasn't even hers to fight. He didn't know what to make of Abhisarika, other than the fact that she was a very remarkable woman. A woman the likes of which he had never seen before.

A long line of men straggling up the mountain slope, men broken in spirit, demoralized.

They trudged along, heads bent and shoulders hunched, eyes on the trail at their feet, one foot following another in perfect monotony. They barely exchanged words, saying nothing about the battle from three days ago, in the hope that the memory would fade and the wounds would heal. Many had lost friends, some had lost close relatives, and what rankled was the fact that they hadn't even brought the dead back with them, leaving the bodies to rot on that distant riverbank. So, they kept to themselves on the long road back home, nursing their wounds, their anger, and the humiliation that the River Kingdoms had dealt them.

None probably felt the mounting loss and fury more than Nagnajit, plodding along on his horse somewhere in the middle of the concourse. Not fifteen days ago, he had left Kapisi with a grand vision of subduing the River Kingdoms and planting Gandhara's flag of expansion in the fertile soil of Jambudvipa. The River Kingdoms were supposed to have been his first gift to the people of Gandhara; they had put their faith in him and blessed him from both sides of Kapisi's streets as he had led the troops out; they had promised to welcome him with drums, cymbals and flutes on his return.

But now, instead of being welcomed home with sounds of triumph and jubilation, he would be greeted by the deafening silence of defeat. A defeat that the wily Kekeyans had dealt him in a most unexpected manner.

It was not as if his troops had been routed and destroyed in battle; they hadn't even lost all that many men this time. They had been undone by craft and surprise, out-thought by the Kekeyans in ways that had sapped his men's morale. They had lost the battle in their minds the moment that first boatload of men had blundered into the fishing nets set in Mithuna. From there, the battle had progressively gone downhill.

Nagnajit saw he had badly misjudged Kekeya's resourcefulness and resolve to defend the River Kingdoms. Fed by intelligence that clearly wasn't up to the mark in terms of reliability, he had assumed that the campaign would be little more than a stroll all the way to Sakala. Instead, the Kekeyans had shown a degree of cunning that he hadn't anticipated, employing guerrilla tactics to throw his attack into confusion.

And springing the Bahlika mercenaries on him had been a masterstroke.

Never in his dreams had he thought the Kekeyans would recruit Bahlikas to fight for them. The Bahlikas had unnerved even the ruthless Kambojas who bore the brunt of their attack; Mahasa was so upset that he had refused to ride with the Gandharan troops and had been heard blaming the shoddy Gandharan landing for the fiasco. The thought of confronting Mahasa had crossed Nagnajit's mind, but he had decided to let tempers cool rather than escalate matters. Also, there was no disputing the fact that the landing had been a complete disaster.

Still, the landing could have been salvaged. Kamboja's archers could have given his troops the cover they needed, but that hadn't happened because the Bahlikas had charged —

The Bahlikas. It all came down to the Bahlikas. They had saved the River Kingdoms.

Distracted by the thoughts of his army's failures, the raya was sitting listless, the reins slack in his fingers, so when his mount missed its footing on the narrow trail and stumbled momentarily, Nagnajit nearly fell out of the saddle, saving himself by grabbing the animal's mane while throwing the other arm awkwardly around its neck. The horse took a hurried step away from the steep drop down the mountainside, tossing its head in panic, while Nagnajit's pulse tripped and the metallic taste of fear flooded his mouth. He knew he cut an ungraceful figure, hanging onto the animal for dear life.

With that realization, a boiling rage descended over the raya.

Only vaguely conscious of the men who had come to a stop on the trail to stare at him, Nagnajit leaped out of the saddle and landed hard on both feet. Without pausing to consider what he was doing, the raya turned and lashed out at his mount with his riding whip. *Whack. Whack. Whack. Whack.* Once… twice… a third time… a fourth… this way, that way, sideways, striking with great force, he laid heavy, brutal blows on the beast's side. The raya's face was set in a demonic grimace and his hand was a blur as it flayed the poor animal. The abruptness of the attack and the sheer viciousness that Nagnajit had channelled into the assault sent the horse sidestepping in surprise and terror, and one of its hind hooves scraped the lip of the trail and went over. For a fraction of a second, the horse lost its balance again, and that led to its undoing.

Whack. Whack. Whack.

Again and again, Nagnajit flogged the startled beast as it scrambled to get back up to safety and bolt to freedom, but the raya's weapons and armour, which were hitched to the saddle, weighed the horse down, dragging it backwards. At the same time, the raya's ceaseless whipping forced the animal back towards the drop inch by desperate inch. In a mad stamping and scuffing of hooves, the horse went over the edge, its frightened neigh intertwining with the raya's insane howl of rage over the twisting trail. The wild-eyed beast fought for a footing, but the slope was too sharp and its body too heavy, so down it went to its death in a rain of mud and loose rocks. It twisted and cartwheeled through the sparse trees to crash against the boulders at the bottom, ending shattered and splay-legged as its last neigh shuddered up the mountainside.

Nagnajit stood at the top of the plunge, panting and shivering uncontrollably, the whip gripped tight, his teeth bared in a rictus of rage as he stared at the broken body below. Above and below him on the trail, his men stood still, trying to stay inconspicuous while the storm in their raya's heart abated. Even the wind had died in the hills.

The Bahlikas had saved the River Kingdoms, he said to himself, as his anger slowly dissolved and his breathing returned to normal. He blinked at the dead horse, as if noticing it for the first time, and he became aware of the eyes that were on him.

"Quit staring like a fool," Nagnajit glowered at the petrified soldier closest to him in line. "Find me a fresh horse." He pointed downhill. "And send someone to fetch my swords and armour."

Fifteen minutes later, Nagnajit crested a rise. He sat astride his new mount, and he had regained his composure. The raya reined in to survey a landscape that was familiar from a few days ago. Flat land stretched towards the dark of twilight spreading in the east. Trees twisted out of shape by the elements grew here and there in clumps, while one or two shepherd's huts were visible, smoke rising from one.

It was exactly the same view that had failed to impress Mahasa the other morning. But Nagnajit had known the value of what he was looking at. Now, as night fell over the land, the trees and the huts, the raya of Gandhara swore an oath that he would return to claim the River Kingdoms for himself.

He would find a way to neutralize the threat of the Bahlikas and destroy Kekeya.

I am making a big market *for Kosala, rajan. Don't come in my way.*

Realizing he had underestimated Bharat, Lavanyasurya sighed wearily as he pressed his thumb and forefinger to his forehead, pinching the spot where his eyebrows met to ease the dull pain that pulsed there almost all the time nowadays. It wasn't just that one spot that pained though. So many parts of his body ached and throbbed that it was becoming difficult to distinguish one pain from another. Then, there was the raging acidity, the fits of nausea, the bouts of dizziness. *But the real pain was Bharat*, Lavanyasurya reminded himself bitterly, shaking all distracting thoughts aside.

Bharat was the real pain.

He remembered the young boy from the time he had accompanied his father to Ayodhya some twelve years ago. Raja Dashratha had invited all the allied kings of Kosala to commemorate something that Lavanyasurya hadn't cared the least about. All he recalled was his father insisting he come along to pay his respects to Raja Dashratha. The four princes of Ayodhya had been there, with Rama being his usual superior self, impressing all the elders. How he had hated Rama, the raja of Madhupura thought back, hated Rama for being so full of himself, and hated Lakshmana for daring to talk back to him… *But no, Bharat*… Shy and reserved, Bharat had hardly said a thing, overawed by Rama, *overshadowed* by Rama… Lavanyasurya remembered thinking of Bharat as the pushover, the weak link in the chain, the chink in the Ikshvaku armour…

Which was why he had thought it timely to assert Madhupura's independence once power had passed to Bharat in the wake of Rama's exile and Dashratha's death. That decision had seemed to play out well. When he had raised taxes, Kosala had made a few feeble noises in protest — all the kingdoms of Jambudvipa had — but there had been no real resistance from Ayodhya. Bharat, it appeared, had forgotten about Kosala's preeminence and power. Then, when Kosala had pushed back, he had retaliated by seizing Kosala's garrison in Madhupura and turning out all of its soldiers. For a while, it had looked like that gamble had backfired when reports came of Kosala assembling its army for war. But then, Lavanyasurya's opinion of Bharat's weakness had been further vindicated when news arrived that Bharat had capitulated on his decision to wage war against Madhupura, favouring instead a more pacific — and downright *pathetic* — form of dissent: building a market on the Yamuna.

The idea had seemed laughable until guild master Amulya had pointed out that a second market in close proximity of Madhupura could dent the city's earnings over a period of time. So, when it became known that a workforce from Kosala was indeed heading west to build the market, Lavanyasurya had taken notice. Hearing that Bharat himself was leading the expedition, he had decided to bully the boy into changing his mind about the market, but things hadn't gone quite as planned. First, Bharat had refused to receive his emissaries. That in itself should have warned him, but

Lavanyasurya had imagined Kosala's young king would be cowed once he intervened in person.

That hadn't happened.

I can't be bothered by such little-little things as procedure and protocol.

Bharat had sounded cool and flippant right through that disaster of an interview. Gone was the shy, unsure kid he had seen a decade ago in Ayodhya.

I really think you need better people advising you on how to run your economy.

There had been an assertiveness — a brazenness — that he hadn't thought existed in the boy.

I am making a big market *for Kosala, rajan. Don't come in my way.*

More than assertiveness and brazenness, a newfound resolve. Steel in the sinews.

Bharat was the real pain.

Lavanyasurya saw that Bharat was right in saying Madhupura could do little to prevent anyone from trading with Kosala once the new market was up and running. He'd already been hearing about Kosala's merchants buying and selling wares in smaller markets down the Yamuna. Once they had their own market going, nothing would hold Kosala back...

Of course, in the time it took Kosala to build its market, he would have destroyed Ayodhya, Lavanyasurya reminded himself. Things were going according to plan, and in a matter of a few months, he'd be ready. Still, the raja hated the thought of not being able to do anything about the market. The market was like a slap on his face, being built as it was right under his nose, a challenge to Madhupura, a dare that needed to be met and shown its proper place.

The good news was that he had hit upon the right antidote for the market, and the antidote now stood before him, looking at him uncertainly in the gathering gloom of sunset.

Lavanyasurya roused himself from his ponderings to peer at the man. He looked familiar, the raja thought, as he waved his hand above his head. A globe of magic-fuelled light dispelled the shadows.

"You..." the raja wagged a finger at the man, his face scrunched as he tried hard to remember. "You were the one who spoke up on the day of the riot at the city's gates. You apologized for the behaviour of your mates."

"That was me, rajan," the man nodded.

"And you brought us news about Kosala planning a war on Madhupura."

"Yes, rajan."

"What did you say your name was?"

"Swagata, rajan."

"*Upanayaka* Swagata of Kosala, yes." Lavanyasurya slouched back in his seat. "I'm told you have a loving family here in Madhupura."

"Indeed I do."

"Hmm... that's good." The king was quiet for a moment. Then, leaning forward, he planted his elbows on his knees and clasped his hands, fingers knitting into one another. "I would like you to do something for me, *upanayaka* Swagata," he said with a conspiratorial smile. "Would you?"

The soldier hesitated for a fraction of a second before nodding.

"Good. Actually, I want you to do *two* things. *Three*, actually. First..." Lavanyasurya counted on his fingers, "...I want you to go to the market that Kosala is building to the north. You know of the market, don't you?" Seeing Swagata nod, he carried on, "Good. Join the station there. Give them some reason for joining them, spin them a story, I don't care. Just make yourself a part of the operation. Clear?"

Though he looked doubtful, Swagata nodded.

"Good. Second, I want you to furnish me with regular reports from the market. How the construction is progressing, what kind of issues they're facing, any shortages of materials or manpower, any illnesses... You will report everything back to me. Is that understood?"

The *upanayaka* blinked uncertainly. "You want me to... spy on my own people?"

"I want you to spy for *me*, your *wife's* king, your *children's* king. Surely you can do that?" The raja made a face. "I mean no harm. It's just reports I need."

Swagata looked less and less convinced, but he nodded again.

"Wonderful," said Lavanyasurya. "Third, I want you to slow down whatever progress they are making. Create issues for them, manufacture obstacles, put up hurdles, conjure hindrances..." Seeing the *upanayaka's* eyes widen, the raja nodded vigorously. "*You* will create shortages in materials and manpower. *You* will cause sickness and disease there. *You* will sabotage Kosala's plans, and *you* will make sure that the market does not take shape."

"But rajan... this... you..." Swagata swatted around for words, "You said you meant no harm."

"I lied," Lavanyasurya cackled in delight. "Pardon me, but what are you going to do about it?"

The soldier paled. "Rajan… I don't know if I can do what you ask of me —"

"Of course, you can do what I ask of you. You are a man of talent and imagination. You'll find ways to do what the occasion demands."

"Rajan, I don't know *a thing* about sabotage," Swagata pleaded. "How can I —"

"You are a man of talent and imagination," Lavanyasurya said again. Then, rising theatrically, he waltzed up to the *upanayaka* and whispered in his ear, "Let me show you the power of your imagination. Do you know what will happen to your lovely wife and loving children if you fail to do as I say? How they will suffer in slow, agonizing detail if you don't meet my expectations —"

"Rajan… please don't… they are harmless…" Swagata blubbered. "Rajan, please…"

"See? That is the power of your imagination," the king grinned mirthlessly. "Now talent? That you will find now that your imagination has been unlocked."

"Rajan… please… my family…"

"They will be safe in my care. Go now. Leave. My men will escort you out of the north gate."

"Rajan, I… wish to see my wife and children."

"Of course," Lavanyasurya stared at Swagata in astonishment. "What do you take me for — a fiend? You will see your family, as soon as you begin achieving what you are setting out to do. That will be your reward. Now, go."

He waved his hand and the light went out. The room plunged into darkness. An uneven orange line marked the horizon where the sun had set some time ago. Swagata whimpered as footsteps swished into the room, hands grabbed him by the elbows and pulled him out. The raja listened as the footsteps faded into silence before turning and leaving the room.

He crossed an antechamber and made his way down a hall supported by stone arches. Reaching the end of the hall, he unlocked a door that opened on a flight of stairs going down into a deep, yawning darkness. Without breaking his stride, without looking back even once, Lavanyasurya slipped through the doorway. Then, snapping his fingers to conjure up a bubble of illumination, he descended into the blackness below.

Had he looked back though, the raja would have noticed a figure detach itself from the shadow of one of the stone pillars and make its way towards the door, following in the king's footsteps.

Darkness clung to the mansion in Ayodhya's old quarter, darkness three shades darker than the surrounding night, so the building would have appeared like a black smear to anyone who cared to look, its lines and edges blurred and blotted. No light shone at its windows; no sound spilled from within its walls. The house just sat there at the end of the street like a terrible saturation, a blight, the physical manifestation of a possession.

Inside, the darkness was even deeper and fouler, a space light had never permeated, a bleakness untouched by hope. All that existed here were shadows, dark and vile and formless, full of hate and violence, filling the mansion to bursting so they seeped out here and there into the night. And at the centre of all the darkness, creating the shadows and controlling them, was Simhika, Mother of Shadows. She brooded in silence, paying only passing heed to the wordless whispers of the shadows that slithered around her, telling each other things that weren't meant to be heard or contemplated. Ideas and schemes meant to corrupt the souls of humankind, plans that were intended to bring about the downfall of the human race.

Except for the shadows, Simhika was alone. The women who worked the looms had left for their homes, and three days after Nandana's disappearance, even the kindly *nagarapalas* who had been coming and going had stopped visiting her. In a city full of disappearances, there was nothing unique about Nandana's disappearance, and the *nagarapalas* had other things to attend to. Dileepa was the only one who dropped in twice a day to enquire after her — though Simhika knew it was chiefly the hope of Nandana's return that kept drawing the fool to this doorstep.

Which was fine. In fact, she had been counting on the *dandapala's* lovesickness when she had decided to do away with Nandana.

"We can't give up hope," the sorceress had said to Dileepa no more than half an hour ago. They were seated in the inner courtyard, and the *dandapala* has been nursing a cup of buttermilk and looking miserable. "And why give up hope?" she had asked, forcing brightness into her voice. "Many of those who had disappeared have come back, and more are returning every day. You'll see it will be no different with Nandana."

The *dandapala* had nodded, reassured, though not fully. He was hopelessly lovelorn, Simhika could tell.

"We must carry on with our lives," she had insisted. "It'll take our minds off Nandana and help the passage of time. Then, before we know it, she will be back." Seeing Dileepa nod again, she had taken a chance. Three days were enough to mourn the girl's disappearance, and she needed the investigator to help advance her plans. "I have a small gift for Rani Kaikeyi. Will you give it to her on my behalf?"

The palace was next on her list now that the intrusion of the Sanctum was well underway. The sorceress had paid the Sanctum a visit earlier that day with a collection of stunning sari designs, and she had been warmly welcomed into the rishis' homes. The women had commiserated with her on Nandana's disappearance, but the mood had lifted the moment Simhika had brought the saris out. Every sari had found a buyer, and every woman in the Sanctum had found a sari she loved. As a consequence, rakshasa magic was well spread throughout the Sanctum, waiting for Simhika to set the shadows on the unsuspecting women and their husbands. Soon, the sacred fire of the *homagriha* would darken and wane, and Ayodhya would become vulnerable again.

She might as well set that process of destruction in motion, the sorceress decided, as she stirred and rose. The darkness draped over and around her like a veil, thick and blind, but the sorceress walked with a firm tread, letting her magic guide her to the well located at the back. The dry whispers multiplied in pitch the nearer she drew, and when she leaned over the water, Simhika was greeted by a frenzied rush of forms that leaped out of the well and cavorted around her in glee, hankering for her attention —

mothermothermothermothermother

How are you, my children? Simhika asked, running her hands over the forms that were shape, smoke and sinuous shadow all at once, slipping through her fingers like silk and running amok in delight.

thirstythirstythirstythirstythirstythirsty hungryhungry hungryhungry

The shadows clamoured and spun around her, delirious in their desire for destruction.

I know, the sorceress replied. *You have been very patient. It is time for a reward.*

rewardrewardrewardreward

The forms writhed and wrapped around one another and around Simhika in anticipation, their non-existent mouths slobbering and smacking obscenely at the prospect of a feeding.

Yes, but first, tell me about her, said Simhika, peering into the depths of the well.

She had wondered what to do about Nandana, where to hide her, and how to explain her sudden disappearance from the city. The solution had been blindingly simple. Ayodhya was in the grip of a mysterious epidemic of disappearances. People were anyway vanishing from everywhere. Nandana's disappearance could be attributed to the same cause, and as long as her remains weren't found, no one would suspect a thing. The bottomless well at the back of the mansion had come in handy, and the plan had worked marvellously. In all these days, no one had even once questioned Simhika's claims. The women who worked for her, the *nagarapalas*, Dileepa, everyone had accepted that Nandana had gone like all the others…

prisonerprisonerprisoner

She isn't dead yet? the sorceress asked, her expression clouding over.

The girl had put up an unexpectedly spirited fight, and it had taken Simhika every ounce of her strength to throw Nandana into the well and force her down to its very bottom, where she now lay, broken and trapped, incapable of rising to the top. She had left Nandana down there in the hope that she would die quickly, but…

nonononono notdeadnotdeadnotdead

Simhika felt rage build against the girl inside her. She had been punished for betraying Lanka's cause, but instead of dying, she was still alive…

Guard her for me. Don't let her escape, ever. She must die here in the dark.

diediedie darkdarkdarkdark mothermothermother

Perhaps it was best that the girl was still breathing, the sorceress thought to herself as she stared into the well, the shadowy forms spinning in a tizzy around her. Nandana could dwell over her decision to side with the humans; she could rue turning her back on Lanka and its lord, Ravana. She could regret deceiving Simhika, Mother of Shadows, as she waited for death to claim her.

six

TWO FIGURES APPEARED AT A DARKENED DOORWAY AND stood for a moment at the threshold of a grey dawn, peering out unhappily into the wide, vacant courtyard before them. Then, hunching their shoulders under their woollen *pravaras* and bracing themselves against the cold, they set off across the courtyard, their wooden *padukas* clacking loudly on stone. The morning was still and heavy with smoke from the many fires that had been lit all over the palace grounds to keep the sentries and palace guards warm through the night.

"No sun today as well," Sheelabhadra said gloomily, casting a quick glance at the overcast sky.

"Humph," Kushadhwaja grunted in reply, keeping his bare head down and his feet moving.

"I can't remember when we saw the sun for the last time," Sheelabhadra remarked. "Must have been a month ago."

"Longer," the *kshatri* mumbled. With a shiver, he added, "What a terrible winter this is proving to be!"

Giving his head a sad shake, Sheelabhadra looked around the courtyard. Every door was closed and every window shuttered to keep the cold out, and where just months ago palace hands would have been seen running errands and discharging their duties, now there was only silence and inactivity, brought on by a winter unprecedented in its harshness. And not just in the palace, all over Ayodhya and Kosala, the winter had brought enterprise and industry to a standstill. The sky was perpetually hazy and the sun had ceased trying to break through, so the blanket of mist over the Sarayu never lifted, making navigation hard and even perilous. People stayed indoors longer, and even when they did venture out for work, they sought warmth by huddling around fires and cursing their fates. Frost, which invariably lay thick on the ground all mornings, had destroyed crops all over the kingdom, and the prospect of food shortages had once again reared its head. Meanwhile, at least twenty lives all over Kosala had already been lost to the cold, and although efforts were on to distribute warm clothing among the populace, the shortage of woollen *pravaras* and blankets was acute. Conditions were so bad that Kosala's citizens had taken to remembering the sweltering heat of the summer with fondness, preferring its familiarity to a cold that they were unaccustomed to and hopelessly underprepared for.

"At least the wind isn't blowing today," Kushadhwaja stated, his eyes already watering as they fixed on the door they were approaching.

"We should be thankful for small mercies," agreed Kosala's guild master, drawing his *pravara* tighter around him and tucking his arms deeper into the cloak for warmth. When it swept down from the north, the wind brought the bite of snow from the Himalayas, slipping through cracks, forcing itself under vestments, burrowing all the way to the marrow and freezing the blood in the veins.

The two men shuffled up to the door, but instead of opening on its own accord, it stayed closed, and Kushadhwaja had to push it open with his shoulder. "The magic is definitely on the wane," he muttered in annoyance as he stepped through.

Sheelabhadra followed the *kshatri* inside, shutting the door on the cold and feeling the relative warmth of the indoors wrap around him. Squaring his shoulders in relief, the guild master blinked in the gloom until Kushadhwaja snapped a globe of light to illuminate the passageway they stood in. The men set off down the passage, the light bobbing along over their heads like a miniature moon, dimming now and then before gaining back its strength.

"It's been only four months since the new *homagriha's* consecration," Sheelabhadra remarked. "There was such a vast improvement in the quality of magic back then, I remember." He paused to consider the matter. "Nothing has changed since then, so I wonder why magic is dipping in Ayodhya."

"Something is definitely wrong," Kushadhwaja agreed. "Look at the weather. Kosala has never faced such a severe winter in living memory."

The men walked in silence for a moment. "Is it possible that the unrest in the Sanctum garrison is linked to this?" Sheelabhadra mused. "Or even the quarrel amongst the rishis' wives, for that matter?"

"Everything is connected to magic, always has been. So…" Kushadhwaja shrugged, letting the word hang ominously. "The trouble is even the rishis aren't being able to fathom why the magic is becoming less and less potent despite the consecration of the new *homagriha*."

Sheelabhadra gave a thoughtful nod, but before he could add to what the *kshatri* had said, the globe flickered and nearly went out before reviving. The men gave the light sour looks as they continued on their way, the passage turning and opening into a hall with doors leading in every direction. A figure waited in the hallway, and seeing the *kshatri* and the guild master approach, the man bowed and did a *pranaam*.

"The rajan has asked me to tell you to wait," said Atibhanu. The bodyguard was dressed in his usual summer attire, tattooed biceps exposed to the elements. The cold didn't seem to have any effect on him.

"Where is the rajan?" asked Kushadhwaja.

"He has gone to see mahamuni Vashishtha… Oh, there he is."

Kushadhwaja and Sheelabhadra turned to the sound of *padukas* and saw Bharat approaching them. They joined their hands and bowed to their king. The guild master observed how Bharat too wore no woollens, and concluded that growing up in Kekeya had perhaps made the young king immune to the cold. He had heard stories about winter in the River Kingdoms and how the rivers sometimes froze over—

"How is the mahamuni?" Kushadhwaja enquired. From his expression, it didn't look as though the *kshatri* was expecting a favourable response, and he was proved right when Bharat shook his head and began walking. The courtiers fell in step beside the king, Atibhanu following five steps behind.

"Not good, I'm afraid," said Bharat in answer to his father-in-law's question.

"And the *vaidyas* aren't being able to put a finger on what's gone wrong?" Kushadhwaja asked.

"They're clueless." Bharat was silent for a moment. "I don't understand what's wrong with the mahamuni. He was showing sure signs of recovery right after the sacred fire had been instituted in the *homagriha*. He had started following movements with his eyes and responding to sounds. Then, suddenly, all progress stopped, and his condition regressed to the way it was earlier…" The king shook his head again. "I don't get it. The rishis had said things would get sorted after the consecration of the *homagriha*. Why has everything gone wrong again?"

Sheelabhadra and Kushadhwaja exchanged glances but said nothing. The four men left the hall and trooped down a gallery that took them in the direction of the Throne Room.

"Why did you wish to see us so early in the day, rajan?" Kushadhwaja broke the heavy silence.

Bharat didn't reply immediately. They crossed the gallery and were halfway down another hall leading to the Throne Room's annex before he spoke. "Yadudeva has gone," he said. "*Adhipati* Sudhanva's son," he added, just so there was no doubt.

"Gone?" The *kshatri* blinked rapidly. "As in *disappeared*… like everyone else?"

The king nodded.

"When?"

"It seems he hasn't been seen since last evening."

"He could have gone somewhere without informing anyone…" Sheelabhadra began, but stopped on seeing Bharat give his head a firm shake.

Everyone walked in silence for a moment, deep in thought.

"Where is everyone going?" Kushadhwaja muttered, half to himself. "Will there be no end to this?"

"*Adhipati* Sudhanva is beside himself with grief and is demanding answers," Bharat shot quick glances at his companions. "I am told he has been heard saying the palace has done nothing to stop the disappearances and he is angry about it."

"What are we going to do about it, rajan?" Sheelabhadra asked guardedly.

"I have asked Mitraka to meet us," the king pointed ahead with his chin. "The *dandapalas* were supposed to have been working on the case. Let's see if they have any answers." From his tone, it was plain his expectations were very low. Bharat lapsed into silence, and the others followed suit.

"We also have a representation of farmers here, seeking redress," the king said suddenly.

"Redress?" The *kshatri's* eyebrows crawled up his forehead. "For what?"

"For the actions of the city's moneylenders… who are also waiting for us."

Kushadhwaja and the guild master looked at each other in mystification.

Bharat stopped and turned to face the two men. "I also received news from Shatrughna late last night." He switched his gaze from Kushadhwaja to Sheelabhadra and back. "It seems they have had another accident at the market construction site."

"What sort of accident?"

"A barrier on one of the canals they had cut from the Yamuna broke in the middle of the night, flooding the whole place," the king said. "It took them nearly a day to rebuild the dam and stop more river water from flowing in, but the place is submerged in water up to waist level. Heaven knows how long it will take to drain the entire place and resume work."

"Did a breach in a barrier cause so much damage?" Kushadhwaja looked dubious.

"Not a breach," said Bharat grimly as he resumed walking. "It looks like the whole barrier gave way."

"Oh," the *kshatri* exclaimed. After a moment's reflection, he added, "A second accident, hardly a month after the fire that broke out in the timber yard."

"These accidents are affecting the construction of the market," Bharat nodded. "We are already behind schedule by a month, and we've barely started."

Having reached the annex, Bharat opened the door without waiting for the magic, which would probably have misfired anyway. He entered the room, and the *kshatri*, the guild master and the bodyguard came in his wake, the door shutting heavily behind them. Bharat stopped to survey those gathered in the annex: two groups of people standing apart from each other, hostility and mistrust shimmering in the space dividing them. The group to the left comprised over a dozen farmers, their feet scarred from years spent tilling the fields, their hands callused from wielding the plough, their faces tanned like leather by Kosala's sun. The set to the right was smaller and consisted of wealthier individuals, their expensive tastes showing in their clothes and manners. A couple of them clearly knew Sheelabhadra well enough to exchange discreet nods with him.

Drawing his breath, Bharat addressed the farmers. "I gather you have a complaint against these gentlemen," he nodded in the direction of the moneylenders.

"Rajan, we haven't come here to complain," one of the farmers said with a humble bow. "We're here to petition for fairness and respite."

The king's eyes drifted to the richer crowd. "Are you here to complain against *them* then?"

"We came because they came here to complain about us," the oldest among the moneylenders spoke, bowing low. "We thought you should hear us as well, and not just the farmers."

"Neither side has complaints against the other, yet here you all are," Bharat sighed wearily. He looked at the farmers. "So, what brings you here?"

"Rajan," one said, his hands folded in a *pranaam*, "We farmers have been scraping an existence from an unforgiving earth for the last two years on account of the drought. We have cultivated little and earned even less, and many of us have been reduced to living in poverty. But we have never complained or sought relief from the throne. We believed the tide would turn, and to our great relief, it did, when the rain finally arrived four months ago. Overjoyed, we took to tilling our lands with hope. But because the last two years had been harsh, there was no money left to buy seeds. So, we went to them," he pointed towards the moneylenders, "and borrowed money to purchase seeds. We had thought we could repay them after harvesting the new crop. But rajan, the frost and the cold have destroyed all of our crops. We have grown nothing that can be harvested; there is nothing to sell to raise money. But the moneylenders are insisting that we honour our promise and return their money with interest, rajan —"

"Money that has been borrowed must be returned, rajan," the old moneylender interrupted. "It is a sacred pact between lender and borrower that cannot be broken."

Voices broke out in protest on the farmers' side until Bharat raised a hand, calling for order.

"Borrowed money must be returned," he said. "You cannot refuse to pay —"

"We are not refusing to pay the money back, rajan," the farmer who had spoken first said. "We are willing to return the money and we *can* — but the moneylenders aren't letting us settle our debts."

Bharat blinked and turned to Kushadhwaja and Sheelabhadra in confusion. "What do you mean they aren't letting you…?" he asked, shooting a glance at the moneylenders.

"Rajan, when we borrowed money for the seeds, we gave the moneylenders our cattle as surety, against which they lent us the money. If we had those cows and buffaloes back, they could earn us an income with which we could clear our debts. We could sell milk and even dung cakes for the fires to drive away the cold, but the moneylenders refuse to give us our cattle back, insisting that we first repay the money we have borrowed."

Bharat turned to the moneylenders. "Is this true?"

"The cattle they have pledged is surety, rajan," the old moneylender replied. "One doesn't just return surety. After all, surety is what protects the lender's interest. Surety is returned when the loan is repaid. Those are the rules."

Bharat weighed the matter for a moment before addressing the moneylenders. "You know what the last two years have been like. You have endured endless summers; you have seen the Sarayu shrink; you have witnessed the earth turn to dust. You can imagine how hard it has been on the farmers. And you only have to visit the countryside to see what the cold has done to the crops. These men are desperate, but they're honourable. They are willing to repay you. Give them the opportunity to clear their debts. Let them have their cattle back."

The moneylenders exchanged unhappy looks. Their leader cleared his throat and raised his chin defiantly. "Rajan,

Kosala's laws are very clear in this matter," he insisted. "The farmers should first repay the money they have borrowed to free their cattle from bond."

Bharat's eyes narrowed on the moneylender. "Laws are created to serve the rich and the mighty, but justice must be upheld to protect the weak and the powerless," he said in a voice sharp with displeasure. "You have possession of their cattle, which is undoubtedly profiting you even now in the form of milk and dung to fuel fires. Meanwhile, the farmers have nothing, so they cannot repay you, and the interest on the loans accumulates. When it becomes impossible to return the money, they are forced to part with their land, their primary source of income. This is unfair on the people who work so hard to put food on our plates. This is an injustice I will not tolerate. Return their cattle and let them clear their debts." He paused to look at the moneylenders' faces. "And if it is surety that you seek, the palace will reimburse the money that you are owed should the farmers default," Bharat's voice thundered. "I believe you will take the word of your king."

The moneylenders all bowed their heads, surprised by the sudden sternness in Bharat and wary of provoking him further. The young king turned to the farmers. "I have staked my word because I believe you are honourable men," he said. "Please don't disappoint me."

"You have our gratitude and our blessings, rajan," the leader of the farmers said, the relief plain in his voice. "We will ensure the palace and the moneylenders have no reason for complaint."

Bharat waited for both groups to depart before turning to the *kshatri* and the guild master. "My apologies for not consulting either of you, even though I had asked both of you to be here," he said. "I did what I thought was right."

"Standing by the farmers was the right thing to do," Kushadhwaja nodded in approval. "But at the same time, by promising to reimburse them in an eventuality, you assured the moneylenders that the palace wasn't unsympathetic towards them." The *kshatri* turned to Sheelabhadra. "The matter was handled well, won't you say?"

The guild master nodded slowly. "Indeed. There was a moment where the moneylenders might have felt a bit let down… when you took the side of the farmers, rajan."

"I took their side because they are in a hopeless situation," said Bharat.

"I know, I know," Sheelabhadra said hurriedly. "But the moneylenders are influential, and it is good to have them on *our* side."

"On *our* side?" asked Bharat. "Against whom?"

Sheelabhadra darted a glance at Kushadhwaja. "Against anyone who wishes the palace ill." He paused and smiled. "The good bit is that like the *kshatri* said, the palace was able to demonstrate that it cared about the moneylenders' interests as well."

The king gave this a moment's thought, then let it pass. "Where are we with the distribution of *pravaras* and blankets among the public?" he asked, changing the subject. "Is there enough of both to keep everyone warm?"

"The demand for warm clothes is high, and the supply is still short," the guild master confessed. "No one had anticipated such a severe winter in Kosala; no one had thought there'd be a market for woollens here. The guild is doing what it can to ramp up the import of cloaks and blankets, but supply isn't enough to meet demand. We are tapping into markets as far north as Srinagara and even Cina to source consignments."

"Let us do whatever is possible to speed up the imports," said Bharat. "We can't have any more people freezing to death for lack of warm clothes." He considered the *kshatri*. "We should also subsidize the price of woollens. Let the treasury bear part of the cost so they're more affordable to everyone." He turned back to Sheelabhadra. "The guild should also ensure no one is hoarding woollens to be sold at a profit. If I discover another Pushyanta trying to turn the situation to his advantage, I will have him stripped and left to freeze in the cold."

The guild master bowed in acknowledgement, but before he could say a word, the door opened and a palace hand stepped in. "Rajan," he announced, "Mitraka, the chief of the *dandapalas*, is here to see you."

The plain around the Bahlika settlement rang with the beat of the *dhol* and the crash of cymbals, and the air was festive with song, dance and laughter as Yuddhajeet left his lodging and stepped out into a bright winter morning that was both cold and cloudless, the sun's warmth welcome on his face. He stood for a moment, watching ox-cart caravans bring in guests who were greeted with food and drink, the men embracing and slapping each other's backs hard while the women held hands and chatted excitedly. Children weaved and darted everywhere, making the most of the lack of parental supervision. The scenes of cheer brought a smile to the prince's face as he set off in search of his hosts.

"Hey," he grabbed a young boy scooting past him by the arm. "Where can I find Ambareesha?" Seeing the boy's wide-eyed stare, he added, "The bridegroom. The man who is getting married. Where can I find him?"

Instead of answering, the boy wriggled out of the prince's grasp and galloped away, yelling to his friends at the top of his voice. Heaving a sigh, Yuddhajeet decided to try his luck elsewhere when a voice hailed him by name. The prince turned, his face lighting up with delight on seeing his friend.

"Ambareesha," he grinned as they embraced, the giant stooping down to hug Yuddhajeet.

"Your beard has grown a lot greyer since summer," Ambareesha said, peering at the prince.

"Old age and older sins finally catching up," Yuddhajeet chuckled as he ran his fingers through his beard. Both men laughed.

"I'm glad you made it," Ambareesha nodded in approval. "I was told you came in late at night."

"The idea was to reach before sundown, but I left Rajagriha late," the prince shrugged.

"And Raja Ashwapati?" the Bahlika asked. "He didn't come?"

Yuddhajeet shook his head. "Father suffered another stroke last month."

"Oh, I hope he is… getting better."

Yuddhajeet only shrugged in response. Ambareesha nodded in understanding.

A moment passed before the giant turned to the woman standing two steps behind him. "This," he said, his face brightening, "is Devadatta, whom I will wed this afternoon." He addressed the woman. "And this is my friend Yuddhajeet of Kekeya."

The woman stepped forward and bowed to the prince. Yuddhajeet returned the *pranaam*.

"I must thank you," Devadatta said in a voice that brought to mind the dainty tinkle of anklets. "I owe you a debt of gratitude, yuvaraja."

"For what?" Yuddhajeet asked in surprise.

"For saving his life," the woman said with a quick glance at Ambareesha. "Abhisarika told me how you risked your life at Mithuna to rescue him from Gandharan swords."

"Oh, that. I would have done that for any ally. And this was Ambareesha." The prince smacked the giant on the shoulder.

"That is why I thank you," said Devadatta.

Yuddhajeet inclined his head. "Abhisarika said a lot of good things about you too," he said, but before he could expand on that, another voice cut in.

"I wonder what's being said about me in my absence?"

All three turned to see Abhisarika approaching them, with Smara holding her hand and walking beside her. The child's face was solemn as usual.

"Nothing that isn't complimentary, sister," Devadatta said with a smile.

"I can trust you on that," Abhisarika replied. She turned to Yuddhajeet. "I just got to know you were here."

Yuddhajeet bowed. "I have something for both of you," he said to Ambareesha and Devadatta. "Come with me."

The prince led the way and the others followed him to the rear of the house where he had been put up for the night.

There, tied to a post, stood a pair of fine white horses, their manes blowing in the cold wind. "Good wishes from Kekeya to the two of you," he said, pointing to the steeds.

"They are beautiful," Devadatta exclaimed, going over to the horses. One promptly nuzzled her hand in search of edibles. Ambareesha joined her, stroking the horse's neck in admiration.

"We thank Kekeya and Raja Ashwapati… and you," he said, bowing to Yuddhajeet.

"Didn't you bring anything for me?"

Yuddhajeet turned to find Smara considering him seriously, her head cocked to one side. Taken aback, he blinked, then crouched before her. Stretching his hand towards her head, he pretended to pluck something from behind her ear. He extended his hand towards the child, his fist closed around something. "For you," he said, opening his fist.

In the middle of his palm lay a delicate silver pendant studded with emeralds. Smara gasped in wonder as she picked the pendant up and inspected it closely.

"You shouldn't have —" Abhisarika protested, but Yuddhajeet stopped her with a shake of his head.

"It's nothing," he smiled as he stood up. "It was always meant to be a gift."

"We should go," said Devadatta, glancing at Ambareesha. "There are ceremonies that are still to be performed…"

"Yes," the giant nodded. He addressed Yuddhajeet. "I will see you later, my friend."

"Go ahead," said Abhisarika. "I shall make sure our guest is properly looked after."

With a smile, Devadatta looked at Smara. "Will you come with us?" she asked. The girl thought about the offer, then nodded. Ambareesha and Devadatta left with Smara in between them, the child intent on admiring the pendant.

"Be careful with that. Don't lose it," Abhisarika called after her, but the girl showed no sign of having heard her mother.

"I didn't think she'd be with anyone but you," Yuddhajeet remarked, staring at Smara.

"She was happy at Rajagriha with your father," Abhisarika reminded him.

The prince nodded. Abhisarika went to the tethered horses and the beasts stretched their necks towards her. "Smara and Devadatta are quite fond of each other," she said, caressing the horses' foreheads. After a small pause, she looked again in the direction of the three departing figures. "I'm so glad for Devadatta," she said. "Ambareesha will make a caring husband. He looks like a monster, but he has a heart of gold."

Yuddhajeet couldn't stop himself from grinning at the woman's description of her cousin. "You are very fond of him," he observed.

Abhisarika nodded. "He and my—" she checked herself. "He and Smara's father were the best of friends."

The silence that ensued was finally broken by Yuddhajeet. "I'm sorry about your loss," he said. "Ambareesha told me."

"It couldn't be helped," Abhisarika said with a slight shrug. Turning away from the horses, she started walking and the prince was obliged to follow. They walked side by side, small oases of silence amidst the noise and gaiety of the settlement. Their attention was drawn briefly towards a rider who came charging over a rise and made a beeline for the settlement. The man was too far away to be seen clearly, and once he had ridden into the settlement and dismounted, he was lost in the crowd. He was forgotten almost the same instant.

"What about you?" Abhisarika asked, glancing at Yuddhajeet. "Were you never married?"

"No."

"That's unusual for a prince."

"I guess I never found the right person."

"But Raja Ashwapati would have wanted you to have a son, an heir to succeed you…"

The prince didn't say anything. They walked some more in silence.

"How would you know if you had found the right person?" Abhisarika asked at last.

Yuddhajeet gave this some consideration. "I think we know," he said at last. "If we are honest to ourselves, we know." He looked at the woman. "With Smara's father, you knew, didn't you? You knew he was the right one."

Abhisarika nodded. For a long while, neither of them spoke. Drawing a deep breath, she finally said, "That pendant you gave Smara… You said it was always meant to be a gift. Not for Smara though, was it?"

Yuddhajeet blinked and stared into the distance, conscious that the woman's eyes were on him. He cleared his throat to speak when they heard someone hail Abhisarika. They looked around to see a short man running towards them on bandy legs.

"What is the matter, Uchhara?" Abhisarika asked.

"Your father wants to see him," the man panted, gesturing towards Yuddhajeet. "Now."

The prince of Kekeya and the daughter of the Bahlika chieftain exchanged puzzled glances as they hastened after the messenger. When they were escorted into chief Sailusha's presence, the room was already crowded with other Bahlika chieftains and warriors. Ambareesha was also there, the tallest and broadest among tall, broad men.

"Salutations from Kekeya," Yuddhajeet offered Sailusha and the other chieftains a *pranaam*.

"Salutations," Sailusha said in response. "It is a pleasure and an honour to have you partake in our joy, yuvaraja. I wish we had nothing but good tidings to share on a happy occasion such as this, but unfortunately, we have just received news that is upsetting."

"What is it, father?" Abhisarika asked, suddenly tense.

The old chieftain glanced at his daughter, then back at Yuddhajeet. "This man here," he pointed to a man standing quietly to one side, "has ridden in from your father's court in Rajagriha." He addressed the man. "Tell them what you just told me."

Taking in the man's dusty appearance and mud-spattered clothes, Yuddhajeet realized he must have been the rider he and Abhisarika had spotted earlier. "You are not from Kekeya," he said. "Who are you?"

"I am a rider from Sakala, yuvaraja. Raja Sampada had sent me to Rajagriha, where I learned from your father that you are here. He asked me to come and deliver the news to you."

"What is the news?"

"Some traders who were recently in Kapisi reported that an army was being amassed in Gandhara. They had occasion to visit a garrison town, where troops were being readied for battle." The messenger cast a look around the room. "In the opinion of these traders, Gandhara is preparing for an attack on the River Kingdoms."

"When was this?" Yuddhajeet asked, his tone and his body rigid. "How long ago?"

"The traders were in Kapisi a fortnight ago, yuvaraja. Perhaps even earlier. We are not sure..."

"Why did they take so long in bringing this to our notice?" Yuddhajeet snapped. Then, realizing the traders had done the River Kingdoms a favour, he softened his tone. "Still, they did well in sharing the information with Raja Sampada."

Sailusha looked at the rider. "Could these traders tell how close Gandhara was to marching on the River Kingdoms?"

"They couldn't say for certain," the messenger replied, "but judging by the level of preparation, they felt that the troops were all set to take the road."

An ominous silence fell over the room. Even the *dhol* in the background sounded threatening.

Sailusha fixed his gaze on Yuddhajeet. "Fifteen days ago, and fully prepared to march. I don't think the River Kingdoms have a lot of time to organize themselves before another Gandharan invasion."

"Do you know how the people of Ayodhya keep themselves entertained nowadays?"

Mitraka glared at the faces in front of her one by one, waiting to see if anyone was prepared to hazard a guess, but all she got in return was stiff, awkward silence.

"They crack jokes about us," the chief of the *dandapalas* snapped in annoyance. Then, without skipping a beat, she asked, "Can you tell which is my favourite joke of the lot?"

The investigators, who had assembled in answer to her summons, shuffled their feet and glanced at each other from the corners of their eyes. This time, the chief let the silence prolong, allowing it to settle uncomfortably over their shoulders.

"I'll tell you," her nostrils flared in indignation. "The *dandapalas* are so incompetent that even if they have *nothing* to do, they will make a complete mess of it." Mitraka grinned at them, but there was no mirth in her eyes. "Funny, isn't it?"

No, it wasn't funny. Not if one was an investigator of the palace.

"We have been reduced to a laughing stock," Mitraka roared. "Five months ago, we were given the charge of investigating the attack on the king. Five months ago, the king and everyone else expected us to solve the case and help make an arrest. Five months later, we are being laughed at, and the king no longer bothers to call us for reports and updates. He knows we have nothing to share with him, and he doesn't want to waste his time with us anymore. But…" She paused theatrically to look around the room, her face brightening in a big, showy, insincere smile. "But this morning the king called me to his court… Do you know why? Yadudeva, son of *adhipati* Sudhanva, has disappeared," Mitraka snapped her fingers. "The *adhipati* is accusing the palace of inaction… and whom do you think the palace is blaming for not having made any progress in investigating the disappearances?" The chief nodded and offered a curt little bow. "You should be proud of yourselves, the way you have all covered yourselves in glory," she smirked.

Dileepa, standing one row behind and a little to the side so he was not directly in Mitraka's line of sight, stared at his feet as he felt shame and anger burning him up. Shame at being labelled incompetent and knowing there was some truth in it; anger at Mitraka for rubbing salt into their wounds with her sarcasm. They had done their best and worked their hardest, he wanted to say in everyone's defence. He had wanted to say the same thing to Rani Kaikeyi three months ago, when she had made a cutting remark about the *dandapalas* plodding through the investigation into the attack on the king. He had wanted to defend the *dandapalas*, but then, the rani had flung the sari that he had brought as a gift from Ma Parnalata back at him, reminding him that he was an investigator of the palace and not a messenger bearing gifts for the queens. Listening to the rani tick him off, he had turned red with shame and embarrassment, and had lost the courage to speak up for the *dandapalas* —

"Let us keep the attack on the king aside for a moment," Mitraka pressed on. "Let's go back to more than a year ago, when the rakshasas attacked the Sanctum. We were assigned the task of figuring out how that attack happened and who aided the rakshasas in getting into the Sanctum. Today, everyone has more or less forgotten about the attack, but the answers to those questions are yet to be found. I can't remember the last time we successfully solved a case. It's a question of time before someone realizes we *dandapalas* are totally redundant..."

Their chief had good reason to be miffed, Dileepa realized. Investigations into two high-profile cases that had struck at the heart of Kosala and shaken its foundations had run out of steam and ground to a halt. The palace investigators had been expected to unearth the conspiracies behind each incident, but so far, they had achieved nothing. Mitraka was under immense pressure, and as the head of the *dandapalas*, her career and reputation were at stake. If they didn't find a lead quickly —

"Are you even listening to what I am saying?"

Dileepa's eyes focused on Mitraka, and he saw she was staring straight at him. He blinked and blushed in embarrassment.

"I… yes," he mumbled.

"*You* came to me with this theory that the killing of the four people in the old quarter might be linked to the attack on the king. *You* offered to investigate those killings. What progress have you made in your investigations? What conclusions have you drawn?"

As the chief waited for his reply, Dileepa felt the weight of everyone else's gaze on him. Some of his colleagues were undoubtedly pleased to see him being knocked down like this, especially those who had resented his being taken off the probe into the disappearances and those who had envied him for having been picked by the king to investigate the hoarding scam. For them, this was his comeuppance, the upstart from faraway Kusinagara getting what he deserved—

"I see you have nothing to say," Mitraka's eyes flashed. She looked away from Dileepa. "The attack on the Sanctum, the attack on Raja Bharat, the killings in the old quarter, and yes, the disappearances. Four cases, but not a single explanation or solution in sight." She paused to look at the faces before her slowly. "I hope you understand that you are still *dandapalas* only because those who are disappearing are also coming back of their own accord. Otherwise, by now, you would all have been stripped of your ranks and sent home." As the men hung their heads, her voice rose in pitch, "I want you to renew your efforts. Find me something that cracks open one of the cases — *any one of the cases*. Find a clue or solve something so that I can show the king we can be depended upon. Go."

Dileepa stepped out into the cold day, drawing his *pravara* around himself and feeling miserable. *I hope you understand that you are still* dandapalas *only because those who are disappearing are also coming back of their own accord.* It was true. The return of those who had disappeared had eased public pressure on the *dandapalas* to find the reason behind the disappearances. The people of Kosala had, in fact, stopped expecting the *dandapalas* to solve the mystery; they just waited for the loved ones who had gone to come back. And they did return. Always, all of them.

All but one.

It was more than four months since Nandana had disappeared. Many who had gone *after* her disappearance had since returned and were reunited with their friends and families. But not Nandana. There was no sign of *her* coming back.

Once the initial shock of her going had worn off, Dileepa had settled to wait for the girl to show up. The first month went by in an edgy mix of agony and anticipation, the prospect of her return strengthening with each passing day. The second month left Dileepa more stressed than hopeful, and when Nandana failed to show up for the third month, the *dandapala* slipped into a state of despondency. Now, four months into her disappearance, the prospect of her return had dimmed to nothing. Even Ma Parnalata appeared to have abandoned the notion of having Nandana back — and for someone so badly stricken by the loss, she seemed to have reconciled to the fact with surprising ease. The woman hardly spoke about the girl anymore, and whenever Dileepa mentioned her, Ma was apt to change the subject brusquely. Ma Parnalata didn't accord him the old warmth either, and the *dandapala* was left with the growing impression that he was no longer welcome in the old mansion, though he had no idea why.

Having lost interest in his work, lacking the drive to carry on, and at a complete loss over what to do with himself, the investigator had wondered if he should visit his parents in Kusinagara. He hadn't been home in a while, and a change in scenery might do him good, he thought, helping take his mind off Nandana. But he knew there was no taking Nandana out of his thoughts, no matter where he was. So, he had decided to stay on in Ayodhya, driven by the hope that the girl would eventually — *inevitably* — come back, like the others had. A small flame burned in him, refusing to be extinguished. He had lost the girl once, but she had come back, he told himself. This time, he would not give up hope.

She was strong. She was spirited. He had seen her fight off the men who had attacked him with her magical powers. She would overcome whatever situation she was in and return to him…

Lost in his thoughts, Dileepa turned into the path that led to the *nagarapalas'* headquarters next to the palace grounds. *Find me something that cracks open one of the cases — any one of the cases*, Mitraka had begged them. Not knowing where else to start looking, Dileepa had decided to retrace the investigation from the *nagarapalas* who had first discovered the bodies in the old quarter. The place wasn't particularly busy, and the investigator found Baladitya munching on roasted water-lily seeds. The *mahanayaka* greeted Dileepa and listened patiently to his request.

"You can meet the men who found the bodies, but if you're hoping to discover something new, you will be disappointed," the chief of the *nagarapalas* shrugged. "My men pursued every lead to identify the four bodies, but they got nowhere..."

"I am sure they did their best," Dileepa said, quick to assuage any hurt to *nagarapala* pride. "I don't doubt the work they put in and I'm not questioning their capabilities. I'm just... Honestly, we are at a complete loss, and we have run out of ideas —"

"I understand," the *mahanayaka* gave a sympathetic nod as he got to his feet. "You have to do *something*, so you might as well start here. Come with me..."

A little while later, Dileepa was seated opposite the three men who had investigated the deaths in the old quarter. Lying on the low table between them was a cloth purse of the kind that could be tied around the waist.

"Was there nothing else on the men to help identify them?" Dileepa asked. "No possessions or personal items, no tattoos... nothing but this?" he pointed to the purse.

All three militiamen regarded the *dandapala* with the weary tolerance of the middle-aged when forced to deal with the foolishness of those younger in years. One of them finally nodded.

"Nothing distinctive about the weapons that were found in their possession?" Dileepa pressed.

"Common *khangas* that could have been forged anywhere in Jambudvipa." The oldest member in the group heaved a sigh and pointed at the purse. "That is all we found, and it's not much."

The *dandapala* reached for the purse. It was old, the fabric fraying where its drawstrings had rubbed against cloth. The purse felt heavy, the coins it held shifting and sliding under Dileepa's fingers. Untying the knot, the investigator upended the purse and *rupas* fell on the table with a loud clatter. Dileepa counted the coins, twelve in all. He picked them up one by one and studied them closely.

"Common *rupas*," he muttered. He looked up to catch the militiamen looking at each other and shaking their heads. "What?" he asked.

"We have investigated every aspect many times now," the man who had spoken before replied. "There is nothing to work on here. It's a dead end. You are wasting your time here."

Knowing the *nagarapalas* were right, Dileepa made a face and tossed the empty purse onto the table in frustration.

It landed with a muffled *clink*, a softly padded sound of something metallic striking against the wooden table. It definitely wasn't a sound that an empty cloth purse was expected to make.

The *dandapala* picked up the purse and felt along its seams and edges.

There! His fingers found something round and hard and smooth nestled in the folds of the cloth. He opened the mouth of the purse wide and peered in. The three militiamen were leaning forward in their seats, their mouths open as they watched Dileepa probe the insides of the purse. The *dandapala* pushed a finger past a seam and touched an object hidden in a recess. Carefully, he pried the gap wider and extracted the thing that had made the noise as it had struck the table. The investigator held the object up between thumb and forefinger so that the *nagarapalas* could also see it.

It was a ring.

"Where did that come from?" one of the militiamen gaped in surprise.

"We had no idea this was inside the purse," swore another.

"It was inside a secret compartment sewn into the purse," said Dileepa. "You must have missed it because even though you might have heard it clink, you'd have thought it was just the *rupas* jangling inside."

The *nagarapalas* drew even closer to inspect the ring. It was made of gold, the band shiny with age, its head flat at the top where a pair of leaves had been etched into the gold. No other design elements were discernible.

"That is a strange design," the oldest *nagarapala* remarked as he examined the twin-leaf motif. "It looks familiar, but I can't seem to remember where I've seen it." He passed the ring to his mates. "Does it strike you fellows as something you have seen?"

Dileepa watched the other two militiamen shake their heads. They all looked at him as he took the ring back and tucked it into the purse along with the silver coins. "This gives us something to work on," he said, buoyed by the sense of hope and relief. "Let us see what this ring can tell us about the men who —" he stopped himself from saying the men who had attacked him, "— who died in the old quarter."

Yadudeva's disappearance couldn't have been better timed, Sudhanva thought to himself as he cast a sly glance at the men seated around him, warming their hands over the broad iron brazier. The north wind had picked up an hour before sundown, blowing through Ayodhya and sending its citizens scurrying for shelter. Gaining severity with the coming of the night, it now whistled in the eaves and tore through branches outside his palatial home, making everyone huddle close to the fire.

Not only had the boy's going brought his friends and sympathizers to his doorstep, it had also given his flagging rebellion a fresh lease of life, channelling everyone's individual angst into collective dissatisfaction with the throne. For the first time since the attack on Bharat and his son nearly five months ago, the *adhipati* felt a rekindling of the discontent that had first brought this company together. All he had to do now was tap into everyone's anger and mistrust so that it built towards a crescendo that would oust Bharat and lay the foundations for a new order in Kosala where — *and here, Sudhanva's heart fluttered at the sheer audacity of the thought* — he could be more than just *kshatri* to some king.

An order where he could be Kosala's next king, Sudhanva shivered in excitement at the idea.

The prospect of becoming king had crept up on him one chilly evening a couple of months ago, surprising him at first, before solidifying slowly and laying claim to his waking hours, growing from possibility to distinct certainty — *an inevitability* — in a matter of weeks. He remembered Mihiradutta asking him whom he had in mind to replace Bharat as king. He hadn't had a definite answer that day. Today, he did. Who else was more qualified to rule Kosala?

He had been Raja Dashratha's trusted right hand, riding into battle to unify Kosala. He had seen the kingdom rise to eminence; he was its most powerful *adhipati*. His contribution to Kosala's glory couldn't be discounted, years of blood and sweat... It was time to reap a harvest. The Ikshvakus had ruled long and well, but with the passing of Dashratha and the banishment of Rama, their time was reaching an end. A change in kingship was due.

"The palace first oversaw the murder of one son of mine by the *dandapalas*," Sudhanva's eyes blazed with the heat of outrage. He shot a glance at Mihiradutta to judge the effect of his reference to Pushyanta on the uncle, but the *adhipati* of Sravasti merely rubbed his palms as he stared at the embers in the brazier. "Now, due to its colossal inaction over the disappearances, the palace has ensured that my second son is also taken from me." The *adhipati* forced a quaver into his voice. "A father outliving his sons is the ultimate curse..." he clutched his forehead in grief, "What did I do to deserve such misfortune?"

"Yadudeva will be back, my friend," said Gajakarna, placing a comforting hand on Sudhanva's shoulder. "All those who've gone have returned, so don't despair."

"Have they?" the *adhipati* asked, looking bitter. "Perhaps they have, but are they the same ones that left? What about the young man from Sravasti that Jayabhama was telling us about..." he looked at Pushyanta's elder brother seated beside Gajakarna, "...the one who has been walking in his sleep every night since his return? Or the daughter-in-law of that grain merchant here in Ayodhya? The one who attacked her father-in-law with a sickle as the poor man slept? She had nothing but respect for her father-in-law, then why the attack on him days after she returned? And she had no recollection of what she'd done."

"There's also a story about a woodcutter in one of the hamlets in the hills," Jayabhama pointed to the north. "According to the family, he's been found walking around the house at night with an axe. Going from room to room in a daze, talking to himself. Everyone is too scared to sleep, it seems, not knowing what he'll do —"

"Stories, that's all they are," Gajakarna interjected. "These are all just stories."

"The woman's attack on her father-in-law is *not* just a story," Sudhanva retorted. "That matter was brought to the court's notice, and the *nagarapala* who went to investigate it confirmed the incident. The old man was treated for the wounds that were inflicted on him. The wounds are very real. Anyone can go and take a look at them."

"Alright, alright," the *mahanayaka* raised his hands to pacify Sudhanva. "The woman attacked her father-in-law. Agreed. There is a man in Sravasti who sleepwalks. And there's a woodcutter somewhere who walks with an axe. That's *three* people. Hundreds have disappeared and come back, and except for these three, everyone else is fine and none the worse for having gone away and returned." He looked at the faces around him. "How do we even know if what is happening in these three cases is connected to their disappearance?"

There was a moment's silence. It was broken by Sudhanva.

"We don't," his eyes were hard as they considered Gajakarna. "But what if they are?" He turned to take in the other two men. "What if they *are* connected?" he asked again. "What if, like with the woman who attacked her father-in-law, each one of those who has returned has the potential to harm those around them? What then? Imagine the chaos that will unfold. Due to the inaction of the palace, hundreds…" he eyed the *mahanayaka* deliberately, "*hundreds* of those who have disappeared and come back present a danger to all the rest of us."

This time, the silence was deeper and longer, filled by the crackling of the fire and the howling of the wind.

"What I say may or may not come to pass. But considering the behaviour of the woman and the two men, there's a strong possibility of things turning out exactly the way I describe them. And that is something we have to exploit to our advantage," the *adhipati* said softly. His eyes shone with firelight and malice. "This fear that we might all be at risk from those who have returned should spread among the people. The subjects of Kosala mustn't view the palace as being *incompetent* at stopping the disappearances. They must start seeing the palace as being *responsible* for doing nothing to halt the disappearances… and as a consequence, putting everyone's life in jeopardy."

Another long, meditative silence followed. Sudhanva took the opportunity to throw two slivers of wood into the fire.

"You want panic to spread throughout the kingdom?" Gajakarna said at last. "You want people to start viewing their own family members and friends who have returned with suspicion? You want to spread alarm over something that might not even be true?" The hint of disapproval was plain in the *mahanayaka's* tone and in the way he slanted his gaze at the *adhipati* of Sankasya.

Murky shadows began closing in on Sudhanva, obscuring his sight, while a bolt of anger surged through his veins, setting his face on fire and obstructing his breathing. Curbing the overriding desire to strike out at the *mahanayaka*, the *adhipati* wrested back control of his senses, waiting for the shadows to recede and subside. He stared at the fire for a moment longer before turning to Gajakarna.

"What do you want?" he asked, his tone gruff at the edges. "Do you or do you not want Bharat removed from the throne of Kosala? Do you want a man who doesn't have the guts to stand up to a lightweight like Lavanyasurya to be your king? Are you willing to let the man who let the morale of *your* men down by refusing to stand up for their mistreatment at Madhupura be the ruler of this great kingdom? Tell me..." the *adhipati's* eyes bored into Gajakarna, "Do you or do you not want to put the spine back into Kosala's leadership?"

The *mahanayaka* looked down into the fire and said nothing. Sudhanva swung his gaze towards Mihiradutta and Jayabhama. "And *you*? Do you not want Pushyanta's killing avenged? Do you not want the man who presided over Pushyanta's murder removed from the throne? Don't you want him to pay with his blood?"

Sudhanva was pleased to see Mihiradutta and Jayabhama nod. They didn't need convincing. It was only Gajakarna who needed some working upon. He turned to the *mahanayaka*. "We have to do whatever it takes to remove Bharat... for Kosala's sake. We can't have an indecisive king ruling us. It is his indecision that led to a loss of face against Madhupura. It is his fumbling that led to the unchecked disappearances, which could still become a problem and cost us all dearly. Bharat has enjoyed the people's sympathy after the attack on him and Taksha, but it is time we took that away and planted antipathy in their minds. We want the people of

Kosala on our side and against Bharat when we make our move to remove him as king. We are laying the ground for that by turning the public against the palace. We must not waste any opportunity that comes our way. Remember, we are doing this to secure Kosala's future."

"I am in agreement with you," said Mihiradutta, finally breaking his silence.

"Yes," Jayabhama chimed in with a nod.

Sudhanva shrugged and looked at Gajakarna, who frowned. "And how do we spread the word that those who have returned might pose a threat to the rest of us?" the *mahanayaka* asked.

"It takes nothing to start a rumour. However," Sudhanva gave the commander an understanding nod, "I agree with you that we can't have the people turning against those who have come back. It is critical to give the story the right spin. We are at risk *not* because of those who've returned, but because the palace failed us. Those who have returned are as much the victims of the king's carelessness and lack of will." His voice choked with sudden emotion. "My son can't be blamed for anything when he returns. It is all on Bharat. Bharat needs to be the target of the people's ire. That is how we will succeed in overthrowing him."

Gajakarna gave a slow nod. It wasn't all that Sudhanva had been hoping for, but it was the best he could expect from the *mahanayaka* for now, he realized. It troubled the *adhipati*. Gajakarna wasn't throwing his entire weight behind the rebellion, and he was posing too many questions, picking too many faults and sticking to too many principles for comfort. But Sudhanva needed the man and his army for the push against Bharat, so he would have to keep chipping away at the commander's resistance by invoking Kosala's cause —

"Our man is waiting," the *mahanayaka* said, interrupting Sudhanva's thoughts. "Let's see what he has to say."

"Call him in."

Drawing his *pravara* tight, Gajakarna rose and went to the door connecting to an antechamber outside. The *mahanayaka* let a figure in, quickly closing the door to keep out the cold, and both men approached the circle of warmth and light.

The man who had followed the commander inside was short and muscular, and had tattoos all over his arms and neck. A pale scar trailed down one of his cheeks like a teardrop.

Atibhanu.

Mihiradutta and Jayabhama looked at the king's bodyguard curiously. Atibhanu did a *pranaam* and waited to be addressed.

"I hope the king isn't expecting you to be in the palace," said Gajakarna, cautious as usual.

"No, he was clear that he didn't want me around today," the bodyguard replied. "He told me I could have the night off, which is why I'm here."

"The raja doesn't suspect you or something, does he?" Sudhanva butted in, looking concerned.

"No, *adhipati*."

Gajakarna and Sudhanva nodded. "So, what's happening at the palace?" the commander asked.

Atibhanu first told them about the dispute between the farmers and the moneylenders, and the king's arbitration in favour of the farmers. Sudhanva looked pleased with the outcome, smiling to himself when he heard that the moneylenders had been forced to give the farmers back their cattle. The bodyguard then filled them in about Bharat's interview with Mitraka. "The raja took the *dandapalas* to task for failing to solve even a single case," said Atibhanu. "He insisted that the *dandapalas* find out the cause behind the disappearances."

"Did he give the *dandapalas* a deadline?" Sudhanva probed. "Did he explain the consequences of not finding the cause to Mitraka?"

"No, *adhipati*."

"See?" Sudhanva smacked his thigh and looked at the men around him. "Words, words, words. That is all the palace is good at. Where's the action, and where are the results?" He snorted in disgust.

"What else?" asked Gajakarna.

"There has been another accident at the market construction site," said the bodyguard.

"We've heard about that," said the *mahanayaka*. "Some dam breach that flooded the place."

"That market is a joke," Sudhanva chortled in delight. "It's doomed to fail, mark my words."

Atibhanu concluded his report by telling the group about the shortage of *pravaras* and blankets, the king's order that the treasury subsidize the price of woollen clothes, and his warning to the guild to guard against the hoarding of blankets and *pravaras*. Sudhanva kept silent through this account, looking sullen. Then, suddenly his eyes acquired a scheming glint, and he could barely sit still and wait for Atibhanu to take his leave.

"Can he be trusted?" Mihiradutta asked once the door had shut and the bodyguard's footsteps faded into silence.

"Absolutely," vouched Gajakarna. "Atibhanu believes Bharat has betrayed Kosala and its army by reversing his decision to march against Lavanyasurya. In his opinion, Bharat isn't fit to rule Kosala. I picked him for the post of bodyguard precisely because he thinks so poorly of Bharat, yet is clever enough to keep his dislike well concealed. So much so that in a short while he has gained Bharat's confidence, which is so critical. We can definitely bank on Atibhanu to spy on the king for us."

"I am hoping he can be relied upon to do more than that when the time comes," said Sudhanva. Even as the others exchanged meaningful glances, the *adhipati* switched the subject, a cunning smile lighting up his face. "This shortage of *pravaras* and blankets has given me another idea… Why do we have such a shortage of woollens?"

Mihiradutta, Jayabhama and Gajakarna looked at each other and shook their heads slowly. "No one expected the winter to be so harsh, so the guild and the traders didn't stock up on woollens," said Jayabhama.

"That might have been true when the cold set in, but the gap in supply ought to have been filled by now," Sudhanva maintained. "No, I think the real reason for this shortage is Lavanyasurya."

Seeing the men stare, the *adhipati* nodded. "I believe Madhupura is intentionally blocking the supply of woollens to Ayodhya. Lavanyasurya knows we are in the grip of a fierce winter, and he knows all woollen products have to come to Ayodhya through Madhupura. By stopping the flow of woollen *pravaras* and blankets, he is adding to the misery and suffering of our people. Once again, who is to blame for this?"

"The palace?" Jayabhama ventured, picking the drift of the *adhipati's* arguments.

"Of course, the palace," Sudhanva exclaimed with a grunt of satisfaction. "Had Kosala attacked Madhupura when we had the chance, we wouldn't be facing a shortage of woollens today. But instead, here we are, building a market that is nowhere close to completion, and our people are dying of the cold. That's the trouble with pacifism. The subjects of Kosala deserve to know the truth, and it's on us to inform them. Let us spread the news about Madhupura's strategy; let the people realize they're again suffering because of the incompetence and lack of decisiveness on the part of their king."

Gajakarna eyed the other two men before returning his gaze to Sudhanva. "But is it true… this theory about Madhupura preventing woollen clothes from reaching Ayodhya?"

"Does it matter whether it is true?" the *adhipati* countered. "It sounds possible, and if it sounds possible, people will buy it. And if people buy the story that the palace is ultimately responsible for their misery, we have everything to gain." He leaned forward to look at the face of the men around him. "We must employ every tactic to discredit Bharat and lower his esteem in the eyes of the people of Kosala. Only then will we succeed in ousting him and restoring Kosala's glory across Jambudvipa." He paused, his gaze intense as it shifted from face to face. "Isn't that what true patriots like us want, the glory of Kosala?"

Sudhanva looked on with satisfaction as all three heads rocked in emphatic nods. Relief flowed through him, knowing this battle was won, at least for now, and that the rebellion was back on track. His heart was set on becoming king of Kosala, and he was prepared to go to great lengths to sit on the throne of the Ikshvakus.

Fog from the Sarayu had laid siege to the Sanctum of the Fire, creeping over the walls, flooding the Sanctum's grounds and pressing into the spaces between buildings in an endless surge. The wind had little impact on the fog, which eddied with each gust before settling into a slow drift; only the fires burning in the sentries' posts flickered and flared in the draught, nearly going out at times. Not a soul was about, so the sentries were the only ones to observe their king part the curtain of fog and head for the *homagriha*, a small bauble of light illuminating his path through the gloom.

Bharat made his way to the same hall where he had been received by rishi Surochi in the earlier visits to the Sanctum. He was met by one of the apprentice rishis who ushered him in and seated him before a small brazier which had a fire going. Bharat was left by himself, and it was a good while before the clack of *padukas* were heard approaching the hall and Surochi's bulky figure filled the doorway, swaddled in a *pravara*.

"Rajan," the middle-aged rishi joined his hands in a *pranaam*. "Pardon me for making you wait for so long. I wasn't expecting a visit at this time of the night."

"My apologies for coming unannounced at such a late hour," said Bharat in reply. "It's kind of you to have agreed to see me, munivar."

Surochi lowered himself opposite the king and stretched his hands towards the fire. "I am sure you have good reason to come at this time," he said, eyeing the king keenly. "How can I be of service, rajan?"

It took a moment for Bharat to reply. "The magic... something's wrong with it."

A frown formed on Surochi's brow. What had been said was not a question. It wasn't an astute observation either. Everyone knew something was the matter with the magic; they had known it for the last couple of months, at least. The issue had been raised in court, the rishis had been asked about it, and it had become a frequent point of discussion among people. There was something obviously wrong, so the rishi didn't quite know how to respond to the king's statement. All he did was nod in agreement and let Bharat fill the silence.

"And we don't know what is weakening the magic?" the king asked.

Surochi felt a twinge of unease run through him. The king hadn't come this far this late at night only to make general enquiries about the depletion of magic in Ayodhya. The rishi instinctively understood there was some other agenda on Bharat's mind...

"We don't know," he admitted, "but we are doing all we can to rebuild the magic."

"I don't doubt that," Bharat replied, but he showed no signs of being reassured by what he had heard. He just continued sitting there, a meditative look on his face. There was definitely more to this visit, Surochi surmised, even as the silence in the room grew awkward and stifling.

The rishi cleared his throat. "If something's on your mind, please speak freely, rajan," he urged.

Bharat thought for a moment and nodded. "I wish to perform the *agnimanasa*," he said, locking his eyes with Surochi's.

The rishi didn't reply immediately. Instead, he sat on the other side of the brazier with his hands on his lap, studying the king minutely. At last, drawing a deep breath, he shook his head.

"No."

Bharat stared. "What do you mean by no? Magic holds everything together, and we have to get the magic back over Ayodhya. I can perform the *agnimanasa* again and —"

"You can't perform the *agnimanasa homa*."

"Why not?"

"Because I won't let you, rajan."

Bharat's eyes narrowed in displeasure. "What do you mean you won't let me?"

Surochi heaved a tired sigh. "You can't do the *agnimanasa* again, rajan," he said patiently. "It is too dangerous."

"But it's *not* dangerous," Bharat exclaimed. He threw his hands wide open. "Look at me. I did the *homa* five months ago, and here I am. Nothing's happened to me —"

"Rajan, you nearly lost the yuvaraja," the rishi reminded the king urgently.

"Taksha?" Bharat threw his head back and chuckled. "The *vaidyas* say it was just a seizure."

"But you nearly lost him —"

"But he is still here with me," the raja was adamant. "You said I would lose something precious when I performed the *agnimanasa*, something dear to me. But look at me," Bharat straightened his back so he was fully upright. "*Look at me.* What have I lost? Nothing. Isn't Taksha still with me? You were wrong about the *agnimanasa.* We have nothing to fear —"

"The *agnimanasa* will claim its price —"

"What if you are wrong about the *homa*?"

"I know we are right, and I cannot allow you to put the lives of those close to you at risk —"

"It is not for you to decide whose lives are at risk —"

"And it is not for you to decide which lives *you* can put in danger… rajan."

The two men glared at one another, hot in the face and a little out of breath.

"Munivar," Bharat spoke at last, tempering his voice and speaking in a gentler, more reasonable tone. "I don't mean to contradict you, but it has been close to six months since I performed the *agnimanasa.* Nothing has happened to Taksha, and I haven't lost anyone. It is possible that the *homa* is perfectly harmless —"

"Rajan," Surochi interrupted, though his pitch too had dropped. "I have said it before, and I am saying it again… The *agnimanasa* will claim its price. Perform the *agnimanasa* again, and you will put *one more* life on the line." The rishi held Bharat's gaze. "You can't just sacrifice those dear to you like this, rajan. And where is the end to this? Every time the magic drops, you can't do an *agnimanasa* that ends up risking someone else's life. No, rajan, *I will not let you do it.*"

Bharat felt something inside him sink as he looked away in despair. On his way to the Sanctum, he had been certain about doing what needed to be done for Kosala's subjects. He had expected the rishis to cooperate — maybe grudgingly

— and cede to his wishes, but instead, here he was being stonewalled by Surochi…

"Look at what's happening in Kosala," the king spread his hands in helplessness in another bid to convince the rishi. "Look at this cold. People are dying, farmers aren't being able to cultivate their crops, and there are prospects of food shortages. Meanwhile, people continue to disappear from all over the kingdom, while the magic is diminishing again. And mahamuni Vashishtha… he had shown an improvement after the last *agnimanasa*, but his condition has slipped since." The raja leaned forward to stare at Surochi earnestly. "Don't you see it? Things had improved after the *agnimanasa*. Everything had got better. The rain came, the mahamuni's condition had improved, the magic had returned. The *agnimanasa* fixed everything."

"It almost took the yuvaraja," the rishi insisted flatly.

"Almost, but it *didn't*," Bharat flailed his hands in exasperation. He paused to recalibrate. "I can make things better for Kosala, for my people, for mahamuni Vashishtha. Let me do the *homa*. I owe it to my people."

"Not by playing with the lives of those dear to you," Surochi maintained. "You can't trade with human lives like this, rajan."

"Let me take that call."

The rishi shook his head, refusing to budge an inch.

Bharat's face darkened and his jaw went rigid. "You forget I'm your king," he said softly. "The rishis have to do as I command."

Surochi stared back levelly. "In that case, you will have to issue the order officially in court."

The young raja glared at the rishi, knowing he had been

outsmarted. Were he to issue the orders officially, everyone would know that he was performing the *agnimanasa*, and it could no longer be kept secret, particularly from the members of the royal household. And if they came to know that he was performing the *homa*, they would step in to prevent him, and he would be powerless to go against them.

"Where was all this righteous posturing when you helped me perform the *agnimanasa* the last time?" the king's lips twisted in a scornful smile. "The thought of those dear to me who would be put at risk by the *homa* didn't seem to affect you back then."

"It was a mistake," Surochi admitted. "We shouldn't have given in to you. We won't make the same blunder again."

The stalemate stretched between the men, the silence awkward and unyielding. Even the wind seemed to have ceased blowing to eavesdrop on the outcome of this exchange.

"Kosala and its people need our help and it is in our power, *yours and mine*, to give it to them, but you stand in the way and refuse to assist me," Bharat said bitterly as he gathered his *pravara* around himself and stood up. "It is unfortunate that I have to walk away empty-handed." He joined his palms in a *pranaam*. "Still, I will find a way to achieve what I have set out to do; that is a promise. My salutations, munivar."

Bharat stepped back into the cold, and he was immediately swallowed by the fog and the night.

Simhika couldn't decide whether to feel pleased with her progress or frustrated at the slowness with which things were taking effect.

She sat in the darkness of the mansion, caressing multitudinous shadowy forms, counting the gains she had made and totalling her losses.

In the four months since she had let her shadows loose in the Sanctum — since the soldiers had first worn their dashing new uniforms and the rishis' wives had sought out her wondrous wares — magic had once again dwindled in Ayodhya. The resurgence that had brought on the sudden rain — and made her terribly anxious about the success of her mission here — had died quickly. Now, four months later, everyone in Ayodhya agreed that the magic had sunk to distressing levels. Light globes routinely flickered and went out, doorknobs didn't always respond to touch, and the magic propelling the newer boats on the Sarayu often died without warning so that the vessels bobbed lamely in the river until they were towed to either bank. Even the listening bells that the humans used had lost some of their efficiency, often failing to transmit messages properly. Crucially, there were unconfirmed reports about the magic misfiring during military drills, with a rising number of complaints about weapons failing to respond effectively to mantras. These reports pleased Simhika in particular, assuring her that she was doing the right things to retard Kosala's military capabilities.

The shadows she had unleashed had tainted Ayodhya's sacred fire enough to affect the *rta*, or the cosmic order, bringing an exceptionally harsh winter to Kosala. If the women who worked her looms were to be believed, this was the worst winter ever in the kingdom's history, the cold already having claimed more than a handful of lives even as crop cultivation suffered, creating pressure on food stocks and supplies.

The shadows had also had a more direct impact on those who had come under their influence. Disagreements had sprung up between the rishis' wives over the allocation of responsibilities, and the war of words had escalated into a spat, with one of the wives accusing the husband of another of laziness and dereliction. Their quarrel had been brought under control, and the issue appeared to have been resolved amicably, but the fissures were there to be exploited. Similarly, there had been trouble at the Sanctum garrison, with some soldiers leading a protest against the garrison's administration. No one knew what had triggered the confrontation; some said it had to do with the quality of food that was being served, while others ascribed the root of the trouble to the shortage of blankets, with soldiers alleging that the garrison's administrators were selling blankets meant for them to the general public for a profit. Whatever the reason, tensions within the Sanctum garrison were heartening news to Simhika.

What the sorceress found unsatisfactory was the speed at which the decay was setting in at the Sanctum. The shadows that beset the Sanctum were many in number and of a virulent type, but the fire in the *homagriha* had proved pure enough to hold out against their corrosiveness. And to make things harder for her, the rishis who tended the fire seemed impervious to the shadows. Sure, their wives had exchanged heated words, but the rishis themselves appeared incorruptible and well beyond her reach. Which explained why the quarrel among their wives and the unrest at the garrison hadn't flared up, and had been so easily contained. The rishis, Simhika realized, were keeping her shadows at bay, stopping them from tarnishing the fire. She had to find a way of neutralizing them. They were the ones tending the fire, so once they were corrupted, the fire would lose its purity and lustre.

Only then would Ayodhya's foundations begin to crumble.

On the positive side, all signs of resistance from Nandana at the bottom of the well had ceased. She had asked the shadows to keep a watch over the girl, and it had been two months since the shadows had told her the girl had stopped fighting for her life. Two months since Nandana had breathed her last. The girl had been resolute, it had to be said. With her gone, the sorceress had one less thing to worry about.

But on the other hand, she had failed to make any inroads into the palace. Simhika had gambled on breaching the palace by charming Rani Kaikeyi, but Dashratha's youngest queen had proved to be quite the opposite of what the sorceress had expected and hoped for. Kaikeyi had rebuffed the gift that Simhika had sent through Dileepa, and though the rakshasi didn't know if that had to do with the *dandapala's* incompetence, she understood that that door into the palace had closed permanently for her.

Her inability to make headway into the palace was preying on the sorceress's mind, and she had begun fearing she would end up letting her lord in Lanka down when, just that morning, one of the women who worked for her had said something that had caught her attention. The women had been comparing weaving techniques when one of them spoke of a unique style from Videha that she quite liked, adding that she had heard that the raja's queen, who hailed from that region, was adept at weaving fabrics in that style.

"You mean Rani Mandavi?" Simhika had asked, her ears perking up. "She knows weaving?"

"Yes. The rani is a skilled weaver. Even our raja sometimes wears garments woven by her."

Mandavi. Wife of Ayodhya's last remaining *mahayoddha* and king. A weaver by passion.

It had been over a year since she had set foot in Ayodhya, but only now was she getting to hear what she should have learned at the very start, Simhika thought ruefully. There was so much she could have done differently with this information, homing in earlier on the palace and the king, springing her shadows sooner on the royal household to widen the divisions between its members… Had she only known a year, even six months ago…

It still wasn't too late, the sorceress said to herself, smiling in the dark. *Even our raja sometimes wears garments woven by her*. Sensing her excitement, the shadowy forms wriggled in delight, coiling around her in a crush of mindless ecstasy.

mandavimandavimandavimandavimandavi

Yes, Mandavi, Simhika whispered to the forms.

Mandavi was a far better target than any to get to Bharat. And she was the perfect tool to bring to an end the reign of the Ikshvakus and the humans over Kosala, and help establish the rule of the rakshasas over Jambudvipa.

seven

THE GANDHARAN ARMY WAS ENCAMPED ACROSS THE VITASTA, two miles to the west of Mithuna. The camp sprawled across the river plain in full view of the defenders of the River Kingdoms, Gandhara's flaming-torch banners fluttering in the sharp breeze atop tents and fancy pavilions, cooking fires sending smoke into the cold, cloudless sky, soldiers armed with *kuntas* practising battle manoeuvres, horses being fed and exercised, and exotic war drums beating erratic tattoos that echoed eerily every time the wind changed direction.

The Gandharan army had been encamped across the Vitasta for six whole days now, occupying the riverbank in plain sight and making no effort to conceal its activities — yet showing no real intent to mount an attack on its intended target.

The Gandharan encampment just sat sunning itself idly across Mithuna.

Exactly like the other two Gandharan camps located further to the north across the Vitasta, one opposite the river market of Saumudri half a day's ride away, the other near the forested slopes of Manglapuri.

Three Gandharan encampments idling in the sun for six days instead of fording the Vitasta and launching their assault on the River Kingdoms.

"What are they up to?" Ambareesha wondered aloud, not for the first time, as he squinted against the glare of the midday sun to peer at the camp in the distance. "Why haven't they made a move so far? What is keeping them?" He turned to Yuddhajeet, who sat astride his new tan mount. "Do you think they are short of boats, and that's what is holding them back?" The giant returned to scrutinizing the far bank. "I haven't seen a single boat anywhere in the camp, unless they're being kept hidden, though I'm not sure what purpose that would serve."

The prince of Kekeya shook his head. "I doubt it has anything to do with boats. Why come this far and reveal yourself if you don't have boats to make a crossing? Though you're right about boats not being visible." A frown creased Yuddhajeet's face. "There's something here that we are missing."

Ambareesha and Devadatta's wedding a fortnight ago had gone in a blur as the River Kingdoms had scrambled to put up a defence against the Gandharan invasion. Yuddhajeet had ridden back to Rajagriha to ready the Kekeyan army for battle, and days later, Bahlika warriors had arrived to bolster defences along the Vitasta. Kekeyan scouts were dispatched to assess enemy troop movements, and they had soon confirmed that a Gandhara-Kamboja force was indeed crossing the mountains and heading eastward. Sailusha, Ambareesha, Abhisarika and the other Bahlika chieftains had joined the battlefront a week ago, and strategies were still being drawn to defend Mithuna, when scouts had brought news of the Gandharan army being divided into three parts, each part heading for a different spot along the Vitasta —

one towards Manglapuri, one towards Saumudri, and one keeping a straight path for Mithuna.

"Remember how the last time I'd said they might attempt crossing the river at multiple points," said Ambareesha. "It's a more effective strategy."

"Not that they appear to be in any hurry to cross over," Yuddhajeet observed drily. "But you're right." He gave it some more thought. "I think the rout from last time has forced them to relook at their strategy and try something different."

"That's another thing I don't quite get," said Ambareesha. "They got roundly beaten by us just six months ago. *Thrashed* is the right word. One would think anyone would take some time to regroup and recalibrate their plans. Reinforce their army, let memories of the defeat fade, boost morale, wait for the wounds to heal properly. Also, the enemy that has beaten you is on a high, charged with victory, glowing with triumph. Why would you engage with them again so soon? Conventional wisdom says you should go easy and not rush back into battle, but here they are. It doesn't make sense."

"It doesn't," Yuddhajeet agreed, looking solemn. "Like I said before, things just don't add up."

Giving a nod, Ambareesha craned his neck to look beyond Yuddhajeet, and the prince followed the gaze to a small hillock that rose a mile or so behind the little town. A man sat on horseback, silhouetted against the sky at the top of the hill, the last lookout in the line posted between here and Saumudri and Manglapuri. It had been decided that should any of the Gandharan divisions make a threatening move, signals would be relayed to the other locations using flags and drums, intimating everyone about the change in status.

Nearly three hundred lookouts were part of this chain, but so far, none of them had had to beat their drums or raise their flags to alert the others about Gandharan troop movements.

"I hope the fellow's not fallen asleep," Ambareesha nodded in the direction of the lookout and gave a good-natured grin.

"At the rate they're going, the Gandharans are guaranteed to put *all* of us to sleep," Yuddhajeet said with a snort. "Perhaps that is going to be their strategy this time," he added with a chuckle.

As Ambareesha threw his head back and laughed, the prince looked back over the river. "What I'd give to have a spy in that camp, figuring out what's going on inside those dumb Gandharan heads," he said wistfully.

"Hmm..." Ambareesha said, knowing they couldn't afford sending a spy or a scout anywhere near the enemy encampment without him being seen by Gandharan sentries. With a distracted shake of his head, the giant grunted, "Isn't it time for lunch yet? I'm getting hungry."

Yuddhajeet looked up at the sun and shook his head. "An hour to go, at least."

With a disheartened scowl, Ambareesha returned to observing the Gandharan camp. A stillness settled around them, with nothing but the sound of the wind and the muted gurgle of the Vitasta in their ears. Then, Ambareesha suddenly turned to Yuddhajeet. "Did you know that Devadatta is a wonderful cook?" he asked brightly.

"So it is *her* cooking that you've been thinking about?" the prince laughed. "No wonder you're hungry."

"She is fantastic with food. Had you not left the wedding in a rush, we'd have invited you over for dinner. She would have liked that."

"I didn't have a choice. I had to be back here to prepare the troops."

"I know."

They sat for a moment in silence.

"I feel bad that you had to come here instead of being with Devadatta," Yuddhajeet said at last.

"War is never nice that way. Absolutely no sense of occasion," the giant jested. "But it's alright. She's not far from here, and she has the pleasant company of Abhisarika."

"While you are stuck with me," Yuddhajeet said, and both men roared with laughter.

Once the Gandharan strategy of crossing the Vitasta at three different points had become plain, Sailusha had proposed that the Kekeyans undertake the defence of Mithuna with the assistance of Ambareesha and his band of warriors. Meanwhile, the Bahlikas under Sailusha and the rest of the chieftains would protect Saumudri and Manglapuri. Despite being afflicted by an old backache that was threatening to flare up, Sailusha had taken on the responsibility of leading Saumudri's defence, though he had asked Abhisarika to come with him so that she could attend to him should the condition worsen.

"Devadatta insisted on coming here with you?" the prince asked. Seeing the giant nod, he said, "Abhisarika is a medicine woman. She is also a warrior. Does Devadatta have…" he paused, not knowing how to put this.

"…does she have any special skills and talents?" Ambareesha said helpfully. "Other than being a great cook, none at all. So, you may rightly wonder what she is doing here in the battle zone." He chuckled in amusement. "She wants to learn healing. She wants to learn to wield the sword." He grinned at Yuddhajeet. "She wants to be everything that Abhisarika already is."

"She's got an excellent role model," the prince of Kekeya offered.

"Mm-hmm," the Bahlika agreed. Shooting Yuddhajeet a quizzical look, he said, "I can tell that *you* are quite in awe of Abhisarika yourself."

The prince shrugged and nodded.

"Why?"

Yuddhajeet gave it a moment's thought. "Because power neither impresses nor intimidates her. Because despite her many talents, she has no vanity. And because she doesn't crave attention. I have hardly met a person as self-assured as your cousin."

Ambareesha smiled to show he was in agreement, but before he could say anything, there came from somewhere behind the sound of feet pounding the earth. Both men turned to see a pair of Kekeyan soldiers dash between two buildings, swords waving in their hands. At the same time, a shout arose from some distance to the left, sharp in the day's stillness and laden with threat.

"Quick, grab them."

"Drop your swords," another voice called from behind a dwelling to the right.

Drawing their own *karapalas* free, Yuddhajeet and Ambareesha wheeled their mounts around. They rode hard in the direction of the shouts, confused and concerned by the suddenness with which the situation was developing around them. They rounded a corner, their horses kicking dust and rubble into the air. They sat low in their saddles with swords ready to smite, their eyes watchful, expecting to come upon their men locked in a skirmish with Gandharan troops who had somehow crossed the river and launched a stealth attack on Mithuna…

But the sight that greeted Yuddhajeet and Ambareesha was so unforeseen that their eyes opened wide in shock and surprise as they reined in their mounts, bringing the beasts to a skidding halt.

In an open space between a house, a storeroom and a foundry, a group of Kekeyan soldiers had besieged a dozen of Ambareesha's men, *shuls* pointed at the Bahlikas even as the Bahlikas held up their swords in defence. Both sets of warriors glared at each other, watching for the slightest hint of violence in the other and ready to counterattack.

"What is all this?" Yuddhajeet roared. Darting a glance at Ambareesha, he shouted to his men, "Lower your spears."

The Kekeyan soldiers shuffled and looked at one another. *Shuls* waved uncertainly, but the tips stayed up, rooting the Bahlikas to the spot.

"Didn't you hear me?" Yuddhajeet thundered. "Put those *shuls* down."

"Yuvaraja," a senior Kekeyan soldier spoke up from the crowd, "these men can't be trusted."

Yuddhajeet shot another glance at Ambareesha, whose face was growing dark with rage. "What do you mean?" the prince asked, realizing he had to resolve the situation quickly. "The Bahlikas are our allies."

"A man from one of the nearby villages is here, yuvaraja," the soldiers said. "He has something important to say." The soldier looked around him searchingly. "Bring the man to the yuvaraja," he commanded.

There was a scurry of feet, and Yuddhajeet turned to see two Kekeyan soldiers escort a civilian from the back. The man was old, a patched *pravara* hanging over his thin shoulders. He bowed to the prince, wrinkled hands joined in a *pranaam*.

"You have something to say," Yuddhajeet said, returning the salutation.

"Yuvaraja…" the man's eyes flicked uncertainly to Ambareesha and back, "…word coming from the north has it that the Gandharan army has crossed the Vitasta at Saumudri, and perhaps even at Manglapuri, and that it is moving in the direction of Sakala and Rajagriha."

A sharp look passed between Yuddhajeet and Ambareesha.

"Where did you hear this?" the prince asked. "Who's saying this?"

"People, yuvaraja," the man replied.

"They're just rumours."

"Everyone is talking about it. The news is everywhere," the man insisted. "The crossing is said to have occurred early this morning."

Yuddhajeet shook his head as he turned to look first towards the Gandharan encampment across the river, then up at the man on the hillock. "It can't be true. Had any crossings been attempted, we'd have heard about the battle. News would have come from Saumudri and Manglapuri via the lookouts that chief Sailusha has posted."

"Tell the yuvaraja everything," the Kekeyan soldier who had spoken earlier said to the old man.

The man nodded and addressed Yuddhajeet again. "There were no battles anywhere, yuvaraja." Seeing the prince stare blankly, he added, "News is that the Gandharan army just crossed over. The Bahlikas did nothing to stop them."

"That is a lie," Ambareesha roared. He pointed his *karapala* at the informant. "*You* lie."

The man flinched a little at the sight of the sword, then drew himself erect. "I teach the children of the neighbouring hamlets how to read, and I serve god by singing his praise at the temple. I have no reason to lie," he said, looking the Bahlika giant in the eye.

Ambareesha's expression remained surly, but he lowered the *karapala*.

Yuddhajeet looked at the man, his face clouding with doubt. "What else did you hear about the crossing?" he asked. "Tell me everything."

The man cleared his throat. "It is being said that chief Sailusha welcomed the Gandharan raya and the commander of the Kambojas into Saumudri. No swords were drawn and no blood was shed, except that of the local militiamen who tried to stop the Gandharan advance. Some twenty of them were slaughtered and hanged from trees by Gandharan soldiers as the Bahlikas stood by and watched."

The silence was so stark, Yuddhajeet could hear the sound of his own breathing.

The old man kept his eyes averted from Ambareesha's severe gaze. "Yuvaraja, it is the Bahlikas who let the invading army come into the River Kingdoms."

At the sound of footsteps on the wooden staircase outside, Abhisarika hurriedly wiped her tears and leaped to her feet. Taking three long strides, she flung herself against the door and resumed banging on it with her fists.

"Open the door," she shouted, straining against the wood. "Open it. Let me out."

She paused to listen. There was no sound from outside.

"Let me out," she shouted even louder, banging the door hard with all her might. "Right now."

"Stop," Sailusha's voice rumbled from the other side, part order, part plea. "Stop, my child."

Hearing the rattle of a key in the lock, Abhisarika stepped back, and with a sliding of bolts, the door swung open to reveal the Bahlika chieftain's large frame filling the doorway. Abhisarika took another step back as her father slipped into the cramped storeroom, its ceiling so low that Sailusha was forced to stoop to keep his head from bumping against it. He cast a glance around the dusty space before surveying his daughter with eyes that were tired and apologetic, even as she stared back at him in defiance.

"What is the meaning of this?" she demanded.

"I didn't mean to keep you here locked like this, my child," Sailusha began. "All I meant —"

"But you *did* put me here," Abhisarika interrupted hotly.

"I didn't mean you any harm," the old man tried reasoning with her once again. "I only wanted to keep you out of harm's way —"

"No, you wanted to keep me from coming *in* your way," Abhisarika cut in. "Because you knew I would never have approved —"

"Abhisarika… please…" Sailusha took a step towards his daughter. "Listen to me —"

"No," the daughter cried, holding one hand up and stepping back to put distance between them. Pinning her father with a frosty glare, she asked, "Why did you stab the River Kingdoms in the back?"

Instead of answering, Sailusha stared at his daughter in silence. His eyes softened suddenly and he looked concerned. "Have you been crying, my child?" he asked.

"Why do *you* care?" Abhisarika snapped back, fighting against the pricking of tears in her eyes. She didn't want to cry and come across as being weak, but she was so furious she wasn't certain she could hold the tears back either. "You are not answering me. Why this betrayal of the River Kingdoms?"

Awkward and uncomfortable standing bent, Sailusha scouted around for a place to sit. His gaze settled on a rough wooden trunk in one corner, layered in dust. Drawing it forward and brushing the dirt off with his hand, the chieftain sat down with a grunt. Looking at Abhisarika, he pointed to a *manchika*, but the woman ignored him and remained standing, arms crossed over her chest, waiting for her father to speak in his defence.

"I acted in the best interests of the Bahlikas," Sailusha said with a sigh.

Abhisarika waited for her father to say more, but nothing came. "A betrayal?" she smirked. "In our interest?"

Sailusha nodded, his mind going back to a meeting in the mountains nearly two months ago. It had all begun with a rider who came one night bearing a message from Nagnajit — the raya of Gandhara was desirous of meeting Sailusha. The message stressed that the raya had a proposal that Sailusha would find impossible to turn down. His curiosity piqued, the chieftain had agreed to a rendezvous, and the men had met under the stars over a flagon of blood-red *kapisi madhu*, the likes of which Sailusha had never dreamed of tasting.

"Do you know why I have come all this way from Kapisi to see you?" Nagnajit had asked, his eyes glittering in the firelight. Up in the mountains, winter was already setting in, and the wine warmed the body and freed the tongue. "It is because I have the utmost admiration and respect for you Bahlika warriors."

Sailusha had nodded, knowing more was to come.

"Sadly, the River Kingdoms have admiration for you… but hardly any respect."

Sailusha had sipped his wine and listened.

"Look at the amount of wealth amassed by all three River Kingdoms," Nagnajit had said. "They have grown plump and rich, thanks to the hard work put in by the Bahlikas… who have nothing. Sure, you have money. After all, that is what you work for and rightfully earn. But what is your social status in the River Kingdoms, my friend?"

"For the people of the River Kingdoms, we're mercenaries for hire. That is all we are," Sailusha looked at Abhisarika. "Look at us. We depend on the River Kingdoms for everything. We have no lands of our own, so we are dependent on the River Kingdoms for grazing our cattle. We're dependent on their trade to make money. We are the power that holds up the River Kingdoms, keeping them safe from threats, but if you look at it, we are just slaves here, having nothing to call our own."

"We have honour, father," Abhisarika said cuttingly. "Or at least we *had* it until this morning."

Sailusha's faced turned a shade darker. "Honour?" he glowered. "Let me ask you one thing about this honour that you speak of. When have the people of the River Kingdoms ever acknowledged us for our honour? I can't remember the people of these lands ever inviting the Bahlikas to one of their weddings, or to the celebration of the birth of a child. If honour is such a prized quality, why not? Show me one Bahlika who was welcomed into their homes because our honour makes us worthy of their hospitality?" Seeing Abhisarika avoid his gaze, the chieftain raised his voice in anger. "Answer me."

The flagon of *kapisi madhu* was almost over and the fire was burning low when Nagnajit made his intentions clear to Sailusha. "Join my side," he had said. "Join my side, and I will make you a deal that the River Kingdoms will never offer you."

"What can you offer me that they can't, raya?"

"I promise to make you raja of the River Kingdoms."

The stars had stopped in their orbits to look down on Sailusha, the wind had paused in the trees to eavesdrop. The night spun around Sailusha, his breath lodged in his chest in disbelief.

"Convince the other Bahlika chiefs to cross sides and help me conquer the River Kingdoms. In return, I will make you the raja," Nagnajit had sworn. "You will rule the River Kingdoms; their coffers will be at your disposal. All I expect is a nominal tribute sent to Kapisi. Keep the rest, and rule that rich and fertile land. And yes, you will have the armies of Gandhara and Kamboja as your allies in any military conquest you may wish to undertake." The raya emptied the flagon into their jars, measuring out the wine carefully so the portions were identical. "You and I will be equals," he had said, lifting his jar and smiling.

"You agreed to side with Nagnajit because he promised to make you king?" Abhisarika stared at her father.

"I agreed because he treated me as an equal, which is more than the River Kingdoms ever did."

"You think he has made you his equal," Abhisarika's tone dripped with scorn, "but the truth is that he has convinced you to become a vassal of Gandhara. You are still a slave, only now you have a new master."

Sailusha stroked his big, white moustache as he considered his daughter. "No," he said at last. "I am no vassal of Gandhara. Nagnajit made me another offer that guaranteed I didn't end up as one."

Abhisarika's eyes narrowed suspiciously. "What offer?"

The raya of Gandhara had looked at Sailusha over the rim of his jar. "To show my readiness to treat you as an equal, I seek permission to marry your daughter," he had said. "See, we are now of the same status. That is the degree of my commitment."

"Don't tell me you agreed, father," Abhisarika looked aghast. "You didn't…"

"I did, Abhisarika. I agreed for *you*."

Abhisarika stared at her father in shock.

"I can't bear to see you throw away your youth in widowhood," Sailusha ran his fingers through his hair in despair. "Which parent can, tell me. And this was a king asking for your hand. Don't forget that no king of the River Kingdoms has ever sought your hand in marriage. I said yes to the raya because I want the best for you."

"You could have asked me for an opinion," Abhisarika said icily. "But you didn't because you were afraid I would say no."

"I want the best for you —"

"If this were really about me," Abhisarika shook her head vehemently, "you wouldn't have done things so sneakily. This is about your desire to become a raja. Don't make this about me." Her fists rolled into tight balls, she turned to face her father squarely. "I refuse to be a pawn in your game. I will not marry Nagnajit."

Sailusha looked at his daughter sharply. "The choice is out of your hands. I have given Nagnajit my word."

"Your word isn't so hard to break, father," Abhisarika seethed. "You've done it once already."

Sailusha rose from the trunk with a heavy grunt, his knees popping at the effort. "The matter's settled," he said. "The wedding is tonight." He stretched one hand towards Abhisarika. "Come, let us go."

The woman's nostrils flared in anger. "I will never submit to marrying Nagnajit," she said.

Sailusha's shoulders drooped as his face clouded in frustration. Still reaching for his daughter's hand, he said, "You *will* marry Nagnajit."

"No."

The chief shook his head regretfully. "You will marry him if you want to see Smara again."

Abhisarika went pale as her knees wobbled. "What…?" she cried. "Where is Smara?"

"She is here with us, and she is safe."

"Smara is in Saumudri? You had her brought here…" Abhisarika's voice quivered as she stared at her father in disbelief. "You brought her here so you could negotiate with me…" she stopped. "I want to see her," she demanded.

"You will… after the wedding." Sailusha reached his hand out again. "Come."

Fresh tears of rage and helplessness smarted in Abhisarika's eyes. "She is your granddaughter and you have made a *hostage* of her?" she shouted in distress, pressing both hands to her sides, refusing to take Sailusha's hand, and to keep him from seeing them tremble in fear and outrage. "What kind of a man have you become, father?"

Without a word, the chieftain turned and walked out of the room, shutting the door hard behind him. Hearing the lock turn and the footsteps recede down the stairs, Abhisarika slumped to the ground and wept in defeat.

Simhika felt a shiver of excitement run through her as she took in her surroundings in disbelief.

She was inside the palace of Ayodhya, the seat of the Ikshvakus, rulers of Kosala for centuries.

The hall she had been ushered into was moderately large, its floors made of *sala* dark with age. Thick pillars carved with celestial figurines lined the room's sides, while the space at the centre was tastefully appointed with ornate *sayyasanas* and *manchikas* for seating and reclining. Brass braziers burned here and there, lending heat to an otherwise draughty space designed for warm and lengthy summers. The walls were hung with paintings of old Ikshvaku kings, Dashratha's portrait at the centre to Simhika's right. The picture portrayed the dead king in middle age, when he had been at his prime, the feared unifier of Kosala and champion of the wars against the rakshasas. The place beside Dashratha's painting was vacant and reserved for Kosala's next king, and from what Simhika had heard, Bharat had declined to have his portrait made, insisting that Rama's picture would grace the spot when he became king. The sorceress smiled inwardly at the thought of how disappointed Bharat was going to be — she had lied and cheated her way here to make sure that no Ikshvaku king's portrait ever hung on these walls.

Deciding to exploit Mandavi's proximity to Bharat was one thing, but getting an audience with the queen had proved to be quite a challenge. Simhika had pinned her hopes on someone or the other knowing Mandavi well enough to make an introduction, but no one she had cultivated a friendship with in Ayodhya seemed to be acquainted with the queen, directly or indirectly. Not being from Kosala — and being reserved by nature — Mandavi hardly had a single close friend in the city and spent almost all of her time within the palace. Seeing she was making no headway by depending on others, and running out of time and patience, the sorceress had taken matters into her own hands and had shown up at the palace uninvited, asking to see the queen. Luckily enough, Ma Parnalata's reputation had preceded her, so instead of turning her away, the guards had invited her to wait while they sent Mandavi a message, announcing the guest. To Simhika's relief, the queen had agreed to grant an audience, and so here she was, inside the palace —

"Why haven't you taken a seat?"

Simhika jumped and turned in the direction of the voice, which had come from her left. For the first time, she noticed a small door hidden in a recess and saw a woman step out of the shadows. The woman had a slight build and middling looks, but her eyes were striking in their depth and the kindness reflected in them. The sorceress recognized Mandavi from the consecration of the *homagriha* and hurriedly joined her hands in a *pranaam*.

"Greetings, rani," she said.

"I didn't mean to startle you," the queen said, returning the *pranaam*.

"No… it's just that I wasn't expecting you to come through a side door," the sorceress said.

She had been expecting an impressive entry through one of the main doors to the hall. She had been expecting guards and a bevy of handmaids in attendance. She had been expecting fanfare. What she hadn't been expecting, what she found hard to believe despite having taken a chance coming here, was the queen coming out to meet her just like that.

"You are Ma Parnalata?" Mandavi asked, gesturing towards a *sayyasana*.

"I am Parnalata," the sorceress replied as she sat down. "Ma is something I was called by my… my niece. She was… she… disappeared."

"Oh," the queen looked dismayed.

"Yes," Simhika nodded, remembering to inject a histrionic tremble into her voice and call forth a tear or two. "My poor little Nandana…" she touched a finger to one eye and sniffled. "Gone."

"Don't worry, she will be back," Mandavi said earnestly, sitting forward in her seat. "All those who go are returning. Look at Siripala, the palace ostler. He is back. They all come back."

"That's the one hope that keeps me going," the sorceress nodded. Then, blinking away the tears and clearing her throat, she sat straight. "Anyway, the name Ma just stuck. Now everyone calls me that."

"So will I then," Mandavi smiled. Then, her eyes brightened as a thought occurred to her. "*You* designed those uniforms for the Sanctum garrison," she said appreciatively.

"A small attempt at doing something for the brave men who protect our king and our kingdom," Simhika bowed humbly.

"Your designs are striking," the queen insisted. After a pause, she asked, "Is there something I can do for you?"

"I am… I have been meaning to pay my respects to the palace ever since I came to Ayodhya a year ago, but so far, I haven't been able to pay you a visit for some reason or the other. I thought it was time I corrected that, so I came…" Simhika extended her hands, which held a bundle, in Mandavi's direction, "Please accept this. It's a small token of my respect, woven with my own hands…"

"Thank you, but you needn't have," the queen said, accepting the gift. She opened the bundle and out spilled a *pravara* made of silk, cobalt blue in colour, lustrous as the ocean and soft as petals to the touch. "This is simply gorgeous," Mandavi gasped in wonder, running a hand over the fabric. "On second thoughts, I am happy you brought this," she laughed.

"It is my pleasure," Simhika replied. It was, indeed. She was delighted at the queen's response. Oh, she should have done this months ago, just come and given Mandavi her present with some specially crafted black magic infused into its weave. "Only someone truly versed with the craft of weaving can appreciate this. The moment I came to know that you also wove, I decided this one was for you."

"I am a weaver of limited talent," Mandavi chuckled.

"That isn't what I have heard said about you, rani," Simhika protested. "I am told that you —"

"Mother, I'm hungry."

Simhika turned to see a small boy saunter in, a bamboo toy cart tied to a rope clattering behind him. The boy was dark and sported a mop of curly hair, knotted loosely into a bun at the top of his head. When his eyes, which were identical to those of the queen, alighted on the sorceress, he came to an uncertain halt midway to where his mother sat.

Taksha, the king's son, Simhika thought in a flash, furious at her own carelessness. She should have known the kid would be around; she should have brought something for him too. Another gift to bring Kosala's king to his knees...

"Come, son," Mandavi called. "Look, we have a visitor."

Tugging the toy cart along, Taksha sidled up to his mother. Without taking his eyes off Simhika, he snuggled up to the queen and whispered in her ear. Mandavi nodded.

"Yes, but first, what do you do when you receive a guest at the palace?" she asked, looking into the boy's face.

Taksha thought for a moment, then looked at Simhika again and joined his hands in a *pranaam*.

"Greetings, yuvaraja," said Simhika, beaming with delight. "It is such a joy to see you."

The boy leaned shyly against his mother. Simhika turned to Mandavi with a frown. "So foolish of me, not having thought of bringing the prince something," she said, landing a self-chastising smack to the side of her head. "How could I have forgotten —"

"It's alright," said the queen, interpreting the redness in the sorceress's face as embarrassment. "The boy is fine —"

"No, I should have got him something."

"This *pravara*," Mandavi ran a palm over the shawl that still lay draped across one of her knees, "will be for both of us. Please, this is enough."

Drawn by his mother's words, Taksha's attention turned to the *pravara* for the first time. Struck by the colour and lustre of the fabric, his eyes opened wide in admiration, and a small gasp left his lips. Reaching a hand out, the boy gently fingered the shawl.

Simhika heaved a sigh of satisfaction. This was turning out perfect, better than she'd imagined. Her magic would now work on both mother and son. "You are most kind, rani," she said. "May both of you and the king be blessed." She rose to her feet. "The yuvaraja is hungry. I shall not take any more of your or his time. Grant me your leave."

The sorceress stepped out of the palace with the satisfaction of knowing that her plan was one more step closer to fruition.

It all made perfect sense.

It was Sailusha who had proposed that the Bahlikas guard Manglapuri and Saumudri, while the Kekeyans defended Mithuna. Keeping Kekeyan soldiers together in one place made better sense, he had argued, because men who knew each other well in peace fought for one another in war. It was Sailusha who had volunteered to go to Saumudri, and it was Sailusha who had urged his nephew to stay back in Mithuna with his band of riders to support the Kekeyans. It was Sailusha who had set up the signal chain between Manglapuri and Mithuna, and it was his men manning the chain almost up to Mithuna, where the last two lookouts were Ambareesha's men. Sailusha had organized the entire defence of the three river markets, and everyone had agreed with him because everything had sounded like a good idea.

What Sailusha had really achieved was lulling the Kekeyans into believing the River Kingdoms were safe under the protection of the Bahlika army while he paved the way for the Gandharans to enter unchallenged. Not once had a doubt crossed Yuddhajeet's mind about where Sailusha's loyalties lay, not once had he questioned the chieftain's motives. And that's what hurt the most. The sense of having one's trust ripped to shreds, the feeling of being horribly, cruelly betrayed.

"How is it possible that you didn't know any of this was happening?" the prince asked bitterly. "He is your uncle, and it is plain that the other chieftains were in on the plot."

"I *didn't* know," said Ambareesha adamantly, looking grim and unhappy. "They were good at keeping things to themselves, and I had no reason to suspect anything."

Yuddhajeet glared at the Gandharan camp across Mithuna, slouching in the afternoon sunshine. The prince could almost feel a hundred pairs of amused eyes looking back at him over the river, laughing at him for having fallen for their ruse, for having waited here, strong and resolute and prepared for war, while the Gandharans crossed at Saumudri and Manglapuri without breaking into a sweat. The camp's singular purpose had been to serve as a decoy, limiting the attention of the Kekeyans to Mithuna and keeping them from looking elsewhere.

A fierce but unwise urge to cross the Vitasta and attack the encampment took hold of the prince. They could storm the camp and destroy it, he thought, they could slaughter every enemy soldier they laid eyes upon, they could murder the Gandharans to the last man in revenge, a punishment for what the Gandharans had done…

"Issue orders to withdraw," he said to one of his deputies.

"Withdraw, yuvaraja?" the man looked puzzled. "We are abandoning Mithuna?"

"Yes. Make sure no one gets left behind by accident."

"But if we leave, the Gandharans will take the town," the deputy frowned, nodding at the camp across the river.

"All the reports we have received point to the Gandharan and Kambojan troops moving towards Sakala and Rajagriha," said Yuddhajeet. "We must fortify Rajagriha. By staying here, we'll be spreading ourselves thin and Rajagriha will fall. We can't save Mithuna, but we definitely must save Rajagriha."

With a nod to show he had understood, the deputy left to execute the prince's orders.

"I wish I could accompany you to Rajagriha, but I must go to Saumudri to make sure Devadatta is alright," said Ambareesha.

"Why wouldn't she be?" Yuddhajeet asked in an acid tone. "I don't see how the Bahlikas could be in any sort of danger from the Gandharans. Not after everything their chief has done to assist the enemy."

Ambareesha's eyes narrowed at the slight. "Still, I must know she is safe," he said gruffly.

Yuddhajeet turned to observe Ambareesha's men, who sat astride their horses, all set to depart. The men watched the Kekeyan soldiers, who stared right back at them in mistrust. A chill wind had begun blowing, so the sun was no longer as warm on the skin.

"Your leaving for Saumudri would be very… *convenient*," said the prince.

"What do you mean?" the Bahlika giant asked.

"Sailusha lets the Gandharan army in at Saumudri and Manglapuri. You and your men just ride away from Mithuna to join them the moment the invasion is complete."

Ambareesha stared at the yuvaraja. "Are you saying my men and I had a hand in the betrayal?"

"Anyone would find it hard to trust you."

"But we were *here* with you, weren't we?" the giant said, throwing his hands up in indignation.

"You are here because Sailusha instructed you to be here," Yuddhajeet countered. "Perhaps to keep an eye on us."

"You really believe my men and I knew what my uncle and the other chiefs were up to?"

"I don't know what to believe any longer," said the prince. "And it is not just what I think. My men are bound to have doubts. So is everyone in Rajagriha."

The giant looked away in anger and exasperation. Yuddhajeet went back to staring at the camp across the river.

"My uncle ordered me to stay here because he knows I would never have stood by this betrayal. That I would have opposed him, made things messy for him and for everyone else. Not wanting me to send out an alert or put up a resistance when the Gandharans crossed over, he made sure I wasn't even around in Saumudri to upset his plans."

Yuddhajeet chewed on this for a bit, taking in the preparations to withdraw that were underway all around them. "What about Abhisarika?" he asked.

"What about her?"

"Sailusha didn't ask *her* to stay here," the prince assessed the big man shrewdly. "He took *her* with him, though he left you behind. Why?"

"Are you implying Abhisarika knew of this plot beforehand?" the giant stared in outrage. "No, never. You must be out of your mind to think that's even a possibility."

"Well, I was the one at the receiving end of a betrayal," Yuddhajeet snapped back. "Impossible to know whom I can trust any longer."

"For the last time, my men and I had nothing to do with whatever has happened," Ambareesha persisted. "We are firmly on your side and on the side of the River Kingdoms."

Yuddhajeet drew a deep breath and shook his head. Seeing this, Ambareesha's eyes narrowed.

"It's fine if you don't want to believe me," the giant said finally. "But here's something to think about. Recall the day we first met, when you'd come seeking our help to fight the Gandharans." He paused to let Yuddhajeet picture that meeting. "Now, if you remember," he went on, "reports coming from Kapisi had it that the Gandharan convoy your men had intercepted had been being killed before being sent back to Kapisi, their bodies tied to their horses."

"I remember," said Yuddhajeet.

"When I asked you about that, you swore those were rumours spread by Gandhara. But I wasn't convinced you were telling us the truth about letting the convoy go. That's when you told me something. You said I could choose not to believe you, but whenever the truth came to light, the blood of innocents who die in the Gandharan invasion will be on me... because I chose not to believe you."

The prince of Kekeya said nothing.

"I took your word that day," Ambareesha went on. "I decided to believe you were speaking the truth, that you were not lying to me. That day, I decided to trust you." The giant placed a hand on the yuvaraja's arm. "Today, I implore you to do the same. Trust me when I say my men and I have no part in my uncle's betrayal."

Watching Yuddhajeet wrestle with this, Ambareesha's hopes faded. But when at last the prince turned to him, it was with understanding eyes. "You are right," Yuddhajeet said. "You accepted me in good faith, and I must reciprocate. Trust needs to be repaid with trust. There is no other currency."

The giant's face cleared with a surge of relief and he gave Yuddhajeet's arm a grateful squeeze. With a small smile of his own, the yuvaraja asked, "So, what will you do once you reach Saumudri?"

"I will find Devadatta. Hopefully Abhisarika too." Ambareesha stared vaguely into the distance as he smoothed his beard. "I will find out why my uncle and the chiefs acted the way they have. Then, I will join you in Rajagriha, and we can see what to do about getting rid of the Gandharan army. I will do everything I can to set this right so that the Bahlikas can regain their lost trust and honour."

The yuvaraja inclined his head. "If Sailusha knows you would have objected to this conspiracy, he will be doubly cautious of your return, expecting you to stir up trouble. You might even be a marked man with a bounty on your head. You will have to be very watchful."

"I know. That is why I fear for Devadatta and want to rush to her side," the giant's face creased with worry.

"I understand," said Yuddhajeet. He nodded towards the Bahlikas waiting for their leader. "Go, my friend. God be with you until we meet again."

Ambareesha gripped the prince's hand in farewell. "I will be back. Wait to hear from me."

The giant had barely crossed half the distance to his men when a thunder of hooves announced someone's arrival. Turning to look down the mud road that led away from Mithuna, Yuddhajeet saw a pair of riders reining in their mounts as they entered the town's limits. One was a thickset man wearing a scrubby beard, and the other was a svelte woman in her twenties. Both appeared familiar, and it took the yuvaraja a second to place them. The man was Uchhara, whom he had seen at Ambareesha's wedding, and the woman was…

"*Devadatta!*" Ambareesha's voice echoed with surprise and relief in the afternoon's stillness.

Yuddhajeet took a couple of steps forward, but he was quickly overtaken by the Bahlika giant, who rushed to his wife and helped her dismount, lifting her off the saddle and putting her gently down on the ground. "Devadatta," he said again, wrapping his arms around the girl's shoulders, and Devadatta practically vanished into the embrace. "My love, you are alright," he murmured into her hair.

As Yuddhajeet drew near, Ambareesha eased his hold on Devadatta and turned to the man who had accompanied the girl. "Uchhara," he said in acknowledgement, before looking at his wife. "What's the news from Saumudri?"

Seeing Yuddhajeet approach them, Devadatta offered him a *pranaam*. Up close, the yuvaraja noted the anxiety in the girl's eyes, her bedraggled state proof of a hasty flight from

Saumudri. "Not good, I'm afraid," she said as Ambareesha's men gathered around them. Some of Yuddhajeet's deputies and a handful of Kekeyan soldiers also joined in to listen. "The town has been overrun and the Gandharan army is everywhere, but that's not the worst…" She looked ominously from her husband to Yuddhajeet.

"Abhisarika has been made a prisoner."

"By whom?" Ambareesha cried, as his men drew sharp breaths. Yuddhajeet blinked in shock.

"By her own father," Uchhara grunted.

The giant shot a grim glance towards Yuddhajeet. "Because she stood up to what he has done?"

"Because he wants her to marry the Gandharan raya against her wishes," said Devadatta.

Hearing the girl's words, Yuddhajeet felt as though a chasm had opened beneath his feet.

"She would never give in to his demands," Ambareesha gave his head an adamant shake. "He can't make her wed the raya."

"The choice is out of her hands," Devadatta's shoulders drooped. "The chieftain has threatened to separate her from Smara if she doesn't submit to his wishes. He's had the poor child brought to Saumudri to increase his leverage over Abhisarika."

"He has gone insane…" the giant growled and let out a stream of curses, but Yuddhajeet wasn't listening anymore. Sickened by Devadatta's words, he saw Smara in his mind's eye, the child holding two flowers, one in each hand. He remembered her giving him one. *You can have this*, she had said.

"...mean and selfish of him to force his daughter into a marriage —"

"We will go and rescue them," said Yuddhajeet, stopping Ambareesha's rant in mid-sentence.

The giant turned to stare at the yuvaraja. "Go when?" he asked.

"Now. Right now."

"Yes, we must. The wedding is scheduled for later tonight," Devadatta said urgently.

"We haven't a moment to lose then," Yuddhajeet cried. "We must hurry..."

"We march the army to Saumudri to mount a full-scale attack?" Ambareesha looked confused.

"Not the entire army," said the prince. "An entire army will take forever to get there, and it will give us away to the Gandharans. Speed and surprise are paramount. Just you, me and your men here."

"That's less than twenty of us," the giant frowned.

"That's twenty more than what Sailusha or the Gandharans are expecting," Yuddhajeet replied. "Logically, we ought to be retreating to Rajagriha as quickly as possible. The last thing anyone would anticipate is us riding to Saumudri to rescue Abhisarika and Smara."

Ambareesha thought about it and nodded.

"What about the rest of us, yuvaraja?" one of the Kekeyan deputies asked.

Instead of answering, Yuddhajeet ran an eye over the Bahlikas. "All of you will be recognized," he said, speaking to Ambareesha. "We will need a few faces that Sailusha's men aren't familiar with." He turned to the deputy. "Select five of the best men you can spare to ride with me. The rest of you will withdraw to Rajagriha to reinforce the city's defences. And tell Raja Ashwapati that we will be back soon."

As the deputy left to carry out the orders, Uchhara stepped forward. "I will come with you," he offered.

Ambareesha nodded and turned to Devadatta. "Go to Rajagriha along with the Kekeyan troops and —"

"I'm coming along to rescue Abhisarika and Smara," the girl squared her shoulders in defiance.

"No, it's too dangerous —"

"I came here by myself, didn't I?" Devadatta interrupted. "I can take care of myself —"

"No means no."

"You can't stop me."

"Things can get hairy in Saumudri and I don't want you hindering —"

"Nothing doing," said Devadatta, planting her hands on her hips.

"Listen to me —"

"If I may say something," Yuddhajeet interrupted, "it might be good if she came along."

As Devadatta gave a triumphant nod, Ambareesha whirled to glare at the prince. "She is not a warrior," he growled.

"She is definitely a fighter," Yuddhajeet pointed out. "Abhisarika would be proud of her."

Ambareesha scowled in disapproval, but didn't contradict the prince this time.

"Sailusha and his men expect Devadatta to be in Saumudri," the yuvaraja spoke in a persuading tone. "Let us use that to our advantage."

"What do you mean?" the giant asked. "What exactly are you proposing?"

"I think I know how to rescue Abhisarika and Smara, but Devadatta will have to be in Saumudri with us for the plan to succeed."

Very slowly, she opened her eyes in the dark, under water.

Very slowly, she breathed in, absorbing dissolved oxygen from the fetid water through the pair of rudimentary gills she had sprouted on both sides of her neck. That had been one of her skills. Adapting her body to suit her surroundings.

Simhika should have thought of that before trapping her in the well.

She breathed long and shallow breaths so that the water around her remained undisturbed. She wasn't keen on drawing the attention of the shadows, should any of them be watching.

It was her first breath in over a week, and it felt good. It had come down to that, breathing once a week. It was safest this way. Today though, she would be needing more air. She took another breath, slow and shallow.

Slowly, she looked around her, first moving only her eyeballs, then turning her head in minute fractions to take in her surroundings.

Water everywhere. And shadows everywhere. Black shapes in black water.

The shadows were all asleep, she noted with relief. They had been asleep the last few times she had opened her eyes and looked around. That was good. It meant they were letting their guards down, that they no longer thought she posed a threat.

For a long while, she just lay at the bottom of the well, broken and twisted and almost immobile, watching the shadows to see if any of them stirred, if any were only feigning sleep. They were cunning like their mother, the sorceress of Lanka, capable of subterfuge, and she had to be very careful with them. They had kept a close watch on her for months as she had lain there, almost dead but not quite, making sure nothing escaped them and reporting her condition to Simhika. They had played a game, she and the shadows, watching each other as she healed slowly, bones, body and spirit repairing with time. She had plotted her escape many times over while watching the shadows watch her, but the shadows were many, their vigil relentless. There was no getting past Simhika until the shadows had been neutralized. She had to get them to believe she wasn't worth watching over, she realized. That was the only way she could begin defeating Simhika's designs.

So, for all intents and purposes, Nandana had stopped breathing. She simply played dead.

It had taken time, but the shadows had slowly got convinced by her act, and in turn, they assured the sorceress that she was dead. Now, they slept around her as she lay, still broken and twisted and nowhere close to being fully healed, watching them while she applied her magic to the task at hand.

This was her fourth shot at what she was trying to achieve. On the first two occasions, she had failed miserably, but with her last attempt, she had made progress, which gave her the courage and the confidence to try again.

Remember what you will say, she whispered, directing the words inwards so they slipped down past her larynx and into her windpipe instead of leaving her lips. *I am not dead. Don't trust Ma Parnalata. Let me explain everything.*

Keep your messages short, Dileepa had instructed her when he had presented her with the listening bells. The bells were fused with low magic, he had said, so they couldn't convey long messages.

I am not dead. Don't trust Ma Parnalata. Let me explain everything, she repeated.

Casting another look all around to check she wasn't being observed, she spoke a few words of magic that escaped her mouth to form an air bubble. The bubble rose slowly through layers of shadow and water, a glistening orb pushing upwards to the well's surface in the dark. Nandana followed the bubble's progress, praying fervently that the magic would hold and her plan would succeed. She didn't stop praying until well after the bubble was lost from sight.

Nudging past the sleeping shadows, the bubble continued to rise as a nebula formed at its core, ashen in colour and steadily growing in size. By the time the bubble broke the surface, the form inside had taken on lines and contours and assumed the consistency of powdery ash. The bubble itself kept rising, buoyed by magic, lifting itself free of the water and floating upwards towards the mouth of the well. Down below, the shadows slumbered as the tiny ripple left by the bubble died in its wake.

The bubble cleared the rim of the well and burst, setting the form it had encased free in a shower of ash. At the same instant, a pair of wings took shape, beating the air hard, and the ashen entity began to glow, as if lit by a fire from within. Propelled by the wings and still continuing to rise, the entity caught fire, and in the twinkling of the eye, it morphed into a *sarikah*. Still rising, the bird flew towards the mansion's domed ceiling in a flurry of wingbeats.

The *sarikah* alighted on a ledge close to the ceiling, where it waited to see if it had been sighted. Once it was satisfied it was safe to venture into the open again, the bird left its perch and picked a zigzag path towards Nandana's old chamber. Finding the door to the chamber shut, the mynah squeezed its way in through a tiny window meant for ventilation. Once inside, the flaming bird dropped down to the floor and hopped under the bed. It went all the way to the farthest corner, where something lay discarded, wrapped in silk and smothered in dust.

The *sarikah* pecked and pulled at the object, peeling the folds of silk back to reveal the listening bells gifted by the *dandapala*. Copper and wood and hope, waiting in the dark to bear messages that would alert Ayodhya to the threat that the sorceress of Lanka posed.

Desperately hoping she would succeed in her plan, Nandana got the mynah to tug the bells out from under the bed. Listening bells needed to be held up to the wind to work, she remembered. She could make the *sarikah* do lots of tricks, but picking the heavy bells up wasn't one of them. She would have to make do with what she had and hope luck was with her, she had concluded.

Bending its head, the bird brought its beak close to the bells. Taking a deep breath, it whispered the words Nandana had taught it to utter.

I am not dead. Don't trust Ma Parnalata. Let me explain everything.

Light from four torches illuminated the wide courtyard and the twenty-odd Gandharan soldiers standing there, clutching their javelins in one hand and clutching at the throats of their *pravaras* with the other to keep the wind from sneaking in and freezing them where they stood. Huddling into each other for warmth, they cursed the cold under their breaths every now and then while darting impatient glances at the house that loomed at one end of the courtyard, two stories high. The most imposing building in this section of the town, it had until very recently been home to Saumudri's guild master; it was now Sailusha's residence, the Bahlikas having appropriated it for themselves only that morning.

The Gandharans weren't the only ones waiting in the courtyard. To their left and near the house, two men lounged against a small but ornately carved *shiraska*. The *shiraska* was closed at both ends, with ingress and exit to the right and left, though here too, silken curtains had been put up to give its rider privacy. The curtain that faced the house was open, and the flickering torchlight revealed a cushioned space within the palanquin that was adequate for a single traveller making a short journey.

The Gandharans and the two palanquin bearers weren't the only ones waiting in the courtyard. At its far end, where the torchlight barely penetrated the darkness, three men stood in their own little huddle. Two had drums slung around their necks, while the third carried a *been* under his *pravara*.

Judging by their attire — and from the distance they kept from the Gandharan soldiers — the palanquin bearers and the musicians appeared to be natives of the River Kingdoms.

Besides the Gandharans, the palanquin bearers and the musicians, two other people were in the courtyard — a pair of Bahlikas standing guard by the foot of a flight of stairs coming down the side of the house. The Bahlikas, dour men loyal to Sailusha, were wrapped in their shawls and leaned on their *kuntas* as they took in the Gandharans, the palanquin bearers and the musicians with hooded eyes.

The wind blew in hard from the direction of the Vitasta, sending firelight and shadows weaving and scattering around the courtyard. The men all hunched their shoulders and burrowed deeper into their shawls and *pravaras*, their expressions bitter where the light glanced and glimmered on their stony faces. Men and the elements faced each other off in a struggle that was nearly as old as the mountains from where the wind swept down on the towns and hamlets of the River Kingdoms.

There was a sudden drop in the wind, and in the ensuing silence, the sound of a latch dropping and a door creaking open was loud enough to draw the attention of everyone in the courtyard. Heads and eyes turned to look at the rectangle of light at the top of the stairs, where two women stood in silhouette, one very young and bareheaded, the other wearing a nuptial veil that fell to her waist at the back and covered her face up to her chin. The men in the courtyard watched as the women came down the stairs, the anklets on their feet chiming rhythmically with every step they took. They watched the woman in the veil in particular, waiting for her to emerge into the torchlight —

— but as the women reached the bottom step, the younger one pulled the other's hand, forcing her to a halt. The younger woman then stepped into the courtyard and glared disapprovingly at the men, assessing even the Bahlika sentries icily, before aiming her words at the Gandharans.

"Aren't you ashamed of gawking at a daughter of our tribe and soon-to-be queen of Gandhara?" Devadatta demanded, one hand on her hip. "Imagine news of your behaviour reaching the ears of your raya… I'd say he would have your hides strung from the gates of Kapisi and your flesh fed to the dogs." With a dismissive snort and a wave of her hand, she went on, "Look the other way so your queen can take her place in the *shiraska*."

Whether it was because of her tone or the threat of their raya coming to hear of some imagined slight, the Gandharan soldiers immediately took heed of Devadatta's words. Hurriedly averting their gaze, they stared everywhere into the night, while the palanquin bearers straightened and looked reverently down at their feet. Even the two Bahlika warriors drew themselves erect and kept their eyes straight in front of them.

Devadatta reached out to take Abhisarika's hand, and both women walked to the *shiraska*. The wind picked up again and torchlight wavered as Abhisarika stepped inside the palanquin and settled into its confines. Devadatta quickly closed the curtain to shield her friend from the cold before nodding at the palanquin bearers, who had taken their places at both ends of the *shiraska*. Crouching under its beams, the men hoisted the palanquin to their shoulders, bracing their legs to keep their balance. They waited for orders, the *shiraska* creaking and swaying between them.

"Your queen is seated," Devadatta called to the Gandharans. "You may leave."

"Aren't you supposed to come along?" the leader of the escort asked gruffly.

"No. My instructions were to get the queen ready and bring her to you. That's all."

"Humph," the man grunted. "What about them?" he said, pointing to the three musicians. "We were told nothing about them." He sounded particularly petulant, annoyed at himself for having been ticked off by a young Bahlika woman. "Why are they here?"

"They are musicians," Devadatta retorted. "Is any wedding procession complete without them? Come on, your raya won't disapprove of two drummers and a man playing a *been*." She waved her hands. "Go now… hurry. Don't keep everyone waiting."

The leader of the Gandharans gave a curt nod, disgruntled to be taking orders from the girl but helpless to do anything about it. "Let's go," he roared to his men, asserting his leadership as he strode to his horse and leaped onto the saddle. "Hurry up," he hollered, taking his anger out on the horse by laying his whip across the poor beast's rump so it neighed and reared up in protest.

Once the rest of the Gandharans were also on horseback, they fell into formation, half the escort in front of the palanquin bearing Abhisarika, half behind. The three musicians took their place at the head of the procession, and at a signal from the leader, they began walking to the beat of the drums. As the high-pitched notes of a badly played *been* joined in, the cavalcade filed after the musicians, the torches flickering and dwindling as light and sound slowly receded into the darkness. Devadatta followed the palanquin's outline until it was little more than a blurry after-image in her mind's eye.

"There she goes, our chief's daughter, set to become a queen," the girl sighed dreamily, turning to the two Bahlika guards who remained with her in the courtyard. Smiling at them, she added, "You two can breathe easy, now that she is in the care of the Gandharans."

The men nodded, their shoulders relaxing visibly under their shawls. Their job of guarding the chief's daughter was done. Their fingers slackened around their *kuntas*, the knots in their brows eased, and they lowered their defences —

— which wasn't such a good thing because if they had stayed alert, they might have sensed the figure creeping down the stairs and coming at them out of the shadows behind them, curved *kshurika* glinting in the light cast by the solitary torch waging its own battle with the wild wind.

Without warning, the figure stepped up to the first of the guards. Moving at a remarkable speed, the figure whipped the hand holding the *kshurika* around the sentry and brought the dagger up to his throat. Before the man's mind could even register hand and dagger, the blade was slicing through flesh and cartilage, and dark blood flowed out of the widening wound and poured down the front of his shawl, staining it black. A wet, clucking noise escaped the man's lips as his life left him and he released his hold of the *kunta*. The javelin fell with a dull thump, raising a small puff of dust, while the guard himself sagged and hit the courtyard in an undignified sprawl.

The second Bahlika whirled to face the attacker, but before he could bring his *kunta* up to strike a blow, he felt a stab of pain shoot through his lower back. Turning on instinct, he was surprised to see Devadatta wielding a *kshurika* and staring at him with wide, horrified eyes. The girl was either inept at handling weapons, or she hadn't accounted for his shawl coming in the way and blunting the force of her thrust. Or maybe, she simply lacked the stomach for bloodshed, losing her nerve in the middle of the fight. Whichever it was, she had to pay for trying to kill him, the guard decided, as he swung the javelin around.

"Die here," he snarled, driving the *kunta's* point at the girl's midriff.

But the javelin's head never made the full distance. When still only halfway into its murderous arc, the man's arm jerked in mid-air as the attacker's dagger expertly sliced his triceps, severing the tendon all the way to the bone. His hand on fire, the guard dropped the *kunta* with a scream of agony, his eyes focused inwards, no longer looking at Devadatta, all his senses absorbed in his own pain, blind to everything happening around him. As a result, he didn't feel the attacker close in behind him and raise the dagger to his throat.

"*You* die here," Abhisarika whispered into the man's ear as she slit his throat, her eyes sparking with rage and firelight.

She stepped back to let the guard fall. Devadatta stared at the slumped body, scarcely believing she had been able to cheat death narrowly. Her head oscillated between the two dead Bahlikas, the horror of having had a hand in someone's murder settling over her like a fog. "Was it… it necessary to kill them?" she asked.

"This one would not have hesitated to kill you," Abhisarika reminded the girl in a flinty voice. "They were father's men.

They would have gone to the grave for him." She studied the corpses. "So, I let them."

Devadatta successfully fought the urge to throw up. "Do we hide their bodies?" she asked, her stomach still heaving.

"There's no time. Don't forget, we must find Smara before that procession reaches the bridge." Abhisarika cocked her head to listen to the beat of the drums and the nasal pitch of the *been* in the distance. "And with the procession well on its way, I don't expect anyone showing up here and discovering the bodies." She grabbed Devadatta's hand. "Come, we have work to do."

The women ran along the dark streets of Saumudri, passing vacant homes as they searched for the house where they had been told —

"Do you know for sure she is there?" Abhisarika asked.

"Ambareesha's man said… that she was," Devadatta panted in reply.

"Was he certain?"

"I don't know."

They ran down a street and reached a dead end. "Must be the next one," said Devadatta, turning to retrace her steps. Abhisarika pulled an exasperated face and followed.

They came to a junction where three roads converged. Devadatta paused, uncertain which route to take.

"Do you remember nothing of the house?" asked Abhisarika in a voice straining with anxiety.

"This way," said Devadatta, plunging down one road. Two turns to the left, one to the right — "There," the girl pointed, dropping her voice to a whisper, "that's the one."

They ducked behind a wall. Abhisarika peeked at the house. A lone light burned at one window.

"Stay here," said Devadatta. Stepping into the open, she went up to the house. "Anyone here?" she called out as she neared the door. "The chief has sent me. Open the door."

The door opened and a Bahlika emerged with a torch. "What is it?" he asked, raising the torch to peer at the girl.

"Chief Sailusha has sent me to fetch the child," said Devadatta.

"He didn't say anything of the sort to me," the man argued.

"The chief changed his mind. Chiefs can do that. That's why they are chiefs."

The man didn't say anything, but there was stubbornness in his silence.

"The chief wants the child," Devadatta reasoned. "Wouldn't I be mad to come all this way in this cold if he hadn't wanted her?"

The man considered this quietly.

"The mother has agreed to the marriage," said Devadatta, gritting her teeth at the delay. "That's the wedding procession you can hear." She pointed in the direction of the drums echoing in the distance. "The chief sees no reason to keep the kid from her now. He is a generous man, as you very well know."

The man listened to the drums for a moment before nodding. He went in, and moments later, returned with Smara. The child's face lit up on seeing Devadatta. "Come on," Devadatta invited with an extended hand, and Smara ran out and clutched her finger in relief. Holding the child's hand tight, Devadatta nodded at the man as she and Smara turned away.

It wasn't until they had turned two corners that Abhisarika emerged from behind a building to stand in their way.

Smara shrank against Devadatta for a moment, fearing she was going to be taken away again, but something about the figure blocking the path seemed familiar. The child pushed away from Devadatta and took a step forward, staring into the dark.

"Mother?" the child called softly.

Realizing she still had the bloodied *kshurika* in her hand, Abhisarika hurriedly flung the dagger to one side so the child wouldn't see it.

"Smara, my darling," she whispered, her voice breaking under a flood of emotions.

Mother and daughter rushed into one another's arms, their tears flowing freely as they crushed each other in desperate embraces, unwilling to let go out of fear of losing each other again. As Devadatta drew close, the wind tore at the three women, whipping all around them, smothering the beat of the drum that was now little more than an echo.

"We must go," Devadatta said gently, though the urgency was just under the surface. "We have very little time left."

"Yes," Abhisarika nodded as she wiped her eyes and got to her feet. "Let us go. Come, child."

Abhisarika took Smara by one hand, while Devadatta took the other. With the child in between, the two women set off at a rapid pace before breaking into a stumbling run. In no time, all three were swallowed by the night.

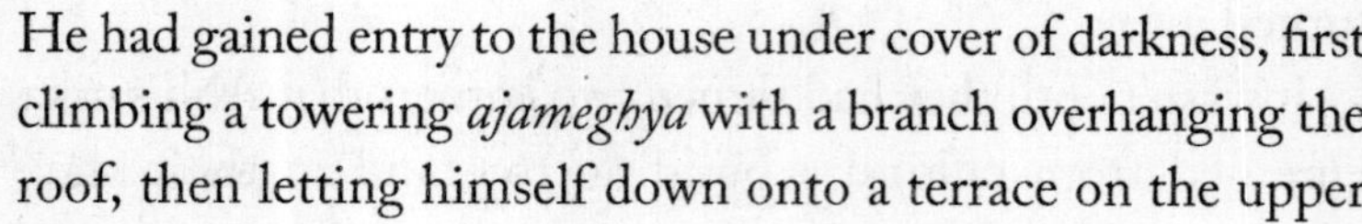

He had gained entry to the house under cover of darkness, first climbing a towering *ajameghya* with a branch overhanging the roof, then letting himself down onto a terrace on the upper floor. From there, he had forced his way in through a window and worked his way to the room where Abhisarika was being held. Both the guards were downstairs, waiting along with the Gandharan escort that had come for Abhisarika.

Devadatta had opened the door to his knock, and stepping in, he had felt a rush of joy on seeing Abhisarika standing there and looking at him with eyes full of wonder.

"I can't believe you've all come this far to rescue me," she had said, taking a step forward, and it had crossed his mind that he would have gone to the ends of the earth for this woman's sake.

"The Gandharans must have begun wondering about the delay," he had said. "They might send someone to investigate. There isn't much time. Devadatta would have told you about the plan." He had glanced at the girl for confirmation, and she had nodded. "Good. I should get dressed then."

He had waited for Abhisarika to begin playing her part in the plan, but the woman didn't budge an inch.

"I need to change into the clothes you are wearing," he had said.

"I should be the one going in the palanquin," Abhisarika had replied. "You shouldn't be putting yourself at risk —"

"No, no, no," he had shaken his head adamantly, "you can't go with the Gandharans. You can't afford getting trapped there —"

"I am capable of defending myself —"

"I don't doubt that," he had said, "but if something goes wrong, you *must* get away. For Smara's sake. For *our* sakes. We didn't come all this way to rescue you only for you to get caught while escaping. No, you must escape at all costs. Find Smara and get away from here before it is too late."

Abhisarika had considered him carefully. "Why did you come for me? *You*, in particular?"

To his surprise, the answer was already on the tip of his tongue. "When we have found the right person, we *know*. And nothing can stop us from coming back for them, no matter what the odds might be."

The odds were a little more than one in three, Yuddhajeet thought to himself as he changed his position inside the *shiraska* to keep the blood circulating and prevent his limbs from going numb. The Gandharans were roughly twenty in number, while they were only six — himself, the two palanquin bearers, and the three musicians up ahead. It was going to be a tight little skirmish, he realized as he eased his *karapala* out from under a quilt where they had previously concealed it. They did have the element of surprise on their side though, which was reassuring.

Replacing the palanquin bearers with his men had been easy, the locals being more than willing to trade places than deal with any Gandharans. Fitting the other three Kekeyan soldiers into the escort had been a challenge until someone had come up with the idea of musicians. Yuddhajeet smiled as he thought back to Devadatta explaining away their presence to the head of the escort, hustling the man into doing what she had wanted. And the way she had bullied the Gandharans into not looking at him very closely — and guessing something was amiss — was sheer genius. He was right about her spirited character, and he was glad he had brought the girl along despite Ambareesha's protestations.

Listening to the beat of the drums and the off-key *been*, the prince wondered whether Devadatta and Abhisarika had located Smara and made an escape. There wasn't much time left. Once the wedding procession reached the bridge spanning the stream that fed into the Vitasta, hell would break loose. In a matter of moments, violence would explode, and in no time, Sailusha and the raya of Gandhara would get wind of the ambush and Abhisarika's flight. There were more than four thousand Gandharan and Kambojan troops in Saumudri, in addition to Sailusha's warriors, who were also present in sizeable numbers. Once the hunt to nab them had been set in motion, it would be virtually impossible to sneak out of the town. They had to be quick, *very quick*, to gain enough of a head start —

A sudden tonal shift in the sound of the horses' hooves alerted Yuddhajeet. He strained to listen over the noise of the drums and the *been* and made out a rumbling hollowness in the hoof beats, as though they were passing over an empty space…

Like a bridge. A wooden bridge.

The yuvaraja gripped his sword and tensed. Across the bridge lay the chunk of the town where Nagnajit had set up residence in the guild hall — where the raya sat preening in anticipation of wedding Abhisarika. Across the bridge lay the lion's lair where both Gandharan and Kambojan warriors prowled. The moment this little cavalcade crossed the bridge, all escape routes would be cut. Everything rested on Ambareesha and his men stopping the procession before it crossed —

There was a sudden shout from up ahead, followed by the sound of something heavy slamming onto the wooden planks of the bridge. Like a sack full of onions falling… or a human body crashing down to its death.

Another shout, this time followed by a single, coherent word of warning.

"Archers!"

Ambareesha's men, Yuddhajeet let his breath out in relief as one more Gandharan rider fell off his horse and hit the bridge hard. The drummers and the man with the *been* continued playing to mask the sounds of war from the enemy across the bridge. The longer it took the Gandharans to realize the procession was under attack, the longer it would take them to send reinforcements, and the more time Yuddhajeet's raiding party would have to flee into the night.

"We're being attacked," someone called. "Take cover."

The problem was that out on the bridge, there was no cover available to the Gandharan escort. Their path across the bridge was blocked by the musicians, while the rear was hindered by the *shiraska* they were escorting. Horses and horsemen milled around in the narrow space, ducking to avoid the arrows that came from the trees nearby, most of them poorly aimed in the dark but serving the purpose of pinning the Gandharans to the spot.

"Guard the queen," one Gandharan shouted, and Yuddhajeet recognized the voice of the leader.

Instantly, the palanquin was lowered to the ground, and the prince sensed the rear-guard of the escort gather around in a crude circle. This was perfect, he thought to himself as he gripped the sword tight and readied to step out. The curtain of the *shiraska* was pulled aside and one of the palanquin bearers looked in. Yuddhajeet handed the soldier a couple of *karapalas*, and the man vanished. Drawing his breath, the yuvaraja swept the bridal veil off. Flinging it to one side, he emerged from the *shiraska*.

The air still echoed with the beat of the drums, loud and erratic, while arrows whistled and sang overhead, Ambareesha's archers intentionally aiming high so Yuddhajeet or his men didn't get hit by accident. The initial shock of the ambush had worn off though, and the Gandharans were now rallying, with the men in front cursing and pushing past the musicians in a bid to get across the bridge and sound an alarm. Meanwhile, the Gandharans at the rear had formed a ring around the palanquin, the soldiers all facing outwards, their horses stamping the ground and whinnying nervously.

Taking a step forward, Yuddhajeet plunged his *karapala* upwards and hard into the back of the soldier in front of him, twisting the blade for maximum impact. Blood sprayed from the wound and the man screamed as bent over his horse's neck before falling right off and landing on his back. He stared up at the sky, his mouth open in an unending scream of agony. Even before his mates could make anything of it, Yuddhajeet slashed a second soldier's back, opening a wound from waist to backbone. As his men unleashed their own attacks, the ring around the palanquin broke and erupted in confusion, the Gandharans scattering as they turned to defend themselves. A couple of them went down to arrows, but the remaining horsemen bore down on Yuddhajeet and his men with their javelins. Having the advantage of both height and reach, the Gandharans attacked fast, and though the yuvaraja parried the thrust of one javelin, a second skewered him near the shoulder, burying deep. Barbs of pain radiated outwards as the javelin was yanked free, and Yuddhajeet felt the ground lurch underfoot as blood stained the blouse he was wearing to pass off as Abhisarika.

"That isn't the Bahlika's daughter," one soldier shouted, finally seeing through the subterfuge. "We have been duped."

Shaking his head to clear his vision, the prince noticed that the horseman had turned his mount around to deal him a deathblow. Yuddhajeet tried lifting his sword, but the strength had left his arm, so all he could do was watch while the Gandharan levelled his javelin as he rode in, aiming for the prince's chest… But the deathblow never landed as a random arrow drilled into the man's throat, killing him instantly. The javelin slipped from his fingers and the horse veered past the yuvaraja, its master jouncing in the saddle, his head thrown back, the shaft of the arrow sticking vulgarly into the night.

"Pull back, pull back."

It wasn't clear whether the command was being followed or whether the Gandharan escort had lost the will to fight and was scattering on its own accord, but the remaining horsemen withdrew in a hurry, some escaping into the tree line, some pushing into the stream to get to safety, some bolting back the way they had come. The ambush had accomplished its end, and for the moment at least, victory was theirs, Yuddhajeet thought to himself through the pain that was setting his shoulder on fire.

But the tide of victory could turn rapidly if they tarried. A clamour could already be heard from somewhere across the bridge, rising steadily in volume; the enemy had figured something had gone terribly wrong. It was a question of time before more Gandharan and Kambojan horsemen poured over the bridge —

A fire appeared at the end of the bridge. Fanned by the wind, it flared within moments, feeding on branches that had been piled one on top of another, forming a wall that would frighten the horses and hamper the Gandharans from immediately giving chase. One of Ambareesha's bright ideas, Yuddhajeet remembered.

"We must go," Ambareesha appeared out of the dark like a ghost. Then, noticing the blood that had soaked through the blouse the prince was wearing, he gasped. "Is that *your* blood? Are you alright?"

"Yes," Yuddhajeet nodded. "And yes and yes," he added, replying to all that the giant had said. "Let's go."

"You need to see a *vaidya*."

"Later, if I don't end up dead," the yuvaraja gave a faint smile. "I know one who can treat me."

"Let us find her then," said Ambareesha.

Drawn by the fire and the evident signs of strife, Gandharan and Kambojan soldiers had started gathering on the other side of the bridge, peering past the eddying smoke to make sense of what was happening. Climbing onto his saddle, Yuddhajeet cast a final glance around him, proud of what they had achieved. His men were all with him, though one had suffered a nasty cut on his forearm and another had received a bad blow to the side of his face. All of Ambareesha's men had made it without a scratch. As he spurred his horse and went after his brave band of warriors, the yuvaraja dwelt upon the words the giant had said to him.

Let us find her then.

Yuddhajeet hoped they would find her. He had much to say to the woman he had come all this way to rescue.

The goldsmith's shop was tiny and tucked into the dreary end of the street where hardly anyone ventured, and observing its state of shabbiness and dereliction, Dileepa's spirits sank. His hopes of learning something about the ring he had recovered from the purse of his attacker were about to be dashed again, he thought, as he descended the narrow, uneven stairs that led to the shop's door.

He had already paid every renowned and not-so-renowned jeweller and goldsmith in Ayodhya a visit, showing the ring around and asking questions, but he had gleaned nothing of value. In fact, he had almost decided to give up this line of enquiry when he had come to hear of the establishment he was now entering.

"Anyone here?" he called as he put his head in through the door.

The place was empty and as rundown from the inside. The walls were crude and dark with age, the marble floor chipped and cracked in many places. A small furnace meant for smelting gold, silver and other precious metals sat in one corner alongside an assortment of implements used to fashion jewellery. There were no items of jewellery to be seen anywhere, however, nor could the *dandapala* find evidence of any jewellery-making work in progress. The place was no more than a shadow of better times, a memory fast fading into oblivion.

"Coming," an ancient voice called from somewhere inside, rich and resonant. "Coming..."

The *dandapala* stepped inside the shop, and at the same time, a dark curtain at the back swished aside to admit a man so stooped with age that he came only up to Dileepa's chest. He shuffled into the light, and Dileepa noticed that he had cataract in one eye. Noticing the man's other eye water weakly, the *dandapala* gave a sigh of resignation, figuring this visit wasn't going to yield anything useful.

"What can I do for you?" the man asked, again surprising Dileepa with the strength in his voice.

The *dandapala* considered making an excuse about having come to the wrong shop by mistake, but he changed his mind at the last moment. He had spent the morning coming here, he thought, drawing the ring from its pouch. He might as well go through with the enquiry before striking this place off his list. If nothing else, he could claim credit for being thorough and professional.

"Are you the goldsmith?" Seeing the man nod, Dileepa handed him the ring. "Is there anything you can tell me about this?"

The man took the ring and held it up to the light. "It's old."

"What else?"

The man squinted up at him. "May I know who is asking? Is this ring yours?"

"I am a *dandapala*," Dileepa pointed towards his official turban. "I am investigating something for the palace."

"Forgive me," the jeweller said. He returned his attention to the ring, running his fingers over its contours. "Give me a moment, please."

Just then, in a rush of footsteps, a young man in his teens burst into the shop. His face was flushed, and his eyes shone with excitement as he searched for the goldsmith in the gloom. On catching sight of the old man, he broke into speech without preamble. "Did you hear the latest?" he asked in a shrill voice. "There has been another disappearance."

Even as thoughts of Nandana rose unexpectedly in Dileepa's mind, stabbing him, the goldsmith waved the boy away, saying, "There's nothing new in that."

"Yes, but this time, it's a *big* one," the young man insisted, gloating at his knowledge.

Dileepa and the jeweller turned in unison to stare at the boy. "Who is it?" the old man asked.

"The daughter of *mahanayaka* Gajakarna."

Dileepa could feel the walls closing in on him as the goldsmith croaked in surprise. "When?"

"This morning. She went to the temple, but she didn't make it back home. The *mahanayaka* is beside himself with grief. His only daughter. Everyone is talking about it."

"What's this world coming to?" the old jeweller lamented, going back to analyzing the ring.

Dileepa pictured the tumult at the *dandapala* headquarters right now. *Mahanayaka* Gajakarna was a very important man, so Mitraka would have been summoned by the palace, and in turn, she would have hauled the *dandapalas* over hot coals. Dileepa was suddenly glad he was here in the goldsmith's shop, away from the heat and the humiliation —

"Aren't you a *dandapala*?" the young man asked, having just noticed the ceremonial turban.

"Yes."

"Aren't you supposed to be investigating these disappearances?"

"I am investigating the attack on Raja Bharat," Dileepa lied, drawing himself to his full height. "But my colleagues are investigating the disappearances."

"They aren't doing a very good job of it," the boy passed judgement with a shrug of superiority. "They've been at it for so long, but people continue to disappear."

Dileepa looked away, not knowing what to say, knowing the boy had a point, and yet bristling with indignation at the slur. It had come to this, he thought: people could utter what they wanted about the *dandapalas* and get away with it because —

"The disappearances must stop," the boy's voice took on a sudden note of urgency. "Otherwise, we are all in danger." Seeing the *dandapala* and the goldsmith turn to him in bewilderment, he said, "The people who are returning… you know they're dangerous, don't you? There's a grain merchant here in Ayodhya whose daughter-in-law had disappeared. One night after her return, she nearly killed her father-in-law with a sickle. Haven't you heard? There's a woodcutter who attacked his family with an axe, another woman who threw her six-month-old baby into a well, a washerwoman who tried to strangle her husband… All of them turned violent after returning. That's why the disappearances have to stop, see?" His eyes focused on Dileepa. "Why haven't you *dandapalas* been able to put a stop to these disappearances?" the boy nagged. "Who is —"

"Mind your own business and stop questioning the *dandapalas*," the investigator snapped. "It's easy to sit around and find fault while we are working our hardest to find out what's happening. And where did you hear all of these stories?" he glared at the boy in anger. "Other than the one about the woman attacking her father-in-law, every story you recounted is made up. Each one is purely fictional. Do you know you are indulging in scaremongering? As a *dandapala*, I can arrest you right now under the charge of spreading false rumours. How about that? Would you appreciate that level of *dandapala* efficiency?" Watching the youngster cringe, Dileepa raised an eyebrow. "What do you do, by the way?"

"Oh," the boy uttered in reply, the *dandapala's* admonishment robbing him of all enthusiasm. Without a word, he turned and hurriedly slunk out of the door. Silence returned to the shop.

"Does this ring have anything to do with the attack on our raja?" the old jeweller asked, looking at Dileepa in awe.

"It may or it may not," the investigator's manner was brusque. He had had enough questions thrown at him. He now wanted answers. "What can you tell me about it?"

"Well… it's old and has been crafted with a lot of care."

"Do you know who could have crafted it… and for whom?"

The goldsmith peered at the ring. "I can't say by whom or for whom. But I can tell you *where* this ring was crafted."

"Where?"

"In Sravasti."

Not one of the jewellers and goldsmiths Dileepa had seen so far had been able to tell him this. "How do you know that?"

"Look at this design here…" the old man pointed and Dileepa looked, although he had no idea about the artistic significance of what he was being shown. "And this indentation here. This is a style favoured by goldsmiths from Sravasti. Not now, not today. I'm talking about forty years ago, during my time. They used to do this a lot. I personally wasn't much of a fan, but the style had its admirers."

"Sravasti," Dileepa repeated. "And made forty years ago."

"Thirty or forty years ago," the jeweller nodded.

"So, if I asked in Sravasti, they might be able to tell me who made it and for whom?"

"I would imagine so."

The *dandapala* emerged from the shop feeling a lot brighter than when he had gone inside. He had a lead, and it led to Sravasti. His attackers had a connection to Sravasti. Kosala's late guild master Pushyanta also had a connection to Sravasti.

His uncle is also an adhipati, *in case you didn't know. Mihiradutta of Sravasti*, he remembered the king telling him.

A shiver went down Dileepa's spine, but his resolve to get to the bottom of the affair had only strengthened after the goldsmith's revelation. He would go to Sravasti and find out all he could about the ring. And he would go straightaway. There was no point in visiting the headquarters and seeking Mitraka's permission. With Gajakarna's daughter also gone, Mitraka would be in the worst possible temper. She would either bite his head off for wanting to go to Sravasti or yank him off this case and put him on the investigation into the disappearances. She'd probably do both, Dileepa feared, so it was best he slipped away unnoticed. By the time he returned, the situation would have cooled down in Ayodhya, and if he were lucky, he would have a solution to his case…

When Dileepa got back to his quarters half an hour later, he went straight to his little room and began readying for the trip to Sravasti. As he pulled a pair of fresh dhotis from the cupboard's topmost shelf, his hand brushed against something.

A muted metallic tinkle sounded in his ears.

Pausing for the span of a breath, the investigator rose on the tips of his toes to look at the bundle he had pushed right to the back. Slowly, he reached for it and brought it down.

It had been a long time since he had touched the listening bells. He had almost given up hope of seeing Nandana again, he realized, as he unwrapped the bells from within the folds of silken cloth. He didn't think she would be coming back like the others ha —

His fingers froze over the bells lying half-uncovered in his hands.

His breath froze in a gasp of amazement that half left his lips.

He stared at the bells, glowing gently in the half-darkness of his room.

A message for him… *from the only person who could send him a message on these bells.*

Holding the bells delicately — as if fearful that the message they bore would self-destruct if he wasn't careful with them — Dileepa went to the window and let the chill breeze brush past the bells. And he listened.

Silence… and then, suddenly, two words in Nandana's voice.

…explain everything.

The *dandapala* frowned, vexed with the magic in Ayodhya. The magic was so poor these days that it was virtually impossible to send or receive messages via the listening bells. No message transmitted properly, so messages had to be sent repeatedly and be pieced together for anything to make sense.

…explain everything. The way Nandana had said the words, it sounded as if they were the last part of a sentence. Like she was going to *explain everything*. But what had she said before that? What did she intend to explain? More importantly,

where was she, and where had she sent this message from?

The questions were pounding inside Dileepa's head when he suddenly remembered something.

Nandana's message to him after the attack on him… after the fiery *shyenas*… after he had seen her standing in the darkened street glowing like a nimbus, her features lit by the glow of the birds…

Please come this evening. I will explain everything.

That had been her message to him that day. *Explain everything.*

Whatever hope had risen in him crumbled under a wave of despair. The magic in Ayodhya had played a dirty trick on him by sending Nandana's old message all over again. A quirk of magic gone bad. A caprice of his cruel fate.

Feeling the sharp prick of tears in his eyes and sensing a storm of outrage building in his chest, the *dandapala* thrust the bells back within the folds of silk. Then, striding over to the cupboard, he flung the little bundle back onto the topmost shelf, where it landed with a jangle and a thud. Dileepa slammed the cupboard door shut, crammed everything that he needed for his trip into a cotton bag and left the house.

He had been foolish to believe Nandana had sent him a message. She was not coming back, he told himself angrily, his eyes smarting with tears that refused to be held back. The girl had been gone far too long. She was gone for good.

Drying his eyes quickly on the sleeve of his tunic, Dileepa wrapped his *pravara* around himself and set off for Sravasti.

The Gandharan soldier struggled at the end of the rope for a long while, legs kicking frantically as he swung from the branch of a sturdy *ajameghya*, fifteen feet up. His face bloated and turned purple as the rope snuffed his life out in fractions, pleas for mercy escaping his mouth in croaks until the noose tightened enough to squeeze out all sounds. Finally, he ceased thrashing around and gave in, dangling over the heads of those who had come to watch him die, the rope twisting and creaking in the silence of the cold, grey morning.

It wasn't until he was fully satisfied the soldier was indeed dead that Nagnajit took his eyes off the body and turned to survey those around him. There were close to a hundred people present, a good mix of Gandharan, Kambojan and Bahlika warriors clustered around the acacia tree that had served as the gallows. Sailusha was there, looking grim, as was Mahasa, staring at the dead body with flat eyes. Straight in front, where Nagnajit stood under the swinging corpse, a dozen men from the previous night's escort quaked and trembled, their eyes switching from their raya to the body of their leader hanging overhead.

"This is what happens when you fail at the job you have been entrusted with," Nagnajit snarled. The men flinched and hastily looked away for fear of provoking the king. "You abandoned the palanquin and fled. Your lives are more important to you than your raya's orders. I should have the lot of you flayed and hanged along with your captain as punishment..."

Hearing this, the men instantly fell on their knees and joined their hands, blabbering apologies and begging for mercy.

"Silence!" Nagnajit commanded. "Stop behaving like women. Get up and get out of my sight!"

The men scrambled to their feet. Bowing to the raya and offering profuse thanks, they hurried to get away, elbowing their way through the crowd of warriors, keen to be gone before Nagnajit changed his mind.

Seeing the men scurry away, the raya spat in disdain before turning to look at the body one last time. Then, very deliberately, he ambled over to Sailusha and Mahasa. "Seven of my men dead. Your daughter and your granddaughter gone. Taken from right under our noses." He paused to make his displeasure felt.

"I too lost two of my best men," Sailusha grumbled.

"All because of that girl your nephew wed… what was her name again?"

"Devadatta."

"Devadatta," Nagnajit repeated the name slowly, savouring it. "Resourceful girl. First, she fools this idiot" — he jerked a thumb at the hanging corpse — "and his men into believing *you* sent her to meet your daughter. Then, she fools your man into thinking *you* wanted the child brought to you. Then, *chhoo*" — the raya opened his fist, miming the magician's trick — "daughter and granddaughter are both gone." His eyes narrowed on Sailusha critically. "You should have kept your eyes on the girl."

"I didn't expect her to pose any problems," the chieftain mumbled. "She is just an ordinary girl —"

"She is anything but ordinary. And you say she and Abhisarika were friends." Nagnajit showed his disappointment with a shake of his head. "You should have paid closer attention to her."

"When I find her, I will make her pay."

The raya was about to say something, but checking himself, he turned to study the men standing around and listening. "Why is everyone still here?" he demanded, clapping his hands irritably. "Don't all of you have things to do?"

In a matter of seconds, the place cleared. The raya, Sailusha, Mahasa and a few of his Kambojan horsemen were the only ones left.

"You will make the girl pay," Nagnajit said, returning to the conversation, "and if *you* don't, I certainly will. But that is not my point. My point is, for a potential raja of the River Kingdoms, you have acted quite foolishly. You let this Devadatta run around unsupervised. I shall let that pass; you didn't foresee her being a threat. Fine. But your nephew, Ambareesha… You should never have let him out of your sight, whereas you sent him straight to the enemy's side?" The raya's eyebrows rose in disbelief. "What were you thinking —"

"I did not want him interfering with our plans," Sailusha said in defence. "I didn't want him alerting the Kekeyans —"

"If you feared he wouldn't support you, if you had doubts about his loyalties, you should have had him killed," the raya cut in heatedly. "At the very least, you could have locked him in chains. But instead, you had to send him to the exact spot where he would pose us the greatest risk."

"Ambareesha is… like a son to me…" Sailusha groped for words. "I couldn't make myself…"

Nagnajit gave his head a pitiful shake. "This," he gestured towards the bridge, the pile of burned branches and the abandoned *shiraska* with a sweep of his hand. "This is the price we've had to pay for the love you have for your nephew."

The Bahlika chieftain flinched at the raya's words and straightened. "I will make him pay too." He paused and repeated himself. "*I* will make my nephew pay."

"Ambareesha and the girl are all fine," Mahasa spoke for the first time in his sleepy drawl, "but let us not forget the man who led the ambush, the one who switched places with Abhisarika in the palanquin and tricked us all…"

"Yuddhajeet…" the raya of Gandhara nodded, cold rage in his eyes, "the yuvaraja of Kekeya."

"I wouldn't have expected the Kekeyan prince to be part of something like this," said Sailusha. "I mean other than a friendship with Ambareesha, what is in it for him?"

Nagnajit looked at the chieftain sideways. "You really must be foolish not to know the answer to that one," he said, a bitter, reptilian smile forming on his lips. "It's all got to do with love. A man would go to great lengths and put his life in immense danger for the woman he loves. The prince is clearly in love with your daughter."

The raya turned and began walking, deep in thought, and everyone else fell in step behind him. They walked through the charred remains of the fire, stirring up cold ash and soot as they went. Crossing the bridge, they approached the palanquin, its curtains billowing in the wind, empty inside except for the quilts and the cushions. No Abhisarika waiting to be wedded to him, Nagnajit thought, his cheeks burning with rage and embarrassment.

It didn't matter that he had never set eyes on the chieftain's daughter, that he had no idea what she looked like. It didn't matter that he had already married twice and had numerous mistresses as well, waiting for his return to Kapisi. It didn't matter that he had offered to marry the chieftain's daughter on an impulse, that too only to sweeten the deal and seal the bargain with the Bahlikas. What mattered was that she had been promised to him. She was his now, and he was bent on possessing her.

But she had been taken from him. Something that was his by right was with someone else. That really stung him.

"The prince may be in love, but he has made a terrible mistake by crossing me," the raya spoke through gritted teeth. "He has taken what is mine, and I shall not rest until I have it back. I shall go to the very ends of this earth to find the woman who was meant for me," he swore savagely, "and I will destroy the man who took her from me. I will destroy all that he has ever held dear — and I will destroy everything that comes in the way of my revenge."

The crowd in front of Gajakarna's house was mostly made up of soldiers, *nayakas*, *upanayakas* and fighting men from Kosala's army, who were there to share their sympathy and show solidarity with their commander in his moment of crisis. Kushadhwaja could feel the baking heat of their resentment as they parted to allow him and Bharat to pass through, the most severe of their glares and sniggers reserved for him. Word had got around that he was the one who had forced a change in Bharat's mind about attacking Madhupura, and the *kshatri* knew it was natural for these soldiers to feel cheated. Still, the hostile glances directed at him unnerved him, and he was thankful that Atibhanu was accompanying him and the king, watching their backs. For the soldiers all seemed to hold the bodyguard in great esteem, greeting him and exchanging pleasantries as he passed by.

The visitors were ushered into the presence of Gajakarna, who rose from his *sayyasana*, mighty as a mountain and grim as a thundercloud, to greet them with joined hands. The *mahanayaka* wasn't alone though. In addition to two *nayakas*, who were clearly men he trusted and confided in, there was one more person present in the room — *adhipati* Sudhanva of Sankasya. The men rose and bowed to their king, and Bharat did likewise, offering everyone his *pranaam* in return.

"Please be seated here, closer to the warmth," Gajakarna said, pointing at a brazier that burned brightly to one side, and Sudhanva shifted to make enough room for everyone. "What can I get you..." the *mahanayaka* continued, playing host though his heart was not in it. "Something hot to combat this cold —"

"Nothing please... nothing," Bharat insisted as he sat down. "We don't mean to impose on you —"

"Oh, it's nothing —" Gajakarna began, but seeing the king raise both hands, he nodded. "Please sit," he directed Kushadhwaja to the *sayyasana* before lowering himself next to Sudhanva. The two *nayakas* and Atibhanu took their places discreetly, standing with their backs pressed to the walls.

"I am distraught to hear about you daughter," Bharat said, once they were comfortably seated. "I... spoke to Mitraka just before coming here, and I made it clear to her that I'm most unhappy and dissatisfied with the investigation she has been running. I've told her these disappearances *have* to stop."

Gajakarna nodded quietly, keeping his thoughts to himself, but looking out of the corner of his eye, Kushadhwaja thought he saw Sudhanva's lips twitch into a sneer.

"Putting a stop to the disappearances now isn't going to miraculously bring the *mahanayaka's* daughter back to him," the *adhipati* said blandly. "Or my son to me, for that matter."

Bharat inclined his head in agreement. "What you say is true, but I am hoping we can prevent more disappearances."

"We should have found a way to prevent every one of the disappearances that have occurred over the last so many months," Sudhanva said with feeling, his eyes on the coals burning in the brazier. "If we had, we wouldn't be here today, commiserating with the *mahanayaka* about his loss."

The king meant to say something, but he was interrupted by a wail from inside the house. "My poor daughter," it was an older woman's voice. "Where are you, my darling?"

Listening to the voice trail away, the men looked at one another.

"A mother's heart is so tender, so easily broken," Gajakarna said by way of explanation.

Bharat nodded, but again, before he could speak, the woman's voice rose in lament, shrill with grief. "Why us? What have *we* done to deserve this? What did our daughter do…?"

"Pardon me, rajan," said Gajakarna. He rose and hurried out of the room, leaving everyone else to sit and wait in the awkward silence that ensued.

The stillness did not last long. "Ayodhya is jinxed after Dashratha's death," the woman's voice rose sharply. "The curse of the gods is upon us. It's no wonder the magic is failing us and everything is going wrong. Woe the moment that struck Raja Dashratha down —"

"Shh… Quiet," the *mahanayaka* said in a low, muffled voice that was still loud enough to carry outside. "The rajan is here," he added urgently. "Stop your lamenting."

"Then ask the rajan to bring back my daughter —"

"Quiet…" Gajakarna hissed. Speaking to someone else, he said, "Take her inside." The sound of doors closing was followed by the clack of the commander's *padukas*.

The *kshatri* looked at the faces around him. Bharat sat with his hands folded in his lap, his eyes hooded, his expression stoic. The *nayakas* and Atibhanu stood studying the floor. However, on Sudhanva's face, Kushadhwaja detected a fleeting sign of… *something*. Was it satisfaction he had seen there, the *kshatri* wondered, was it triumph, or was it pleasure? Or, could it have been the gleam of pure malice…?

"My apologies, rajan," Gajakarna said as he returned and assumed his seat. "The wife has taken this badly. She didn't mean to —"

"I understand," said Bharat. "There's no need for apologies. I only wish it was in my power to bring your daughter back as your wife demands."

"It is alright," the commander said in a heavy voice. "I guess she will come back anyway. They all do. We must be patient, that's all."

There was a moment's silence, and Kushadhwaja was wondering if this would be a good time to take the *mahanayaka's* leave when Sudhanva spoke.

"It's not the curse of the gods that is upon us," he said in a tone that was defiant and challenging. "It is the inefficiency of men. So many gone, and no sign of it stopping."

"I guess those who haven't lost anyone dear to them simply won't understand," said Gajakarna.

Again, for the smallest fraction of a second, something skimmed over the *adhipati's* face, swift like a hawk in motion. Kushadhwaja struggled to decode it, but he thought it had resembled an expression of relief —

"You forget that I almost lost my son not six months ago," Bharat said, the words spilling from his thin lips, hurried and hard-edged. "I too have borne the pain; I too have wept the tears."

"Yes, you have, rajan," Gajakarna admitted. "My intention was not to remind you of that pain. If I have, I regret it and I am deeply sorry."

"Not at all," said the king. "And my intent was not to trivialize your agony by bringing Taksha up. All I'd meant to say was that we have all suffered in some way or the other." He got to his feet and Kushadhwaja, Sudhanva and the *mahanayaka* rose as well. Bharat took a moment to study the *adhipati* and the commander. Then, stepping close to Gajakarna, he laid a hand on the man's shoulder.

"The disappearances should have stopped a long time ago, I agree," he said. "I agree that we've been clueless over what's happening. I agree this has run longer than it should have. So, I make you a promise. I will spare no effort to get to the bottom of this, and I will put an end to these disappearances."

The mare pranced along the periphery of the palace ground in easy, loping strides, kicking mud and grass into the air and snorting playfully in delight. On its back sat Taksha, bouncing in the saddle in perfect rhythm with the beast, his hair loose and whipping in the wind, his face flushed as much with excitement as from the cold. Reaching the far end, the horse made a turn towards the royal stables, where Bharat lingered in the company of Siripala and Angara, the ostler filling the troughs with water for the horses, the dog lolling idly in the grass. Atibhanu stood ten paces away from the king, watchful as he surveyed the surroundings.

The mare dropped its pace as it neared the stable, and Bharat took a step forward to help his son off the horse. But at the last moment, the boy spurred the animal back into a gallop and veered away, grinning at his father, his eyes wild and shining with mischief.

"Ah, careful," Bharat called out in mock annoyance as the mare thundered past. Then, injecting seriousness into his voice, he shouted, "Keep your elbows closer to your knees."

Taksha and the horse were already away, nearly out of earshot, but the boy narrowed his elbows in accordance with his father's instructions. Horse and yuvaraja sped away to the diminishing thrum of hoof beats.

"That boy rides like his father," said Siripala, limping up beside the king and looking at Taksha with admiration. Chuckling to himself, he added, "Also, it's almost impossible to separate him from that horse."

"It's a good horse Shatrughna gifted the kid," Bharat observed. "As if they were made for each other."

The two men watched the boy and the horse as they banked to the left where the ground ended.

"How come you aren't riding today, rajan?" the ostler asked. He had taken to addressing Bharat as rajan ever since Atibhanu had joined the king's service, and Bharat sometimes missed being called 'kumara' the way Siripala used to.

"I don't feel like it," the king replied.

Siripala gave Bharat a slow, sidelong glance. Letting a moment pass, he said, "That is so unlike you, rajan. Is something troubling you?"

Bharat looked down at Angara, who chose that moment to stand up and wag its tail, demanding attention. The king bent to scratch the dog on its head, and the animal closed its eyes and folded its ears back in pleasure. Bharat remained silent for a moment, lifting his gaze from Angara to Taksha, who was coming around another bend, the mare graceful and controlled in its movements.

"There's just so much that is wrong, Siripala," the king said at last. "The magic that is no longer in Ayodhya. The disappearances and all the absurd rumours associated with them. This cold..." he waved a hand and glanced up at the trees, their branches quivering in the wind. "Everywhere, the people are so unhappy."

The old ostler didn't say anything. Taksha came around, and Bharat raised one hand, signalling him to stop. The boy drew near, but he was already begging and beseeching, his face scrunched in appeal. "Father, *one* more round..." he pleaded, "Just *one* more... please father... please..." Seeing Bharat nod, the kid's face brightened, and he was off before Bharat could even entertain a change in mind. Angara, as if realizing that this was to be the last shot at play, bounded after the horse, a black streak of lightning chasing a dark-brown rumble of thunder.

"Did you know that *mahanayaka* Gajakarna's daughter has disappeared?" Bharat asked.

Siripala nodded. "I heard."

"How long can things go on like this?" the king snapped in frustration. "These disappearances have to stop."

The old man said nothing.

"And have you heard the rumours?" Bharat asked. Seeing Siripala nod, he shook his head. "It's ridiculous, the kind of things that are being said. They're making it sound as though the… those who have come back are a threat to everyone else." He turned to the ostler. "*You* are back, but you're nowhere near a threat to anyone. Tell me, who makes up these rumours?"

Siripala shrugged. "That woman did attack her father-in-law, rajan —"

"Can it be proved her attack was linked to her disappearance? Only last week, a case came up in court. A cobbler from Ambapuri had a disagreement with one of his patrons, and the two came to blows. Neither man had ever disappeared, so why did they attack each other?" Bharat paused to see how Taksha was faring, then turned back to Siripala. "People have been attacking one another from the beginning of time, definitely from a long way before these disappearances began. Using that poor woman's example to spawn rumours and sow fear in people's hearts is reprehensible."

"You are right, rajan," said the ostler.

"You —" Bharat continued, barely pausing for breath. "You disappeared and came back. Tell me, have *you* ever felt a murderous desire in you after coming back? Have you wanted to attack anyone, kill anyone? Tell me."

Siripala felt a sickening sensation slosh over him as something stirred in his memory. A hunger and a thirst. And an intense, overwhelming need to feed. Something else stirred along with that memory. The scent of blood from a freshly severed artery filling his nostrils and almost making him salivate. And a gluttonous void in the pit of his stomach that craved tender, succulent flesh.

Tell me…

Siripala blinked through the rising waves of insanity besieging him to see Bharat gazing at him intently. "…have you felt the need to kill?"

"Rajan, the yuvaraja is here," Siripala managed to blurt out, waving a hand in the direction of the horse and the young prince.

Distracted, Bharat turned to see Taksha and the mare draw to a halt. The king went over, picked the kid off the saddle and put him down. "Had fun?" he asked.

"Yes, but I want to play with Angara," the boy launched into his next demand without wasting a breath. "Just for a little while, father… plea —"

"Alright, alright," Bharat waved the kid away, and Taksha, pleasantly surprised and even more elated, flicked his fingers at the dog and took off on a run. Angara ran at the boy's heels, barking with excitement.

By the time Bharat turned to face him again, Siripala had overcome the bizarre urge to kill that had possessed him. He stood there, composed, but gripped by a mortal fear that the king would pose the same questions again, probing him about how he felt — *hunger and thirst* — after his return…

"Tell me, Siripala… What do you remember about the time you were not here?" Bharat asked. "Is there anything you can tell me about… *anything*? Where you were, who was with you, what you did… *anything*?"

The old man looked away. The day was drawing to a close. Darkness was not far away. "I have told the *dandapalas* that I can't remember anything, rajan," he said at last.

"Yes, I know, but try and remember."

"I have tried, but I can't. There is nothing to remember in my memory."

"I have made Gajakarna a promise," Bharat's lips were thin lines, so the words came out harsh. "I have sworn to stop these disappearances. For that, I must know what is going on. You must help me. So for *my* sake, please try and remember."

Siripala nodded and opened his mouth to speak. Then, his gaze turned inwards, and he paused. At last, he shook his head. "I… can't remember. I just can't."

Bharat blinked to conceal his frustration. "Okay… how do you feel when you think of the time you were away?" he asked, groping desperately for an answer. "*What* do you feel? Do you feel happy, sad, angry…"

Empty. And hungry and thirsty. For blood.

"Empty, rajan," the ostler answered. "Like there is nothing inside. Nothing at all. No memories, no words, no feelings…"

"Okay," said Bharat, letting the matter drop, although his disappointment was obvious. "Should something ever strike you, let me know." Turning around, he hailed the boy. "Taksha, it's time to go," he shouted, his voice so uncharacteristically harsh that the kid hurried over without any argument.

"Shall we brush down the horse?" Taksha asked his father, pointing to the mare.

"Let it be, yuvaraja. I shall do it," said Siripala. "You should go now. It is growing dark." Then, noticing the *pravara* around the boy's shoulders for the first time, the ostler exclaimed, "That's one magnificent *pravara*! Was it made by your mother, yuvaraja?"

"No, that woman gave it to my mother."

Seeing Siripala's confusion, Bharat said, "The woman who made the uniforms for the Sanctum garrison paid Mandavi a visit and gifted her this *pravara*." He ruffled Taksha's hair in affection, and the boy grinned back at his father. "This little imp liked it so much he has claimed it as his own."

"He looks quite grand in it," Siripala remarked. "Like a little king."

Bharat smiled proudly. "Come, let's go then," he said to Taksha with a pat on the kid's back.

Father and son hadn't taken more than six steps, and Atibhanu had barely fallen in behind them, when Siripala hailed the king. "Rajan," he said, "I remember darkness."

Bharat stopped and turned to look at the old warrior.

"And I think there was a voice, rajan."

"What did it say?"

"I can't remember. But I promise to try and recall what was said, rajan."

As twilight descended over the palace ground, the wind assumed an edge. Bharat drew his own *pravara* close and took Taksha by the hand. They began heading towards the palace, Atibhanu half a dozen steps behind.

Noticing Taksha's departure and not yet ready to halt play, Angara began trotting after the boy. Siripala whistled at the dog, ordering it to stop, but the animal ignored the ostler and went after the king and the prince, its tail up, jaunty and defiant.

Suddenly, without the slightest warning, a red rage flooded Siripala's mind. The dog was being disobedient. It needed to be disciplined.

"Angara!"

The dog's name was shouted out so loud and with so much viciousness that Taksha gave a start and the blood drained from his face. Even Bharat was so taken aback that he grabbed his son's hand hard and drew the kid close. Angara, for its part, gave a high, piteous whine as it crouched low on the path, frozen in its tracks, its ears flat and its tail between its legs.

Bharat, Taksha and Atibhanu turned to look at Siripala, who stared back at them and at the dog, his ears ringing with the echo of his own voice, harsh and strident, brimming with a foreboding of violence. With an effort, he got ahold of himself and licked his lips, conscious of the king's eyes boring into him.

"Angara," he said, trying to sound as endearing and gentle as possible. "Come here, Angara."

Recognizing the voice as that of the other Siripala, *the old Siripala*, the dog got up and turned, its tail wagging uncertainly as it looked at the ostler.

"Come on," Siripala called, limping towards the dog, hand outstretched in a bid to make peace. "Your dinner is ready."

"Go, Angara," Bharat said softly. "Go."

The dog blinked at Bharat and Taksha, its tail wagging with greater confidence on seeing them, but it didn't budge from its spot.

"Go, Angara," Taksha called out. "Go, eat your dinner."

Showing great reluctance, Angara turned and threaded its way back, squeezing past Atibhanu, cowering as it neared the ostler. The dog finally went down on its belly before rolling over onto its side in surrender, whimpering and mewling as it gazed at Siripala with eyes that were awash with terror that was ancient and atavistic, terror that knew and recognized evil in its vilest form. When Siripala bent down to rub the dog's stomach, it let out a tiny yelp of fear that was heard by none except the ostler.

"I'm sorry, Angara," the old man whispered. "I didn't mean to scare you. I love you, silly dog, don't you know that?"

The dog wagged its tail and clambered happily to its legs. Whatever had scared it was no longer there. Everything was fine in its trusting little world.

Siripala straightened to see Bharat and Taksha standing and watching him. He waved. Whether it was the wave or the sight of Angara in front of him acting normally he couldn't tell, but the king and the young prince turned and walked away, with Atibhanu trailing them. Watching the king and the prince meld into the twilight, Siripala was overcome with a bout of shivering that had nothing to do with the evening's chill. Sweat beaded his wrinkled brow and his palms were damp with fear. He looked down at Angara, seated before him, its tail wagging in anticipation of dinner.

He feared for the dog. Nothing was fine in its world.

He feared for himself, the king and the little yuvaraja. Nothing was fine in his world or in theirs.

He crept along the dark, uneven passageway, his hands trailing the cold stone walls for support. Tripping here, stubbing a toe there, but always pressing forward, not slowing down lest he lose sight of the bubble of light bobbing twenty paces ahead of him, illuminating the bent back and shoulders of his king Lavanyasurya.

Down and down the winding passage they went, the king and his guild master, the latter trailing the former surreptitiously and not for the first time. Amulya had made this journey a couple of times already, always without Lavanyasurya's knowledge, always careful not to make a noise or get too close. On all the previous occasions, he had struggled to make sense of what was happening, though he instinctively understood there was something dark and malevolent afoot, having an outcome that would be utterly destructive. Destructive to whom and how, that was what he was intent on deciphering.

Amulya knew what lay at the end of this subterranean passageway, though the first time he had tailed the raja down here, he had had no inkling such a place even existed beneath Madhupura. If the passage and the cavernous hall at its end had come as a surprise, what he'd witnessed *in* the hall had shocked him, leaving him with disturbing dreams and sleepless nights. Even now, as he descended the last flight of stairs that would bring the hall into view, Madhupura's guild master steeled himself for the sight that was to unfold before his eyes.

Reaching the foot of the stairs, Lavanyasurya disappeared into the hall, and for a brief moment, darkness swamped Amulya, making his heart leap in fright. The guild master hurried down the last few steps, sighing with relief as the light glimmered in front, outlining the king's back —

— and then, as he emerged into the hall, he gasped at the enormity of what he saw before him.

The first time he had been down here, he had gawked at the scene with an open mouth, staring at the freakish shapes that filled the hall, swaddled in what appeared to him to be giant strands of cobweb. The shapes were everywhere, some standing erect, some prone on the ground, some leaning against or sitting with their backs to the walls. It had taken Amulya some time to realize the shapes bore distinctly human proportions — *head, arms and torso, and legs, all encased in cobweb*. He hadn't been able to count, but the guild master's guess was there had been a hundred of those shapes that first time. That number had increased the second time he was here. Definitely a few hundred more, he'd thought, wondering where they had all come from.

Now, standing at the edge of the hall and observing Lavanyasurya head towards its centre, Amulya was overawed by the sheer number of cobwebbed shapes before him.

They were in the thousands, he could tell.

Sitting, standing, lying on their sides, fallen on top of one another. They were so many piled in here, there was hardly place left to walk, and the guild master could see Lavanyasurya nudging and squeezing his way forward in places.

The guild master no longer had questions regarding the origins of the shapes trussed in cobweb. Reports about the strange disappearances occurring in Kosala had reached Madhupura over the months, borne by a variety of sources. He'd heard about people vanishing without a trace, their numbers having swelled rapidly in the last month or so. Now, staring at the shapes rocking and swaying in Lavanyasurya's wake, Amulya was left in no doubt what — *no, who* — these things were.

I will give them a war they won't forget, he remembered the king saying to him. Lavanyasurya had threatened to annihilate Kosala and turn Ayodhya into a city of the dead. The guild master was quick to understand that what he was seeing before him was part of Lavanyasurya's grand scheme.

Thousands of shapes — *heads, arms, torsos and legs* — in mindless slumber. Barely breathing, hardly alive, he could tell. Yet, waiting to awaken like moths in their cocoons, only savage and ravenous like birds of prey. The notion made Amulya's skin crawl.

Afraid of setting another foot into the hall — he shrank back at the thought of brushing against the shapes, which he refused to think of as human bodies — Amulya craned his neck to follow Lavanyasurya's path until king and light disappeared once again, lost in the press of cobwebbed shapes. But the thought of being left in the dark with only the shapes for company was far from comforting, and the guild master plunged into the gap in front of him, shrivelling and recoiling whenever his arm or shoulder made contact with the shapes. The cobweb encasing the shapes didn't feel cobwebby and sticky, which was a mild relief, but it didn't muffle the wet, laboured breathing of the shapes, reminding him that there were living things inside, which was terrible.

The light reappeared ahead, and Amulya slowed his pace, careful to stay out of Lavanyasurya's sight. He watched the raja make his way to the centre of the hall, where another dark shape sat cross-legged on the floor, still as the night, yet trembling with raging currents and forces under the skin. The guild master did not need light to know who was seated in the centre of the hall. He had recognized her the first time he had come here.

It was Naika, his king's wife and queen of Madhupura.

Only this was a Naika so dark and fierce that Amulya had quaked when he had set eyes on her.

Even now, he quailed, seeing her seated with her eyes closed while tempers rippled around her, storms raged in the wrinkles on her brow, and poison churned in her breath. The queen sat there at the vortex of the slowly breathing shapes like a spider, spinning threads of such malignancy that Amulya shuddered in terror and revulsion. He watched as Lavanyasurya went to his wife's side, bent down and put his lips to her ears, as if telling her something. As he spoke, the queen's frame shook, her skin became mottled and started smoking, and then, her eyes flew wide open, revealing pale white orbs with everything else missing. Yet, Amulya cringed back, certain she could see everything.

Then came the whispers, spilling from Lavanyasurya's mouth and amplified through whatever powers Naika was channelling, gushing forth and flooding the hall like the beating of bat wings. There were no words in the whispers, though. Only sound and emotion. Emotion so strong that even Amulya felt it, like a breath on his skin, tickling the hairs, then a hot flush, then a singeing that made him reel, then a furnace blast that slipped under the skin and vanished into the blood.

The next instant, Amulya felt the rage rise in him. Uncontrollable rage, rage that would find its peace only in destruction.

He also felt hunger gnawing at him. In his stomach, in his blood, in his bones.

A hunger for flesh. And blood.

And all around the guild master, the cobwebbed shapes also woke and writhed, incited by anger and hunger.

Rage and hunger. A craving for flesh. A thirst for blood. And Rani Naika at the centre of it all, watching everything with her wide, sightless eyes. Watching him…

Amulya's eyes snapped open. He had seen and heard and felt enough. He had to get away from the madness before it consumed him, he realized. Shaking himself free of the whispers and the rising tides of anger, he turned and pushed past the writhing human bodies, running blind, not caring if he was making a noise, not caring if his presence had been noticed by Lavanyasurya…

He ran with only one thought in mind.

To be out of that wretched hall with the cobwebbed human bodies and the murderous whispers, and Madhupura's grotesque queen at the centre of it all.

The fires in the three iron braziers burned so low that they hardly emitted any light, which was good, because that way, they were hard to discern by enemy lookouts searching for them in the dark. The problem, however, was that the fires barely gave any heat, so everyone had to huddle around the three braziers to keep warm — which was good, because the fires were shielded by everyone's bodies as well, making it even harder for enemy lookouts to sight them.

A full day and half a night had passed since their flight out of Saumudri. They had all regrouped a mile to the east of the market as planned, and riding hard to stay ahead of their pursuers, they had made for the safety of Rajagriha.

But barely halfway into the journey, they'd begun hearing rumours of Rajagriha's fall, and the sacking of the palace by Gandharan and Kambojan troops. Yuddhajeet had wanted to press on regardless, and so they had until conjecture turned into cold facts and they'd had to accept the grim reality of Rajagriha's capitulation. Yuddhajeet had still insisted on riding to his father's rescue, but then they had received reports that Raja Ashwapati was no more: Even as the city had fortified itself, the king had suffered another stroke and died in his bed. Leaderless and at a loss, the beleaguered city had surrendered, and its attackers had then overrun Kekeya.

They'd also gathered that the Gandharan troops were on high alert in Rajagriha, fully expecting Yuddhajeet to show up for his father's last rites, while at the same time, Gandharan, Kambojan and Bahlika warriors combed the countryside for them. Nagnajit, it seemed, wanted Abhisarika to be delivered to him unharmed, but he had put a steep price on Yuddhajeet and Ambareesha's heads.

It had taken some effort on Abhisarika and Ambareesha's part to convince Yuddhajeet not to take the bait and go to the capital. "You'll be walking into an open trap," Ambareesha had said.

"It is a son's duty to attend his father's funeral," Yuddhajeet had argued.

"It is a son's duty to safeguard his father's legacy," Abhisarika had pointed out. "And you can't safeguard your father's legacy by becoming a prisoner of Gandhara. To free Kekeya from these invaders, you must first be free of chains yourself."

Having talked Yuddhajeet out of going to Rajagriha, they had spent the rest of the day evading capture while formulating a plan of action. Smara's safety was paramount, and everyone agreed the child had to be protected from Nagnajit and Sailusha. The challenge lay in finding a suitable place to hide. Rajagriha was under Gandharan control, and the rest of Kekeya would inevitably follow. They could seek sanctuary in one of the many independent market towns on the Vitasta, the Chandrabhaga or the Iravati, but these market towns were frequented by traders with an ear for gossip. News of their whereabouts would travel faster than the monsoon wind, and they'd be left with no choice but to move from market town to market town, perpetually at the mercy of the local *adhipati* or guild master. Moreover, attracted by the bounty on their heads, someone was always liable to betray them to a Gandharan or Bahlika unit.

With night almost upon them, the small band of refugees had chanced upon the abandoned huts that had once served as a waystation until a shorter or safer route had been discovered and the place had been left to ruin. They made camp, and to their luck, they found the old iron braziers, which they had lit to cook a meal and warm themselves.

"Among our tribespeople, there must be some who oppose what my uncle and the chiefs did," Ambareesha muttered, rubbing his hands to keep them from growing numb. "I must find them."

"What good would that do?" asked Yuddhajeet, eyeing the giant's silhouette seated across him.

"We could start building a resistance to Gandharan rule."

"All resistance to Gandharan rule you can find among your tribespeople is right here, around you," the prince remarked dryly, alluding to Ambareesha's loyalists.

"There have to be others," Ambareesha insisted.

Yuddhajeet shifted to bring himself closer to the brazier, but the movement put pressure on his shoulder and he winced. Abhisarika had stitched the wound and treated it with a herbal poultice, but it still hurt awfully. She had said he'd been lucky the Gandharan javelin hadn't broken any bones.

"Do you think we will find a safe haven in the hills beyond Trigartha?" Devadatta asked from where she sat, next to Abhisarika, who had just put Smara to sleep with a haunting little lullaby.

"It's a chance we must take," Ambareesha replied. "Honestly, it's also the only option we have. The hills offer hiding places like no other. Here in the plains, we will be discovered in no time."

"Sakala has been taken by the Gandharans," Abhisarika said quietly. "Trigartha should be next on their list. How safe will our passage be, brother?"

"I don't know. But wherever we travel, we must be careful." The giant was silent for a moment. "I can't believe the chief betrayed us like this," he said with sudden feeling. "He was so noble." He looked in Abhisarika's direction. "Remember father?" he asked.

Yuddhajeet saw Abhisarika nod in the dark. When neither cousin said anything for a while, the prince asked, "Whose father were you referring to?"

"My father," said Ambareesha, following it up with more silence. Then, at last, he spoke. "My father was the older of the two. But he wasn't a strong man. Let us put it this way, he wasn't a natural leader of men. He was weak, indecisive. Not like uncle, I mean chief Sailusha. So, our people wanted uncle to be chieftain instead of father. But uncle refused. He was a loyal younger brother until the very end, when illness took father. And afterwards, he was good to me. Raised me like his own son. He wanted me to become chief after him." The giant shook his head. "He was always so principled... Why did he do this?"

"He said he did it because for the first time, someone treated him as an equal," said Abhisarika, "someone treated a Bahlika as an equal."

"Nagnajit treated him as an equal?" Yuddhajeet could hear his own voice squeak in disbelief.

"Well, he promised to make father king, which is a lot more than anything father has ever been offered before."

Yuddhajeet couldn't tell Abhisarika's expression in the dark, so he kept his thoughts to himself.

"I believe Nagnajit's proposal was so unexpected that it blinded father," Abhisarika added. "He became so enamoured with the idea of being someone he had never imagined he would become — *a king* — that it warped his faculty to tell right from wrong. Father was tempted and seduced by evil." She went silent, although only for a moment. "Nagnajit's biggest crime is that he took the goodness out of father and corrupted his soul," she said, her voice quivering with anger and sorrow. "We must make Nagnajit pay for it."

"We will, sister," said Ambareesha. "Nagnajit will answer for all of his crimes against us and the people of the River Kingdoms."

Silence took over as everyone introspected on the vagaries of life. Many minutes passed before Yuddhajeet broke the silence by addressing Ambareesha. "If we mean to follow up on that oath to make Nagnajit suffer for his sins, we will need to do more than build a resistance of Bahlika warriors. We will need an army to overthrow the Gandharans, and I don't expect to find enough men anywhere in the River Kingdoms."

Yuddhajeet sensed everyone's attention shift towards him as his and Ambareesha's men turned in their places around the braziers to listen to him better.

"My friend, what do you have in mind?" the giant asked.

"If the intent is to raise an army, let us go to Ayodhya, where my nephew Bharat rules as king," Yuddhajeet replied. "Let us seek his help to fight Nagnajit and reclaim the River Kingdoms for ourselves."

"Do you think your nephew will help us?" Ambareesha asked, hope kindling in his voice.

Yuddhajeet paused as an image of the boy in a saddle, his hair blowing behind him in the wind, came suddenly to mind. "Bharat spent much of his childhood in Rajagriha," Yuddhajeet smiled fondly at the memory. "These lands are his lands; the palace is his palace. Bharat won't sit back and allow some invader from Gandhara to take it all away."

He turned to look at the faces staring at him in the dimming firelight. "Bharat will do everything to help us rid this land of Nagnajit's shadow," he promised.

eight

WHEN DILEEPA STEPPED INSIDE THE *DANDAPALA* headquarters, he was mentally prepared to be screamed at for having been away for close to a week without anyone's permission, but much to his surprise, he found Mitraka in a vastly improved mood.

"Where have *you* been all these days?" the chief of the *dandapalas* asked, looking him up and down. Swaddled in a heavy woollen *pravara*, she seemed bulkier and even more imposing than usual. "I'd begun to wonder if you had also disappeared like all the others," her eyes twinkled with hilarity that had been missing a long time. "I must confess I was hoping you had, so you'd be able to find out what's happening," she chuckled.

Dileepa was still wondering what had changed for Mitraka to make light of the disappearances when one of the senior *dandapalas* appeared at the door. "Is it true?" he asked the chief, looking and sounding hopeful. "That *adhipati* Sudhanva's son has returned?"

"Yes, Yadudeva returned early this morning," Mitraka said with a broad smile.

The older *dandapala*, who had clearly been investigating the disappearances, exhaled in relief. "That should get *adhipati* Sudhanva off our backs," he said. "There hasn't been a day he hasn't taken a dig at us these last few weeks since his son disappeared."

Mitraka nodded. "I am hoping the palace will also ease up on us a little," she said, "considering so many have come back in the last few days."

"How many have come back in the last few days?" Dileepa asked, realizing the gossip he had picked up on the road from Sravasti was not all rumour.

"Well over five hundred, all over Kosala. Three hundred in Ayodhya alone. In just three days," said Mitraka. Raising her eyebrows, she asked, "Haven't you heard?"

Three hundred in Ayodhya alone, Dileepa's heart leaped. *In the last three days.* Could Nandana be among the three hundred, he wondered, his hopes rising. He would visit the old quarter right after this interview, he decided. Perhaps she was back and was waiting for him…

"Why are you looking so lost?" Mitraka eyed him closely. "Don't tell me you didn't know."

Seeing Dileepa give a vague shrug, the other *dandapala* asked, "Where have you been? It's the only thing everyone is talking about. Wait…" he grinned, "…had you also disappeared? Is that why this is news to you? If you had, please tell us what's happening…"

"I was in Sravasti," Dileepa snapped in reply, beginning to tire of the joke.

"Sravasti?" Mitraka's eyebrows rose even higher this time.

Conscious of the senior *dandapala's* eyes on him and eager to be rid of the man, Dileepa turned to look at him. "What about the disappearances?" he asked. "Have they stopped?"

The man's face deflated. "They're still happening," he said stiffly, "but more are coming back."

"Let's hope *mahanayaka* Gajakarna's daughter returns soon," said Mitraka. "That would really be welcome."

Taking that as a cue, the older *dandapala* nodded and left. The chief of the palace investigators turned to Dileepa. "And what were you doing in Sravasti?"

"I was investigating the killings in the old quarter. I have made progress."

"Enlighten me, please."

In quick, broad strokes, Dileepa recounted his visit to the old goldsmith in Ayodhya who, based on the ring maker's craft, had determined that the ring had been forged decades ago in Sravasti. "I followed the trail to Sravasti," he said, "and visited almost all the goldsmiths there, but none of them could tell me anything remotely useful. Here too, it was an old jeweller who provided a breakthrough. According to him, the ring is typical in design and is commemorative of loyalty to an *adhipati*."

"What does that even mean?"

"It means the ring was forged at the behest of an *adhipati* who would have gifted it to someone who was loyal to him."

"Oh, I see. Did this jeweller have any idea which *adhipati* it could have been?"

"The *adhipati* of Sravasti. He recognized the twin-leaf design on the ring as the old emblem of Sravasti before it was changed to the lion's head that we now associate with Sravasti."

"The *adhipati* of Sravasti… meaning Mihiradutta?" Mitraka stared.

"Or his father, who would have been Sravasti's *adhipati* thirty or forty years ago, when the old emblem was still in use."

"Wait a minute," the chief of the *dandapalas* backed away as she tried to get her head around this. "You are telling me a ring forged years ago, on behalf of the *adhipati* of Sravasti, was found in the purse of an unidentified man who was killed brutally along with three others in the city's old quarter. Is that right?"

"Yes."

"So the dead man — or should we say *dead men*? — might have had something to do with the *adhipati* of Sravasti."

"Directly or indirectly, yes."

Mitraka chewed the matter over for a moment or two. "You were in Sravasti," she said. "Didn't you try to dig deeper?"

"I didn't want to confront anyone without more evidence. I mean, the ring was stolen to begin with, so it would've —"

"Stolen?" Mitraka sat up straight. "How do you know it was stolen?"

"If this ring had belonged to the man in whose possession it was found, why was it in his purse and not on his finger?" asked Dileepa. "It clearly wasn't his ring."

"It could have been given to him," Mitraka argued. "A gift for his loyalty towards the *adhipati*."

The adhipati *of Sravasti's ring of loyalty in the possession of a hired killer, Dileepa thought to himself with a shudder.*

"If it were a gift, the ring would have been kept in the purse with the silver *rupas*," he said, "and not hidden away inside a secret compartment sewn into the purse. There can only be one reason why the ring was so carefully concealed — it had been stolen, and the man didn't want it found in case the purse was searched."

"So, what are you saying? What do we do next?"

"I'm saying we have to find out where the ring came from, whose ring it is. If we advertise the fact that we found it on one of the dead men, we may never learn who the ring's real owner is. But if we announce that such a ring has been found *without mentioning where and how it was found*, its owner might come forward to claim it. That way, we'd at least have established some link between the dead men and the world they inhabited."

"Yes, and perhaps we will find a thread that leads to those who killed them," said Mitraka. "Do that then… put out an announcement about the ring, and let us see who comes forward to claim it."

Ayodhya is jinxed after Dashratha's death…

Standing on an open terrace and soaking in a weak, colourless mid-afternoon sunshine, Bharat contemplated the woman's words with a deep sense of dejection.

The curse of the gods is upon us. It's no wonder the magic is failing us and everything is going wrong. Woe the moment that struck Raja Dashratha down —

Gajakarna had apologized for his wife's behaviour, ascribing it to a mother's broken heart, but the words stung, opening old wounds afresh. The citizens of Ayodhya still hadn't accepted him as their own, he realized. Far from it, they were more than ready to attribute any suffering they had to endure to the passing of his father and the exile of Rama, thus holding him indirectly responsible for their plight.

Sucking distractedly on the seed of an *amalakam*, Bharat wondered for the hundredth time why Kaikeyi had been so bent on seeing him made king. She had said it was because Dashratha had promised to name her son as his successor, and she was holding him accountable to his word. She had also said it was because she loved him, Bharat, that she *always had*, though he failed to remember even one kind word or touch from her. Nothing except the unending comparisons to Rama…

The memory of another winter afternoon — warmer, brighter, pleasanter than this one — came to Bharat from the mists of the past. The archery contest for the kids of the palace. The red clay bird suspended from the branch, pivoting on its axis. His own breath suspended as he carefully took his aim to draw even with Rama's tally. Four birds successfully shot, one more to go. The last one. If he got this, it would make his father, who was watching the contest so attentively, proud of him, and Bharat desperately wanted to make his father proud…

He had loosed off the arrow and missed.

You missed, he remembered Kaikeyi saying later. No mention of the four birds he had shattered. It was the one shot he had missed that had counted the most. That one arrow that had failed to find its mark and marked him as a failure in his mother's eyes… and in his own. Never as good as Rama. Always second-best.

"What are you doing here?"

Bharat turned to find Mandavi by the door to the terrace.

"Nothing," he replied. "Just enjoying what little warmth the sun has to offer." Finding she was alone, he asked, "Where's Taksha?"

"With Atibhanu," Mandavi said, joining Bharat by the parapet. "They get along well. Atibhanu made Taksha a play sword out of wood. He's told the kid he'll teach him how to wield a sword."

Bharat nodded and looked away.

"Any further news of Shatrughna's arrival?" Mandavi asked after a few moments had passed.

"No, but he should be here later tonight or early tomorrow," said Bharat.

"It's been a while since he left Ayodhya, so he should be excited about coming back," Mandavi smiled. "He must be particularly eager to go to Rajviraj and see Shrutakirti before the delivery."

"When is she due?" Bharat asked.

"The *vaidyas* are expecting her to go into labour in the next ten or twelve days." Mandavi eyed her husband sideways. "You will come, right?"

"To Rajviraj? Of course. Send a message and I'll come."

"Father or Shatrughna or I… one of us will inform you as soon as the child is born."

Bharat gave a distracted nod and looked away.

"Try and bring the queen mothers as well," Mandavi suggested. "Mother Sumitra, at least."

Bharat managed another vague nod.

"What's the matter?" Mandavi asked. "You look preoccupied."

"Nothing."

"Don't lie to me. Something is bothering you." Mandavi reached out a hand and ran her fingers along Bharat's forehead, easing the frown lines etched on his brow. "Tell me… what is it?"

"It's… these disappearances."

"But more and more people are coming back, aren't they?" Seeing Bharat nod, Mandavi asked, "So, what's the problem?"

"The problem is I have failed to put a stop to these disappearances. I have failed my people as king."

Mandavi didn't immediately know what to say. As she scouted around for the right words, her husband spoke again. "I have been king for three years now, and I've done the best I could for them, but they still don't want me here." He spat the *amalakam* seed into his hand and looked at it with distaste for a second before flinging it into the bushes lining a pathway directly below him.

"What has happened for you to suddenly think such thoughts?" Mandavi asked in a gentle tone.

"Can't you see for yourself?" her husband answered harshly. "Look at the weather. Kosala has never faced such a severe winter before. People are dying from the cold. Over fifty dead across the kingdom. We are doing all we can to provide warmth to the people, but there is a growing rumour that the palace is responsible for the deaths because Madhupura has blocked the supply of woollen *pravaras* coming to Ayodhya. The implication is that such a situation would never have arisen had Kosala gone to war against Madhupura six months ago. There isn't a shred of truth in the rumours about Madhupura blocking the supply of *pravaras*, but there is no stopping those pointing fingers at the palace."

Mandavi placed a hand on Bharat's shoulder. "Remember what Yuddhajeet mama told you the night he left Ayodhya for Kekeya two years ago?" she asked. Giving Bharat a few moments to think, she said, "He said the elephant isn't bothered by the barking of dogs, and as a king, you too should not be bothered by loose talk."

"It's hard not to be bothered when the talk is based on fact though," Bharat countered.

"Like what?"

"Like the magic failing us… or these disappearances. These are real."

"These things are happening for no fault of yours."

The curse of the gods is upon us. It's no wonder the magic is failing us and everything is going wrong. Woe the moment that struck Raja Dashratha down —

"Unfortunately, the people of Kosala don't seem to share your opinion," Bharat grimaced. "They think father's death has brought a blight on Ayodhya. And as the one responsible for his death, I am to blame for the misfortunes that have befallen this kingdom. The magic going away, the disappearances… it's all my fault."

"Is that what *you* believe to be true?" asked Mandavi. "That it is all your fault?"

"What I believe is of no consequence. What matters is what the people see as the truth, and for the people of Ayodhya, the truth is that I will never be good enough a king, no matter how hard I try." Gripping the parapet hard with both hands, Bharat shook his head vehemently. "I should never have accepted the responsibility of becoming king of Kosala."

"What should you have done then, Bharat?" Mandavi asked in a voice suddenly stern, her gaze steely. "Should you have left Kosala to its fate? Imagine you had done that. What would have happened the night the rakshasas attacked the Sanctum of the Fire? Who would have saved the Sanctum from the rakshasas, Bharat? Who would have protected the sacred fire and kept the magic from dying? And what would have happened to the people of Ayodhya if Pushyanta's hoarding scam had not been uncovered? They would have been bled dry by rising prices. And those poor farmers and the cattle they had mortgaged to the moneylenders… who would have given them justice, Bharat? By accepting the responsibility to be king, you have saved Kosala from ruin."

The king stared into the distance for a while. Then, without taking his eyes off the horizon, he said, "The people still only want Rama."

"Is it the people, or is it you who is obsessed with Rama?" Mandavi asked.

"What do you mean?" Bharat looked at his wife sharply.

"You have always run away from your brother and comparisons to him," Mandavi dropped her voice and placed her hand over Bharat's on the parapet. "There is a reason you love Kekeya so much and spent much of your childhood there. Kekeya is your refuge, Bharat, your sanctuary. A place away from Rama and comparisons to him."

"That's not true —" Bharat began to counter Mandavi, but she tightened his grip on his hand.

"It is," she whispered. "You weren't with me when I was expecting Taksha. You weren't even in Ayodhya with Rama, Lakshmana and Shatrughna. You were in Kekeya, where you are safe from being measured against Rama."

With an angry shake of his head, Bharat tried pulling his hand free, but Mandavi held on tight.

"I am not blaming you, Bharat," she insisted. "That fear, that insecurity is real, but you have to stop being afraid of coming up short. No matter who says what, stop making those comparisons in *your* head. You have to realize that you are different from your father and your brother, and you must let that difference define you. That's when the people of Kosala will grow to like and respect you."

Bharat remained silent. Mandavi turned to face him square. Then, taking him by the shoulders, she turned him around so he faced her. "Raja Seeradhwaja used to tell us girls something," she said. "Every day is a battle between who you are, who you want to be, and who you *can* be." She paused to look deep into Bharat's eyes. "The question is, which one of these will you help win today?"

Bharat looked back at Mandavi, the anger in his eyes slowly melting.

Mandavi gave her husband a moment to think. "We know you want to be a yuvaraja in Kekeya, where your heart resides. We know you are the raja of Kosala. But you *can* be much more than these, Bharat. You can be Ayodhya's hope, its saviour. Embrace that destiny."

Drawing a deep breath, the king placed his own hands on his wife's shoulders and drew her to himself. "Has anyone ever told you that you are probably the most intelligent woman in all of Jambudvipa?" he asked. Before she could laugh, he added, "I dearly wish someone had warned me before our marriage. I would definitely have told father that I did not want to wed a woman who would tell me what to do, and tell it in such a way that I'd want to do it nonetheless."

Mandavi burst out laughing, and Bharat grinned. Then, as they sobered down, Bharat squeezed Mandavi's shoulders. "Who I *can* be..." he said thoughtfully. "That made a lot of sense."

Mandavi was on the verge of a reply when she was interrupted by signs of sudden activity from further down the path towards the palace gates. There arose the muted rumble of many hooves treading the ground in a slow, leisurely walk, while voices were raised in conversation. A pair of palace guards came into view, escorting the visitors who had arrived, and half a dozen palace hands ran out to help with the horses.

"I wonder if that is Shatrughna," said Mandavi, perking up.

"It must be, though it's a bit early for him," Bharat remarked. "He must be very eager to get to Rajviraj and Shrutakirti," he added with a grin.

The small cavalcade rounded the copse of trees that hid them from the terrace, and the first few riders came into view.

"It can't be," the king gasped in surprise, recognizing the face riding right in front.

"It's Yuddhajeet mama," Mandavi exclaimed.

"You were just speaking about his last visit to Ayodhya," said Bharat. "What a coincidence!"

He had been running as hard as his spindly little legs would allow him, trying to keep ahead of Shatrughna or one of the other children in their game of catch-the-bandits, when he had tripped and fallen, scraping both elbows and a knee. The cut on the knee had bled, and he remembered bawling his eyes out as a palace *vaidya* had tended to the wound. His nana, who had been trying to calm him down, had suddenly bent over him, reached behind his ear and plucked out a round *draksha*, holding it up triumphantly between his fingers.

He remembered being so surprised that he had ceased crying almost immediately, staring open-mouthed at the shiny fruit under his nose.

"How did you do that?" he had asked between whimpers.

"Magic," Raja Ashwapati had replied, popping the berry into his mouth, his eyes twinkling.

"Show me how," he had said, wiping his tears, the injury to his knee forgotten in his excitement.

Bharat had been six or seven, and he had instinctively known there was no magic in this. It was all sleight of hand, and his grandfather had taught him half a dozen other tricks that Bharat had practised over the years. He'd never become very good at them, nowhere as good as his mama Yuddhajeet, but that trick was his earliest memory of Raja Ashwapati, Bharat remembered, as he watched the flames dance in the brazier that warmed the room.

"Father died alone," Yuddhajeet broke the silence, his voice heavy with regret. "It should never have been so."

Kaikeyi sniffled and dabbed at her eyes with the corner of her *uttariya*. She hadn't spoken since she had come rushing to meet Yuddhajeet, the news of Raja Ashwapati's death already having reached her ears. Brother and sister had held onto each other in a long, tearful embrace, grieving their shared loss before Kaikeyi had slowly pulled away to compose herself.

His nana had died alone, Bharat thought. He should have taken time to make a trip to Rajagriha and visit the old raja, Bharat realized. He had meant to, he knew, but the bottom line was that he hadn't. He had missed a chance to see his nana one last time. His mama was right. It should never have been so.

"I wish I had at least been able to perform his last rites," Yuddhajeet said for the third time, not willing to let it go. "Father deserved that."

"Stop it," said Kaikeyi, her tone a trifle sharp in the stillness of the room. Modulating her words and her voice to a gentler pitch, she went on, "You did what was right under the circumstances. Father taught us to be sensible, remember? He would have approved of your decision. And the girl is right," she looked in Abhisarika's direction. "You can't hope to free the River Kingdoms from the confines of a dungeon."

Bharat let his gaze wander to the three Bahlikas standing to Yuddhajeet's left. The woman his mother had made a reference to had an enigmatic quality about her, her poise and self-assurance marking her out. She had a daughter, he knew, though he had no idea where the child was at the moment. He had also understood it was the woman's father, a chieftain, who had betrayed Kekeya. The big, brawny man next to her had been introduced as Ambareesha, and Bharat had gathered he and the woman were related. The bright young girl by the giant's side was his wife.

Bharat was wondering how the three Bahlikas and their entourage fit in with his uncle's escape from Kekeya — and how best to broach the topic — when Kaikeyi spoke again.

"Do we know whether Nagnajit's commanders granted father a dignified farewell?" she asked. "Or," and here her eyes flashed dangerously, "did they obstruct or desecrate his last rites in any way?"

"From what we have learned, it appears father's last rites were performed by his senior council, in accordance with tradition and without hindrance," Yuddhajeet replied, the relief plain in his voice.

A collective sense of thankfulness settled over the room, but everyone's spirits dampened right away on hearing what

Yuddhajeet said next. "But that's where the good news ends, I'm afraid."

"What do you mean?"

"Conditions in Rajagriha are far from good under Gandharan occupation."

"What do we know of the situation?" asked Bharat, speaking after a long time.

"Nagnajit seems to have been nursing a severe grudge against Kekeya, especially after his army was thrashed at Mithuna," said Yuddhajeet. "So, his commanders have been singling Kekeyans out for harsh punishment, with our soldiers bearing the brunt of their abuse. We have been told that captured Kekeyan soldiers are being treated like animals, herded into cramped cells, hardly being given enough to eat and being forced to toil without rest. There have been stories of our soldiers being tortured as well."

Bharat's eyes narrowed in anger at the account of Gandharan atrocities, but Yuddhajeet wasn't quite done yet. "That's only part of the suffering being inflicted on our people. Laws have been passed ordering the common people to fall on their knees and salute passing Gandharan troops and commanders, failing which they are liable to be whipped and thrown into prison. Also, all sorts of taxes and fines are being levied on Kekeyans; there are penalties for looking Gandharan soldiers in the eye, would you believe it! There have been reports of Gandharan troops forcibly entering homes and taking away provisions and money under the guise of taxation."

"This is outrageous!" Kaikeyi said through gritted teeth.

"There's more," said Yuddhajeet. "The guild at Rajagriha was sacked and burned to the ground by Gandharan troops.

Sections of the palace suffered a similar fate before someone decided to convert the place into a garrison for Gandharan and Kambojan soldiers."

"Our home is a barrack for enemy troops?" Kaikeyi remarked, seething with rage.

Yuddhajeet nodded. "And yes, all the fine horses of Rajagriha have been seized and sent off to Kapisi. I'm told there's not a single horse to be seen anywhere in Kekeya other than those being ridden by Gandharan or Kambojan warriors."

An image of finely bred horses galloping along the banks of the Vitasta and the Chandrabhaga flashed through Bharat's mind, and he was gripped by a sudden, crippling sadness, and a sense of irreparable loss. His nana was no more, while his mama had had to flee his home. The horses of Kekeya were gone, its people no longer free. The land of his childhood had been subjugated, and his memories of that land were being defiled.

With that realization came rage. And steely resolve. His land, his people, the memories of his childhood... everything had to be liberated from the oppressor.

"We must rid the River Kingdoms of foreign rule," said Kaikeyi, echoing Bharat's thoughts.

Bharat nodded, but before he could say anything, Kushadhwaja stepped into the conversation.

"While on the topic of freeing the River Kingdoms," the *kshatri* said, "what I am unclear about is the role the Bahlikas will be playing. Pardon me," he glanced at the giant and the two women, "you are Bahlikas and you are with yuvaraja Yuddhajeet here, but what about the rest of you? From what I understand, your tribespeople are firmly behind Nagnajit —"

"By switching loyalties, my father and the other chieftains have betrayed the Bahlikas as much as they have betrayed the River Kingdoms," said Abhisarika. Placing a hand on Ambareesha's arm, she continued, "My brother and I are on the side of the River Kingdoms, and I believe we will find more Bahlikas willing to part with the chieftains and come to our side once we mount a campaign on Gandhara. The Bahlikas are people of honour and they mean well. They've just been misled by my father. They need a better leader, that's all."

"And why are *you* on the side of the River Kingdoms?"

"That was the original deal that my father agreed to. Fighting on the side of the River Kingdoms in exchange for money." Abhisarika paused to look at the *kshatri* levelly. "But there's more to it now. Yuvaraja Yuddhajeet risked his life to save my brother, and he came to *my* rescue when I was on the verge of being married off to Nagnajit of Gandhara against my wishes. My brother owes the yuvaraja his life. I owe him my daughter's freedom, and mine."

With a small nod of satisfaction, Kushadhwaja reverted to silence.

Yuddhajeet took a step forward. "We must move quickly if we are to free the River Kingdoms," he urged. "The more we delay, the more we give Gandhara time to consolidate, and the harder it will be to pry the enemy out." He turned to Bharat. "Kekeya's force is scattered and will take time to regroup. Meanwhile, as Abhisarika just said, Bahlika warriors could turn their backs on Sailusha and join our cause. But be it the Kekeyan army or Bahlika warriors, people will join our side only when they see us making a concerted effort to drive Nagnajit out." He paused to draw breath. "We need an army of our own to take on the might of the Gandhara and Kamboja armies."

A few moments' silence followed as everyone waited for Bharat's reaction, knowing fully well what Yuddhajeet was proposing, and knowing even better that the outcome hinged on Bharat's willingness to back a war on Gandhara. The raja of Kosala took his time organizing his thoughts before he finally spoke.

"We must wage war against Nagnajit to free our land of the invaders," he said. "Kosala will go to war on behalf of the River Kingdoms. I shall convene a war council at the earliest."

Relief played on Yuddhajeet's face, and Ambareesha and Abhisarika's shoulders slackened as the burden of expectations lifted suddenly. Pleased with the decision, Kaikeyi gave her brother a reassuring smile as she went up to Abhisarika and took her by her hand. "I would like you to come and stay with me," she said. "Your daughter too, and," she reached to touch Devadatta's cheek gently, "you are also welcome to my quarters, child."

"Arrangements have been made for them to stay in the east wing by the pond —" Bharat began, but he was cut short by his mother.

"In all these years, it's the first time my brother has brought a girl home," she insisted. "I would like to get to know her better."

Abhisarika coloured and quickly dropped her gaze, while Yuddhajeet developed a sudden and consuming interest in the decorative patterns on the marbled floor.

And just like that, Bharat understood.

He nodded at his mother.

"I shall have Smara sent over," Mandavi gave Abhisarika a warm smile, and Abhisarika bowed her head in return, grateful for the welcome they were being afforded.

"You could have Taksha come over as well," Kaikeyi said. Watching Bharat stiffen, she added, "Smara is of roughly the same age. They might get along and be good for each other."

Bharat gave this a moment's thought before catching Mandavi's eye. He nodded. Then, looking over to Yuddhajeet and Ambareesha, he said, "You must all be tired after such a long ride. Rest and refresh yourselves. I shall see you later."

"Let me understand this…" Sudhanva paused to peer into the faces around him before focusing again on Gajakarna. "The raja has summoned a war council to deliberate over waging a war on Gandhara. Is that correct?"

"Yes," the *mahanayaka* replied.

"Except that from what we know, the raja has already made up his mind about waging this war, which means there will be no debate on the matter. Is that correct?"

"Yes," Gajakarna said again.

"In other words, this war council is a sham. And despite commanding Kosala's army, you will have no say in this. You will have no choice but to do as directed by the king."

The *mahanayaka* said nothing, a deep frown forming at the corners of his lips and on his brow.

Sudhanva sat back and assessed Mihiradutta and Jayabhama. "Look what we've come to," he said, throwing his hands up in helplessness. "The *mahanayaka* of Kosala has no authority over the army he commands. I doubt this would ever have happened under the rule of Raja Dashratha or Rama."

Seeing Mihiradutta and Jayabhama shake their heads at Gajakarna in commiseration, Sudhanva was filled with delight. When he had heard about Yuddhajeet's arrival in Ayodhya, he had had no idea how much he could benefit from it. The rebellion he had been planning had hardly any momentum, and despite successfully spreading rumours against the palace, resentment against Bharat hadn't peaked as he had expected. He had even reached out to the moneylenders against whom Bharat had ruled, hoping that the ruling had antagonized them enough for them to desire a change in regime. But he had quickly realized the moneylenders were a gutless lot, unwilling to go against their king, not while he graced the throne at any rate. They would come fawning and grovelling once power had shifted, Sudhanva was certain, but as things stood, the rebellion was cold and dead like early-morning ash in the braziers.

Then, Yuddhajeet had come, and a few hours later, he had heard about the Gandharan invasion of the River Kingdoms and Bharat's decision to march an army to liberate Kekeya. There! In one unexpected stroke of good fortune, he had been presented with the spark to reignite his rebellion. The *adhipati* was hard-pressed to tell which of the two was a reason for greater joy — Yuddhajeet's arrival in Ayodhya, or the return of his son Yadudeva early that morning.

"Do you even see what's happening here?" Sudhanva asked, leaning forward to get everyone's attention. "Six months ago, soldiers of our garrison in Madhupura were beaten and thrown into a dungeon. Madhupura then appropriated our garrison and kicked our soldiers out. Kosala was humiliated by a tiny market city, but when it came to holding Madhupura accountable, our raja showed no inclination to fight. But now, a foreign kingdom from across the Sindhu has invaded Kekeya — our king's favourite Kekeya, mind you — and he springs into action, summoning a council, calling for war. Look at his priorities. He is king of Kosala, but its humiliation means nothing to him. But his beloved Kekeya… that's a different story."

The other men in the room nodded in the brooding silence.

"And look at our *kshatri*," the *adhipati* continued, not wanting to miss a single roll of the dice. "Just when we'd convinced Bharat to march against Madhupura, Kushadhwaja used some silly logic to talk the king out of war. Where is that *kshatri* now, and why doesn't he have any objections to war this time?"

More silence filled the room.

"I have one simple question," Sudhanva continued, raising the rhetoric. "Why should the blood of Kosala's soldiers be shed in this war against Gandhara? This isn't Kosala's war. Kosala has not been invaded. Why should Kosala wager its men then? Let Kekeya fight Gandhara. Let the king lead the Kekeyans if he so wishes. But he cannot play with the lives of Kosala's subjects. He cannot use our brave men as pieces in his move to protect Kekeya."

"You are absolutely right," Jayabhama said, slapping his thigh in agreement.

"How will you justify this campaign to your men?" Sudhanva asked the *mahanayaka*, needling him out of his silence. "What will you say to them? That they are expected to lay down their lives in a war that has nothing to do with them? Can you sell that to your men?"

The commander sat deep in thought, twiddling his thumbs, his chin on his chest.

"Remember how you had to tell your men they weren't marching to Madhupura to avenge the insults their mates had suffered there?" Sudhanva pressed on. "Remember how cheated they'd felt? Remember how humiliating it had felt to you? And now, you will order them to march to Kekeya instead, so they can fight in a war they don't care the least bit about. What respect will your men have for you, *mahanayaka*?"

Gajakarna shook his head, his face darkening in anger and frustration. "I cannot let my men go into this war," he said.

"I don't know how you can prevent it," said Sudhanva.

"The time to act has arrived," the *mahanayaka* snapped, squaring his shoulders and glaring at the others. "That rebellion we've been speaking of..." he flicked his fingers in rapid succession, "...its time has come."

Sudhanva let his breath out softly. "I agree with you," he said in a voice no more than a whisper.

"I will need to take the *nayakas* and *upanayakas* loyal to me into confidence," said Gajakarna. "We shall devise a plan that I can share with all of you. The change in power should be swift... but it should also be bloodless, if it can be helped."

"Remember that we don't have much time," Sudhanva cautioned, ignoring the *mahanayaka's* reference to a peaceable transition of power. "Bharat wants to move against Gandhara quickly, so we'll have to act fast as well."

"Bharat has convened the war council tomorrow," said Gajakarna. "Once he makes his decision public, I can start planting unrest and discontentment among the ranks. The men are already an unhappy lot. It won't take much to rile them."

"Maybe we can overthrow Bharat and seize the palace in two or three days," Mihiradutta said, rubbing his hands for warmth — and perhaps also in anticipation of what was to come.

"We probably can," said Gajakarna.

"In which case, we most definitely should," Sudhanva stressed as he rose to take leave.

"Let me start by talking to my men," said the *mahanayaka*, also rising.

Sudhanva was halfway to the door when, remembering his last visit to the commander's house, he stopped to face Gajakarna. "How is your wife faring?" he asked, placing a hand on the man's shoulder.

"She weeps for our daughter while she waits for her to return." Gajakarna looked at the *adhipati* of Sankasya, his eyes slowly lighting up with hope. "Your son… how is he?" he asked.

"He is back, and so will your daughter be," Sudhanva said, comforting the *mahanayaka* with a gentle pat. With a tight squeeze to the commander's shoulder, he added, "But we won't forgive those who did nothing to prevent our children from being taken. Vengeance has to be ours, my friend."

Gajakarna wore a blank expression as he swore under his breath, "Vengeance will be ours."

"I knew nothing about the market garrison being built on the Yamuna."

Day was turning to evening as Yuddhajeet and Bharat sauntered through the palace grounds, deep in conversation. Taksha and Smara walked a dozen paces in front of the men, not really saying anything at all, but happy to be in each other's company. Taksha had started off shy but excited to make a new friend, and he'd been eager to introduce Smara to Angara, and it was to that end that the little procession now wound its way. The wind had shifted and gained an edge with the lowering of the sun, and everywhere, long grass bent and swayed and rustled, while the leaves in the tress shivered at every draught.

"Had I known about the market and about Shatrughna, I'd have stopped there instead of coming through Madhupura," Yuddhajeet continued. "Then we could have arrived here together."

"It's good you came when you did," Bharat replied. "You were all able to rest a bit. Shatrughna is not expected until tonight or tomorrow."

Yuddhajeet inclined his head in agreement and they walked in silence for a moment. "It's hard to believe Shatrughna is going to be a father," Yuddhajeet chuckled. "I remember him running around the courtyard in Rajagriha, waving his play sword and screaming at the top of his voice. He was really skinny back then, and I get the feeling he was always coughing and sneezing. It feels like yesterday."

Bharat smiled at the memory. "I think he will make a good father. He's good with kids. He is incredibly excited, I know, and he's looking forward to the responsibility."

"How is he otherwise?" asked Yuddhajeet.

"He is growing up," Bharat smiled and shrugged. "We all are, aren't we?"

"I'm not growing up. I'm growing old," Yuddhajeet said with a wave of his hand.

"But not old enough to avoid falling in love," Bharat grinned, shooting a sidelong glance at his uncle.

Yuddhajeet looked sharply at his nephew and they both burst into laughter.

"Forget Shatrughna becoming a father… I find this harder to believe," Bharat said with a shake of his head. "I remember asking you what you had against women, and you said they were too much trouble. Now, here you are —"

"But they *are* trouble," Yuddhajeet grinned, spreading his hands. "Look at me, the yuvaraja of Kekeya, run out of my home and living as a fugitive in my nephew's kingdom. All because of a woman."

"What does she have to do with it?" Bharat looked at Yuddhajeet in surprise. "The Gandharan invasion isn't linked to Abhisarika, is it?"

"Well… yes and no. I mean, her being given in marriage to Nagnajit was part of the deal struck between Nagnajit and Sailusha. By rescuing her and preventing that wedding, I haven't exactly won the love and admiration of Nagnajit and Sailusha."

With a chuckle, Bharat shook his head. "I also remember telling you that when you fall in love with someone, you'll discover that the trouble is worth it." He glanced at his uncle. "Something tells me I was right."

Yuddhajeet shucked his shoulder in response and winced instantaneously.

Watching his uncle's face scrunch in pain, Bharat said, "You should let the palace *vaidyas* take a look at that wound, mama."

"Abhisarika has fixed and mended me once already," Yuddhajeet said with a shake of his head. Nursing his shoulder tenderly, he added, "She'll do fine."

"She is a medicine woman as well?" Bharat asked, clearly intrigued.

Yuddhajeet swished his *pravara* to one side so Bharat could glimpse the scar running along his midriff, still reddish in colour. "I got that in Mithuna," he said. "The healing is her handiwork."

Bharat's eyebrows rose and fell in appreciation. "I guess finding a woman like her was worth the wait, mama," he smiled, impressed.

Yuddhajeet merely nodded in reply.

"What about the daughter?" Bharat asked, looking at Smara marching solemnly beside Taksha. "Has she accepted you?"

"Phew," Yuddhajeet blew his cheeks out. "She was harder to impress than the mother," he said. "But eventually, I got through to her as well… with your nana's trick, of all things."

"You mean his magic trick?" Bharat laughed as the memory resurfaced. "Well, that's one trick that never fails."

Smara had stopped to investigate a trail of ants crossing the path, and Taksha squatted next to her, observing the insects with an interest he had never displayed before. Bharat could see the two learning from each other, and the thought warmed him. It reminded him of Kekeya, where he and Shatrughna would go off every morning exploring the fields and the countryside…

"You had better hurry if you want your friend to meet Angara, young man," he said, addressing Taksha. "It's getting dark and cold, and we have to get back for dinner."

Smara turned to look at Bharat, but his father's words spurred Taksha into action. Taking Smara by the hand, he rose and began pulling her down the path, and the girl let herself be dragged a bit before falling in step beside him. The children skipped and ran, free like the wind scything through Ayodhya, and the two men had to lengthen their strides to keep pace.

"What about you?" Yuddhajeet asked suddenly. "How are you doing?"

Bharat shrugged. "Okay," he replied, instinctively huddling into his *pravara*.

"Okay?"

Bharat nodded. They walked in silence for a bit. "I mean as okay as it can get," the raja admitted finally.

"What's troubling you?" Yuddhajeet asked.

"Everything. This cold… the crops are failing and people are dying. It's never happened before. Then the magic. It's just… dwindling… it's *dying out*. And I'm powerless to do anything about it."

"If it is not in your power, why blame yourself at all?"

You can't perform the agnimanasa homa. *Because I won't let you, rajan.*

"It's not…" Bharat checked himself with a frustrated shake of his head. He couldn't tell anyone about the *agnimanasa*, not even Yuddhajeet. He cursed Surochi under his breath.

"It's not what?" his uncle asked.

"It's… never enough," said Bharat. "Whatever you do is never enough. I don't understand why people yearn to become kings and rule over kingdoms. It's hardly worth the effort."

"The way some women are worth the trouble, some kingdoms are worth the effort," Yuddhajeet remarked with a smile. "Kosala is worth the effort… at least for the promise you have made to your brother."

Bharat shot a glance at his uncle and then looked away.

"Also, these disappearances," he said, changing the subject. "They haven't stopped, and we're clueless about what to do to prevent them. People just go and just come back. It can be anyone. Totally random. And none of them have any idea where they'd been when they'd gone away."

"We heard about the disappearances in Rajagriha, though I had no idea they were so widespread," exclaimed Yuddhajeet. He gave it a moment's thought. "And those who come back are… fine?"

"Absolutely, and that's the bizarre bit," said Bharat. "Take Siripala… you'll see him now. You wouldn't be able to tell he had disappeared. He's perfectly normal… ah, there he is…"

The old ostler was sweeping the ground in front of the royal stable. On hearing Taksha's trilling voice, he looked up to see the children and the two men approaching. Taksha ran up to Siripala, and Bharat saw the man bow down and greet Smara with a *pranaam*. He then straightened and waited for his king to draw near.

"Salutations," the old man said, putting his hands together for Bharat and Yuddhajeet. His eyes dwelled on the latter, carefully taking in the prince as he tried to figure who this visitor might be.

"This is Siripala," Bharat said by way of introduction, "and this is my mama, Yuddhajeet."

The old man's eyes sparkled in recognition. "*You* are yuvaraja Yuddhajeet," he said in wonder, bowing low again. Then, as an old memory of Bharat as a young boy came back, Siripala lapsed into an earlier form of address. "You are the mama who taught the kumara how to ride so well," he said.

"I am that mama," Yuddhajeet laughed.

"It is an honour meeting you," said Siripala with yet another bow. "I have heard so much about you."

"I have heard about you as well," said Yuddhajeet. "Bha— your rajan has told me of your love for horses. And how you helped him train to fight on horseback."

"You taught him how to ride. The rajan already had all the skills needed to fight on horseback."

"Okay… how about giving *me* some of the credit for the riding and the fighting?" Bharat butted in with a good-natured laugh.

The men were still laughing when Angara made an appearance from around the stable, wagging its tail as it trotted towards Taksha and Smara. The girl took a wary step back, but seeing Taksha run to embrace the dog, she followed, and for that, she was immediately rewarded with a nuzzle and a big lick on the face. Smara giggled at the attention Angara was lavishing on her, and Taksha watched with a proud smile, happy to see that his old friend was getting along well with his newest friend.

"Is that… the pup from Manglapuri?" Yuddhajeet asked in astonishment. Seeing Bharat smile, he shook his head. "It's really grown." He snapped his fingers and Angara turned and made its way towards the men, tail wagging merrily until it noticed Siripala and slowed, its tail drooping and a timid look in its eyes. Bharat stared, wondering what the matter was, but by then, the dog was at his and Yuddhajeet's feet and they were petting it, and then it had turned and gone back to the children, bounding after them.

"It is lovely to see children taking to animals," said Yuddhajeet, watching the three run around. "Bringing Angara to Ayodhya was a good decision. Perhaps I should look for a pet for Smara."

"Maybe you could take Angara to the palace," Siripala said in a small voice.

Bharat turned sharply to the ostler. "Pets aren't allowed inside the palace, you know that. That's why Angara has been left here in your care."

"Yes... I... I know..." Siripala looked flustered. "It was only a suggestion, rajan. I thought the children could play with the dog... I am sorry."

"The kids will come here and play with the dog," said Bharat, looking at the old man squarely. "Just take good care of the animal, that's all."

"I will, rajan," said Siripala, dropping his gaze.

In another five minutes, the sky had turned dark except for one patch to the west, and the palace grounds were in shadows. Bharat called to the children to halt their play, but it was a couple of minutes before they obeyed and Taksha, Smara and Angara returned to where the men waited. As Bharat took Taksha's hand and Yuddhajeet took Smara's, the dog waddled off into the dark. The men and the kids were about to leave when Siripala called from behind.

"Rajan," he said, "I would like a word with you in private."

Ordering Taksha to go with Yuddhajeet and Smara, Bharat returned to the ostler's side. "Yes?" he asked.

"Rajan… you had asked me if I remember anything from the time I… I wasn't here."

"Yes," said Bharat. "And you'd said you remembered darkness, and maybe a voice." He leaned closer in sudden excitement. "Have you remembered something else…" he asked, "…like what the voice said?"

"No," the old man shook his head. "Not the voice. But I remember something else, rajan."

"What?"

"The place I was in… there were many of us there. Lots of us. And everywhere, there was pain and misery and sorrow, rajan. It was the saddest, most terrible place to be in. Like prisoners. It made us all sad and desperate and angry, rajan. That's what I remember."

"Sad and desperate and angry?"

"Sad and desperate and angry," Siripala nodded. "And I fear we — we who've come back — might have brought that sadness and desperation and anger with us. I do truly fear that, rajan."

The east bank of the Yamuna was a dark silhouette against a dark, star-studded sky, its contours and features fading rapidly as night fell around the little boat making a lonely, perilous crossing of the crocodile-infested river. And if darkness wasn't enough of a hindrance, Swagata's vision was further impaired by the tears that kept pooling in his eyes and flowing down his cheeks — which were already burning with shame at the thought of what he was going to do once he had forded the river and landed on safe ground, half a mile north of the market garrison that he had been trying his level best to destroy.

"I have been doing my best, rajan," he had whimpered, standing before Lavanyasurya less than an hour ago. "I have... I set fire to the timber yard, rajan, and that fire destroyed a whole week's supply of wood. I sabotaged the dam that led to the flooding of the market's foundations, rajan. I introduced venomous *vrischikas* into the workers' tents and over a dozen of them were stung, forcing a halt to the construction until the *vrischikas* were found and killed. I have delayed the building of the market by many days —"

"And yet, looking across the Yamuna, I can see the market rise from the floor of the forest like a curse, a blot on the horizon, an eclipse over Madhupura," Lavanyasurya had said in his grating voice. The king's face had grown even more ashen since the time the *upanayaka* had last seen him, and his features were even more twisted in protracted pain. "Your fires and *vrischikas* and whatnot haven't discouraged the men building the market, sapping their will to work anymore, and that is why you have failed in slowing the construction of the market. Your sabotage has to hurt the men, *upanayaka*, not the process."

"Rajan, I can't hurt those men. They are my own people, citizens of Kosala. Even the *vrischikas* — it was wrong on my part to have —"

"Where are your priorities, *upanayaka*, where are your priorities?" Lavanyasurya had turned away from Swagata with a theatrical flourish, his face anguished by the spectacle of so much human folly. "You will not hurt those men because they are your own people... Is that what you say, *upanayaka*?

Then what of them —" he flung an arm to point to one side, "— what are *they* to you?"

With his breath trembling on his lips, Swagata had followed the king's finger, already knowing what he would see there, knowing what the king was pointing at…

"Father," a tremulous voice had called out, and Swagata had felt his knees buckle. His daughter's voice.

Asmi's voice.

His eyes already swimming with tears, the *upanayaka* had turned to see Vedika, Asmi and Nari at the far end of the hall, huddled together and looking small and intimidated in the shadow of the three large men who held them hostage, calloused fingers hard and unforgiving around their arms and on their shoulders. Vedika had dark circles under her eyes from crying, and Asmi and Nari's sunken cheeks and haunted eyes told him they were not eating or sleeping well. A sob had escaped Swagata's lips, and he had taken a step towards the three people who were dearer to him than life when a hand had clamped down on his wrist, yanking him back.

"What are those three to you, *upanayaka*?" Lavanyasurya had whispered into his ear. "Nothing, I would imagine. So, perhaps we should dispense with them. Starting with… the woman? How about the girl? Or maybe the boy?"

"Rajan, please…" Swagata had begged, "please let me meet my family. It has been so long and you had promised —"

"Yes, indeed. But your priorities have changed —"

"No, rajan —"

"You no longer care for these three —"

"Rajan, they are everything to me —"

"You want to save the men building the market —"

"No, rajan, no —"

"Why should I feed and protect these three when *you* don't care about them —"

"Rajan, I will do what you ask of me —"

"But you said no to me —"

"Rajan, I was foolish —"

"There should be a price attached to foolishness —"

"Rajan, no… *please* —"

Seeing the king nod at the men holding his family imprisoned, Swagata's eyes had grown wide in horror, and he was overcome by a sense of time becoming viscous and coming to a standstill. He remembered turning ever so slowly to look at Vedika, Asmi and Nari… and seeing the men draw curved *kshurikas*. He remembered screaming as he watched the daggers come up towards the necks of Vedika, Asmi and Nari; he remembered straining to break free of Lavanyasurya's vice-like grip; he remembered the flash of steel and a shrill cry of pain. Then, his legs had given way and he had suffered a blackout…

When Swagata returned to consciousness, he had found the hall empty. Pale, oblique light from a setting sun entered through the windows, and the floor felt cold against his cheek. There was no sign of his family.

"Vedika… Asmi…" he had called as he scrambled to his feet, his eyes searching wildly. "Nari…"

"Don't get so worked up," Lavanyasurya's voice had said from the shadows where he had been standing. "Your family is fine."

"I want to see them, rajan. Please…"

"But you just did."

"Rajan… they… the men had *kshurikas*…"

"Nothing has happened to your dear wife and children, I promise you." Lavanyasurya had stopped, as if remembering something. "No, that is not entirely correct, and if nothing, I am an honest man. Something has happened —"

"Rajan…" Swagata had wailed.

"Something *small*…" The king had walked over, and the *upanayaka* noticed he held something in his hand. The raja had thrust the object under Swagata's nose for inspection, and on realizing what it was, the *upanayaka* had gagged and nearly emptied the contents of his stomach all over the floor.

Lavanyasurya had been holding a severed ear between his fingers.

A small ear, without piercings, without adornments. A child's ear, cleanly sliced. Nari's ear.

Swagata had reeled at the sight, the floor pitching under him, so he had grabbed Lavanyasurya's arm to keep himself from falling again. The raja had caught and steadied him… and then pulled him close. Swagata had felt Lavanyasurya's hot breath on his cheek, but the words that had fallen into his ear were chilling.

"This is what happens when you don't listen and do as I say. You don't listen, they lose an ear. Remember, I have five more ears left to cut. One by one by one… Do you hear me? Or should I —"

"I hear you, rajan… I hear you," Swagata had panted, eager to please the madman. "I hear you. I will do as you say. I will do as you say, rajan…" And with that, he had collapsed to his knees, his body racked by sobs.

Wiping his tears, Swagata rowed the little boat purposefully, pointing its prow to the spot where he thought it was safe to land. He hated himself for what he was going to do, but he was doing it for those he loved. He was doing it for Vedika, Asmi and Nari, he told himself. Poor Nari… how much pain he must be in…

The boat rammed into an embankment with sudden force, throwing the *upanayaka* forward in his seat. The little craft rocked and juddered precariously for a moment before gaining stability, and Swagata slowly edged it against the bank where the water was shallow and tranquil enough to allow a landing. The *upanayaka* climbed out of the boat and pulled it ashore, away from the river's reach. Then, rummaging around its bottom, he withdrew a small bag made of homespun cotton. The bag was filled with the seeds and leaves of the toxic *dhattura* plant.

"Here," Lavanyasurya had said, thrusting the bag into his hand. "I've made it easy for you. All you have to do is ensure this goes into the biggest cooking cauldron you can find." He had paused to give Swagata an obscene grin. "Make sure you don't end up eating what they serve for lunch or dinner that day."

With a gasp and a shudder of self-loathing, Swagata hefted the bag and stepped away from the boat. He then picked his way through the dark towards the spot where Kosala's market garrison was being built.

Simhika sat at the centre of the mansion and pulled the darkness to her.

She pulled it from the depths of the well in the mansion, and she pulled it from the night lying thick over Ayodhya.

She pulled it from the black pit of vileness and pestilence, and she pulled it from the anger festering in her heart.

our lord is displeased with your progress the wraith from Lanka had whispered in her dream, *he wonders if he erred in sending you to Ayodhya with this task* the wraith had taken the form of Nandana and burst into laughter, *he thinks the girl would have done a better job than you* the wraith's form cycled from Nandana to bear to stork to old man, *he believes he should have sent cunning Maricha instead*

Simhika had woken in a sweat to find the wraith gone. All that had remained was a trail of ash that led out of the door.

our lord is displeased with your progress

Smarting at the words, the sorceress pulled the darkness to herself.

he wonders if he erred in sending you to Ayodhya with this task

She had come to destroy Ayodhya's protective magic, but it had proved to be more challenging than she had expected. She had dampened the magic, without a doubt, but corrupting the rishis and contaminating the sacred fire was really hard, she was learning.

he thinks the girl would have done a better job than you

The lord of Lanka couldn't be serious, she thought to herself heatedly. Nandana's deviousness was the reason she was behind schedule. Had the girl not been smitten by that *dandapala*, they would have gained access to the palace earlier…

he believes he should have sent cunning Maricha instead

No, she would not allow herself to be replaced by Maricha or any of the other rakshasas in her lord's service, Simhika decided, pulling more and more shadows to herself. She would not rest until she had accomplished what she had set out to achieve. She would beset Ayodhya with her shadows and cause the fall of the Ikshvakus. She would destroy this city and its magic to usher in the age of the rakshasas.

our lord is displeased with your progress

She would show the lord of Lanka he was right in picking her for this job, she swore to herself, darkness and anger rising within her in waves. She pulled darkness out of anger and anger out of darkness, and she knitted the two together into shadows that she let loose back into the night. She would destroy Ayodhya and its magic if it was the last thing she did.

destroydestroydestroydestroydestroy

The shadows screeched and tittered to themselves as they slipped from the mansion and spread to the dark, slumbering city.

When Dileepa dragged himself home that night, he was cold and miserable.

Cold because the weather had turned even more severe as the evening had progressed, with the wind getting as sharp as a razor, freezing his extremities and chilling him to the bone. Dileepa had never experienced a winter this bad, and by the time he got home, he was shivering inside his *pravara*, his teeth were chattering in his mouth and he could feel his toes going numb in his open *padukas*. That night, for probably the first time in his life, the young man understood the importance of having a roof and four walls around him.

Getting behind closed doors might have brought the *dandapala* enormous respite from the cold, but it was no salve for the sadness that tugged at his heart. If anything, the silence of the room added to the loneliness he had felt rising inside him all day as news of more and more of those who had disappeared returning came to his ears. If three hundred had returned in the preceding three days, nearly the same number had come back that day alone. Ayodhya was full of reports of returns in every quarter and locality, and Mitraka and the rest of the investigators couldn't stop smiling in relief at this unexpected turn of events. The *dandapalas* may not have played a part in the returns, but at least now everyone would stop abusing and making fun of them. That was the hope.

Dileepa was the only one who couldn't find it in himself to smile.

He had started off fine enough after meeting Mitraka, leaving the *dandapala* headquarters with a spring in his step and hope in his heart. He had gone to the old quarter with visions of finding Nandana back like everyone else, but approaching the old mansion, he'd known that he'd been wrong in getting his hopes up. He was met at the door by one of the women in Ma Parnalata's employ, who told him Nandana wasn't back. Pertinently, she did not invite him in, and Dileepa was given no hint about Ma Parnalata's whereabouts, though he suspected the aunt was within the mansion and had issued instructions that he was not to be entertained.

He had spent the entire day alternating between watching the mansion and waiting for someone to come and claim the ring at the *dandapala* headquarters, but with the day drawing to a close, both vigils had proved futile. The ring remained unclaimed, and though people returned by the hundreds, there was still no sign of Nandana.

Dropping down on his bed in the dark, Dileepa covered his eyes with his forearm and let out a sob. It wasn't until that evening that he had realized how much he missed Nandana, how much she had come to mean to him. She had been his closest companion in this city, and he wanted nothing greater than for her to be a part of his life for all time to come. Yet, she wasn't there, and while everyone else who had disappeared was returning, Nandana hadn't come back. The weight of his sorrow was so hard to bear that Dileepa felt sure his heart would burst and shrivel and die, beating itself slower and slower into nothingness and death.

…explain everything.

That was the last he had left of Nandana, Dileepa remembered. Just two words, a part of an old message the girl had sent him that Ayodhya's flawed magic had somehow brought back to the listening bells.

Two words. A dead echo.

Still, he wanted to draw some comfort from them. He wanted to hold the bells close. It was all he could do in Nandana's memory.

The *dandapala* rose in the dark and went to the cupboard in which he had flung the bells before leaving for Sravasti a week ago. On opening the cupboard, his sight was drawn to a pallid glow emanating from somewhere on the topmost shelf…

Feeling his pulse quicken, Dileepa reached in and retrieved the bells, still wrapped in silk. With trembling fingers, he peeled the cloth back until the bells were revealed, all three glowing richly like moonlight.

It couldn't be, he told himself. *Explain everything.* However faulty the magic, the message had been delivered to him. The bells should have ceased glowing. Unless there was a new message awaiting him, another meaningless thread from the past, another instance of Ayodhya's slowly decaying magic losing its grip over its function. Or… and here the *dandapala* almost suspended his breathing as the possibility occurred to him, maybe it was a new message…

Ever so slowly, Dileepa turned and walked to the window. His heart hammering in his chest, he eased it open. Heedless of the chill wind that struck him flat, buffeting him and blowing the hair across his forehead and making him shudder, he raised the bells to his ears. He strained to hear the words over the whistling of the wind.

Why aren't you replying? …love me?

The investigator stared. This was certainly no message from earlier.

"I love you, Nandana," he said in a voice that was barely above a whisper. "Where are you?"

It was close to a couple of minutes before the bells glowed again. Dileepa realized there were tears in his eyes.

…you at last, he heard the words, discerning relief in Nandana's voice. Then, a burst of silence, followed by…*very important… …she is not Ma Parnalata…*

Dileepa brushed the tears away and cursed the erratic magic. He hadn't the wildest notion what the girl was trying to tell him.

"Who is not Ma Parnalata? And where are you?"

Many minutes later, the bells glowed. The *dandapala* had to strain to hear the girl.

...not my aunt... ...Simhika... ...uniforms for the garrison...

"What is it about the uniforms again?"

...the sacred fire... ...bring an end to the magic... You must protect...

"Whom should I protect?" Dileepa shook his head in frustration. "And tell me where *you* are."

...the well in the mansion... ...is immensely powerful... the *dandapala* detected desperation in the girl's tone. *...have to stop...*

As the message faded, the investigator looked out of the window and got the distinct impression that the night had somehow turned darker than before, churning with shadows that hadn't been there earlier. Out of nowhere, he was overcome by a sense of hopelessness and an inescapable doom.

"This is not making sense," he spoke to the bells, taking a shaky breath to dispel the foreboding. "Tell me again from the beginning."

Minutes passed and Dileepa waited, eyes glued to the bells. But the bells stayed dark, refusing to glow again. And all around him, the *dandapala* sensed the shadows beginning to thicken — *blacker and blacker and blacker still* — squeezing the magic slowly and deliberately out of the atmosphere.

nine

DAY DAWNED OVER AYODHYA, DARK, COLD AND VIOLENT. Three more people had died of the cold during the night, and as the news spread, it gave birth to rumours of a severe shortage of *pravaras* and blankets in the city. The rumours quickly morphed into stories of warm clothes being hoarded for profiteering, and an angry crowd raided one of the city's storehouses, looking for woollens. Finding nothing — and getting even more convinced that warm clothes were indeed in short supply — the irate mob vented its fear and frustration by setting the storehouse on fire.

Anger travelled like a contagion, and in no time, riots had broken out in other parts of the city, forcing the *nagarapalas* to step in to control the crowds and restore order. But the *nagarapalas* only managed inciting public rage, and clashes erupted between the people and the militiamen. Over a dozen injuries were sustained on both sides, some even critical, and the morning quickly became charged with tension. Meanwhile, there were reports of people getting into petty fights that escalated for no apparent reason, and the *nagarapalas* received five such complaints, with one fight almost ending in a fatal stabbing. Ayodhya, it appeared, had turned on itself overnight, bent on its own destruction.

Bharat rode his horse slowly through the city's streets, taking in the signs of violence from the morning, stopping here to inspect a ransacked granary, pausing there to share a gentle word with an old milk vendor whose cart had overturned during a *nagarapala* charge. The king rode at the head of a small bunch of riders, with Shatrughna to his right and Kushadhwaja to his left. Atibhanu and *mahanayaka* Baladitya rode two steps behind, while a dozen palace guards came after them. Everywhere they went, people observed the small cavalcade from street corners and from inside doors and windows with wary, resentful eyes.

Turning a corner, the king's party entered a neighbourhood where people had engaged in a pitched battle with the *nagarapalas*. Trouble had been quelled, but with a heavy hand, and the mood among the locals was still one of belligerence. Kushadhwaja had counselled Bharat against visiting the locality, but the king had refused to listen. "Don't the deepest wounds demand the greatest attention?" he had asked.

Now, riding through the scarred and battered neighbourhood, Bharat took in the faces that lined the streets, watching him as he made his way to a stunted *ajameghya* that roughly corresponded to the locality's centre. Reining in his horse by the tree, the king of Kosala surveyed the houses and trading establishments in the vicinity for a moment, waiting so he would have the people's undivided interest.

"I am here to let everyone know that there is no dearth of woollens in Ayodhya or elsewhere in this kingdom," he said at last, his voice clear in the chilly air. "The palace is also ensuring there is no hoarding of *pravaras* or blankets to drive up prices and profits. So, please don't fall victim to rumours to the contrary, and please do not indulge in violence that springs from belief in such rumours."

"It all started when the *nagarapalas* attacked us," a hoarse voice called out from the crowd that had tailed the royal party and was now assembled by one street corner. Even as Bharat watched, the crowd drew in more and more people, swelling in numbers.

"Yes, the *nagarapalas* are entirely at fault," another voice barked, harsh and strident, and more voices joined in agreement. A rumble rose from the crowd and spread like a wave, rippling out along the streets.

Mahanayaka Baladitya and Atibhanu instinctively reached for their *karapalas* and the weapons were halfway out of their scabbards before Bharat raised a restraining hand. He rode two paces forward so that he was alone and outside the protective ring of his guards and companions. He looked at the crowd until it slowly fell quiet.

"The *nagarapalas* were trying to restore calm," Bharat began, but he was promptly interrupted by a woman.

"They beat my son up," she said. "He just happened to be on the street. He had done nothing."

"They scared the mules I was taking to the market to sell," a man shouted. "When I complained, the *nagarapalas* hit me."

More voices began rising in outrage, but they were stilled by Shatrughna. "Let the raja speak," he roared, his voice echoing like a thunderclap.

The king raised his hand again. "The *nagarapalas* were acting to stop the spread of violence," he said. "They were trying to maintain peace. Theirs isn't an easy job, and at times, it is hard to tell the innocent from the wrongdoers. Yet, the onus is on us to protect the innocent at all times, even as we tackle any offenders. If there has been excess and undue use of force on any of you, I apologize on behalf of the *nagarapalas*. As I said, their intent was peaceful, and I believe that is your intent as well."

He paused for a moment, waiting for the crowd to respond, willing it to respond. Heads nodded slowly and a softer, conciliatory murmur ebbed and flowed along the street.

"We want to carry on with our lives, rajan," someone said, and there was agreement all around.

Bharat sensed the light change around him as some of the darkness of the morning shifted and moved away, like shadows dissolving with the emergence of the sun, though there was no sun in sight over Ayodhya. He sighed in relief.

"Let us all do that then," he said, adding, "And once again, I ask you not to give in to rumours."

Bharat spent the rest of the morning touring each of the city's troubled districts, calming frayed tempers here, allaying rumours there, and winning back peace and good sense, street by street, inch by inch. It was nearly noon by the time the small party turned back towards the palace, its purpose fulfilled.

"My men were struggling to maintain law and order," said Baladitya. "The crowds were out of hand in many places."

"I don't doubt it, and given the circumstances, I think the *nagarapalas* did the best they could," said Bharat. "But the people are scared, and fear prompted the violence. No one is to blame for what happened." He looked at the *mahanayaka* before including everyone in his gaze. "There is something wrong in Ayodhya, and it is affecting everyone."

"Yes, I can sense it too," said Kushadhwaja.

"This darkness..." Shatrughna frowned at the brooding sky. "Who'd believe it is midday now? And the magic has all but drained out of Ayodhya."

"We must find out what is happening," Bharat's tone was grim. "Something tells me our city's future depends on it."

If only Surochi and the rishis could be brought around to an *agnimanasa*, he thought to himself. Perhaps that'd help. But he knew there was no point in asking again. Surochi was unbendable.

He turned to address one of the palace attendants. "I wish to summon a council this afternoon to discuss the situation in Ayodhya. Have word sent to all the *adhipatis*, ministers and courtiers, seeking their attendance."

When they got back to the palace, Bharat was told that Yuddhajeet was waiting to see him over a pressing matter. Bharat, Shatrughna and Kushadhwaja were taken to one of the palace's many guest halls, where Yuddhajeet sat with Abhisarika, Ambareesha and a tall stranger.

"Shatrughna," Yuddhajeet's eyes lit up on seeing Dashratha's youngest son. "I was told you'd come in last night." He rose to embrace the boy. "I was hoping to see you this morning."

"I would have loved that as well, mama," Shatrughna replied. "But we had to go into the city."

"I heard there was trouble," said Yuddhajeet, looking from one brother to the other.

"There was, but it's hopefully under control now," Bharat replied.

Yuddhajeet nodded. Then, noticing Shatrughna glance at Ambareesha and Abhisarika, he made the introductions. Pointing to the stranger, he said, "This is Sayas." He glanced at Bharat. "You may remember him from the palace at Rajagriha."

The newcomer bowed and Bharat returned the salutation with a *pranaam*.

"Sayas has come bearing vital news from Kekeya."

"What news?" Bharat asked.

With a glance at Yuddhajeet, Sayas said, "Rajan, word in Kekeya is that Nagnajit is marshalling his army to march to Ayodhya."

Bharat blinked and looked at Kushadhwaja, taken aback by the abruptness of the development.

"The raya has sent for additional troops from Gandhara, and it seems more Kamboja horsemen are scheduled to join his army as well." The man shot another glance at Yuddhajeet. "The army that Nagnajit is amassing is a very large one, rajan."

"But why is he coming here?" Kushadhwaja interjected, trying to make sense of it.

"The raya is bent on possessing chief Sailusha's daughter," Sayas said, gesturing to Abhisarika. "He has also set his mind on punishing yuvaraja Yuddhajeet. Having learned that they are in Ayodhya, he is coming here to settle scores. I came because I thought the yuvaraja should know about this threat."

"You have been here *one day*," the *kshatri* exclaimed, looking from Yuddhajeet to Abhisarika. "How did Nagnajit get to know so soon that you're in Ayodhya?"

"It's not hard to guess," Yuddhajeet replied. "We took the quickest route here, roads that traders use regularly. We were seen by others along the way. We didn't conceal our identities because we weren't expecting to be followed here. So, anyone could have taken the news to Nagnajit's ears. Even otherwise, Nagnajit would have learned that Bharat is my nephew. Not finding me in Kekeya, he would have figured I would make my way here, so…"

Shatrughna turned to Sayas. "Do you know when Nagnajit plans to start his march?" he asked.

"Preparations for the march were still underway when I left Rajagriha five days ago, yuvaraja," Sayas replied. "That is all I can say for certain."

There was a moment's stillness as everyone digested the news.

"Well, by coming here, Nagnajit is definitely making our job easier," said Bharat, breaking the silence. He looked at the faces around him and smiled. "The raya of Gandhara is saving us the trouble of crossing the breadth of Jambudvipa, without denying us the pleasure of handing him a defeat."

Dileepa had spent a long and fretful night in bed, buoyed by hope and dragged down by despair, tossing and turning as he tried piecing Nandana's messages together into a coherent whole. The girl being alive was a source of immense joy and relief, but he had learned nothing of her whereabouts before the bells had fallen silent, leaving him groping in the dark for answers. He had even kept the bells by his pillow in the hope that they would light up with another message, but there had been none. It felt to him as though magic had finally ceased to exist in Ayodhya. Still sleepless at the crack of dawn, he had risen to apply his mind to what little he had.

...she is not Ma Parnalata... ...not my aunt...

It felt as though Nandana was telling him that the woman in the mansion was not Ma Parnalata, the *dandapala* mused.

...Simhika...

That sounded like someone's name, but who was Simhika?

...she is not Ma Parnalata...

Was Nandana suggesting that the woman in the mansion was actually Simhika?

...uniforms for the garrison...

The girl was referring to the uniforms that Ma Parnalata had designed for the Sanctum garrison. Why was that pertinent? Because Ma Parnalata was not Ma Parnalata but Simhika? What was so significant about Simhika anyway?

...the sacred fire... You must protect...

Something about the sacred fire. And the girl was asking him to protect something. Could it be the sacred fire? From whom? Dileepa had no idea. From Simhika perhaps? It was a possibility, but he could be wrong...

...the well in the mansion... ...is immensely powerful... ... have to stop...

Was the well immensely powerful, or was Nandana referring to Simhika again? The *dandapala* couldn't be sure. He also couldn't shake off the feeling that he was forgetting something crucial that had been said...

He had been wrestling with it nearly all morning when a thought struck.

...the sacred fire...

The sacred fire had been the reason behind the rakshasa attack on Ayodhya two years ago. And his investigation into the attack had led him to Bakula, the diligent clerk at the records office, who had died of a stroke before Dileepa could interview him in connection with the attack. Bakula had left behind a daughter with whom he had fallen in love, and the same girl had saved his life using magic the likes of which he had never seen before — *magic with origins in distant Lanka*. The *dandapala* paled at the realization, the truth about Nandana punching him hard in the gut.

When the girl had returned to Ayodhya after her father's death, she had brought an aunt along…

…she is not Ma Parnalata… …not my aunt…

Which meant the older woman had to be Simhika, and Nandana was now trying to caution him about her. But why do that, Dileepa wondered. Both were rakshasis. Both had arrived in Ayodhya as allies. Why was the girl siding with the humans then?

Because she was in love with him. It was that simple.

And just like that, he realized he didn't care that Nandana was a rakshasi. He loved her anyway and always would. But where was she…

…the well in the mansion…

Could that be where Nandana was, in that well? Was she being held there by force, against her will? Had Simhika put her there, and did that explain the older woman's reluctance to entertain him at the mansion any longer? Was that why the girl had reached out to him using the listening bells? That meant she was powerless to free herself, and he had to find a way of rescuing her…

Dileepa realized his life was set to unravel drastically, permanently. There was no way he could keep all of this to himself, pretending no one needed to know. He would have to tell others about Nandana, about what he'd seen her do one dark and stormy night nearly seven months ago. He would have to admit to not reporting Bakula because he had been smitten by his daughter, and he knew he risked facing censure for that. The other *dandapalas* would know of his dereliction of duty, and so would the king, who had trusted him by choosing him to investigate Pushyanta's hoarding scam. And it wouldn't be his humiliation alone. His parents would suffer the shaming and scarring too. Finally, there was the stigma of having fallen in love with a rakshasi, not that he'd known it then. Still, she was the enemy.

Yet, the investigator knew it had to be done. The truth had to come out. Nandana had reached out to him, expecting him to act. *You must protect...*

He had left home with a mind to take Mitraka into confidence first, but as the riots had broken out, the *dandapalas* were pulled into the task of maintaining order. No one knew where to find Mitraka, and Dileepa had ended up patrolling the city with militiamen most of the morning and afternoon. Following a gradual improvement in the situation, he had visited the old quarter and scouted the mansion, looking for signs of suspicious activity, but the building had just sat there under the gloomy sky. Tiring of his vigil, he had returned to the *dandapala* headquarters where, much to his frustration, he learned that Mitraka still wasn't in.

"But there is a *nagarapala* waiting for you," said a colleague, pointing to a room at the end of a verandah.

"A *nagarapala*?"

"He's been waiting a while," the other man nodded. "He was asking about that ring of yours."

Wondering what a *nagarapala* might want with the ring they had recovered from the dead man, Dileepa made his way down the verandah. Stepping through the doorway, he stared in surprise at the militiaman who sat waiting inside.

It was *upanayaka* Mahulya, who assigned *nagarapalas* to sentry duty all over Ayodhya, who had come under suspicion for having posted the same set of five guards at Ayodhya's east gate when Dileepa had been investigating the hoarding scam. When the militiaman stood to greet Dileepa, he towered over the investigator, his grand beard and bald head adding to his imposing stature.

"Take a seat," Dileepa offered. Once they had settled down, the *dandapala* looked at Mahulya. "You are here in connection with the ring?"

"Yes." The *upanayaka* leaned thick hands on the table. "I think the ring is mine. The description matches the one I have lost."

When Dileepa retrieved the ring and showed it to him, the militiaman's eyes shone with relief. "Yes, it is mine," he said with a smile. He looked at the *dandapala*. "I'm curious to know where it was found."

"Are you certain it is yours?" Dileepa enquired.

"Absolutely. It belonged to my father. I have inherited it from him."

"It must be precious to you then," said Dileepa. With a pause, he added, "I believe it was forged in Sravasti."

"You have a sharp eye," Mahulya replied, quite impressed. "Yes, it was gifted to my father by the old *adhipati* of Sravasti. As an award for his loyalty."

"Mihiradutta's father, you mean?" Seeing the militiaman nod, Dileepa asked, "It was awarded to your father for his loyalty to the *adhipati* of Sravasti?"

"Yes."

"I don't understand."

"We are from Sravasti," said Mahulya. "My family has proudly served the *adhipatis* of Sravasti for many generations. This ring is a symbol of that pride and loyalty, and I was shattered when it was lost. I can't tell you how pleased I am to set eyes on it once again."

My family has proudly served the adhipatis *of Sravasti for many generations.*

That was why the militiaman had done it, the *dandapala* realized. He had appointed the same guards at Ayodhya's east gate to facilitate the entry of food grains into Pushyanta's storehouses not out of greed, but out of loyalty to a scion of Sravasti's royal household. And he had helped the four would-be assassins for the same reason; he, Dileepa, had caused the fall of Pushyanta, and someone in Sravasti had wanted his blood in return. Mahulya's loyalty had almost ensured that payback.

"What I am curious to know is how such a precious ring found its way into the purse of one of the four dead men who were found in the old quarter one morning about seven months ago," said Dileepa. "You remember the incident, don't you? Four men, dead in the street, their faces badly mutilated...?"

"What... I..."

The investigator had the pleasure of seeing the *upanayaka* blink and go pale as he searched for the right words. He waited, watching carefully as the man struggled to get his composure back.

"I… don't understand," Mahulya said, still flailing for words. "How could the ring have… No, there must have been a mistake —"

"As you didn't part with such a precious item willingly, I can only assume it was taken without your knowledge," said Dileepa. "Probably when you sheltered the men in your house?"

"I don't know what you are talking about," the militiaman blustered.

"I'm talking about the men who had come to the old quarter with the intent of killing someone."

"This is ridiculous —"

"The men who knew where to wait for their target… because *you* had shown them the spot."

"I refuse to indulge in such slanderous conversation," said Mahulya, beginning to rise. "I intend to report you to your superiors —"

"Four men who had come to the old quarter to kill *me* that night," Dileepa shouted. "*I* was their intended victim, and we both know it, *upanayaka*. I know it because I was there when the men stepped out of the shadows, *khangas* in hand. It was also the night our king was attacked in the palace," he pointed an accusing finger at Mahulya, "so perhaps *that* attack was also carried out with your assistance."

"No," the militiaman yelped, shaking his head and looking horrified. "I had nothing to do with the attack on the king. I swear…"

"So, you did have something to do with the attack on me," Dileepa pinned the *upanayaka* with an unflinching glare.

Mahulya sagged and crumpled as if the life had gone out of him.

"Who wanted me dead?" Dileepa demanded, leaning across the table. "Why were the four men sent to kill me?"

Before the *upanayaka* could reply, a noise came from the direction of the door. Dileepa turned to find Mitraka leaning against the door frame, scrutinizing him with narrowed eyes.

"Those men were there to kill *you* that night?" she asked, sounding doubtful. "You were present in the old quarter when… you were attacked?"

Seeing Dileepa nod, the chief of the *dandapalas* gave her head a thoroughly dissatisfied shake. "You have a lot of explaining to do, young man," she scowled.

"I meant to anyway," Dileepa replied. "But first, can we take *upanayaka* Mahulya into custody for further questioning?"

"Make it quick," said Mitraka with a curt nod.

"Is it true that the palace has received reports of an imminent Gandharan attack on Kosala?"

Looking at Sudhanva and reckoning how best to phrase his reply, Bharat marvelled at the speed with which news travelled. Sayas had set foot in Ayodhya barely an hour or so ago, but already, next to everyone in court knew what his arrival portended. So much so that as soon as Sudhanva had posed the question, every single courtier in the annex by the Throne Room had sat up and looked at the king in anticipation.

"We have been informed about the possibility of a Gandharan army marching against us," said Bharat.

"Pardon me, rajan, but from what we have heard, this Gandharan march against Kosala is more than just a *possibility*," said Sudhanva. He took in the faces around them. "To us, it looks more like an inevitability."

"The news is premature and needs verification," Bharat replied. "Only then will we know how real or imagined the threat is." Then, eager to switch the council's focus back to discussing the more pressing issues facing the city, he said, "Now, about the rumours that are at the root of the problem—"

"Pardon me once again, rajan, but what if the threat is real?" the *adhipati* of Sankasya persisted in speculating about the Gandharan attack.

Bharat paused to assess Sudhanva. "Well," he said eventually, "even assuming this Gandharan attack is inevitable, as you've put it, there is no cause for concern. Kosala is capable of guarding against any attack."

Sudhanva shucked his shoulders in a way that could only have meant he didn't share his king's sentiment, but he stayed quiet. However, any hopes Bharat had of the conversation ending there were dashed in an instant.

"Nagnajit's army consists of his own Gandharan troops, horsemen from Kamboja, and Bahlika mercenaries," observed Mihiradutta, who was seated to Sudhanva's left. Mimicking Sudhanva, the *adhipati* of Sravasti cast one look at those around him. "If you were to ask me, that is quite a menacing force heading Kosala's way."

"But it is not something that Kosala can't deal with," said Bharat, a frown forming on his brow. "Surely you don't doubt our army's ability to defend this kingdom."

"Not at all," said Mihiradutta, "but I can't help feeling afraid for the people of this kingdom. If war comes this way, they are bound to suffer, no matter who wins in the end. I dread to imagine the plight of our people when Kambojan horsemen and Bahlika mercenaries find their way into Kosala."

"Is that truly you speaking, *adhipati* Mihiradutta?" asked Sheelabhadra, the guild master. "You, whose sword never wavered once in the defence of Kosala?"

"My sword and my words are both forged in the defence of Kosala," Mihiradutta replied. "I do not fear war. But the suffering of our people is not acceptable to me."

"So, what would you have us do instead, *adhipati*?" Kushadhwaja asked.

As tension built in the chamber, courtiers and clerks craned their heads to watch the exchange, their ears perked to not miss even a single word.

"Seeing how you talked the raja out of going to war against Madhupura, it is plain that you are not in favour of war yourself," Sudhanva spoke instead of Mihiradutta. "Perhaps you could try doing that again..."

"Madhupura was a different case," said the *kshatri*. "Here, *we* are being attacked, and we would be within our rights to fight back. Unless you are saying we do nothing to defend ourselves —"

"Wait a minute," said Sudhanva, jumping in. Once again he turned to the crowd, as if in appeal. "Our *kshatri* here defends war if we are under attack, but he opposes it if we are the aggressor. Which is a commendable stance, except that he has no objections to sending Kosala's army to wage war against Gandhara in faraway Kekeya, even though that makes Kosala the aggressor."

"That just shows double standards," said Jayabhama, joining the debate.

"That's not double standards," Shatrughna butted in angrily. "The move against Gandhara was aimed at freeing the River Kingdoms, not claiming Gandharan territory. There is a difference."

"Yet it was a move that would have cost the lives of Kosala's soldiers," Sudhanva pointed out.

"Are you suggesting we should have sat back and done nothing to assist the River Kingdoms?" Bharat asked, fixing his gaze on the *adhipati*.

"I am saying it was not Kosala's problem, so there was no need to jump into war."

A moment of utter silence followed as everyone held their breaths, scarcely believing what had been said. The *adhipati* wasn't just contesting the king's rationale for going to war. By drawing a deliberate distinction between Kosala and Kekeya — between Bharat's father's kingdom and his mother's — Sudhanva was forcing the king to pick a side by proclaiming his loyalty to one over the other… knowing fully well that Bharat would never be capable of turning his back on Kekeya. Being the king of Kosala, Bharat was cornered, and every soul in that court understood that.

Bharat and Sudhanva studied each other narrowly.

"Well, war is coming now, whether we want it or not, so the question of jumping into it doesn't arise any longer," Bharat said at last with a shrug.

"It is still not Kosala's war," Sudhanva insisted.

"What would you have me do?" Bharat asked. "You want me to turn Yuddhajeet and the others over to Nagnajit just to avert a war? They are here as our guests, seeking asylum from a maniac who has overrun their land. There is no question of handing them over to Nagnajit or whoever it may be. That is not the Ikshvaku code." Bharat paused as his eyes swept over the faces in the room. When he spoke next, there was a challenge in his voice. "Whether you stand by that code or not is a choice each one of you must make."

The chamber fell silent, the king's ultimatum ringing in everyone's ears. At last, the man sitting to Mihiradutta's left stood up, arthritic joints creaking with age. It was Naresha, Pushyanta and Jayabhama's father. Mihiradutta and Jayabhama helped him up, and still holding his son's hand for support, the old man looked at Bharat for a moment before speaking.

"The Ikshvaku code also binds Kosala's kings to the contentment and prosperity of the people," he said. "Look around you, rajan. Do you see contentment and prosperity in Ayodhya? We've never had riots in this kingdom before, but this morning…" he shrugged. "The people are cold, they are scared, they are angry. They fret about the magic and agonize over the disappearances. They want answers and solutions to problems, but they have neither. And now, you're speaking of bringing war to their doorstep as well." He paused to assess the king. "It is not we who need to be reminded about the Ikshvaku code, rajan."

Courtiers looked at one another with wary, uneasy eyes, and a murmur ran through the chamber at the prospect of a full-blown disagreement tearing the council in two. No one quite knew how to deal with the predicament, no one knew what it might lead to, so all eyes instinctively turned to Bharat, sitting immobile and watching the old *adhipati*.

"Whether it's the cold, the drop in magic or the false scarcity of food grain Kosala experienced last year, the palace is conscious of the problems facing the people," the king said pointedly to the patriarch. "The palace is doing all it can to alleviate suffering and shall continue to do so."

Naresha glared at Bharat for a moment, the reference to Pushyanta's misdeeds finding its mark. Then, drawing a heavy breath, the *adhipati* slowly looked around the chamber. His legs shook, feeble with age, so he had to grip Jayabhama's hand tight, but his voice rang with steely resolve as he addressed the council.

"In all the years Raja Dashratha ruled, not once did the rakshasas dare attack Ayodhya, and not once did a human dream of marching his army against Kosala." He turned to look at Bharat. "I do believe Kosala is missing the leadership of Raja Dashratha."

Naresha turned to make his way out, helped by Jayabhama and Mihiradutta. Everyone watched, too stunned to speak, as Sudhanva and an entourage of half a dozen other minor *adhipatis* and attendants followed in their wake.

"By invoking the Ikshvaku code in his defence, the king tried to portray us as villains," asserted Jayabhama.

"Yes," Mihiradutta nodded. "By insisting that everyone stand by the code — in effect, stand in support of his decision to let Yuddhajeet and the others stay in Kosala — Bharat was attempting to turn the court against us by painting those who opposed him as the enemies of this kingdom."

"That too when all we were asking for was that this kingdom remain peaceful and free of war," insisted Sudhanva.

After leaving the palace, the rebel *adhipatis* of Sravasti and Sankasya had come to Sudhanva's residence, where they now sat around iron braziers, warming their hands and drinking hot lentil soup. Gajakarna had joined the *adhipatis*, and the commander slowly set his bowl of soup down and looked at the noblemen, one after the other.

"My question is, what do you propose to do next?" he asked.

It was Naresha who answered. "The battle lines are drawn," he said. "Bharat won't overturn his decision to let Yuddhajeet stay. He has made that clear. But *we* cannot let Bharat have his way. It's too late for that anyway. We have no choice but to challenge him. It's the only way forward, the only way we will be taken seriously and be seen as an alternative to him."

"I will add that we must challenge him swiftly," said Sudhanva. "The longer we take, the more we delay in striking, the greater the chances of the palace getting wind of what we're planning."

"It didn't help that you openly challenged him in court today," Gajakarna grumbled. "The king has already been put on his guard, I'd imagine."

"We had to do it," Sudhanva replied. "We had to present our point of view before the court so that when we move against Bharat, we are judged in the right light and our actions come across as being justified."

"We also had to show the court we had given Bharat ample opportunity to correct his course," added Mihiradutta. "We will need the courtiers on our side once the storm has blown over and the dust has settled."

The *mahanayaka* nodded. "My question still is, what do you propose to do now?"

"We act immediately," said Sudhanva.

Everyone else exchanged glances. "How soon is that supposed to be?" asked Gajakarna.

"That depends entirely on how soon you can get your men ready."

The commander spent a quiet moment, doing some mental math. "I could have them ready by tomorrow morning."

"We make our move tomorrow morning then," said Sudhanva.

"So, we storm the palace, the armoury, the Sanctum, and the headquarters of the *nagarapalas*." Mihiradutta looked at the *mahanayaka*. "Is that right?"

"Yes, but I would like there to be as little violence as possible," Gajakarna reiterated.

"Of course, of course," Sudhanva assured him. "These are all our people, after all."

"The queen mothers, Rani Mandavi, Rani Urmila… even Bharat. I don't want anyone harmed," the commander said.

"Still, we should go in expecting some resistance, especially now that Shatrughna is also here," warned Jayabhama.

"Which is why I'm hoping we can use Taksha to negotiate Bharat's surrender," said Gajakarna.

"Your man…" Sudhanva paused, "…you're sure he can take the boy hostage?"

The *mahanayaka* nodded. "Atibhanu has befriended the boy. He has the king and queen's trust. He should be able to bring us the kid without any difficulty."

Mihiradutta looked at Gajakarna. "Tomorrow, when exactly will we move against the palace?"

"If Taksha is with us by mid-morning, we can seize control of the palace at noon tomorrow."

The room fell silent, everyone overawed by the enormity of the decision and the commitment it asked from them.

Sudhanva was the one to finally break the hush.

"Send word to Atibhanu to snatch the kid and bring him tomorrow morning," the *adhipati* said.

"We made a mistake in coming to Ayodhya."

"What do you mean by that?" Abhisarika asked, staring into Yuddhajeet's troubled eyes. "How is it a mistake?"

"Bharat is in trouble because of us."

"What do you mean?" Abhisarika took a step closer and touched Yuddhajeet's cheek. "Tell me what's happened..."

Yuddhajeet drew a breath and surveyed the silhouette of Ayodhya's landscape etched against an early twilight. He and Abhisarika were on a forsaken strip of terrace overlooking a secluded section of the palace grounds, and although it was cold and windy out in the open, they couldn't be easily overheard. Still, Yuddhajeet lowered his voice as he spoke.

"Our coming here has divided the court of Kosala. There's a section of *adhipatis* and courtiers who believe Kosala should not get into the tussle between the River Kingdoms and Gandhara."

Abhisarika's eyebrows rose in disbelief. "You mean they don't care if the River Kingdoms are subjugated by an invader?" she asked in indignation.

Yuddhajeet nodded. "For them, it is not Kosala's problem."

"People never stand up to wrongdoing until it starts hurting *them*," the woman said with a shake of her head. "Self-interest is the curse of the human race."

They were silent for a moment. "So, maybe Bharat won't be able to supply us with an army to take the River Kingdoms back?" Abhisarika asked after a while.

"It could be worse than that," Yuddhajeet replied, nodding on seeing the alarm on the woman's face. "News of Nagnajit's decision to march to Ayodhya has spread around the city. Obviously, no one likes the thought of being the target of an attack —"

"Well, that should tell those not wanting Kosala to get involved that they *should* be supporting Bharat's decision to free the River Kingdoms," Abhisarika interrupted hotly.

"Wait, let me finish," Yuddhajeet said. "What's more worrying is that there are some who think Nagnajit can easily be persuaded not to come here."

Abhisarika stared at Yuddhajeet, her eyes widening in disbelief. "They would like you and me to be handed over to Nagnajit, wouldn't they?" she asked.

The yuvaraja of Kekeya nodded. "That's what I meant when I said it could be a lot worse than not getting an army to fight Gandhara."

Abhisarika chewed the matter over for a while. "Surely Bharat won't give in to such a demand," she said.

"Not in this lifetime or any other," Yuddhajeet spoke the words with absolute conviction.

"That means we're safe," Abhisarika said with palpable relief. "We were right in coming here."

Yuddhajeet took a moment to reply. "*We* might be safe, but Bharat's position as king of Kosala isn't. In fact, there is a real risk of Ayodhya's court getting divided into two factions, one *with* Bharat and the other against him. Even civil war could erupt in Kosala, and it will all be because of you and me."

Abhisarika looked away, suddenly anxious for Bharat.

"Perhaps my fears are unfounded. Perhaps Bharat will find a way of winning over those who're against him. I hope that is what happens. Even then, war will still come to Kosala," Yuddhajeet said, looking disconsolate. "Nagnajit will still come with his army of Kambojan horsemen and Bahlika warriors."

"They can be defeated," Abhisarika countered. "We did that at Mithuna with fewer resources."

"Even so, they will bring unavoidable hardship to the people of Kosala." Yuddhajeet turned to face the woman. "Bharat has sworn to keep Kosala safe for Rama's return. It is an Ikshvaku's promise. If this kingdom suffers on account of war, Bharat's word to his brother will become worthless." Taking Abhisarika by the shoulders, the prince looked at her with tenderness. "That shouldn't happen under any circumstance. You and I shouldn't be why Bharat fails to keep the promise made to Rama."

Abhisarika nodded slowly. "What do you suggest we do?" she asked, though judging from her eyes, she already knew what Yuddhajeet was going to say.

"Nagnajit has nothing against Kosala," the yuvaraja answered. "His only interest is in you and me. If the two of us are not in Kosala, he has no reason to come here. If you and I are not here, Kosala is safe from all threats of war."

Abhisarika looked away for a moment, her eyes sweeping across Ayodhya on the other side of the palace ground. "Is this the only way?" she asked.

"I am afraid so. Every other option will bring Nagnajit and war to Kosala."

"Where do we go from here?" Abhisarika asked after giving the idea some more thought. "East to Angadesh? Maybe Tamralipti? Or south to Chedi or Kasi?"

"We must draw Nagnajit as far away from Ayodhya as possible," the prince said with a shake of his head. "So, I would say we return the way we came, back towards Madhupura, and then decide where to go from there."

The woman nodded and sighed. "Do you think Bharat will agree to this?"

"He won't. Neither will my sister. Nor will Shatrughna or anyone else in the palace." Yuddhajeet gave Abhisarika a long, meaningful look. "Which is why they must not know. We must leave without telling them."

"We go just like that, without even a word of thanks?"

The prince nodded. "It's the only way. If they get even the slightest whiff of this, they're never going to let us out of their sight."

Abhisarika inhaled deeply, filling her lungs with air and her mind with resolve. "When do you want to tell Ambareesha about —"

"No, we don't tell him anything," said Yuddhajeet. "Not him, not *anyone*."

The woman stared hard at the yuvaraja. "He is my brother. He'd never abandon me, and I won't abandon him —"

"If we tell Ambareesha, he will want to come with us. Then, his men will want to come as well. That's all it'll take for everyone else in the palace to know what we're up to. Imagine all of us riding towards the palace gate, one big group, through the palace gate, through the city… News will come back to the palace quicker than we can blink. No… the fewer people who know, the better it is."

Abhisarika didn't say anything.

"There will only be the three of us riding out of Ayodhya," said Yuddhajeet after a moment.

Abhisarika waited, still saying nothing.

"You, me and Smara. Only the three of us." Yuddhajeet cupped Abhisarika's face in his hands. It was almost too dark to make out the woman's features, but the prince could see her perfectly mirrored in his mind's eye. "In the last few months, I have dreamed of little else than a simple life with you and Smara," he said. "Let us run away, the three of us, and start afresh, away from everything we have lived and experienced so far. Come with me, Abhisarika. Bring Smara and come with me where we can build a world only for ourselves, only for the three of us."

The woman was silent for a long time. When she finally nodded, the yuvaraja felt the dampness of tears on her cheeks. "I'd begun to think you would never ask," she said with a quaver in her voice. Then, gaining control over herself, she cleared her throat. "When should we leave?" she asked.

"Tonight," Yuddhajeet replied. "Once the palace has gone to sleep."

ten

"THEY MUST BE INSANE TO THINK I WOULD SIMPLY TURN Yuddhajeet and the others over to Nagnajit."

Bharat paced the room in agitation, his feet measuring the floor in great strides, hands clenching and unclenching by his sides, his shoulders swaying while his eyes swept right and left, burning like hot coals. Shatrughna, Kushadhwaja, Sheelabhadra and revenue minister Sheshagupta stood on one side of the room, their faces brooding and heads bowed in thought, while Atibhanu watched from near the door, his tattooed arms crossed in front of him.

"Forget for a moment he is my mama," the king stopped his pacing to address the others. "Here are people seeking shelter from a usurper and oppressor. Handing them back to their persecutor is the most heartless thing to do, but that's precisely what is being asked of me. The inhumanity of it is appalling."

"Sudhanva has been looking for a way to get back at us ever since the decision to not wage war on Madhupura was taken," Kushadhwaja observed.

"Indeed, he hasn't missed a single opportunity to dredge up Madhupura," Sheshagupta nodded in agreement.

Bharat was about to reply when a palace attendant made an appearance at the door. Bowing to the king, he said, “Rajan, the *dandapalas* Mitraka and Dileepa are waiting to see you.”

“They are still here?” Bharat asked irritably. “I thought I’d said I couldn’t see them.” He waved his hand at the attendant. “Not today. Tell them I’ve got other things to deal with.”

“I did tell them,” the man said with another timid bow, “but *dandapala* Mitraka insists that you hear her out, rajan. She refuses to leave without seeing you.”

Bharat made an exasperated face and turned to the attendant in annoyance, but before he could say a harsh word, Shatrughna spoke. “I can see what they want, brother,” he suggested.

The king nodded, and everyone waited for the door to close on Shatrughna and the attendant.

“Sudhanva has been looking to show the rajan down from well before Madhupura. He has been bitter from the time of Pushyanta’s arrest in connection with the food grain scam,” guild master Sheelabhadra reminded everyone.

“You’re right,” Bharat agreed. “That also explains the support Sudhanva has from the *adhipatis* Naresha and Mihiradutta. They are united by a common cause.”

“And that makes them dangerous,” said Kushadhwaja. “What happened today was a deliberate challenge to your authority.”

The king nodded. “It was also a challenge to basic human decency,” he said.

“Sudhanva, Naresha and Mihiradutta must be shown their places,” Sheelabhadra said hotly.

"We must act with restraint and dignity," the *kshatri* warned, flashing a look at the guild master. "In whatever we do next, our response should be reasoned."

"They insulted our rajan," Sheelabhadra said in defiance. "Their demands to surrender yuvaraja Yuddhajeet are unacceptable to us. The way I see it, they've done nothing to deserve a reasoned response from us."

"The people of Kosala will be watching us closely," Kushadhwaja answered. "Our actions must be seen as fair and just. Only then will we have the people's support."

Bharat was again on the verge of saying something when the door opened to admit Shatrughna. Behind him came Mitraka and Dileepa.

The king's eyebrows rose sharply, but Shatrughna nodded. "We should listen to what they have to say," he said.

"Pardon me, rajan," said Mitraka. "I know there's a lot going on, but this couldn't wait."

"Okay." With a glance at Shatrughna, Bharat spread his hands. "Tell me what you have to say."

"We think there is a rakshasi in Ayodhya," said Mitraka.

Even as everyone in the room stared at the woman, Dileepa said, "*Two* rakshasis, to be correct."

Starting with the rakshasa attack on the Sanctum and Bakula, filling the blanks in one another's narratives, the *dandapalas* took turns to give the king and his council a complete account of all that Dileepa had learned about the woman in the mansion in the last twenty-four hours. Bharat listened without interruption, and it was only when they were done did he look away from the two *dandapalas'* faces.

"That was quite an account," he said, turning to each of his councillors for reactions.

"How do we know this rakshasi… this Nandana… is not lying?" asked Sheelabhadra. "It might be a ruse to trick us into something."

"She has no reason to lie to us," said Mitraka. "They've been here for over a year now. They've had plenty of time to do whatever mischief they had planned for Ayodhya. There's no need to trick us into anything now."

Bharat nodded. "The only real question is whether the woman in the mansion is Simhika." He looked at Dileepa. "Nandana didn't really say as much, did she?"

"I think she was trying to tell me that," the investigator asserted. "That the woman *is* Simhika."

"Even if she isn't, it is too much of a risk to ignore," said the king. He looked around the room. "We must have her arrested immediately."

"We must be careful in ensuring no harm comes to Nandana," said Dileepa. "She is being held captive in the mansion, remember?"

"We can't be sure of that," said Sheelabhadra. "And anyway, she's a rakshasi."

"A rakshasi who is helping us," Dileepa reminded a trifle testily.

Bharat nodded. "You think she has been imprisoned inside the well?"

"It's just a guess."

"Much like everything else here," said Shatrughna. "The uniforms, the sacred fire… what's the connection?"

"Nandana was talking about protecting something and about stopping someone," said Dileepa. "She knows this is important. If it wasn't, why reach out to me through the bells at all, why tell me all of this?"

"You are right," said Bharat. "We must act swiftly to prevent —" he stopped to stare at Dileepa. "What's the matter?"

"I just remembered something else Nandana had said," the *dandapala's* eyes shone with relief.

"What?" Bharat pressed.

"She said something to the effect of bringing an end to the magic."

"Bringing an end to the magic," the *kshatri* rolled the words on his tongue.

"It doesn't make much sense —"

"But it *does* make sense," Bharat interjected, looking around the room animatedly. "She spoke about the uniforms for the Sanctum garrison, she spoke about the sacred fire, and then she said something about bringing an end to the magic." The king stared at the faces around him. "You do remember the consecration of the *homagriha*..."

There were vigorous nods as everyone looked at Bharat in anticipation.

"It was at the consecration that our soldiers wore the new uniforms for the first time. One thing I have always found bizarre and hard to reconcile is how the magic in Ayodhya started *dropping* after the consecration of the *homagriha* — when, logically speaking, the levels of magic in the atmosphere should have increased."

"You're right," said Kushadhwaja. The guild master and the revenue minister nodded as well.

"It didn't make any sense then," Bharat continued, "but considering what Nandana has told us, perhaps there was something about the uniforms... maybe dark magic woven into the cloth or something that nullified the effect of the sacred fire and had an adverse impact on our magic. What if that's what Nandana means by bringing an end to the magic?"

"The rakshasas know that our magic sustains *rta* and protects Ayodhya," Shatrughna said. "It's natural they'd want to destroy it, and maybe that's what Simhika has been sent here to achieve."

"And she is succeeding," Bharat exclaimed. "Look at this strange winter. Look at the magic that's no longer in Ayodhya. Look at the anger sweeping the city."

"Who knows, perhaps even the disappearances are connected to that," Sheshagupta wondered.

"Nandana did not mention it," said Dileepa.

"Unless she meant to, but the magic died before she could," Mitraka shrugged.

"Simhika needs to be stopped right away," said Bharat, his voice suddenly grim. He looked at Shatrughna. "Send word to Baladitya. Ask him to come with a dozen men."

"A dozen won't be enough," the *kshatri* quickly pointed out. "This rakshasi has been subverting something as powerful as the sacred fire. It'll take a lot more than a dozen men to subdue her."

"Shatrughna and I will be there as well," said Bharat.

"Remember, there is no magic in Ayodhya's atmosphere to assist you," Sheshagupta cautioned him, "whereas this Simhika has recourse to whatever dark magic she has brought with her."

"Nandana did refer to something as immensely powerful," Mitraka interposed. "She might well have meant Simhika."

"We can't sit around waiting for magic to come to our aid," said Shatrughna. "We will have to take her down without magic."

Bharat drew a deep breath. Shatrughna was right, but he also knew magic would play a big part in their efforts to deal with Simhika. The rakshasi wouldn't hesitate to use whatever magic she had against them. They couldn't go into this fight without some magic of their own.

Every time the magic drops, you can't do an agnimanasa *that ends up risking someone else's life. No, rajan… I will not let you do it.*

He wondered whether it was worth appealing to Surochi once again. With the sacred fire itself at risk, the rishi might agree to an *agnimanasa* this time. Then again, he might not. If only there was someone else who could help him perform the sacrifice —

— he stopped in mid-thought.

Yes, the king thought to himself. *That* was a possibility worth pursuing. His face cleared.

"Get Baladitya to assemble his militiamen," Bharat addressed Shatrughna. With a glance at the *kshatri*, he added, "Yes, a dozen may not be enough. Double that number, just to be on the safe side."

The king looked at Dileepa. "You know the mansion well. You can guide us if need be. I'd like you to come with us." He turned back to his brother. "Tell everyone to be prepared to leave an hour before midnight."

"Why so late?" asked Shatrughna in surprise. "Why not sooner?"

Bharat weighed his answer carefully before looking at his brother. "The later we go, the greater the likelihood of taking the rakshasi by surprise."

With a nod, Shatrughna left to carry out Bharat's instructions.

The king turned to Atibhanu. "I want to have a word with you," he said.

Taking the cue, everyone else offered Bharat their *pranaams* before making their way out.

It wasn't until they were alone that the king called the bodyguard's attention with a snap of his fingers. "Come with me," he commanded.

"You will not utter a word about what you're about to see and hear. *No one* should get to know. Have I made myself absolutely clear?"

"Yes, rajan," Atibhanu nodded as he padded beside Bharat. He didn't have a clue what his king was talking about, but there was a furtiveness about the raja that intrigued the bodyguard.

They went down two flights of stairs and crossed to a section of the palace that Atibhanu knew was reserved for the queen mothers. The palace was silent, so their *padukas* clacked in the dark hallways, making Bharat wince as he cast his gaze all around, as if checking to see if they were being watched. Finally, they turned down a corridor with a door at one end, and the king turned to the bodyguard.

"The only reason you're with me is because I need a witness for what is going to happen next, should the need arise," said Bharat.

Atibhanu nodded, though he couldn't have been more perplexed. The king had just warned him not to share what he was about to see with anyone… and then said he might have to vouch for what he was about to see. It was all so contradictory that it didn't make the slightest bit of sense to him. Yet, he nodded and trailed his king down the corridor to the closed door. Bharat paused, as if making up his mind one last time, then raised his hand and knocked softly on the wood.

There was a moment's silence before a voice came from within. A woman's voice.

"Who is it?"

"It is I, Bharat. I'm here with my bodyguard Atibhanu." He paused. "I need your help, sister."

Atibhanu waited for the woman's response, but instead, with a click of a latch, the door opened. The bodyguard squinted. Even though the lamplight was faint, he recognized the woman in the doorway.

"How can I be of help?" asked Urmila, looking over once at Atibhanu.

Bharat hesitated. "Well, the other day, Mandavi happened to mention that you are learning to… weave magic?" he looked enquiringly at Urmila.

"Yes."

"And… you've been learning for over a year now?"

"Yes."

"Have you learned all…" the king stopped to clear his throat. "Let me get to the point. Can you help me do the *agnimanasa homa*?" he asked.

Atibhanu saw a flicker of surprise in Urmila's eyes as she stared at the king. "You should come inside," she said, stepping back from the door.

The king and the bodyguard entered a courtyard lit by a single lamp that barely illuminated the farthest reaches of the space, but Atibhanu could see the *sayyasana* and the reading stand, both piled with parchments and palm leaf scrolls.

"Do you even know what the *agnimanasa homa* is?" Urmila asked Bharat, her arms crossed in front of her.

"I do."

"I doubt you do," Urmila shook her head. "Not fully, at any rate. You wouldn't be here asking about it otherwise."

"I do," Bharat said again. "I have already done it once."

Atibhanu saw Urmila's eyes grow wide. "You have *done* an *agnimanasa*?" she asked, sounding incredulous.

"Earlier this year," the king nodded. "When the magic in Ayodhya was ebbing. The rishis at the Sanctum helped me."

"Didn't they warn you about the *homa's* consequences?" There was utter disbelief in Urmila's voice.

"They did."

"You still went ahead and did it?" the woman looked outraged. "And the rishis helped you?"

"Yes."

"Then why are you here?" she said. "Go back to them."

"Rishi Surochi has refused to help me with the *homa* a second time," said Bharat. "I have tried reasoning with him, but —"

"*Reasoning?*" Urmila stretched the word out. "You are the one who needs to be reasoned with." She took a step towards her brother-in-law. "You did the *agnimanasa* the first time, well aware of its consequences. Now, you want to do it *again*? I can see you've taken leave of your senses."

Atibhanu watched the king and the woman. He couldn't help noticing how much she resembled her husband Lakshmana in temper and attitude. It seemed they were made for each other... and that is when the bodyguard realized why his king had wanted him here. Bharat didn't want to be alone in his sister-in-law's chambers, lest tongues wag…

"The scriptures are wrong about the consequences," said Bharat.

"They are perfectly clear about the consequences," Urmila said stubbornly. "The *agnimanasa* exacts a terrible price on the one doing the *homa*. The magic gains strength from someone who is close to —"

"I know how the magic works," the king retorted. "I don't need a lesson on that."

"Good," the woman snapped. "In which case, you know you will lose someone precious to you when you do the *agnimanasa*. Probably why Surochi has sensibly refused to help you."

Atibhanu listened, fascinated. He didn't understand everything, but he got the fact that the king was seeking his sister-in-law's help to do a *homa*, but she was dead against it as it had serious repercussions.

"Look at me," said Bharat, sounding exasperated. "It's been seven months since I did the *homa*. Nothing has happened to anyone dear to me —"

"You lost your nana."

"He died of a stroke and old age."

"What about Taksha?"

Atibhanu thought he saw Bharat pale. "Nothing happened to Taksha. The boy is fine."

Urmila looked dissatisfied as she shook her head and turned away.

"What? I just showed you how the scriptures are wrong," the king persisted. "The *agnimanasa* is safe to perform, but Surochi will not do it, and you will not do it."

"I don't know. Just because nothing has happened, it doesn't mean something won't —"

"Please, Urmila," Bharat beseeched. "The magic has all but gone from Ayodhya. You can see how the people of Kosala are suffering. But we have discovered why the magic is disappearing. A rakshasi, Simhika. She is here in Ayodhya, and she's slowly destroying our magic. We know where she is and we can stop her, but we need magic to combat her. Without magic, we cannot dream of putting an end to her devices. That's why I am here. Please..."

"You cannot keep performing the *agnimanasa* whenever a need arises —"

"But the need will never arise again, Urmila," the king entreated earnestly. "Once Simhika has been defeated, the sacred fire will flourish, and the magic will revive in Ayodhya. There won't be a need for me to do the *agnimanasa* again." He looked at the woman. "Just this once, please. One last time..."

Urmila considered the appeal for a long moment. Finally, she looked at Bharat. "Does Mandavi know?" she asked.

"This will be the last time." With a nod at Atibhanu, Bharat said, "Other than him, you and me, no one needs to know."

"Alright," the woman said with a sigh of resignation. "You will need to bathe before the *homa*."

For the next ten minutes, Atibhanu observed Urmila make preparations for the *homa*, building a platform and placing firestones in a square with the fire pit at the centre. Finally, when Bharat returned from his bath, dripping wet and shivering with cold, he sat between the firestones and

Urmila took her place on the platform. Picking up the sheaf of palm leaves, she paused to assess the king.

"This time, it's the rakshasi," she said. "What made you do the *homa* the first time?"

"I did it for the people of Kosala," Bharat revealed. "The sacred fire had grown feeble following the rakshasa attack on the Sanctum, and magic was dwindling. We'd had two years of drought, and the disappearances had begun in the city. Our people were suffering everywhere. I couldn't sit back and do nothing." He paused, a humourless smile on his lips. "The rains did come," he added, "and the magic did soar after the *agnimanasa*."

"Alright," Urmila nodded. "But you do understand that by doing this, you risk losing someone dear to you."

"I do understand," said Bharat, "but I won't lose anyone."

Urmila sighed and opened the palm leaves. Bharat closed his eyes and Urmila began chanting mantras. Moments later, a fire sprang to life around Bharat, enveloping him. Atibhanu watched, his mouth agape, as his king began glowing inside the fire, turning golden and shedding a light that radiated from within the flames, driving back shadows. And as Urmila continued chanting, particles of light lifted from the raja's body and rose into the air like sparks, only more golden and magical than anything the bodyguard had ever seen before in his life.

Tomorrow morning, Atibhanu thought to himself as he walked behind his king.

Tomorrow morning.

The message from *mahanayaka* Gajakarna had been pithy, but it said everything that Atibhanu needed to know. The plot to overthrow Bharat was in motion. And his was the crucial part, that of kidnapping Taksha so the boy could be held as ransom in exchange of a peaceful surrender. He had wondered what the raja would think of him, having betrayed his trust. He had wondered what the boy would think of him. He had grown to like the kid. He knew the kid liked him too.

Tomorrow morning.

The rebellion was planned for the next day, the bodyguard thought, considering his options.

"I'm going to get my sword," Bharat said, interrupting his thoughts. "Ask everyone to be ready to ride in five minutes."

"Yes, rajan."

The king looked at Atibhanu, eyes flashing a warning. "Not a word to anyone about what you just saw."

"Yes, rajan. Rajan…" the bodyguard hesitated, "I… was thinking…"

Bharat dropped his pace. As Atibhanu came to a halt, the king stopped and turned. "What?"

Tomorrow morning.

"Rajan, if all of us go to the old quarter, we'll be leaving the palace unguarded," said Atibhanu. "I mean, the rani is here, the queen mothers are here. *Taksha is here*. Shouldn't somebody stay behind, just in case the palace comes under attack?"

Bharat's eyes narrowed as he considered the possibility. "You are right," he said slowly.

"I am willing to stay here, rajan," the bodyguard offered, hoping he didn't sound desperate.

Bharat gave the proposal more thought. Then, with a nod of approval, he said, "Make sure that no one in the palace comes to any harm."

"I will, rajan," Atibhanu bowed in relief as Bharat turned away.

The rebellion was planned for the next day, the bodyguard thought to himself again.

I did it for the people of Kosala.

Watching millions of golden sparks spiral from his king's body and disappear into Ayodhya's atmosphere, the bodyguard had been filled with wonder.

His raja had performed a dangerous *homa* to ease the suffering of his people, Atibhanu realized. His raja had been selfless — *not once, but twice, putting someone close to himself at risk* — in his concern for the welfare of Kosala's subjects. His raja had been willing to sacrifice so much in his quest to bring the magic back to Ayodhya.

It struck him that they had been wrong about Raja Bharat. If the Ikshvaku code bound Kosala's kings to the contentment and prosperity of the people, as *adhipati* Naresha had pointed out that afternoon, Bharat was a testament of that commitment to the people. Without their knowing it, he had been working to solve the people's problems and ease their hardships. The king certainly needed no reminders about the finer details of the Ikshvaku code.

I do believe Kosala is missing the leadership of Raja Dashratha.

Once again, *adhipati* Naresha had been wrong. In Bharat, they had a raja who was precisely the sort of leader Kosala needed. The *adhipatis* and the people just didn't know it. Neither did *mahanayaka* Gajakarna.

The rebellion was planned for the next day.

It was time to let the *mahanayaka* know the truth about their king. The king had forbidden him from telling anyone about the *agnimanasa homa*, but Atibhanu knew something Bharat didn't.

Kosala stood on the threshold of a rebellion to overthrow its king. The very king Kosala needed.

The rebellion had to be stopped, the bodyguard decided. Even if it meant disobeying his king.

The mansion rose out of the centre of the old quarter like a spectre, grimly outlined against the black of the night, a silent, hulking mass that seemed to breathe shallow breaths of anticipation as the *nagarapala* contingent approached on horseback. The militiamen were thirty in number, their *mahanayaka* riding in front alongside Bharat and Shatrughna. Dileepa rode to Baladitya's left, looking anxious in the light of the six guttering torches. Palace investigators were adept at tackling problems using their intellect; fighting was not their forte, definitely not fighting that involved fearsome rakshasis wielding dark magic.

The party rode down the street as silently as possible, the only noises coming from the clinking of a harness here or the scuff of a hoof there. Drawing up to the mansion's doorway, Shatrughna signalled a stop, and a dozen *nagarapalas* dismounted and took their places on both sides of the door, ready to make a rush, while a handful slipped into the lanes leading to the building's rear. It wasn't until the militiamen had taken their positions that Bharat and Shatrughna dismounted. Throwing off his *pravara*, Shatrughna took a torch from one of the men and strode purposefully to the door. Meanwhile, Bharat glanced up at the building, which was wreathed in unearthly shadows, and hoped that the magic generated by the *agnimanasa* would take effect in time for their confrontation with what waited inside.

"Open the door," Shatrughna ordered, hammering on the wood with the flat of his hand. Then, taking a step back, he waited, his right hand resting on the hilt of his *khanga*.

There was no response from within. Nothing stirred, other than the shadows, ragged in the light of the torches battling the wind.

Shatrughna motioned Dileepa to his side. "Outer courtyard… then a set of steps up to an inner courtyard," he reconfirmed.

Dileepa nodded.

Shatrughna looked at Bharat and Baladitya. At a nod from Bharat, all three drew their *khangas*. On seeing the militiamen grip their *kuntas* in anticipation, Dileepa hurriedly swept his *pravara* aside to get his *karapala* out. He then stepped out of the way so the *nagarapalas* could rush in ahead of him.

It took one ferocious kick for the door to give way, and Shatrughna pushed through the opening, torch held high, sword at the ready. Bharat, Baladitya and the rest of the *nagarapalas* streamed in on the prince's heels, and the courtyard filled with men and torches, the militiamen spreading out to deal with threats. The courtyard was empty though, the door to the inner courtyard firmly shut.

Shatrughna bounded up the stairs and smashed his way through the second door as well. Bharat and the *nagarapalas* followed, with Dileepa close behind. Spilling into the inner courtyard, the raiding party came to a stop, swords and javelins glinting dully in the torchlight.

The darkness within the inner courtyard was stark, pushing back at the intruders like a physical entity, an invisible curtain, and when the torches came in contact with it, their light diminished. The men almost had to plough their way through, and even then the darkness seemed reluctant to yield, pulling at them from all sides, slowing them down....

"Simhika," Shatrughna's voice boomed in the quietness of the courtyard, startling pigeons into a flurried flight. "Simhika, reveal yourself," the yuvaraja called again as the flapping of wings subsided and the birds returned to their perches.

As if in response to Shatrughna's challenge, the darkness that cloaked them seemed to implode and wash away like a retreating tide. Freed of its influence, the torches flared and burned bright, lighting up the courtyard—

—and there at its centre a figure stood revealed, perfectly still and watching the men, torchlight not quite reaching the face so it was impossible to say if the whites of its eyes were truly visible or were just in the imagination. Bright, neon-coloured whorls and patterns covered the figure's arms, coursing with dark magic.

A rakshasi.

The king stepped forward. "I advise you to yield without a fight," he said. "We are many. You will be overwhelmed."

The rakshasi said nothing, though Bharat sensed that she had smiled a shadow of a smile. Then, before he could make up his mind about what to do next, the darkness seemed to seethe around them. It bubbled and unravelled, tearing apart into skeins that wove and spun thickly, morphing into sightless beings with talons and jaws. The men gasped and floundered, smothered in pitch darkness, and Bharat felt something shift and rend inside his body as he fought to retain control of his senses. An unfathomable grudge seemed to rise from deep in his core, a hatred and anger that he didn't know he had in himself, a gluttonous urge to harm and destroy, and he felt a shadow tear from him and spill outwards. All that anger and hatred left him the same instant, and Bharat reeled, nearly losing his grip on his *khanga*. From the corner of his eye, he saw Shatrughna, the *mahanayaka* and the militiamen also stagger as the shadows that had beset them leached away, back towards the rakshasi and past her, to merge into the infinite darkness that rose behind her.

Curling his left hand into a fist, Bharat whispered a mantra, testing the magic. There was none. The *vajramushti* strapped to his forearm remained cold and unresponsive.

"Kosala's rajan visiting me in person," the rakshasi said in a silken whisper. "I am honoured."

Still swaying a little on his feet, Bharat cursed and waved his sword at Simhika.

"Surrender now," he commanded.

The king sensed the rakshasi's smile again as she raised a lazy hand to beckon something from behind her. As the darkness in the background rearranged itself into distinct shapes and forms, the men got their weapons up and braced themselves.

"You say you are many," the rakshasi said, her smile broadening. "You are correct."

Shadows detached from the dark and drew abreast of Simhika. Bharat noticed that the shadows resembled men.

"Let me introduce you to yourselves," the rakshasi chuckled as she motioned with her hand.

The shadow men stepped forward, their *khangas* and *kuntas* raised.

Bharat's breath caught as the shadow men entered the ring of light cast by the torches. His eyes locked on the figure facing him.

The shadow figure was his double almost down to the last, minute detail.

The same height and lean, muscular build. The same groomed beard. The exact same hairstyle, knotted into a bun. The one difference lay in the deathly pallor on the shadow Bharat's face, as though it had freshly risen from a pyre. The other striking aspect was the hatred in the replica's eyes, an insane urge for bloodlust of the sort that Bharat had experienced just moments earlier.

Unable to comprehend what he was seeing, the king shot a glance at the other shadow men. He saw Baladitya's duplicate, vile and violent, facing the *mahanayaka*. Shatrughna's replica stood opposite Shatrughna, big and powerful like the original, but significantly more malevolent. The rest of the *nagarapalas* were lined up against their doubles, and even Dileepa's shadow version was in front of him.

"You are many," Bharat heard Simhika whisper in amusement. "You *will* be overwhelmed."

Teeth bared in mad, bottomless rage, the shadow figures launched themselves upon the raiding party, their swords and *kuntas* seeking out torsos and throats to skewer and cut and cleave open.

Listening to Kosala's commander speak, the first crush of disappointment stirred in Sudhanva's chest, and he sensed the shadows beginning to form in the periphery of his vision.

"— hard to imagine that the rajan has subjected himself to an *agnimanasa* to bring magic back to Ayodhya," the *mahanayaka* was saying in an awed voice. "And not for the first time, mind you. He has done it before. He has done it *twice* now, knowing what is at stake."

Sudhanva had to make an effort to stop himself from snapping in reply. "Doing the *agnimanasa* is fine," he said, "but it's an undeniable fact that Bharat has failed on so many counts. He failed to stop the disappearances," he began counting on his fingers, then paused to look at Gajakarna. "Look at you. Your daughter is missing, your wife is inconsolable, and you have no idea what's become of her. Then, by shying away from war, Bharat failed to avenge Lavanyasurya's insult of Kosala, and he failed to get justice for the men of the garrison. *Your men, mahanayaka*. His reluctance to act against Madhupura also led to the scarcity of woollens that resulted in deaths and suffering throughout the kingdom. More spectacular failure."

"The shortage of woollens was mostly rumour and very little fact," Gajakarna interjected.

"Then that decision to gamble with the lives of our men to free the River Kingdoms," Sudhanva persisted, ignoring the *mahanayaka*, though his face flushed in anger at the lie being called out. "And now, he is bringing war to Ayodhya by giving asylum to Yuddhajeet and that treacherous band of Bahlikas."

"I still think we must rethink our decision to overthrow Bharat."

Opening the door to Gajakarna so late in the night, Sudhanva had never imagined his dream of becoming Kosala's next king — a dream so close to becoming reality — was on the verge of being destroyed. He had welcomed the *mahanayaka* into his home thinking they would discuss the finer points of the coup, but instead, the commander had launched into a commendation of Bharat because the king had risked the life of a dear one to perform a stupid *homa*. If that hadn't been bad enough, Gajakarna was now blabbering about reconsidering the coup...

"I don't see what has changed for us to rethink the decision, my friend," he said, trying to sound amiable. "Didn't I just list all the reasons why Bharat has to go?"

"We might have been hasty in judging him," said the *mahanayaka*. "Yes, some of his decisions appear rash and not well considered, but then, it's hard to blame him for everything that's been going wrong. I don't know if he can be held responsible for the disappearances because *no one* has a clue why they've been happening in the first place. It's not as though there was an evident solution to the problem which Bharat wilfully ignored or overlooked. And about that shortfall in the supply of blankets and *pravaras*... there's no evidence of that. It was just your theory..."

Sudhanva felt the shadows closing in on him from all sides, even as a tidal wave of resentment swelled from deep within his heart. All of his life, he had wanted to be nothing more than a *kshatri* to the kings of Kosala, but fate had denied him that simple wish. He had never ceased cursing his fate until that evening three months ago, when it had suddenly struck him that fate might have bigger plans for him.

That fate might have been paving the way for him to become king of Kosala.

For three months, he had been nursing that dream, plotting and planning his moves to have the powerful and influential *adhipatis* of Sravasti on his side. He had worked tirelessly to sow seeds of mistrust in the minds of the people of Kosala, planting rumours about the king's incompetence, and these had finally borne fruit in the form of the previous day's riots. He had cultivated Gajakarna with a lot of care and patience so that the army would be on his side when he moved against Bharat. Yuddhajeet's arrival had given his plans stimulus, and his rebellion was moving at the right pace and in the right direction. But just when it looked like his destiny as Kosala's new king was finally being forged, the *mahanayaka* was pulling everything apart for no good reason…

"…we should perhaps give Bharat some benefit of the doubt. He has done the *agnimanasa* for the people, so his heart is in the right place —"

"Catch your breath, my friend," Sudhanva interrupted Gajakarna, laughing, "Catch your breath before the life slips from your lips." He walked over to the commander and put his hand on the man's shoulder. "Fine, I get your point," he said mildly. "So, what do you suggest we do next?"

"For starters, I will have my *nayakas* and *upanayakas* order their men to stand down," said the commander.

"Right," Sudhanva nodded, letting the shadows swamp him and letting himself sink in the mad urges that they bore to the surface of his consciousness.

"You should speak to *adhipati* Mihiradutta and the others about the king's *agnimanasa* and tell them we should give Bharat some leeway."

"Absolutely," the *adhipati* of Sankasya agreed as the last dregs of good sense left him, replaced by a ravenous desire to shed blood and revel in it. "Absolutely," he repeated, as he took a tighter grip of the commander's shoulder and drew him close, narrowing the distance between them…

"What are you —" Gajakarna began, but the words froze in his throat when he saw Sudhanva's lips twist in a horrible, mirthless smile that kept spreading unnaturally to the sides so that a row of teeth — *or was it many rows of teeth?* — split his face into two. "Wha —" the *mahanayaka* tried again, but this time the words turned to a gasp as searing pain exploded on the left side of his chest. "Wha —" he said a third time, as he gawked at the *kshurika* protruding from between his ribs, Sudhanva's fingers around the weapon's hilt. "Why?" he managed asking the *adhipati*, his vision already starting to blur and fade.

"Why?" Sudhanva asked, the smile turning into a hateful snarl as he twisted the *kshurika* deeper into the commander's chest. "Because you are in my way, stopping me from becoming the new king of Kosala, and I cannot, *I will not*, tolerate that. I have worked hard to get to a point where this rebellion can become a reality, and I cannot, *I will not*, have you undoing all that work. Do you know what it's taken for me to get here? I've had to cheat, lie… and kill." He paused and gave his head a regretful shake. "I owe you the truth before you leave us for good, so listen carefully. Your daughter… she didn't disappear." Seeing Gajakarna's eyes open wide, he nodded. "Well, she did, but not like the others, so she won't be coming back… *ever*."

"What did… you… do?" the *mahanayaka* wheezed as the dagger burrowed into him.

"I had her killed," the *adhipati* confessed with a chilling smile. He bent to listen to Gajakarna's gasps. "Why? Oh, because you were being a pain, arguing against the rebellion, not committing yourself to it. Totally unacceptable, so I thought a personal loss might serve as the right sort of motivation for you. And I was right. Once your daughter disappeared, you turned firmly against the king."

A croak escaped the commander's lips.

"What?" asked Sudhanva. "You wish to know where she is? In all honesty, I don't know," the *adhipati* shrugged. "Probably at the bottom of the Sarayu, or perhaps buried somewhere outside Ayodhya. I didn't ask the men what they did with her." He looked into the *mahanayaka's* eyes. "Don't look so outraged. There was nothing personal there. I'd happily kill anyone to get what I want. I killed my own son-in-law so I could rally Naresha, Mihiradutta and Jayabhama against Bharat by blaming Pushyanta's death on the *dandapalas*." He twisted the blade in one last time, relishing the ooze of warm blood over his fingers and down his hand, dripping off his elbow to splatter at his feet. "My destiny is to be king of Kosala. No one can stop me from realizing that destiny."

Gajakarna made one futile attempt to break free of the *adhipati's* grasp before his body sagged. Sudhanva let the commander fall, wrenching the dagger out of the body as it yielded to gravity. The shadows began to thin out and withdraw, and Sudhanva was left staring at the man he had just murdered.

A noise from somewhere above and behind him snapped Sudhanva out of his daze. He turned, but he saw nothing in the gallery above. Probably a window banging in the wind, the *adhipati* said to himself, realizing he had work to do. The body needed to be fixed. Then, there was the king's bodyguard who had told Gajakarna about the *agnimanasa* and pivoted the stupid commander's mind away from rebellion. The fellow was supposed to have been on their side, but because he had been so awed by the king's *homa*, the *mahanayaka* was now dead and the rebellion was in jeopardy. Sudhanva wondered how much damage he might already have done, before realizing that the bodyguard probably hadn't told anyone else anything yet. Atibhanu was Gajakarna's man, which is why he had come straight to his commander, expecting Gajakarna to do whatever was needed to halt the rebellion.

Which meant that in all likelihood, Atibhanu knew Gajakarna had come to see him, the *adhipati* realized.

That could have presented a problem, but Sudhanva already had a plan in place for the meddlesome bodyguard.

No *mahanayaka* or bodyguard would come in the way of his aims and ambitions. The rebellion would happen, and he would be king of Kosala.

Let me introduce you to yourselves.

Seeing the shadowy figures emerge from the darkness behind Simhika, Shatrughna had been struck by a sense of familiarity, but it wasn't until he had laid eyes on Dileepa's double that he had realized what was happening, and understood what the rakshasi's words had truly portended.

Let me introduce you to yourselves.

Now, seeing his own replica bear down on him with a raised *khanga*, the prince braced himself and waited for the swing of the sword. The swing came as expected, a scything downward chop aimed at cutting him in two from shoulder to midriff, but Shatrughna parried the blow expertly before ducking in close and driving his own sword into the shadow's stomach, a killing stroke. But the shadow twisted out of the way in the nick of time and brought its *khanga* up, stabbing at Shatrughna's throat.

Another block and deflection from Shatrughna, another swift thrust of the blade, another dodge by the double, another slash at an unguarded torso, another deft side step, another miss by mere inches… The yuvaraja and his shadow thrust and parried in attack and counterattack, drawing together in a deadly grapple, then pulling away to create room for wide, arcing cuts and slashes. They were evenly matched, shadow and original, both expert swordsmen so neither had an advantage over the other. Once or twice, Shatrughna tried resorting to magic, hoping to squeeze a tiny amount out of the atmosphere to use against his double, but no matter how hard he uttered the mantras, there wasn't sufficient magic to draw from, and the effort only left him weakened. So, on and on they fought, and around them, feet scrambled for purchase on stone, *khanga* rang against *khanga*, and men panted while their limbs grew weary and their thinking turned leaden with fatigue.

Fuelled by anger and hatred, the shadows, however, showed no signs of flagging.

"The *dandapala* needs assistance," Bharat's voice sounded in Shatrughna's ear. "He won't last long by himself."

The prince risked a quick glance around. Everywhere, *nagarapalas* were locked in duels with their doubles. He glimpsed Dileepa straining against his shadow version, fear plain on his face.

"At this rate, many of us won't last long, brother," Shatrughna shouted back.

They needed more men, he reckoned, before realizing there was no advantage in numbers here. Each new man would be perfectly matched with *his* double. Simhika would see to that. More men would change nothing.

"We need magic," he shouted, parrying another blow from the shadow Shatrughna.

There had been so much strength behind that strike that a jolt ran along Shatrughna's arm, and his *khanga* slipped from his fingers and landed in a clatter. His double moved in to deliver the death blow, but Bharat's *khanga* swept out, deflecting the blade. Shatrughna bent and retrieved his fallen sword, amazed at the speed of his brother's response.

"Don't get distracted," Bharat yelled as he beat back his own replica.

Angry at having been bested in a sword fight, Shatrughna locked eyes with shadow Shatrughna. And in that moment, the prince saw every shred of hatred he had ever experienced manifested in his double, and he understood what these shadows really were — meaner, more wrathful, *more vengeful* incarnations of primitive rages and resentments, brought alive by rakshasa magic. The shadows were the basest versions of the self, drawing sustenance from wells of anger, mistrust, jealousy and violence, and that's what made them so invulnerable, so hopelessly hard to defeat.

Seeing his shadow prepare to lunge at him, Shatrughna said a mantra and closed his fist — and to his sheer surprise, a shield formed in his hand, shimmering with magic. Even as his duplicate swung its sword at him, the prince took the blow on the shield and counterattacked, hacking at the double and driving it back with newfound vigour.

"The magic," he screamed. "It's back. Use it."

Hearing his brother's cry and seeing the shield in his hand, Bharat experienced a huge surge of relief. The *agnimanasa* had worked. He had taken a big chance by banking on Urmila's mastery over magic, but his faith in her had paid off.

The king raised his left hand and whispered a mantra. Two bolts blazed out of the *vajramushti* and struck his double in the chest, and Bharat had the satisfaction of seeing the double erupt in flames and stagger away. But the next instant, a wave of tiredness crashed over Bharat, and he realized he was losing energy in his effort to tap into too little magic. It didn't matter, the king told himself. His shadow was on fire, and no matter how little magic there was in the air, *it was working and…*

…Simhika had to be stopped.

Bharat spun around, looking for the rakshasi, but there was only billowing darkness where she had stood just moments ago. The king's gaze swung wildly, searching for Simhika, but his eyes alighted on Dileepa instead; the *dandapala* was sprawled on the cold floor of the courtyard, his shadow looming over him, poised for the kill. The investigator lay motionless, staring up at his double in horror, helpless and waiting for the sword to descend…

Bharat loosed off a volley of bolts on the investigator's double. The double failed to catch fire, but it did drop dead. In rapid succession, Bharat brought down the doubles of four *nagarapalas*.

The shadows could be killed. The thought elevated the king's mood, igniting hope in his heart, but another giddy spell got the better of him and he teetered on his feet. He was still recovering when out of nowhere, he was overtaken by a surge of bitterness. Floundering in its wash, trying to make sense of it, Bharat felt something being tugged from within him, and the next moment, another shadowy form peeled away from his body. With astonishing swiftness, it reconstructed itself into another replica of him, impossible to tell apart from the one that had caught fire and burned on the cold stone floor of the courtyard. Watching this replica appraise him with hate-filled eyes, Bharat understood the full impact of what the rakshasi had said.

You are many. You will *be overwhelmed.*

All around Bharat, more doubles of the *nagarapalas* manifested. There was anger and violence in plenty, he saw, enough for Simhika's sorcery to create new replicas to replace the dead ones. Endless sources of strife, an endless stock of shadows.

That's what the rakshasi had gloated about, he realized, as he aimed his *vajramushti* resignedly at his new double. They were many, and that was why they would be overwhelmed.

The magic... It's back. Use it.

Running from his double, knowing it was futile trying to fight it and win, veering one way and then the other, scanning his memory for doors, looking for a way out, Dileepa had been focused on his survival, when someone had called out about the magic. The *dandapala* had instinctively shot a glance over his shoulder to see who it was.

That was a mistake.

Because he wasn't looking where he was going, Dileepa hurtled into someone, tripped, lost his balance and went down on the cold stone of the courtyard. He sprawled, face down, his sword knocked out of his hand. He lay there for a second or two, winded and hurting while he gathered his wits.

That too was a mistake.

His duplicate hadn't been far behind him to start with. Now, as he squandered precious seconds gathering his wits, the double bounded up to his side, its *karapala* raised to end the matter. The *dandapala* watched his shadow in horror as it prepared for the kill when, all of a sudden, it was struck on the head by bolts that went in deep, slaying it where it stood. The *karapala* fell from its hand, and the shadow toppled right on top of him.

Dileepa heaved and hoisted until he was free of his double. Around him, *nagarapalas* brawled with shadow *nagarapalas*. Thankful for being saved in the nick of time and eager to make that count, the investigator sprang to his feet and looked towards Bharat by the doorway, *karapala* in one hand, *vajramushti* strapped to the other. He saw the king shoot a pair of bolts into a pair of shadow *nagarapalas*, bringing both down.

Realizing the magic was back and the fight was going in their favour, Dileepa began to rejoice, but within a moment, he was seized by loathing and mindless rage, neither of which had cause to exist. Sick with the sensation, the investigator lurched around blindly until the loathing and rage went out of him, blown out like a flame. The *dandapala* gasped in relief, but stopped as a fresh double formed in front of his eyes, full of the loathing and rage that had birthed it.

His new double was already swinging its *karapala* at him, and the *dandapala* stepped back just in time, the tip of the blade missing him by a whisker. Turning around, Dileepa scooped up his sword and leaped away, trying to put some distance between himself and his shadow. The clang of *khanga* against *khanga* and *kunta* against *kunta* rang around the courtyard, and even without looking at them, Dileepa sensed the exhaustion and hopelessness in the militiamen, locked in tussle with their doubles.

In a surge of fury, Dileepa wheeled around and swung his sword, taking his double by surprise, slashing its cheek from ear to mouth. The anger behind the stroke only served to strengthen his double, however, and it came at Dileepa with unexpected force. The *dandapala* tried to counter the attack, but he was outdone by the sheer fury of the assault, and his *karapala* was knocked out of his hand.

Dileepa turned and fled once again, his double on his heels, swinging the *karapala* in wild arcs in the hope of cutting the *dandapala* down. Shadows milled around him and the darkness grew as Dileepa ran from the courtyard, his duplicate right behind, manically focused on killing him. Desperate to shake his pursuer off, the investigator blundered from room to room until he found himself by the well at the rear.

The well.

Maybe he could throw himself into the well to save himself, the *dandapala* thought. Maybe his shadow wouldn't follow him there. He might drown, of course, but it was better than being cut into pieces by —

Dileepa pulled up short and stared. He blinked, and he stared some more.

The well was radiating from within, as though lit by a fire inside, or as if the water at the bottom had turned molten, burning like lava. Golden-orange lava.

Mesmerized by the sight, Dileepa walked towards the well, his shadow forgotten. The shadow, for its part, stood rooted where it had come to a halt, staring at the slowly widening glow, as if in thrall. The *karapala* dangled loosely from the double's fingers.

The *dandapala* had covered half the distance to the well when the glow suddenly strengthened, and a spectacular figure bathed in dripping golden light rose from its depths on a pair of giant wings. The figure was a woman, and despite being nearly blinded by the brightness she shed, Dileepa recognized her in an instant. He had seen her lit almost the same way the night he had been attacked on the street outside, the night he had been saved by the six fiery *shyenas*... and the woman who controlled them.

"Nandana," the name escaped the *dandapala's* lips in a shiver of relief, disbelief and despair. One part of him was already aware this was the end of them, that they were so different, their love was fated to fail.

Clearing the lip of the well, the rakshasi hovered in the air, oozing light, wings beating slowly. Then, as the investigator watched open-mouthed, she spread her hands wide, as if to embrace the world. Skeins of light unravelled from her, taking the shape of birds in moments. *Shyenas*, *grdhas*, *kakahs*, *atayis*, even *jatukas*, all varieties of winged creatures slipped from Nandana's open arms and flew over the *dandapala's* head in a rush of wings and light, and suddenly, the darkness was pushed back, driven into retreat. Bats and birds swooped and soared through the mansion, parting the darkness like arrows and leaving trails of light and fire in their wake. And wherever they went, the darkness fled.

Nandana alighted in front of the well. Folding her wings, she walked past Dileepa, showing no sign of having recognized him. Crossing his double, she looked at it with blazing eyes, and the double burst into flames. Reduced to soot and ash in no time, it blew away in the wind and into the night. The rakshasi headed into the mansion, trailing golden-orange droplets that sparked and sizzled on cold stone before dissipating.

Too dazed to say a word, Dileepa followed Nandana, skirting the pool of ash that had been his double. In the inner courtyard, *shyenas*, *grdhas* and *atayis* were attacking the shadow doubles, setting them on fire as Bharat, Shatrughna and the *nagarapalas* looked on in wonder. Someone noticed Nandana and a shout went up. Fingers were pointed, and Dileepa saw Bharat bring his arm up, aiming his *vajramushti* at the rakshasi.

"Rajan... *no*..." the *dandapala* shouted, darting forward. "She is on our side."

The king lowered his weapon. The rakshasi ignored him and Dileepa, all of her attention on a pall of darkness that simmered at the centre of the courtyard. As she approached the blob, Nandana eased her hands open, releasing coils of fire that flew towards the boiling blob. As they bridged the gap, the coils opened to take the form of flying *sarpas* that bit and burrowed into the dark form. *Shyenas* and *atayis* lunged at the blot from above, while *jatukas* worried it from the sides. Rays of light skewered through the tears in its surface until, all of a sudden, the blob fell apart, leaving a solitary figure at its centre.

Simhika, a snarl wrenched across her face, magic winking furiously underneath her skin like a network of neon veins.

"You couldn't stop meddling, could you?" she asked, her eyes narrowed viciously on Nandana. "You had to defy me, you had to defy our lord for… for *them*?" The rakshasi swept a disdainful glance in the direction of Bharat and the *nagarapalas*. Then, looking over Nandana's shoulder, her eyes came to rest on Dileepa. "You betrayed the entire rakshasa clan… for *him*?" she asked.

"Surrender now, Simhika," Bharat called, levelling his *vajramushti* at the rakshasi.

Simhika didn't even bother acknowledging the king with a glance. "I didn't realize you had so much light in you," she said to Nandana. "But no matter how much light there is, there will always be shadows. You cannot destroy me with your light because your light creates shadows. You have slowed me down, at best. Not ended me. Your sacrifice will be in vain, Nandana." A cold smile appeared on the rakshasi's lips. "You cannot stop the march of Lanka. You cannot save these people the next time… No, not again, *never again*."

Your sacrifice will be in vain. Dileepa felt a chill go through him. What had Simhika meant? Had Nandana risked her life by coming to their aid —

The thought had yet to form fully in the *dandapala's* mind when a shadow rose behind Simhika. Her own shadow, created by Nandana's light. It reared and swamped the sorceress, smothering her… swallowing her…

Everything happened in the space of a heartbeat. Then, she was gone.

Shadow and rakshasi, both were gone.

Nandana's light dimmed… diminished… and went out. The fiery *shyenas*, *grdhas*, *atayis* and *jatukas* blinked in mid-flight, went dark and disappeared.

Night returned to the mansion and its inner courtyard.

Night returned to Nandana as her legs gave way and she slumped to the ground.

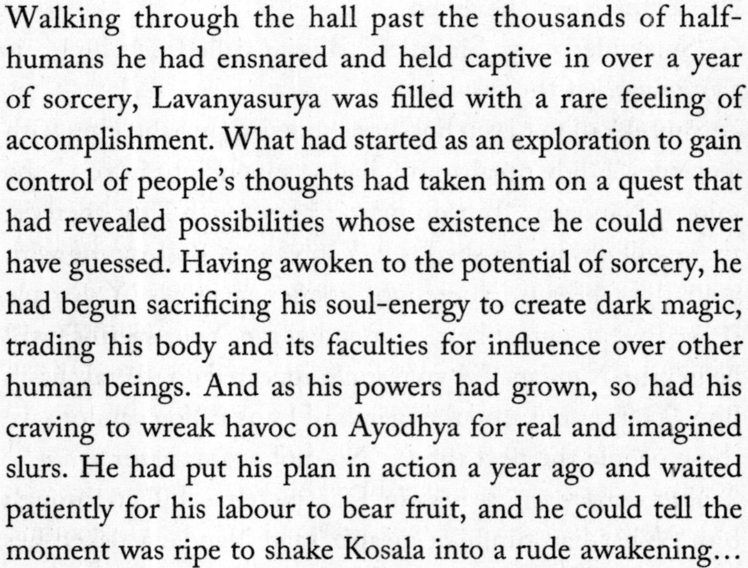

Walking through the hall past the thousands of half-humans he had ensnared and held captive in over a year of sorcery, Lavanyasurya was filled with a rare feeling of accomplishment. What had started as an exploration to gain control of people's thoughts had taken him on a quest that had revealed possibilities whose existence he could never have guessed. Having awoken to the potential of sorcery, he had begun sacrificing his soul-energy to create dark magic, trading his body and its faculties for influence over other human beings. And as his powers had grown, so had his craving to wreak havoc on Ayodhya for real and imagined slurs. He had put his plan in action a year ago and waited patiently for his labour to bear fruit, and he could tell the moment was ripe to shake Kosala into a rude awakening…

Proud of what he had achieved and bursting with guile and expectation, the king walked to the middle of the hall, where Naika sat with her eyes closed, dark as a storm cloud, keeping all his prisoners alive. Naika had become a part of his plan when he had found out that his soul-energy wasn't sufficient to generate the kind of magic he'd aspired for. Fortunately for Lavanyasurya, his queen had his best interests in mind; after all, hadn't she been the one to ask for a *vatika* on the banks of the Yamuna with his statue at its centre? Naika had agreed to do what was wanted of her, though Lavanyasurya admitted that he hadn't been entirely truthful about her role in the scheme of things. Had he told her the truth, he suspected she might have been a whole lot less amenable.

But all that was in the past. What mattered was that he was on the cusp of unleashing something terrible on unsuspecting Ayodhya, and he simply couldn't wait to hear about its outcome. Proud and mighty Kosala was on the verge of being overrun. If Lavanyasurya had a regret, it was that he couldn't be in Ayodhya to witness the carnage with his own eyes.

Going up to his queen, the raja of Madhupura squatted by her side and took her hand in his. He regretted what was going to happen next, he said to himself. By no means was he a cold-hearted monster. It was just that circumstances demanded this sacrifice. Had it been possible, he would have traded places with his queen, but he needed to be alive to receive reports about the horrors that were soon to befall Kosala. After all, wasn't that the whole point — *his enjoyment of Ayodhya's suffering and imminent obliteration?* He couldn't be the one dying and missing out on all the fun, so…

Lavanyasurya looked up at Naika's face, observing the rage and hunger and yearning for blood that boiled inside her, feeding the same urges into his prisoners. It was time to free all that thirst and hunger so it could run savage through Ayodhya, stoking primal passions and drenching the city's streets in blood…

Taking her by the chin, the raja lifted his queen's head, exposing the soft of her throat. He said a mantra and drew a dagger right across. As Naika's blood spilled and soaked her *uttariya*, the bundled half-humans all around the hall shook and came awake, hungry and thirsting for blood.

eleven

"THEY KILLED HIM RIGHT AT MY DOORSTEP."

The crowd around the pathway to Sudhanva's mansion consisted mainly of soldiers of Kosala's army, men loyal to *mahanayaka* Gajakarna. There were about a hundred of them, *nayakas* and *upanayakas* and common soldiers, clustered in a circle around Sudhanva and the dead body of their commander, which lay on its side halfway between the gate and the mansion's main door, mortal wound bared to the sky. Flanking Sudhanva to his left were Mihiradutta and Jayabhama, while Yadudeva stood to his right. All eyes were on Gajakarna, everyone's features grim in the pallid light of dawn.

Yadudeva appeared oddly distracted though, his gaze haunted and turned inwards, and neither his father's impassioned speech nor the corpse on the pathway seemed to hold his attention for long. Nobody noticed, however; the spectacle of the dead commander, gruesomely murdered, was too riveting.

"I heard him cry out and rushed outside, but it was too late," Sudhanva continued, holding his hands up to the first rays of sunshine so everyone could see the blood that had dried there. "He died in my arms," his voice choked and he faltered. "I did not… I could not do anything to save him."

Mihiradutta placed his hand on Sudhanva's shoulder. "You did your best, my friend," he said.

A murmur of discontent went through the assembled soldiers. Sudhanva spotted more soldiers arrive as the news of the murder spread quickly. This was going well, he decided. Once he had moved the *mahanayaka's* body onto the pathway, he had dispatched men to tell all the captains, knowing it would stoke passions in the garrisons. It had, and the *adhipati* believed the prospects of this rebellion succeeding had actually improved with Gajakarna's death, making him wonder why he hadn't considered killing off the commander while plotting Bharat's fall. Of course, he couldn't have planned this death any better, so he had no regrets…

"A brave warrior, killed in cold blood," he went on, inciting the soldiers. "Killed by stealth, by deceit… betrayed by a hand he trusted."

"Who killed him?" an angry voice called from the crowd.

"The king's bodyguard, Atibhanu."

"Atibhanu?" The question was sharp, and a shocked silence followed.

"No," someone else in the crowd muttered in disbelief. "It couldn't have been him."

"The truth is harsh," Sudhanva shook his head ruefully. "I wouldn't have believed it either, had the *mahanayaka* not named Atibhanu as his killer before dying in these arms of mine."

Another silence as everyone struggled to come to terms with what they'd heard. "Atibhanu was a trustworthy man," observed one *upanayaka*. "One of the *mahanayaka's* favourites…"

"Who better then to kill Gajakarna?" Sudhanva demanded.

"Why would Atibhanu do it?" asked Jayabhama.

"Probably for some petty reward from the king," the *adhipati* of Sankasya shrugged. He looked at the men around him and spoke with a challenge in his tone. "Treachery can be easily bought when loyalty is so cheap."

There was a perceptible change in the mood of the soldiers.

"The *mahanayaka* must not go unavenged," a *nayaka* shouted.

"Yes, Atibhanu must pay," said another soldier, his words meeting with approval.

Sudhanva raised a hand to summon everyone's attention. The sun was up, radiant for the first time in weeks, and the bloodstains clearly showed on the *adhipati's* clothes. "Atibhanu should pay, and he will. But Atibhanu is just an instrument of death. The hand is someone else's." The nobleman paused to let the meaning soak in. "That hand will be coming for us next. They could have killed the *mahanayaka* anywhere, but they killed him here, at my doorstep. It is a warning, perhaps even an attempt to pin Gajakarna's death on me. The palace has begun moving against us. The only way we can expect to win now is by acting quickly and forcefully."

"If Atibhanu has betrayed us, we won't have Taksha to bargain with Bharat," said Mihiradutta.

"The question of bargaining with Bharat doesn't arise anymore, not after what he's done to our dear friend," said Sudhanva. What he didn't add was that he'd never cared about using Taksha to negotiate a peaceful transition with Bharat; that had been Gajakarna's idea. As far as he was concerned, it made no difference whether the rebellion was peaceful or steeped in blood. Either was fine as long as at the end of it, he became king.

"No negotiations with the palace," swore a *nayaka*. "We want revenge for our commander."

Revenge… revenge… revenge… The word spread like wildfire and was taken up by the crowd like a chant. Sudhanva felt good. The mood enlivened him, the prospect of violence getting the shadows at the edges of his vision frolicking.

"In the *mahanayaka's* absence, who will lead the move against the palace?" someone asked.

A spot of silence. Sudhanva knew he had to time this right. If he spoke too soon, he could come across as being opportunistic. But even a slight delay, and someone else could volunteer, and the opportunity to command Kosala's army would pass him by. Kosala's king and commander. Why not have both titles when they were there for the taking?

"I will," Sudhanva offered. "It will be an honour to lead you in place of the fallen commander." He looked around at the men. "Atibhanu and Bharat will have to answer for Gajakarna's death."

"We are with you, *adhipati*," two of the *nayakas* announced, drawing their swords and holding them aloft. "Long live *adhipati* Sudhanva."

The rest of the soldiers were about to join them in support when a woman's voice cut in, harsh and reproachful.

"He is lying."

Sudhanva froze.

Eyes turned in the direction of the voice, squinting against the sun's glare to see a figure framed in one of the mansion's darkened doorways. No one could tell the person clearly until the figure stepped out into the light.

It was Varnakavi, the *adhipati's* daughter.

"He lies," she said again, pointing an accusing finger at her father. "He has lied about the king's bodyguard; he has lied about your commander's death. The only truth in what he's said is that your commander did die in his arms… killed by a dagger *he* buried in *mahanayaka* Gajakarna's chest."

The cawing of crows in the trees nearby sounded incredibly loud in the silence that ensued.

"Go inside, Varnakavi —" Sudhanva began irritably, but the woman cut him short.

"*You* killed *mahanayaka* Gajakarna," she raged. "I witnessed the murder with my own eyes."

The *adhipati* sensed the shadows beginning to flock around him.

"You have no idea what you're saying —" he began, but he was interrupted again, this time by a *nayaka*.

"We wish to hear the lady speak."

"She is not quite in her senses," Sudhanva said with a wave of his hand. He turned to Varnakavi. "Go back inside, my child. You need rest…" He turned to Yadudeva, "Take your sister inside."

Yadudeva stared at his father for a long moment before looking away in disinterest. Sudhanva's face reddened in anger, but he forced a smile as he took in the faces of the men in front of him.

"I'm afraid my daughter has not been the same ever since the death of her husband —"

"*Whom you killed,*" Varnakavi screeched. "I heard you tell the *mahanayaka* about it —"

"Varnakavi, my child," Sudhanva gave an exasperated sigh before turning to the ring of faces. "I really apologize for this… please." He took two steps in the woman's direction. "Come, let's go in, child —"

"I want to listen to what she has to say," Mihiradutta said in a voice like the rumble of thunder.

Sudhanva turned to Mihiradutta. "You know how it is with women, my friend. She needs —"

Mihiradutta's hand went to the *karapala* hanging from his waist. "I wish to hear her speak," he said.

Sudhanva stopped, his eyes narrowing. He looked around to see the soldiers staring at him with suspicion. When he turned back, he found that a couple of soldiers had taken positions near his daughter, their hands on the hilts of their swords. He sighed. The shadows were taking over his vision.

In a gentler tone, Mihiradutta addressed Varnakavi. "Speak, child," he said. "Tell us everything you saw and overheard."

"It was last night," Varnakavi said, speaking slowly. "I had woken up to check on my daughter. She had a mild fever last evening, so… Anyway, I was passing along a gallery that overlooks the hall when I heard voices. I looked to see my father and the *mahanayaka* in conversation."

Sudhanva remembered the sound he had heard behind him, the one he had ascribed to a window banging in the wind. He cursed his carelessness. He should have investigated the noise —

"I would have moved on, but then I caught the *mahanayaka* telling father that they must rethink the decision to overthrow Bharat," Varnakavi continued. "I was intrigued, so I stayed to listen. Lots of things were said that I didn't understand, but the *mahanayaka* kept insisting that Bharat had done an *agnimanasa* for the people of Kosala, and for that, he deserved credit and a second chance."

"*The king did an* agnimanasa?" Mihiradutta whispered, his voice filled with wonder. "When?"

Jayabhama looked at his father, not comprehending the import of what had been revealed, and many of the soldiers exchanged puzzled glances.

"I don't know," shrugged Varnakavi. "But the *mahanayaka* seemed sure the king had done it. Anyway, father seemed to disagree with Gajakarna, but then he gave in. The *mahanayaka* told father to tell you," she addressed *adhipati* Mihiradutta, "about the king's *agnimanasa*… and that was when father stabbed him with a knife."

Sudhanva felt everyone's eyes turn on him, and a loathing for his daughter was born in the dark pit of his soul. He was doing everything to become king, and the ungrateful creature was tearing his ambitions up by their roots —

"Why…" some stupid soul in the crowd behind wondered, "Why did he kill the *mahanayaka*?"

"Because my father aspires to become the king of Kosala once Bharat has been overthrown."

The shadows were swarming around Sudhanva now, inside and outside.

"He killed *mahanayaka* Gajakarna because the commander wanted to put the rebellion on hold to give Bharat more time to prove himself," said Varnakavi. "And that's not all. Father had the commander's daughter killed so that Gajakarna would turn against Bharat and lend his support to the rebellion. I heard him admit to that as well."

Loud gasps of shock and revulsion were followed by angry murmurs.

"You said something about Pushyanta," Mihiradutta reminded her gently. "That you heard him confess —"

"He told the *mahanayaka* that he killed..." a sob went through Varnakavi's body, "...he killed Pushyanta so that he could pin the death on the *dandapalas* and turn you, *adhipati* Naresha and brother Jayabhama against the king." She paused to judge Sudhanva with anguished eyes. "He killed my husband and orphaned his own grandchildren to further his ambitions. This man is a monster —"

"*Stop whining*," Sudhanva roared, the shadows now running amok in his mind, in his veins, in his very breath. "Stop whining about your husband for once in your life. What was that husband of yours worth? He was a *guild master*. He would have ended up as Kosala's revenue minister at best. Which I highly doubt, for he couldn't keep his thieving hands to himself. No, he went and hoarded food grains for a measly profit. But look at me — I want to be Kosala's raja. *That* is my worth. So, stop moaning about your guild master husband and stand by your father. You can be Kosala's next princess. Don't throw that away."

"My guild master husband might have been a thief," said Varnakavi, her tone icy in the warmth of the sun, "but you are a murderer. *That* is your worth. It's all you will ever be worth, father. You will never become the king of Kosala."

"Stop it," Sudhanva screamed, eyes ablaze with fury. His daughter was wishing him ill, willing him to fail. She was denying him his destiny. For that, she had to die...

He lunged at her.

He felt himself being yanked back by his arm.

He turned to see Yadudeva gripping his wrist, holding him back.

"Let me go, fool," the *adhipati* snarled. Then seeing his son's red, bloodshot eyes and drooling, slack-jawed grin, he paused. A strange fear overcame him. He pulled back instinctively. "What is it —"

"Father, help me," Yadudeva whispered, pleading.

"What's happened, son?"

"Father… I am… beyond help," Yadudeva mumbled. "Forgive me."

"For what —"

The son leaped at the father, grabbing and holding tight as his jaws opened in hunger, the mouth latching onto the side of Sudhanva's throat, teeth sinking into flesh, clamping down hard, biting through into veins and arteries… satiating a hunger and thirst that had throbbed inside for many days now.

A hunger for flesh. A thirst for blood.

A bloodcurdling scream burst from Sudhanva's lips and ripped through the morning air, scaring the men motionless and sending the crows scattering into the sky.

"Has Simhika really gone?"

Sheshagupta's question hung in the sunlit chamber, where all windows were open to admit the light and chase away gloom from the remotest corners. The sun's heat was back, and birds that had been silent these past few months had broken into song.

"It looks like she's gone," said Bharat at last. "I mean, the battle ended..."

"It could be a deception," said Sheshagupta. "She might still be hiding nearby, waiting to strike when our guard is down."

You have slowed me down, not ended me, Simhika had warned Nandana, Bharat remembered.

"There's always a possibility," the king agreed. They could speculate forever and still not reach a conclusion.

"I think she has fled Ayodhya," Shatrughna asserted. He glanced at the windows. "Look at the sun. Ayodhya hasn't seen such glorious sunshine in a really long time. How come it's suddenly sunny this morning? What has changed between yesterday and today? One thing — Simhika."

Bharat wondered whether it was Simhika's departure or the *agnimanasa* that was responsible. Perhaps it was both. Glancing in Atibhanu's direction, he thought he detected a glimmer in the bodyguard's eyes when they met his. Looking again, he saw Atibhanu's face was impassive as usual.

"We can't be certain about anything pertaining to Simhika until Nandana is revived," he said.

"*If* she revives, that is," Shatrughna added.

Sheshagupta and Kushadhwaja nodded. "What do the *vaidyas* say?" the *kshatri* asked.

"Vihari is tending to her," was all Bharat said.

There was a brief silence before the revenue minister spoke. "What do we do when she returns to consciousness? Can we trust her? Here, in the palace of all places? She is still a rakshasi..."

"She helped us fight Simhika and our shadows," Bharat reminded him. "Without her assistance, I doubt we'd have been able to get the better of Simhika."

"She also warned us about Simhika," Kushadhwaja pointed out. "But then, if she did what you said she did — all that light and birds and whatnot — why didn't she do that earlier, by herself? Why wait until you and Shatrughna showed up with the *nagarapalas*? Could it all be for effect, just to gain our trust?"

It was possible, Bharat had to admit. "We won't know until she is fit enough to be questioned," he said, worn out by the doubts and uncertainties that lurked at every turn in the road.

"I think the two of you should get some sleep," Kushadhwaja suggested, assessing the king's tiredness correctly.

"Yes, that's probably a good —"

Bharat broke off as a clatter of *padukas* brought Sheelabhadra through the door, wild-eyed and short of breath. The guild master didn't waste a second to launch into speech.

"Have you heard?" he asked without preamble, peering at the faces around him in excitement. "It seems *mahanayaka* Gajakarna has been murdered by Sudhanva."

The announcement was so sudden and shocking that all anyone could do was stare at the guild master in astonishment.

"Where did you pick this up?" Kushadhwaja asked, breaking the silence.

"From one of the garrisons," Sheelabhadra replied ambiguously. "The news will be everywhere in no time."

"Why would Sudhanva kill the *mahanayaka*?" Shatrughna pondered aloud, not knowing that there was one man in the room who might have guessed the answer.

"Word is that the *adhipati* himself was bitten by his son," the guild master added.

"*Bitten* by his son?" Sheshagupta mimicked the words as everyone exchanged baffled glances. "Why would Yadudeva bite Sudhanva? That's so *absurd*."

"This isn't making sense," Bharat scowled. "We must find out what's happened for ourselves."

Making for the exit, he glanced at Shatrughna, who interpreted the look correctly. "I shall fetch Baladitya," the younger brother said.

The brothers had reached the door, with everybody else coming close behind, when Shatrughna collided with a man who was rushing into the chamber from outside. It was the courtier Vijaya, who looked flustered.

Mumbling an apology to Shatrughna, Vijaya bowed to Bharat. "I was coming to see you."

"Is it about *mahanayaka* Gajakarna?" Bharat asked.

Vijaya shook his head, not comprehending. "No… it's the returned, rajan."

"The returned?" the king grew tense, sensing a new threat.

The courtier nodded. "From all over the city, there are reports of the returned attacking people without reason."

"You mean those who had disappeared?" Bharat's voice rose, sharp with concern.

"Yes, rajan. They are everywhere, biting people like animals."

"Biting people?" Bharat's eyes widened as he turned to Sheelabhadra. "Didn't you just say that Sudhanva was bitten by Yadudeva?"

"And Yadudeva is one of the returned," Kushadhwaja remarked softly.

"They are..." Vijaya blanched for a second before recovering. "Rajan... the returned appear to be hungering for flesh and thirsting for blood..."

As his blood turned to ice in his veins, Bharat stared at the courtier, waiting for him to complete what he was saying. But the implication was never in doubt, hanging in the air like a bad omen.

"*...the returned of Kosala have turned into vetalas.*"

"We shall get the palace *vaidyas* to tend to her."

Nandana's confrontation with Simhika had left her nearly unconscious, and all efforts to revive her had so far proved futile, so the raja's words hadn't come as a reassurance to Dileepa, more so because the same *vaidyas* hadn't been able to do much for mahamuni Vashishtha in close to two years of treatment. But the investigator realized that it was the best Bharat could offer, and though he didn't have a lot of faith in the palace *vaidyas*, he was relieved that the girl was under the king's protection. The *dandapala* knew that opinion could turn against Nandana once news of her being a rakshasi went public, even though she had come to Kosala's aid in the end. Being in the palace would give her some protection from the people's ire.

Having nothing to do in the palace but wait, and realizing he still had to interrogate *upanayaka* Mahulya in connection with the attack on himself, Dileepa slipped out of the palace as the sky turned pink to the east, ushering in a dawn so dazzling that it made the *dandapala* stop and stare in wonder. In the bright light of day, the night that had passed seemed almost like a fevered dream, and were it not for the hurts and bruises he could feel all over him, Dileepa might have believed he had imagined it all.

In truth, the *dandapala* was reeling from the previous night's experiences. Having ridden up to the mansion, fully aware that they were up against a powerful rakshasi, Dileepa had nonetheless been wholly unprepared for the forces unleashed by Simhika. The detestation he had felt before his shadows had parted from him, the unbridled hatred that had filled him, lingered like a foul aftertaste. And the dread that had seized him when he had seen his double raise its *karapala* to kill him still made him shiver and shut his eyes. The young investigator wasn't certain he would ever be able to overcome the horrors of the night gone by.

Caught up in its own thoughts, the *dandapala's* mind initially failed to register the screams that were coming from somewhere ahead of him. It wasn't until a man veered into view from a side street and dashed frantically towards him that Dileepa took notice, his hand instinctively going to his *karapala*. Despite being contorted with fright, the man's face looked familiar, and it took the *dandapala* no more than a few seconds to place him. He was the aging moneylender whose eldest son had been among the first few people to disappear. The moneylender had approached the court, and that was how the palace investigators had commenced their fruitless investigation into the disappearances.

Dileepa was still wondering what had scared the old man witless when a second figure bounded into view, hot in pursuit of the moneylender. One look at this man was all the *dandapala* needed to recognize the moneylender's son — *the one who had disappeared*. The younger man's face bore a strange expression, his eyes vacant, yet full of lust. He came after his father hard, gaining ground rapidly on stronger legs, his hands extended to grab the old man.

"Help me," the old moneylender shrieked on seeing Dileepa. "Help!"

Confused about what was happening, the investigator managed to take a couple of unsure steps forward, when the son made a desperate lunge at his father. The two men went down in a tangle of limbs, son on top of the father, wrestling him into submission even as the old man screamed again.

"Somebody… please help!"

"Hey!" Dileepa shouted as he drew his sword and finally broke into a run. "Stop."

The *dandapala* hadn't taken more than five steps when he slowed, his eyes widening in horror at what he was witnessing. The moneylender's son had managed to pin his father's hands down and straddle him, and as Dileepa watched, the son bent down to sink his teeth into the old man's throat. The moneylender squealed in abject terror, the echo bouncing off the houses bordering the street.

"Stop," Dileepa screamed as he hurtled towards the thrashing figures. "Get off him."

Hearing Dileepa's footsteps draw closer, the son lifted his gaze to the investigator. Fresh blood coated the man's lips and stained his teeth, while a single rivulet ran down the side of his mouth and dripped off his chin, splattering red on the stone pavement beneath. His eyes were crazed, content yet ravenous, his grin vulgar with delight. Dileepa was so repulsed by the sight that he struggled not to turn on his heel and run. Under the son, the moneylender continued to screech at the sky, the side of his throat torn and bleeding.

"Get off him," the *dandapala* shouted again as he came up to father and son. Then, on realizing that his words were having no effect, he raised his leg and stamped the son hard across the side, kicking and shoving him off his father. Thrown off balance, the son fell and rolled over — then came up in a flash, his eyes on Dileepa, full of malice. Dileepa instantly brought his sword up.

"Back off," he growled.

The grin on the son's face widened, and without sparing a moment's thought, he threw himself at Dileepa with a fierceness that took the *dandapala* by surprise. The man nearly broke through the investigator's defences, clawing his way forward, but Dileepa stopped him by thrusting his *karapala* at the man's chest. The point of the sword went in, burying deeper and deeper as the man strained against it, blood welling from the wound and oozing down his stomach. The man should have been in sufficient pain, but there was no evidence of it in his expression. Onwards he came, flailing and clawing, leaving scratch marks on Dileepa's arms. He thrust his face into Dileepa's, teeth gnashing and lips smacking obscenely, his grin growing perverse and maniacal with every passing moment.

Taken aback, the *dandapala* decided to disengage. Drawn by the racket, people from the houses nearby had flocked to their doors and windows to see what was happening, and some passersby had stopped to stare. Dileepa yanked the *karapala* out of the son's chest, sending fountains of blood squirting. He took two hurried steps backwards, but this proved useless as the son lunged forward freely, forcing Dileepa to thrust his sword out again, plunging the tip this time into the base of the man's throat. The blade went in smoothly, parting muscle and cartilage to go almost all the way to the back. Blood sluiced down the blade and sloshed down the man's chest.

The wound should have killed the moneylender's son. It should have stopped him in his tracks, at the very least.

Neither of those things happened.

The son kept pushing forward, grinning and leering at Dileepa, reaching for him, blood pouring from his wounds in torrents…

Another scream issued from somewhere, full of agony and terror. It so unnerved the *dandapala* that he wrenched the sword out of the man's throat and whirled around, seeking its source. The suddenness of the move cost the moneylender's son his balance, and he fell face down behind Dileepa, sprawling on the pavement that was already slick with blood.

The investigator felt a hand grab hold of his ankle.

Looking down, Dileepa saw the moneylender staring up at him. The old man was trying to rise, using the investigator's leg for leverage. Dileepa bent to assist the old man but stopped halfway on noticing the expression on the man's face. Crazed. Cunning. And hungry. The moneylender opened his mouth and lunged for Dileepa's leg, ready to take a big bite of the flesh —

Pulling his leg out of the way, the *dandapala* hacked down with his sword, using all his might. The sword cut into the side of the moneylender's head, burying sideways from the right temple to midway up the scalp. Again blood spurted in the morning sun; again, this was to no avail as the moneylender only tightened his grip on the leg and attempted another bite.

Vaguely conscious of the screams that were starting to go up around him, Dileepa realized that these things — *whatever they were, they were no longer human* — craved flesh and blood, and would not be stopped by swords. But the scariest part was that once bitten, their victims seemed to turn into monsters themselves, in turn seeking fresh victims and multiplying like the vetalas of old.

There was only one thing left to do. *Run.*

Dileepa used all of his strength to wriggle out of the moneylender's grasp and pried his *karapala* free at the same time. The neighbourhood had erupted in violence, and everywhere around him, people were running, screaming in terror, chased by the crazed, bloodthirsty things.

Wondering if Ayodhya was in the grip of a curse, the *dandapala* cast a look at the moneylender and his son. Both were staggering to their feet, scarred and drenched in their own blood, ghastly creatures out of some nightmare. Within moments, they would be up, and they would come for him.

Dileepa did the only thing left to be done. He turned and ran to save himself from the ravenous, bloodthirsty things that were taking over Ayodhya.

"The returned have to be products of horrendous sorcery," Kushadhwaja stated with certainty.

"Maybe they're linked to the rakshasi Simhika," Sheshagupta suggested, and a hush descended over the group at the possibility that the rakshasi might still be exerting her influence on Kosala.

"No matter what they are or where they've come from, the returned are overrunning Ayodhya," said Vijaya. "They are spreading faster than a contagion, and there's no stopping them, rajan."

"If the returned are displaying the properties of vetalas, there's only one way of stopping them," said Kushadhwaja, exchanging grim looks with Bharat.

"They must be beheaded," said Sheelabhadra, putting into words what nobody wanted said.

Sheshagupta and Vijaya flinched as they trained their eyes on Bharat. But the king said nothing.

"Beheaded right down to the last vetala," Kushadhwaja stressed. "It's the only way to end this."

"Then that's what must be done to the returned before they turn Ayodhya into a city of vetalas," declared Sheelabhadra.

Bharat shot the guild master a sharp glance. "Let us not forget that the returned are our people."

"Once they've turned into vetalas, they are no longer our people — *they are no longer people*," said the *kshatri*. "Sheelabhadra is right. We have to stop them to save our citizens from harm."

Your role as king is to protect the people from harm, Rama's words spoken on the banks of the Mandakini, guiding him on the responsibilities of kingship, came back to Bharat. *Anything you do to achieve that end will be worth the time and effort.*

Bharat nodded, looking stricken nevertheless. "Then let's do what needs —" he stopped, seeing Ambareesha and Devadatta come hurrying towards them. Noticing the frown on the Bahlika's brow, he asked, "What's happened?"

"Yuddhajeet, Abhisarika and Smara are nowhere to be seen," said Ambareesha. "We've looked everywhere in the palace, but…"

"They could be out in the grounds —"

"We've searched there too. Your mother is worried, rajan."

Bharat spread his hands. "They couldn't just disappear. Maybe…" as the thought formed in his mind, he went pale. He looked at the faces around him with trepidation. "Could they have gone into the city for some reason?"

"It's possible," Kushadhwaja whispered in dismay. "It is a bright, sunny morning after all, ideal for taking in the city's sights."

"Their lives could be in danger then," Shatrughna insisted. "We must find them before it's too late."

Bharat nodded at his brother. "Get Baladitya to put a contingent together. The best swordsmen. Baladitya probably knows how to tackle vetalas. Tell him to spread the word among his men all the same. The only thing that works is a beheading." He turned to the *kshatri*. "Please have word sent to Kosala's garrisons as well. We'll need every man and woman capable of wielding swords, choppers and cleavers hunting the vetalas. People must know it is a fight for Ayodhya's survival."

"What about us?" asked Sheelabhadra, pointing to himself, Sheshagupta and Vijaya.

"Arm yourselves and help Atibhanu defend the palace with the palace guards," said Bharat. He looked at Atibhanu. "The palace is in your charge. I leave everything I hold dear in your hands."

"I will protect the palace with my life, rajan," the bodyguard said, aware that he would have to make a confession to his king and hope for a pardon once this madness got over. *If this madness got over*, he corrected himself.

Bharat reached his chambers to find Mandavi on one of the terraces, looking out over the palace grounds in the direction of the city. Hearing his step, she turned and Bharat saw concern on her face.

"Is it true?" she asked. "That those who had disappeared have turned into vetalas?"

Bharat nodded, ceaselessly amazed at the speed with which news spread.

"What about Yuddhajeet, Abhisarika and Smara?"

Bharat shook his head this time. "We're going to look for them in the city."

Seeing Mandavi go pale, Bharat took her by her shoulders. "I want you to take Taksha, mother, the queen mothers and Urmila to a safe spot, where you cannot be reached," he said. "Atibhanu and the guards are here to keep the palace secure, but we must be prepared for any eventuality." He lifted her face to his. "Can you do it?"

"I can."

"Good." Bharat took his queen into an embrace, then released her. "Where is Taksha?"

"I am here," the boy announced from near the door. "Where are we going?" he asked, indicating he had overheard at least a part of Bharat and Mandavi's conversation.

Bharat knelt before the boy and held his little hands in his own. "You are going with mother to keep everyone else in the palace safe," he said, peering into the kid's face. "Will you do that?"

Taksha nodded. "Can I take my *karapala*?" he asked, pointing to the wooden sword Atibhanu had made for him.

"You must," said Bharat, handing the kid the sword and marvelling at the rapid development in the boy's speech.

"Where are *you* going?"

"To keep everyone in the city safe," Bharat answered.

"And Smara?"

"We will find Smara and bring her back," Bharat said with a level of assurance he didn't exactly feel. Not wanting Taksha to see the doubt in his eyes, he hugged the boy, then rose and nodded at Mandavi. She nodded back. Taking Taksha by the hand, she left.

Bharat went into an antechamber and opened an iron-bound chest. Inside it lay a length of thick chain made of chunky iron links. At one end of the chain was a spike six inches long, also made of iron. Slinging one half of the chain over his shoulders, the king wrapped the other half around his right forearm. Then, slamming the chest shut, he left his chambers.

Bharat exited the palace to find Shatrughna, Baladitya and over a hundred *nagarapalas* waiting for him, mounted and ready to ride into the city in search of Yuddhajeet, Abhisarika and Smara. The king strode towards his horse and was about to mount when a stable boy came out running, looking scared.

"Rajan..." he huffed as he pointed towards the royal stables. "Rajan... Siripala... he is..."

Bharat felt the world start to cave in around him. *Siripala was one of those who had returned...*

Heaving a sigh of despair, Bharat motioned to Shatrughna, telling him to proceed with the men. "I will find you," he said, his face cast in stone. The tremor in his voice, however, betrayed the immeasurable sadness that had already laid hold of him. Without uttering another word, he turned and headed for the royal stable.

For a moment, Shatrughna watched his brother go. Then, spurring his horse, he led his men out of the palace and into the city.

The thunder of departing hooves barely registered in Bharat's mind, all his thoughts centred on Siripala. He didn't know what he was going to do when he got to the stable, but he was certain he couldn't let the old bodyguard just die at anyone's hands…

The stable yard was vacant. The stable boys watched from a safe distance, ready to take to their heels at the first sign of danger, while some palace hands stood near the palace, observing what was happening.

Bharat set foot in the stable yard.

You ride well, kumara.

The stable was silent. The horses in their stalls were silent too, as if dreading what was to come.

My name is Siripala, and I am the new caretaker of the stable.

"Siripala…?" Bharat called.

"You've come, rajan," a gravelly voice called from inside one of the stables.

Before Bharat could reply, Angara slunk out of the stable and darted towards him, whimpering and wagging its tail furiously. As the king bent and petted the dog, the voice spoke again.

"I am relieved you came, rajan. I was afraid for the dog."

Bharat unwound the chain from around his forearm as he walked to the stable. Angara followed two steps behind. "Siripala?" the king called again. "Are you alright?"

"Come in, rajan," the ostler invited. As an afterthought, he added, "I cannot harm you."

Bharat ducked into the stable's doorway. Coming in from the bright sunlight, it took a moment for his eyes to adjust to the darkness inside, and he stood at the doorstep, unsure what to expect. Then, as his vision grew accustomed to the dark, he saw… and he experienced a sharp pang of distress.

Before him stood Siripala, shackled by his ankle to one of the upright posts of an empty horse stall.

"Siripala," Bharat gasped and took a step forward. "Who did this —"

"I did this to myself, rajan," the old man said. "I chained myself up. I threw away the key."

"Why?"

"When I understood it would turn out this way, I didn't want anyone coming to harm, especially not you or Taksha or the dog. The dog…" the ostler chuckled, "it knew all along that something was wrong. But it wouldn't leave my side. It wouldn't go away." He smiled at Bharat. "We are not worthy of such loyalty."

The king glanced at Angara and nodded. "You knew this would happen?" he asked slowly.

"I didn't, not consciously. But I think, unconsciously, I always knew. We all always knew. We, the returned. We knew this was why we had been returned."

"By whom? Who did this to you, who made you…" Bharat searched for a kinder, gentler word.

"Who made us vetalas?" Siripala said bluntly. He paused to think for a moment. "I don't know, rajan. It is all —"

Without warning, in mid-sentence, the old bodyguard's expression changed and a lunatic gleam entered his eyes.

With mouth open in hunger, teeth bared, he lunged at Bharat. The king stepped back in reflex, but he needn't have. The manacle on Siripala's ankle snagged and he was pulled back, snapping and snarling at Bharat in frustration. Angara crouched low and whined in fright. It took a few moments for the madness to ebb. Slowly, Siripala's eyes cleared.

"I will find whoever did this to you," Bharat swore, trembling in anger.

"Maybe later," said the ostler. "First, you must save the people of Kosala." He looked at Bharat meaningfully. "You know what must be done with vetalas, rajan. Do it."

Bharat said nothing as he glanced at the shackle on Siripala's leg. The ostler saw him and shook his head. "Kumara," he said, "this chain will hold me back, but it won't make me human again. When you come back after saving everyone, I will still be here, the last remaining vetala. And you will have to kill me. Otherwise, no one will be safe. You might as well do it now than later."

You ride well, kumara. The first words Siripala had said to him, so many years ago.

Bharat tried to blink back the tears and failed. "I cannot," he sobbed.

"Kumara, you and I both know that I would rather die at your hands than anyone else's."

You ride the best. Better than the others.

"I cannot," Bharat sobbed. "You were a ray of kindness in my darkness… How can I…?"

"Be a ray of kindness in *my* darkness and do it, kumara."

Bharat shook his head, the tears streaming down his cheeks.

Angara growled low in its throat.

"Rajan, there's someone outside…" Siripala called sharply, and Bharat heard the scurry of feet on mud.

Bharat whirled around, the chain already unspooling in his hands. Two figures were in the yard behind him, both with crazed expressions on their faces, mouths hanging open, the side of their necks chewed and bloodied. They stared at him for a moment, then broke into a run, drooling as they came at him while he stepped out of the stable and strode towards them…

Bharat said a mantra, and twin blades fanned out of the sides of the iron spike at the end of the chain to form a two-headed *parshvadha*. Without wasting a moment, and calibrating his moves with precision, Bharat swung the chain-axe at the two figures. The axe arced, its edges dazzling in the sunlight. It sliced through the neck of one vetala, severing its head clean off the shoulders. Another flick of Bharat's wrist, and the *parshvadha* detached the second vetala's head as well.

Both vetalas dropped to the ground dead, their heads rolling in the mud.

Bharat straightened and drew the chain-axe in, its blades retracting into the spike. He stared at the two decapitated bodies. Both had had their necks chewed open, he thought; both had turned into vetalas *after* being attacked by the returned, or by other vetalas who would have been victims of the returned. Whichever way one looked at it, it had started with the returned…

First, you must save the people of Kosala, Siripala had said. Bharat realized he was right.

You know what must be done with vetalas, rajan. Do it.

The king turned back towards the stable.

You are bound to lose something precious.

The king's feet were suddenly heavy, as though clamped with invisible irons. It was impossible to walk.

The loss is inevitable. It is a sacrifice that the magic demands and exacts.

The brightness of the sun and the starkness of the shadows made Bharat's head spin.

The agnimanasa *will claim its price. Perform the* agnimanasa *again, and you will put* one more *life on the line.*

Surochi had been right all the time, the king realized. Urmila had been right too about the *homa.*

Bharat stepped through the stable door. The weight on his chest was unbearable, making it hard for him to breathe, but he managed to utter the mantras and tap into the magic. The *parshvadha* formed at the end of the chain.

The king and the ostler looked at each other, and the latter smiled.

"It was an honour knowing you, kumara," he said.

His eyes were so full of tears that all Bharat could make out of Siripala was a glistening outline. Bracing himself, he swung the chain-axe at the outline, his heart breaking into a million pieces.

End of Book Two

JAICO PUBLISHING HOUSE

Elevate Your Life. Transform Your World.

ESTABLISHED IN 1946, Jaico Publishing House is home to world-transforming authors such as Sri Sri Paramahansa Yogananda, Osho, the Dalai Lama, Sri Sri Ravi Shankar, Sadhguru, Robin Sharma, Deepak Chopra, Jack Canfield, Eknath Easwaran, Devdutt Pattanaik, Khushwant Singh, John Maxwell, Brian Tracy, and Stephen Hawking.

Our late founder Mr. Jaman Shah first established Jaico as a book distribution company. Sensing that independence was around the corner, he aptly named his company Jaico ('Jai' means victory in Hindi). In order to service the significant demand for affordable books in a developing nation, Mr. Shah initiated Jaico's own publications. Jaico was India's first publisher of paperback books in the English language.

While self-help, religion and philosophy, mind/body/spirit, and business titles form the cornerstone of our non-fiction list, we publish an exciting range of travel, current affairs, biography, and popular science books as well. Our renewed focus on popular fiction is evident in our new titles by a host of fresh young talent from India and abroad. Jaico's recently established translations division translates selected English content into nine regional languages.

Jaico distributes its own titles. With its headquarters in Mumbai, Jaico has branches in Ahmedabad, Bangalore, Chennai, Delhi, Hyderabad, and Kolkata.

SINCE 1946